Bad Origins

The Hellborn Series, Volume 4

Sammantha Anderson

Published by Sammantha Anderson, 2020.

This is a work of fiction. Similarities to real people, places, or events are entirely coincidental.

BAD ORIGINS

First edition. May 22, 2020.

ISBN: 978-1393801795

Written by Sammantha Anderson.

Also by Sammantha Anderson

The Hellborn Series
Bad Witch Walking
Bad Karma
Bad Origins

Watch for more at https://www.facebook.com/authorsammanthaanderson.

Dedication

I would like to give special thanks to Dez Purington. Dez thank you so much for the beautiful cover you created. I am so grateful for the work you did for this book. I would also like my ARC readers. The support all of you show me on a regular basis is amazing. I am thankful to all of you. You guys show support not just for me but also how much you love Savannah. Words cannot express how grateful I am to all of you.

I would also like to thank Rita Ryan for all the work she has done on this book. You have spent weekend after weekend with me on the phone editing this book. Thank you for all that you do.

I would like to give special thanks to my kids who have been patient with me as while I have dedicated so much time to writing these books. You guys are wonderful and I love you.

I want to give a special thanks to my friend L.E. Martin, who is always willing to chat with me when I need it and is supportive. I am so lucky to call you my friend.

Lastly this book is dedicated to one of my students, JaSarah. I am so happy you have found the joy in writing. It warms my heart to see how much you have grown as my student and as a writer. I love you Little Miss.

Chapter One
Seven Days Before the Ceremony

Our new home was far enough away from all of the ambient noise of the city, maybe not far away but enough that you could forget that you lived in the city. My home was peaceful with only my mate and myself occupying it. Meri, my best friend and the closest thing I had to a sister came here to work daily. Meri had joined my company three months ago. As much as I enjoyed working by myself, working with her was even better.

As of late, my home was chaotic and filled with more noise than normal. Santiago and I had been planning our mating ceremony for the past three months and it was crunch time. I was ready for all of it to be done and had grown tired of all the calls to florists, boutiques, the venue, caterers, and any other individuals I had to speak to during the planning. I was ready for this damn thing to be done. Most females were the ones who did all the planning for these events and turned into nightmare mates. I was the opposite. I had been part of the planning but so had an entire team of planners. We were technically already mated under vampire law. I had given my vow to the head of the Black Grove Vampire Clan three months ago and Santiago had marked me that night. In my eyes this was all for Hugo. Santiago was Hugo's second in command, which meant we had to have a public ceremony with all the big names of the city present. It was in many ways a political event. I had insisted on adding a few other names to the list that had nothing to do with politics and everything to do with them being my friends.

The ceremony was to show the human world the clan was growing not just in numbers but in strength as well, in accepting my mating to Santiago. I was a leyline witch and a hunter for the city of Sweetclover. I carried my own power outside of the clan. Santiago and I were two powerhouses becoming one. Our mating told the humans we were not to be screwed with or taken lightly. Soon enough I would make the transition to a hybrid. If all went well, I would be witch and vampire. We hadn't set a date yet for when that would happen but Hugo would want it to happen sooner rather than later.

It also showed the wolves we could be an even stronger ally or one hell of an enemy if the treaty were to end between the two groups. Most of the vampires enjoyed the treaty and so did the wolves. My addition to the clan I believed made them content we were allies. My friendship with the wolves helped to ensure the treaty stayed in place. Santiago had been one of the creators along with my ex-lover Damian, the Alpha of the Falls Pack. The two had spent weeks creating the treaty and it had been in place for over five years now. Damian and I were still friends or at least I believed we were. In truth, we hadn't talked in months. After his mate had been killed for trying to kill him and her twin had tried to rape me, it had put a strain on our relationship. There had been a lot for Damian to deal with and I was giving him the space to do so. I knew the wolves well from my past with Damian. I respected them and Damian. I would work with Santiago to keep the treaty in place.

The mating ceremony was also a reason to have a party and Hugo loved parties. Hugo would take any opportunity to show off. This was no different. For me the entire ceremony and party was too much like what humans did for my liking. I didn't understand why females of any species would sign up for this. Taking my vow and being given my mark was enough for me. The ceremony would be for the witch part of me or that was what Santiago argued. We would be mated in both traditions. I thought it was crap. I was perfectly content with being mated under vampire law. I had no family outside Santiago, Meri, Duncan and the clan. They were all vampires. This was one of those moments when I had to compromise. I hated those moments. Being part of the clan, I would have to face more compromises ahead. Being Santiago's mate brought more responsibility. I was given the same level of respect he received from other vampires. I also was considered part of Hugo's inner circle. The clan was no longer Hugo and Santiago's people but mine as well. I was still learning how to handle it all.

I had spent most of my life trying to be alone. Then I met Meri, she became my best friend. I had made a deal with myself she was it. She and Duncan that was it, then came Damian. I had loved him or at least a part of me had. When I ended the relationship, I was once again content with having only Meri and Duncan in my life. From there it snowballed to my human friends within the police department, I worked closely with. Cain had shown me we were not just colleagues, we were friends. I was one of them.

Santiago and I had known each other for years before he had made his feelings known to me. When he did, I fell hard for him. In some weird way, I felt the same for him without even realizing I had until he had opened up to me. Mating him had brought a slew of others who were tied to him. It was a lot for a female who had wanted to be alone for the rest of her life to take on. Adjustments were still being made to say the least. I had to admit, even with the adjustment of being part of the clan, the adjustment of being Santiago's mate felt natural. More times than not I could find a way to compromise with him and he did the same for me. He never asked me to be anyone but who I was, which made me love him more. It was probably why I was able to give into the public mating ceremony so easily.

Today was the day for my last fitting of the dress I would wear in seven days. I wasn't a dress person. I was a female who wore clothes for hunting hellborns who had broken the law. Dresses didn't fit into that equation, ever. The only time I wore dresses was when Santiago wanted to take me out. Neither of us had a lot of free time between my job and his but we made it happen. He liked me in dresses and I liked wearing them for him. The dresses I wore were cocktail dresses. The dress for the ceremony was a formal gown. Not a dress. Definitely not something I wore ever.

I will admit the gown Meri and I had picked out was breathtaking. The down side was about seven inches of the dress had to be cut off and the entire dress had to be altered , due to my short stature. The seamstress had worked the last two months on the dress and today I would see the finished product. The dress was royal blue with an empire waist. The top of the dress had capped sleeves and tight bodice. Silver beads sat at the top of the bodice and along the bottom of it under my breasts. The dress flowed fluidly from the bodice to the floor. It was simple but elegant.

When I was dress hunting, Hugo had sent a team of shoppers to my home with racks upon racks of dresses. I spent hours trying on dress after dress while Meri sat and made faces. Depending on the degree of ugliness of the gown I had on her facial expressions got funnier. By hour three, I had had my fill and began to comb through the dresses on my own. I had reached my limit of being told to put this one on, try this color. I found the gown tucked away in a back of a rack. A number of the shoppers had tried to stop me from even trying it on. They did not feel the dress made enough of a statement. I tried it on anyway, ignoring all of their assessments and concerns. As soon as I tried the dress on I knew it was the dress for me. The color was stunning against my skin. It made my red hair look breathtakingly bright. It was also one of my favorite colors to wear. There were more arguments with the shoppers about it not being the right type of gown for my mating ceremony. I proceeded to lose my shit at that point, reminding all of them that it was not Hugo's mating ceremony, it was mine and Santiago's. I would wear any goddamn thing I wanted. That shut all of them up. They left shortly after.

I contacted Santiago and told him I had the dress I was purchasing and would need to find a seamstress. Within the hour one was at my door with an assistant, a stool, and a sewing kit. The seamstress, Ms. Radmaker was a hellborn who was smaller than I was. She stood at four feet nine inches, if she was lucky, and had a sharp eye. She was also a female not to argue with, which I learned quickly. I had tried to send her away saying I would make an appointment when she shoved past me and informed me she was to see the dress and start working on it immediately. I would not delay her from executing her duties. Her hard aqua eyes told me to do what I was told for once. I put the dress on and stood on her stool as she walked around the dress. Ms. Radmaker spoke with her assistant quickly and the two went to work pinning the dress. It took her less than thirty minutes to mark how much would be taken off at the bottom and along with taking in the bodice half an inch. She then ordered me to find a corset to go under the dress. When I tried to say that wasn't going to happen, she fixed me with that death stare once more. I agreed to buy a corset. I wasn't sure what the female was outside of a hellborn but she was not a female I would ever cross. I bought a black corset later that afternoon.

Today, Ms. Radmaker was back with my dress. Meri cinched me into the corset and then helped me into the dress. I stared at myself as Meri zipped up the gown, astonished at how I looked. I didn't want to admit it but Ms. Radmaker had been right about the corset and taking in the bodice. I loved the dress before she did anything. Now I saw how those small adjustments made a difference. The bodice now wrapped perfectly around my torso almost like a second skin. I walked to the spare bedroom we were using for a fitting room and climbed onto the stool. She walked around the dress saying nothing. One arm across her chest with the other on top, her chin resting on her small fist.

"It is perfect. Don't you think Cissy?" she asked her assistant.

"Yes, madam."

"Now, you will need to purchase a pair of silver shoes to match the stones on the dress," she said with a rough voice.

"I was actually going to wear black..."

"Cissy go retrieve the silver heels we brought. Your mate gave us your size a month ago."

I looked at Meri frustrated by the whole thing. Why tell me to buy something when she already did? I think it was a test. Cissy was back in minutes carrying heels with two straps that criss-crossed at the toe and a thin ankle strap. The heel was thin and stood about three inches high. I had to admit they were nice. I stepped into them with Meri holding my hand as Cissy fastened them.

"Yes. Beautiful. You will need to wear your hair up and a choker or a necklace at the base of your throat would go wonderfully with this. You are quite a stunning female Ms. Woods," she pronounced as she circled me once more.

"Thank you."

"Now go remove the dress and make sure all of it goes in this bag." She said, indicating the black plastic dress bag.

I did as I was told and came back out of the bathroom to hang the dress in the closet.

"No, Ms. Embers will take it. Your mate is to not see it until the day of the ceremony."

"Isn't that a human tradition?"

"No. It is a tradition vampires began with long before humans created the excuse it was bad luck. This dress is how you will be presented to your mate and society. Ms. Embers you are to bring the dress to the venue and help her dress. Do you understand me?" she ordered.

"Yes, madam," Meri replied.

"And what will you be wearing?" she asked Meri.

"I have a dress in my..."

"No, what color?"

"Green."

"No you will be wearing a shade darker than our fair Ms. Woods. I have an eye for sizes. I brought a gown that will fit you perfectly. Cissy, bring Ms. Embers her dress."

Cissy bowed out of the room once more. She returned minutes later with a black garment bag in her arms. Hanging the garment bag, Cissy began unzipping the garment bag, revealing Meri's new gown. The gown she had picked out for Meri was a darker blue. The bodice of the dress wrapped around the upper body, draping over her right shoulder leaving the left shoulder bare. The bottom of the dress flowed down loosely as my own did. There was a small trail of silver stones along the shoulder draping and at the top of the bodice. Ms. Radmaker zipped up the bag, making Cissy hand it over to Meri along with a shoe box holding her shoes.

"The shoes are the same as Ms. Woods. Now, I will see you when I come to dress Santiago for future events. I have wanted that male to find a mate for years and now I will have the opportunity to dress the two of you," the excitement in her voice was evident as she hustled out of the room. Cissy on her heels. Meri and I followed behind.

She took her leave of us. Meri and I stood watching Ms. Radmaker and Cissy leave, dumbfounded at her ability to handle every detail. I was confident no one ever said no to her.

"I guess we should put these in the car and go find jewelry for Saturday," Meri finally said.

"I guess so but let's take the dresses to your place first."

As we loaded the dresses into the back of Meri's car with the shoes, my phone went off. I looked at the screen seeing it was Ryan.

"Ryan, I took the week off," I said without a hello.

"I know. We have a situation, I need you to come in."

"No, I do not have time to solve a murder."

"It's not a murder, it's a kidnapping. A hybrid child has been taken from her bed in the middle of the night."

I closed my eyes as I let the words sink in. A young had been stolen from their bed. I could not say no to this one.

"Send me the address."

I hung up as Meri looked at me as if I had lost my mind.

"Don't look at me in that way."

"Savannah we still have a lot to do," she said with her hands on her hips.

"I know Meri but a young has been taken, I can't say no."

"Damn."

"Yeah. Let's drop the dresses at your place and head to the scene."

"Alright," she replied.

I locked the house up and climbed in Meri's car as the text from Ryan came in. I had planned to be off for the next week. Technically, I could have sent Meri. She had learned how to handle a murder scenes and petty crimes. While working on my own case, she had learned the grueling task of rape cases and the toll it took. Kidnapping was a different beast entirely so this would be new for her. I didn't feel comfortable sending her in on a kidnapping case with no experience. I called Santiago as we drove.

"Mi Amor, I take it that everything with your dress went perfectly," he said.

"Yes, it did. Ms. Radmaker can't wait to dress me for the next event."

"I can imagine. She is very good at what she does."

"Yeah, she is," I answered. I took a breath before I pushed on. "Uhm...The reason I'm calling you is not to talk about Ms. Radmaker but to tell you I have been called in for a case."

"Savannah, our mating ceremony is in seven days. This is not the time to be working."

"First off, you are working right now so please do not give me that Santiago. Secondly, a young has been taken from their home. I cannot sit back knowing a young is missing."

He was silent for a moment before he took a deep breath. "Do you know yet what species the young is?"

"Only the young is a hybrid and nothing more."

"I understand why you said yes. I know of only a few hybrids within the city. One of them is part of our clan. I pray it was not them. Please be safe and let me know when you will be coming home."

"I will. I love you," I replied.

"I love you, too."

The call ended. I sat in silence as we drove. I had no desire to take on this case but the thought of a young being scared and with a monster, doing God knows what was terrifying. I couldn't say no. I dialed my phone once more, calling my new shadow, Antione Watts. He was a detective with the Hellborn Crime Unit. He had joined the team a year ago and wanted to learn more about hellborns. He was a good cop, who knew he would be with the HCU for the rest of his career. He had made peace with it and wanted to know everything he could about hellborns. The police department provided little education for how to handle the other species, so he asked if he could shadow me. The department had said no and forced him to take a sabbatical if he wanted to work with me. For the next six months he would be working with Meri and I on cases and hunts. My business had gone from me working by myself, to me working with two other individuals. At first I had fought it, hating every minute of it. Now I was enjoying it. Watts still had four months with me and I had grown used to having him with me. I didn't know how I would feel when he finally went back to the police department.

"Watts," he answered, his bass voice was heavy with exertion.

"It's Woods. We have a case."

"I thought we were taking a week off for your mating ceremony."

"We were until Ryan called with a kidnapping."

"Shit. Okay, give me ten and I'll head out."

"Good man, Watts. I'll send you the address."

"Cool."

I hung up and sent him the info I had. Meri and I dropped our dresses and shoes off at her place before we headed to The Gallery. I was not looking forward to this case and hoped I could solve it quickly with a happy ending for the young and the family. I hated cases where kids were involved.

Chapter Two

The address Ryan sent was located in The Gallery, in the center of the hellborn homes. It was a working class neighborhood with modest homes and vehicles. Some of the yards were full of green grass, while others were brown and dry. Fall was moving in slowly this year with temperatures still in the seventies on most days. The trees were beginning their change from green to vibrant reds, yellows, and oranges. The normally quiet street was full of police activity. The neighborhood was blocked off with wooden barriers and uniform officers. Meri pulled up to the barricade.

"Ma'am we need you to..."

"We're here to see Lieutenant Ryan," I said showing my identification.

He examined my I.D. looking from it to me. He looked at Meri then.

"This is Meri Embers, she is my associate," I explained. Meri handed him her identification as well. He examined her I.D. with the same attention he had given mine. The uniform officer looked young, telling me that he was probably a boot. Most people within the department knew who I was.

"I need to radio you in."

He took a step back speaking into his radio. It took him only a couple of minutes before he handed our I.D.'s back to us and waved us around the barricade. Set in the middle of the street was a large command post. There was a large white and blue trailer with a blue canopy set up. At least twenty police cars were taking up spots on the block. I could see uniformed officers milling around the neighborhood. A few were knocking on doors. Ryan had already set up a canvass. Normally I would say it was a good thing if this was a human neighborhood but this was a hellborn neighborhood. Most hellborns would be leery to even speak to the police. The few that would speak to them would more than likely provide them with little or no information. Meri and I were better suited for the job, we were part of their community. Since I had mated Santiago, there had been more of an acceptance of me. Yes, I was still a hunter but now I was part of a vampire clan. It meant I had more of a connection to hellborns as a whole. Some were seeing me as a possible ambassador for their causes. I could be used as a middle man between hellborns and the police. In some cases, between other hellborns and Hugo. I didn't want any part of that. I just wanted to do my job as I had always done it.

Meri parked four houses down from the confusion, trying to ensure we would be able to get out of the chaos if something went down. If the perp was found or if the child was, it would become difficult to leave the neighborhood with all of the cops trying to do the same thing, at the same time. Meri and I approached the trailer finding Cain sitting at a table with a laptop in front of him. There were other detectives and officers in plain clothes next to him working on computers as well. Every officer had a job. The amount of background on any individual who had contact with the young would be looked at. Cain was wearing a white polo shirt with his police jacket. His badge hung around his neck as he focused on whatever he was doing. He looked up on our approach.

"Woods, Embers, glad you guys to make it."

"How bad is it?" I asked.

"I'll let the Lieutenant fill you in."

"Where's Ryan?" I asked looking around.

"In the trailer talking to a negotiator."

"Have we gotten a ransom call?" I asked.

"No, but the department sent one down just in case."

I looked around the neighborhood thinking no call was coming. This was not a rich neighborhood. Chances were the parents were just trying to get by. It meant we had to work even faster. If there was a ransom, we would have a timeline set for us. This was a snatch and grab it meant we had hours to try and find her. Within the first three hours of a stranger abduction over seventy percent of children were murdered. The first few hours were the most critical in terms of saving a child's life. After that the chance of survival decreased the longer the child was missing.

We went inside, leaving Cain to his work. The inside of the trailer was like a small office. There were steel cabinets on one end with counter tops. Coffee makers were set up with donuts and small bags of chips to snack on. The food of the gods for cops. The other end had a table with three chairs. Ryan was with a female officer speaking low. She was tall, her head coming level to his shoulders. Her brown hair was pulled back in a bun with bangs hanging low over her brows. As the door shut behind us Ryan looked up. We began our approach as he stopped their conversation.

"Thanks for coming."

"What do we have?" I asked.

"Not much. The child is female, seven, and a hybrid. Her mother is a hybrid as well and was turned during her pregnancy. The child was born shortly after and has characteristics of both species."

"Father?" I asked.

"He is a vampire."

This could mean the family was one of ours.

"How long has she been gone?" Meri asked.

"The parents don't know. They put her to bed at eight, checked in on her at ten last night. Mom went to check on her this morning at nine to find her missing. They searched the house and found nothing. That's when they called us."

"So far there has been no ransom call but we can't rule it out," said the woman next to Ryan.

I looked at the woman with confusion on my face.

"Sorry, this is the negotiator Rita Bridges. Bridges, this is our consultants, Savannah Woods and Meri Embers."

"Hi," I said, shaking her hand.

"I've heard of you. You do good work from what I understand."

"Thanks."

"Your name I don't know as well. I did hear something about you taking down a vampire in the middle of a shop," Bridges said as she addressed Meri.

Meri smiled before she spoke. "I just joined Savannah's company. Give me some more time, you'll know my name soon enough."

As our niceties were winding up, Watts came flying into the trailer.

"What took you so long?" I asked.

"Sorry when you called I was just leaving the gym. I didn't want to show up in my gym clothes," Watts apologized. I looked at him, taking in his jeans and standard T-shirt. It was better than his gym clothes but I would have to get him to go shopping for better hunting clothes and a go bag.

"Nice to see you, Watts," Ryan answered, his voice a little hard.

Ryan had not been happy about Watts taking a leave of absence from the department to learn from me. For Ryan, the department was everything. He had the expectation that Watts should learn the way he did, on the job. I got it but I disagreed with him.

"Hey, Lieutenant," he replied with a nod.

"Okay, let's get to work. Can we go in and see the kid's room?" I asked.

"Yeah. Get Cain to take you in. I have a few things I need to handle here."

"Got it," I replied.

The three of us left the trailer as Ryan went back to his conversation with the negotiator.

"Watts, before our next case I need you to get a go bag together and leave it in your car," I said.

"Why?" he asked.

"Because you never know when you are going to get a call or when your clothes could get ruined. You wouldn't want to be on a hunt with us and say your pants get torn to shreds and have to see fellow officers that way. Right?"

"I got it. Sorry."

"Don't be sorry just take care of it." I turned my attention to Cain. "Ryan wants you to show us into the house."

"You know you could just walk yourself inside Woods. I shouldn't need to be your tour guide," he said slightly irritated as he stood from his hard metal chair.

"But you do it so well. It's like having my very own manservant."

"Bite me, Woods!" Cain growled.

The house was older but in good condition. The outside paint was tan but faded. The grass was green with a small flower-bed, still full of brightly colored flowers that were pink and purple. We walked into the house finding the parents huddled up in the living room. The mother was my height but rounder, her black hair was straight, worn long running down her back. I could see where her hands had been in her hair as strands sat at odd angles. The female's eyes were dark blue, almost navy in color. I could see she had been crying, from the red circles around her eyes. The whites of the female's eyes were red as well. She had reached the catatonic stage, the fear gripping her would not allow her to do anything else but let the fear eat away at her.

Her mate was only a few inches taller than she was, with sandy brown hair and black eyes. His eyes held a hollowness to them. His small build looked as if he was about to collapse. He had his arms wrapped around his mate as he sat trying to hold both of them to-gether. His fear spread throughout the room. I recognized the couple but couldn't recall their names. My stomach dropped at the realization they were one of our clan. I needed to call Santiago and Hugo. This made this case worse.

"Mr. and Mrs. Daring this is..." Cain began the introductions. The couple gasped at my presence, standing, and bowed their heads at my approach. Cain looked confused at the reception I was receiving.

The bowing had started after Santiago and I were mated. He is a high ranking official in the clan, which made me one as well. For those who were civilians, they tended to bow as a sign of respect. I hated it. It would have been different if I had earned the respect but I hadn't, at least not yet. Who am I kidding, I would still hate it.

"We had no clue you would be coming. We..." Mr. Daring started to speak.

"No stop, please," I interrupted him, trying to soften my voice. "I am not here for the clan. I am here to help find your daughter. This is my team, you may know Meri Embers," I said pointing to Meri. "She and I work together as consultants for the police. This is Antione Watts, he also works with us. May we ask you a few questions before we look around?" I spoke delicately.

"Of course," he said as he tried to offer the couch to us.

"No, you sit there. Please?" I insisted.

He sat pulling his mate down onto the sofa. They sat as the female leaned into her mate once more. I pulled a small red chair in front of them. Meri and Watts stood behind me as I leaned towards the two, placing my elbows on my knees. Their names finally came back to me, Brian and Emma. Their daughter's name? I had no clue what her name was.

"Lieutenant Ryan has already told me some of your story but I would like you to tell me. Is that alright?"

"Yes."

"Okay, good. So what time did you put your daughter to bed?" I asked.

"Isobel went to bed around eight last night," Brian Daring started to speak. His voice cracking slightly. "We had taken her to the fair and spent the day. By the time we got home, she was exhausted. I carried her to bed from the car."

"What fair?" I asked.

"The one at Sweetclover High. It's to help raise money for the school. I saw signs for it and thought it would be fun for us to go," Brian Daring answered. The guilt in his voice was heavy.

"Did you go check on her at any time through the night?"

"My mate did just after ten. She was sleeping."

"Can you tell me what Isobel was wearing?"

"Uhm...uhm... she had on her pink shirt, it has a rainbow unicorn on it... and... and a pair of black leggings with stars on them. She loves them. They're her favorite," Brian explained.

I switched my line of questioning to give them a moment.

"Have you had any problems or disagreements with any individuals recently?" I asked.

"No," he said looking at his mate for confirmation. She kept her head low, not looking at anyone in the room.

"No problems with anyone in the clan or maybe in the neighborhood?"

"We keep to ourselves mostly," Brian answered.

I nodded my head and waited before I shifted back to the night before.

"Let's go back to last night. Did you notice anyone paying too much attention to your daughter or your family? Maybe someone who made you uncomfortable?" I asked.

"No, I don't think so," Brian answered, shaking his head at the same time. "What if I missed something?"

"We don't know that you did Brian. I have to ask just so we can find a starting point," I reassured him.

"Have you contacted the Clan yet?" Meri asked.

"No. We're just members, not a ranking member, there is no need to."

"It doesn't matter, Hugo could be of help," Meri said.

"We don't wish to bother him or Santiago," Brian replied looking at me.

"At some point, we may need to connect them. Are you okay with us doing so on your behalf?" Meri asked.

"Yes."

I would have to contact Santiago and Hugo as soon as possible. This was the balancing act I had to walk between hunter and a member of the Black Grove Clan.

"I have to ask this. Are you Isobel's birth father?" I asked Brian.

"Yes. My mate and I got pregnant before I went through the transition," he paused then started to speak again. "When she was eight and a half months pregnant she went through the transition. She had been having complications with the pregnancy and..."

"I just needed to know if you were her birth father. No explanation is needed. Isobel is a hybrid then, correct?" I inquired.

"Yes."

"Does she require feedings?" Meri asked.

"No. She has vampire senses and that's all, so far."

Hybrid children were different from adult hybrids. They carried both sets of characteristics of vampire and witch but they also went through a second change when they were around twenty. They stopped aging and you never knew if anything would change when it came to what they required for their existence. They could even develop more of the vampire side than they had as children. Some would still be fertile and could produce children where others could not.

"What kind of magic does she have?" I asked.

"Earth magic."

"Is there anything you can think of that was out of the ordinary. Maybe in the last week or so?" I asked.

Brian paused as he thought over what I was asking.

"No, everything has been normal," Brian answered.

"Emma, I need to ask you if the house felt off when you got up to check on Isobel?"

Emma shook her head saying nothing. She was a hybrid and he was a vampire, one of them should have sensed something.

"When you realized Isobel was missing, was the front door or a window open?" I asked.

"We found the bathroom window open. The screen broke weeks ago and I hadn't fixed it yet," he explained. Red tears were starting to fall down his face. The guilt was thick around him as he looked away from me. I didn't think they could tell me anything else, at least not right now.

"Okay, we may have some more questions for you later. For now if it is okay with you both I would like to look around Isobel's room?"

"Of course."

I got up, returned the chair to its original place and turned from them.

"Please find her," Brian pleaded. I turned back to face them.

"We will do everything we can to find her. I promise you the police and my team will do our best."

"I know how human police look at us. I..."

I walked back over to them and squatted down in front of them.

"Lieutenant Ryan and his officers work with hellborns everyday. They are the best humans I have ever met. They do not care if you are hellborns. All they want to do is help you. My team and I are the best hunters this city has. I swear we will do everything we can to find her and bring her home to you."

"Thank you."

I gave them one last look of reassurance before I stood up again. I walked out of the room following Cain down a narrow hall filled with family pictures. Isobel looked like her mother with the same black hair and navy blue eyes. You could see the slender build of her father in her body structure. Her face was still carrying some of the baby roundness. From the look of the pictures on the wall she was a happy young who liked to dance. I pulled my eyes from the pictures when we got to her bedroom door. It was covered in stickers.

The room was all pink and white with bright pink walls and a white twin bed sitting in the middle of the room. Dolls and stuffed animals decorated most of the floor. She had a small table in the corner under her window where she had coloring pages and crayons spread out. The table was crooked with only one corner of it against the wall. I looked at the window finding it locked and the screen intact.

"Cain was there any signs of forced entry or a broken window lock?"

"No, just the bathroom window they told you about. I don't know how anyone could get a kid out of the bathroom window easily."

"Where's the bathroom?"

"Next door," he replied with his thumb pointing to the right.

I headed for the bathroom, seeing the window open wide. It was a decent sized window for a bathroom. Not as large as Isobel's window but big enough that if the kidnapper was small enough they could squeeze inside. This didn't feel right.

"Do we know how the screen broke?" Watts asked.

"Dad saw that it was loose and tried to fix it. He said it broke as he tried to get it back in the window frame."

"That's interesting isn't it?" I replied.

"From what I can tell the house is older and hasn't had many upgrades, so it could be as simple as the frame broke," Cain offered.

"Or it could be someone did it intentionally," I replied.

"We dusted the window and found no prints?"

"No prints?" I asked.

Cain shook his head. "The perp wiped the window sill down. We found some smudges, nothing else."

So we knew how he got in but how did he leave? I looked out the window and saw that the window sat at least six feet from the ground. It would be difficult to climb through the window by yourself but with a small child there was no way. I walked out of the bathroom heading back to the young's room.

"Do you smell anything that doesn't belong?" I asked Meri.

"Yeah but the problem is there's been too many bodies in here since she was taken. It muddies up the scent. I can't tell what it is."

"Okay," I stood looking at the room thinking. There was something that made this feel off. Something was not right with the entire scenario. The problem was I didn't know what it was. "Meri I want you to call Santiago and tell him who they are and what is happening, but do it quietly. I don't want to upset them more. Let him know as of right now they didn't want the clan to be involved but we may need help later."

"Got it."

"Watts, I want to ask the parents a couple more questions. Come with me."

I waited for Meri to step outside before we walked back to the living room. The parents were still sitting where I'd left them, frozen.

"Brian, can I ask you just a few more questions?" I asked.

"Yes," he replied as if snapping back into reality.

"When you went to Isobel's room this morning did you smell anything?"

"I was in a panic when my mate came and got me. Dear, did you smell anything?"

"Lilacs, I smelled lilacs," she said in a hollow voice.

"Anything else?" I asked.

She shook her head.

"Did you notice anything missing?" I asked

"No," he said as he shook his head, his eyes closing. I waited a moment before I asked anything else.

"Does your daughter have a favorite toy she may sleep with or play with all the time?" I inquired.

"Uhm... yes she has an orange stuffed animal, its a cat. She named it Max."

"Watts, can you go and check to see if it's there?" I ordered him.

"On it," Watts responded softly.

I waited until he was gone before I moved on.

"Did you notice if your front door was closed this morning?" I asked.

"I... I... know it was shut," Brian answered.

"How about locked?"

"I know it was shut but I don't know if it was locked. As soon as we couldn't find her we were running around yelling for her. Emma ran out of the house yelling her name. It's all a haze after we found her gone," his voice cracked.

"Okay, thank you. I may have more questions for you later. Is it okay if we come back and speak with you?"

"Yes. Anything we can do to help."

I nodded to Brian Daring and stepped out of the room. The two grieving parents went back to sitting as still as statues. I met Watts at the entrance to the hall and motioned for him to follow me outside. We shut the door and began to move away from the house. Cain followed us out.

"There was no cat. I couldn't find it in the bed or around it. I even looked through the toys on the floor," Watts said as we moved down the walkway.

"Chances are they took it with them." I turned my attention to Cain. "Anyone find a stuffed animal?"

"No. But it looks like the kid has a lot of stuffed animals."

"The girl has a favorite stuffed animal, an orange cat. Watts looked and we couldn't find it. I think maybe the kidnapper may have taken it."

"They said nothing was missing," Cain complained.

"They're distraught. They probably didn't notice."

"You know they could have done something to her?" Cain suggested.

"I don't think they did but we need to search the street for the stuffed animal, maybe it was dropped." I looked over to Meri who was still on the phone waving me over. "Give me one second guys."

I joined Meri as she was standing to the side of the house.

"Santiago wants to speak to you."

I took the phone from her.

"Hey," I said.

"How are they doing?" he asked.

"Not well. The female is a zombie and the husband is trying to hold it all together."

"Do you have anything that could help find their young?" he asked.

"No. The room smelled like lilacs according to the mother and the female's stuffed cat is missing, she always sleeps with it. We think we know where the kidnapper entered the house but that's all we have."

"Mi Amor, I try to keep out of your work but this one..."

"I know. What do you need from me?"

"If you find anything, I need you to keep us abreast of any new information."

I took a deep breath before I responded. This was one of those situations that it was like walking a tightrope. I had a job to do and that was to find Isobel Daring but I also had a responsibility to the clan as well. They were members, which meant they were my people. Santiago would have to be involved in this no matter what happened to Isobel. I would also need background on the family. The only one who could give me that was Santiago. We were both walking the same tightrope. Shit!

"Look, I can to a point but if I feel it may endanger her, I won't tell you anything," I offered.

"Agreed."

"I may need to come see you at some point to do background on the parents, more than likely within the next few hours. Can you help me out with that?"

"Of course. Anything to help find the young."

"I'll call you as soon as possible."

"I love you," he said with a heavy voice.

"I love you too."

I hung up. I had a terrible feeling about this one. Whatever I was feeling, so was my mate, which didn't help ease the feeling in my gut.

I returned to the small group. We needed to work fast to find Isobel Daring.

"Cain, I take it you are doing background on the parents?" I asked.

"Yeah."

"Have you found anything?"

"Nothing criminal. The husband has a few parking tickets but nothing worse than that. We are waiting for their financials to come through," he informed us.

"Okay." I took a minute to think about what was next. "As soon as those come in, send them our way. We can help you comb through them," I told Cain.

"Got it."

"What about school?" Watts asked.

"We are doing a background on staff right now. So far, nothing is panning out with any of the teachers or staff. If this was a sexual predator then they probably don't have a record," Cain answered.

"I want us to help canvass the neighborhood. Have your guys finished the block yet?" I asked.

"Yeah, they got nothing from anyone."

That wasn't shocking. If anyone did see anything they were less likely to tell the humans.

"Meri, you take this half of the street," I pointed to the right. "Watts and I will take the other half. We will then cross the street and meet in the middle."

"Why are we recanvassing?" Watts questioned.

"Because there's a chance a neighbor did see something but aren't willing to talk to the humans. We have a better chance of them talking to us," I explained.

"I'll get started on my side of the street," Meri added.

"Make sure you ask them if they saw anything over the last few days or even weeks. If this was a stranger kidnapping, the perp could have been here before last night."

"Yeah," Meri replied as she walked away.

"The search dogs are on the way and should be here within the hour. We're also running plates of all the cars on the street," Cain informed me.

"Okay. After we finish talking to the neighbors, I'll head over to Obsidian to get background from the clan."

"You know it's nice to have someone so closely tied to the clan now. It cuts through the red tape with the vamps," Cain replied with a smirk.

"Like you ever had to deal with the red tape with the hell-borns," I shot back.

With that, Watts and I headed over to the neighbors to the left of the Darings, hoping someone may have seen something that would lead us to finding Isobel Daring.

Chapter Three

We spent two hours banging on doors getting a whole lot of nothing from the neighbors. No one seemed to see anything odd or out of place in the neighborhood the night before or during the week. It was damn frustrating. To add to the situation the temperature was sweltering, more than it should have been, according to the calendar and the trees it was fall. I guess someone forgot to tell Mother Nature.

We walked back to the trailer, finding Ryan and Cain inside. The trailer was air conditioned, which gave all of us a relief from the heat, even if it was just for a few minutes. I dropped my ass in one of the chairs as I enjoyed the cool air.

"Did you get anywhere with the neighbors?" Ryan asked.

"No. No one saw or heard anything. How about the search dogs?" I inquired.

"The dogs were able to track the scent to just outside The Gallery. But they became confused as to where it went after that," Ryan informed us.

"What do you mean they got confused?" I asked, feeling my frustrations growing.

Dogs could track even if a car was used in the kidnapping. It didn't make sense that the dogs had lost the female's scent. There were stories of dogs tracking a scent for thirty or forty miles but our dogs couldn't? What did we have the JV squad of dogs?

"The handlers don't know why the dogs lost the scent, all they know is they did," Ryan answered.

"Which direction did they travel?" Watts asked.

"North east of The Gallery. The dogs traveled to Maker Drive and Milton Boulevard," Cain answered. "In the middle of all the shops and eateries."

"Too many scents in the area, the dogs couldn't separate them?" Watts speculated.

"The Gallery is our biggest tourist area. There is a mixture of hellborn and human scents, why didn't the dogs get confused here?" Meri asked.

"He stayed away from the commercial area of The Gallery, staying within the residential area," Cain said.

"Still doesn't make sense. The dogs should have been able to track, even with the other scents," I added.

It did not make sense what our kidnapper was doing. Why would you go to the busiest human area of the city? Was it to confuse us? Does our perp live in that area? Is he human? I filed away the questions and moved on.

"We're getting surveillance videos from the local businesses, maybe they caught something on camera," Ryan informed us.

"Did you get the financials on the parents?" I asked Cain.

"Yeah, they just arrived. Cain is about to start going through them." Ryan answered "What's your take on this so far Woods?" Ryan replied.

"I don't know what to think yet. The parents seem genuine in their grief. It could be a stranger abduction but no one heard anything or saw anything different in the past week. It appears organized, so if it is a stranger, they would have to know at least something about the Daring's movements. Which could mean they were watched. There is also a possibility it could be someone they know. It could explain why no one saw anything unusual."

"Chances are better that it was one of the parents who did something to her," Cain offered up.

"Normally I would agree with you Cain but I'm with Woods on this one. A stranger would be my bet. What if it was someone at the carnival? They saw the kid and followed the parents' home," Watts offered.

"More times than not it's the parents that did it," Cain replied.

"Maybe for humans that's true," Meri added.

"Okay, enough people. We look at the parents, once they are clear, we can move on to other theories. Cain get to the financials. You three..." Ryan said.

"We will head to the clan to get some background on the parents," I offered.

"Good. I want to have them cleared or something on them in the next three hours. Got it?" Ryan replied.

"Got it," we all chimed at the same time.

I waved my team out of the trailer and walked towards the car. I waited until we were out of ear shot from the lingering police presence, before I turned to my team.

"Meri, I want you here talking to the parents. Find out about their family outside the clan. Maybe there is something there."

"Didn't the cops already start looking at them?" she questioned.

"Right now, they are focused on the parents, until they can say the parents are guilty or innocent," Watts answered.

"My gut says those parents didn't harm her. Once they realize the cops are looking at them, they'll shut down. I want them to trust us. Best chance of that happening is one of us getting as much background information from them."

"Savannah, I have never questioned a victim of a kidnapping," Meri pointed out, uncertainty in her voice.

"You have been doing this job for three months, you know how to do this. Besides, I need to go to get more background from Santiago, one of us needs to do this. I can't be in two places at once

Meri. There is a better chance they will open up to you than they would to me. Just talk to them about their extended family, friends, and Isobel's teachers. Anyone they spend time with."

"Alright. I'll see what I can find out," she nodded.

"We'll be back in an hour and we'll go from there."

WATTS AND I PULLED up at the club ten minutes later. I had called Santiago to let him know we were on the way. He had sounded just as excited as I was with the fact our personal life was colliding with my professional life. Cristian, one of our vampires, was standing at the club's door. He was Santiago's right hand man or at least he was now. Santiago had developed a trust with the vampire and in doing so he was taking a much bigger role in not just the club's affairs but the clan as well. I didn't know Cristian well. He said little, but seemed to observe everyone and everything around him. I could respect that trait for the simple fact that I did the same thing. That I didn't know more about the vampire was a concern for me. I reminded myself if Santiago trusted him so should I. Cristian was on the young side, compared to Santiago and Hugo. Only having been a vampire for the last eighty-three years. He was as tall as my mate with lighter skin than Santiago's. He was built with wide shoulders and a narrow waist. His body was in a fighter's shape. His soft grey eyes were bright against his tan skin and red highlighted brown hair. When he became angry those eyes seemed to light up, becoming a different color. I had seen him angry only once. The anger had been directed at Dante. It seems Dante had tried to fire him, when Cristian had refused to remove a patron. The patron was a vampire who Dante had had an altercation with. Cristian had refused Dante's demands. It took Santiago stepping in to force Dante to back off. Shortly after Santiago moved Cristian from the front of the club to the back of the club with him.

Cristian bowed to me as we approached the front door.

"Cristian, this is Antione Watts," I said making introductions.

"It is nice to meet you," he replied, shaking Watts' hand. "Santiago is in his office, would you like me to escort you down?" He offered.

"Thanks. I got it from here."

"If you need anything, let me know," he bowed once more.

As we moved across the empty club, waitstaff bowed their heads to me. I gave a wave to Abel as I passed, he was the head of floor security. Kabel was also there, checking an order of alcohol. He waved at me, giving me a wide grin, as always. I waved back and kept moving. I punched in the security code and heard the click as the door swung free. Watts grabbed the door pulling it open as I went in first. We moved in complete silence as we reached Santiago's office. As soon as we were at the door of Santiago's office I knocked on the open door. His head was bent over a stack of papers. He looked up from his work at us.

"Have you found anything?" he asked as he stood from his chair. I walked in the office with Watts hot on my heels. Santiago met me halfway, embracing me. I returned the embrace taking in the scent of him. The embrace was quick but it was enough for me to enjoy him for a moment. I stepped back so he could shake hands with Watts. Two chairs sat in front of his large desk. I took one as Watts sat in the other. Santiago returned to his seat. He always looked good sitting at the desk in his fine tailored suits. His eyes narrowed as he took in my scent. I wanted to be on the other side of the desk with him but reminded myself this was a business call not a social one.

"No, we have no leads at this point," I answered his question. "Were you able to find out anything about the Darings?"

"They joined the clan about seven years ago. They are not high ranking and do not wish to be so. From the small information I have they have filed no complaints nor have they had any filed against them."

"Is the little girl part of the clan?" Watts asked.

"No, she is not old enough to take an oath to Hugo. She will become a member when she turns eighteen, if she wishes to," I answered.

"But she is considered under our protection," Santiago added.

"Is there any way you can ask some of the members if they know anything about them?" I asked.

"Mi Amor, I have spent the last two hours calling members, none of them seem to know much about the family other than to say they are very nice and their daughter Isobel is a delight."

"Sorry. I should have known you had already made those calls."

"Do you have any suspicions who would have done this?" Santiago asked.

"Not yet. The police are looking into the parents right now," I answered, a hint of irritation in my voice.

I understood they needed to check every angle but it felt as if they were ignoring all the other possibilities. Statistically, when a child goes missing it is usually because of a parent. The problem was if it was a stranger who took her, they could be hundreds of miles away with Isobel or she could already be dead because no one was looking at the other possibilities. Law enforcement tended to get tunnel vision too often.

"You do not believe they have anything to do with this?" Santiago questioned.

"No, I don't."

"Has there been any demands for a ransom?" he asked.

"Not as of yet, which probably means there won't be," Watts answered.

"If there is, Hugo has instructed me to let you know he will help pay the ransom. I would also like to offer a reward," Santiago informed us.

"I will let the family and the police know. I have to ask, how much were you thinking of offering?" I asked.

"Fifty thousand."

Watts let out a whistle at the amount.

"Can I make a suggestion?" I asked.

"Of course."

"I would start at ten and add little by little. I would also coordinate with the cops to do a press release regarding the reward money. Reward money could encourage someone to come forward but it will bring out all of the crackpots and those looking to make a dime."

"Can you set up a meeting with your Lieutenant?" Santiago asked.

"Yes, I can."

"Also, I must ask you, are you fine with you and I assisting with the financial part of this?" Santiago looked at me.

As of three months ago I had become not only Santiago's mate but also became quite rich, like a millionaire rich. I was still adjusting to the fact I had more money than I ever thought was possible. This was an easy decision for me. I wanted to find Isobel as soon as possible. There was a chance a reward would help in finding her.

"Yes."

"I will make the call to set the money aside. Can you speak with your Lieutenant?"

"I'll take care of it. If you find out anything about the family, call me," I said as I stood up.

Santiago came around the desk embracing me. I placed my head against his chest finding a calmness, as I leaned into him. I reached up on my toes giving him a quick kiss. I should have known as soon as our lips touched, I would want more than a quick peck. My body tightened with the need I was feeling. It was enough to cause a reaction in my mate. I felt as he grew hard in response to my scent change. This was so not the time but neither of our bodies seemed to care. I should have been embarrassed by the reaction but I wasn't.

"Will you be home later?" he asked.

"Yes. I don't know what time."

"I will be waiting for you."

"I'll see you tonight," I gave him one more peck and forced my feet to move away from Santiago. I felt his eyes as he watched me walk to the door. I waited for Watts to exit first before I gave Santiago one more glance as I left the room. Damn, he was gorgeous as he stood there with those dark eyes. I would have Santiago later tonight, right now I had a job to do and I needed to focus on Isobel Daring.

Chapter Four

We left the coolness of the club and were greeted by the hot sun. The family had no enemies within the clan that Santiago could find. The neighbors we spoke with, had said they were a nice family who tried to help any neighbor who may be in need. From the look of their house and where they lived money was tight. The wife was distraught to the point of almost being catatonic. The husband, his grief was written all over his body, from the down turn of his mouth to the way his body seemed to be ready to collapse, his shoulders were hunched. The meeting with my mate did nothing but confirm the belief they were free and clear of all of this in my head.

I moved onto the next possibility of a stranger abduction. Ransom seemed out of the question, unless the abductor expected the clan to pay it. If that were the case, I was confident they would have called by now. Maybe they were waiting to see what the clan was going to do before they made their move. It was possible but highly unlikely. That left a sexual predator as an option. He could have seen the girl at the fair or maybe coming home from school. Generally, sexual predators groomed their victims, they spent weeks and months building a relationship with the child but not always. If it was a phedophile, then there was a good chance Isobel was already dead. The thought of her final moments came crashing down on me, making me wish I had not gone there.

I moved away from that line of thought to other options. It could be a hate group. But why? I mean she was a hybrid. Why not take out the entire family? I guess it was possible a hate group could be involved but I didn't know how likely it was. There was a witch group who hated hybrids and had been speaking out about hybrids lately. They were vocal about the fact they felt hybrids were mudding up the witch species. It was disgusting the way hybrid children were called defects. Someone like me who was willing to become a hybrid, we were abominations. We were betraying our species. The question was did they have the guts to take a hybrid child? If they did, there was only one way for it to end for poor Isobel. What would be the point of taking her?

There was always a chance a female took Isobel. There were desperate females, who took kids to raise them as their own. They usually took infants, not seven year old's but it was possible. The size of the window in the bathroom was narrow. It wasn't impossible for a male to get in through the window but I didn't see how one could, unless they were built like Dante. It made more sense that a female would be the kidnapper if the window was the entry point. I was hoping Meri learned something new about the family.

I was so trapped in my thoughts, I didn't hear Watts trying to get my attention. He tapped my arm, startling me back into reality. We were almost back to the police barricade.

"You okay, Woods?" he asked.

"Yeah... just... thinking about where we go next. Sorry. What were you trying to tell me?"

"I was asking about hybrids actually. Meri asked the parents in the interview if the girl needs to feed? And Santiago said she was under the vampire's protection. Aren't hybrids their own species?" he asked.

"To humans they are, maybe even to some hellborns, but they are actually a part of whatever species they want to be part of. For this young it sounds like Hugo is wanting her to be part of his clan but it will be up to her to decide what she wants, when she is old enough," I explained. "The feeding thing is because hybrids vary in what they become. Some need to feed like vampires, others can but don't need to. There are some that develop no fangs at all. The body or rather the DNA decides what each hybrid will become."

"How likely is it that witches would accept her?"

"Not very. To be honest, hybrids have it more difficult than any other hellborn species because they aren't one or the other in terms of species so they are shunned a lot of times."

"Why don't they come together to create their own community?"

"That's a good question, maybe it's because they're so few. The last census that was done said there were less than ninety thousand in the country. It could be sheer lack of numbers. It could also be because in certain parts of the world hellborns are discouraged from creating hybrids. I don't know the answer or if there is even one."

"Are you planning on becoming one?" he asked.

I wasn't sure how to answer that one. Watts had been working with me for the last two months and in that time I had gotten to know the guy well. He learned quickly and always wanted to learn more. I liked having him on my team and dreaded the day he went back to the police department. He was a good fit for Meri and I. The problem was he would be going back to the police department and telling him I was about to become a hybrid could mean the entire department found out. Or maybe just Ryan. I hadn't told Ryan about it because I was worried about his reaction. He hadn't liked the idea of Santiago and I being mated. Now I was going to be more than a ley witch if I survived the transition. I wasn't sure what he would say. Watts was more than just a human I worked with. He was a human I trusted with my life. He was someone who wanted to learn about hellborns to be more effective in his job. He was a friend. I guess I was about to find out if he saw me the same way or just a colleague.

"Yes, I am. It was a requirement of Hugo's when I mated Santiago," I said as I watched his reaction.

"Is it safe to become a hybrid?" there was uneasiness to his voice.

"No, it's not," I said, showing my I.D. to the cop once more at the barricade. The uniform nodded, moving the barricade out of our way.

"Why do it?"

"Because I want to be with Santiago. I wouldn't be okay if he asked me to give up who I was. I can't ask him to walk away from who he is."

"But isn't Santaigo asking you to give up who you are to become a hybrid," Watts pointed out.

I thought about what he was saying and I guess to Watts it looks that way. I saw it as a compromise. Santiago never asked me to do it. In fact when Hugo had demanded I become a hybrid, Santiago had become upset at the idea. He didn't like the idea any more than I did. He was fine with me staying a witch. Hugo had wanted it and the more I thought about it over the last three months, the more I was inclined to agree with Hugo. I was part of a vampire clan, I couldn't stay witch. There would be vampires who would have a problem with it. Unfortunately, those problems would become Santiago's. I wasn't willing to put any of that on him. There was also the chance I could be challenged by a vampire. I wouldn't be allowed to use my magic against another in a challenge for my position. It would be bare knuckle fighting. I was good and trained regularly but I wouldn't be able to last forever against a vampire. Being a hybrid gave me a better chance.

"No, he's not. I will still be a witch after I go through the transition. I'll just have a little different DNA makeup than I did before. Besides, Santiago didn't ask me to do it, Hugo did."

"Maybe hybrids see it the way you see it, that's why they don't consider themselves a different species," Watts added.

"Maybe." We parked in the same spot we had left. Police were everywhere, just as they had been before. I was confident nothing had changed while we were gone. "Watts, I want you to go in and let Meri know we're back and meet me in the trailer with Meri. Can you do me a favor?"

We climbed from his car and began to move towards the trailer and house once more.

"Yeah?"

"Don't say anything to Ryan or Cain about my becoming a hybrid. I want to tell them."

"You got it," Watts replied.

I watched as Watts entered the house before I headed inside the command post. Cain was sitting inside, with papers spread across the table. Ryan was with him, leaning back in his chair looking over some documents in his hand. They both looked up as the door shut behind me.

"Find anything?" I asked.

"Their financials look pretty straight forward. They have little in savings and they have a college fund set up for the kid. No life insurance on any of them. No hidden money I can find," Cain answered.

"How much in the college fund?" I asked.

"Three hundred dollars," Ryan answered.

"It's not much of a college fund," Cain replied.

Meri and Watts walked in as we talked.

"Santiago is still doing a little digging but so far he has nothing. The parents and young have been part of the clan for the last seven years. They have had no complaints filed against them nor have they filed any. People think they're a great family," I reported.

"Damn," Ryan cursed.

"We need to start looking at other possibilities," I said.

"We still can't say they're innocent Woods," Cain pointed out.

"I get that Cain but every minute we waste on them, Isobel is with a perp possibly being harmed. We need to move on," I retorted.

"Chances are good they..."

"Enough you two," Ryan snapped at us. We all fell silent as he thought about what to do next.

"Woods is right. We need to start looking at other possibilities." Cain looked like he was about to argue his point one more time when Ryan stopped him with a hand gesture. "Cain, I want you to keep digging into their past. I will get Houser to start looking at the carnival people. I have him doing background checks on the neighbors to see if we come up with criminal records on any of them."

"We can start looking at hate groups," I offered.

"Actually, Savannah, I think we need to go see Emma Daring's parents," Meri finally chimed in.

"Why?" I asked.

"They disagree with their daughter's choice to marry Brian Daring because he was human. When he was turned and she chose to become a hybrid, the parents disowned her. Maybe they had something to do with this. From what Mr. Daring said they are part of a group called Witches Preservation Group."

"They don't sound like an accepting group," Watts said.

Witches Preservation Group was a hate group. They were about preventing witches from marrying outside their own species. They were against hybrids and felt the witch species would die out if we all didn't start breeding with one another. Just the hellborns I didn't want to deal with. I had dismissed the idea in my head as far fetched, maybe I was wrong.

"What is Witches Preservation Group?" Watts asked.

"They're a hate group," I replied.

"They're an organization nothing more, Woods," Ryan shot back.

"They are a group who wants to stop witches from mating anyone who is not a witch. They call hybrids defects and abominations. They're a hate group Ryan," I argued.

"Not according to the federal government," he argued back. "I can send a detective over to talk to Emma Daring's parents this evening. But if they hate their daughter, I can't see why they would take their granddaughter," Ryan offered.

"No, we'll go," I offered.

"Woods I don't think that's a good idea," Ryan pointed out.

"They didn't like that she mated a human. Do you really think a human detective is going to get anywhere with them? You'll be lucky to get past the front door. No, we'll go and I'll let you know what they say."

Ryan thought about what I was saying before he spoke. He leaned forward and rubbed his face with the palms of his hands.

"I don't know if you will have a better chance with these people than we would but they are hellborns so I'll let you do it. Embers did you get the parents' names?"

"Emerson and Jemma Brazen," Meri answered.

"Find an address for Woods," Ryan ordered Cain.

"I'm on it, Lieutenant."

Cain went to work on his laptop. I turned to Ryan.

"The clan is offering to pay any ransom, if one, is demanded," I said as we waited for Cain.

"I don't see a ransom call coming in at this point," Ryan said.

"Me either but I thought I would let you know. Also, Santiago is wanting to offer a ten thousand dollar reward to anyone with information to help find Isobel."

"Okay," Ryan grumbled. He was rubbing his face again. He sat back in the chair saying nothing for a moment. "We're setting up a press conference tomorrow at eight a.m. I need the bl... I mean your mate and all of you there for it. I will announce the reward during the press conference. I have CSU guys combing through footage right now from the intersection where the dogs lost the scent. We're hoping to have something by then. Phones are being set up at the precinct now. We will be leaving a handful of officers here while we work from the office."

"I'll let Santiago know and we'll be here," I replied.

Cain handed me a slip of paper with the address of Emerson and Jemma Brazen. I took it from him reading they were in a home not far from Meri's place. It was a mostly human neighborhood, which I found interesting.

"Do you want us to meet you back at the station?" I asked.

"No. Call me as soon as you're done with the parents. If anything changes I'll call you."

"Okay. See you in the morning."

The three of us headed out of the trailer. I waited until we were near the cars before I said anything to my team.

"Watts follow us over to the address," I ordered. "I want Watts and I to take the lead when we question them. If we fail to get cooperation from them, Meri will step in. I don't want you to be nice about it either," I pointed at her.

"How mean do you want me to get?" she asked with a smile.

"No physical violence but anything above that is fine with me."

"Not a problem," she shrugged.

"Wait if Ryan finds out..."

"Isobel has been missing for hours. If we don't find her soon, chances are good she will die. There is a good chance these people are going to be less than helpful. We have to make sure they had nothing to do with this, so we can move on. If you're uncomfortable with this I suggest you go home. What will it be, Watts?" I asked.

He looked from one to the other as Meri and I stared back at him. I could tell he was wondering how far we were willing to go.

"I won't cross the line, no harm will come to them unless they are involved but you need to understand that they are not going to want to help us. Hellborns play by other rules, this group plays on an entirely different plane," I explained.

"Fine...I'm in," he said slowly.

Chapter Five

With the shift in the seasons came a shift in the sun's clock as well. The sun was starting its western descent as we pulled in front of Emerson and Jemma Brazen's home. The house they lived in was a one story, ranch style home. The wide house had a small yard with grass that was still green. I could see small patches of grass on their way to turning brown.

The front door was protected by a glass storm door. I tried the small black handle first, finding it locked. I rang the bell, unsure if they would hear a knock on the storm door. It took a moment for a male with a round gut and dark hair to answer the door. His dark hair was thinning on top, neatly trimmed around the base of his skull. I met his eyes, seeing the same midnight blue eyes Emma and Isobel Daring had. The male looked me up and down when recognition dawned on his features. His eyes went from shocked to disgust at the sight of me. I flashed my credentials at him. He pushed open the glass door far enough to stick his head out. His pudgy body blocking the opening prevented us from entering.

"What can I do for you?" he asked curtly.

"I'm Hunter Savannah Woods. These are my associates," I indicated Meri and Watts behind me. "I was wondering if we could speak to you about your granddaughter, Isobel Daring?" I tried to be polite first.

"We don't have a granddaughter," he denied.

"Are you the parents of Emma Daring?" I asked.

"We used to be until she married that male. We have no children now," he sneered as he tried to step away from the door bringing it with him. I grabbed onto the door taking a step closer to the witch. My politeness didn't last long.

"Isobel Daring is missing and we need to speak to you and your mate," I snapped.

"She is my consort, not mate. Only wolves and vampires have mates, something you have forgotten."

This guy was really starting to piss me off.

"You can talk to us or you can talk to the humans but either way you are going to have this conversation. Which will it be?" Meri said from behind me.

He gave Meri a hard look before he released the door and stepped aside. We walked past him into the entryway. As I came level with Emerson, I saw he was only five nine, making him closer to my height next to Watts. The male looked at Watts unsure if he could trust the human. Watts gave him a polite smile.

The living room was large with well used, clean furniture. The chairs were yellow with pillows to match. The walls were white with no pictures hanging on them.. The carpet was beige, covering the living room. It looked like no one used the room. There was no homie feel to this place. Nothing out of place or a hint of dust on any of the surfaces. It was the polar opposite of the Darings' home.

"Stay here. I'll be back with my consort," he ordered tersely.

I wanted to point out manners even by witch standards meant you at least offered your guests a place to sit but I restrained myself. This was already going terribly and I didn't think it was going to get any better.

I looked around the room while we waited for Mr. Brazen to return. A small table sat next to the door with a pile of mail on it and a set of keys. I pushed the mail, fanning it out, reading all of the return addresses and names. It looked to be your everyday household bills. One did not look like everyday mail and got my attention. There was an envelope from a H&W Clinical Research. I had never heard of this medical practice. Most witches didn't go to the doctor unless it was an emergency. I filed the information away in my head promising to check the place out. I turned my attention to the keys. They looked like any other set of keys with a key chain that was face down. I flipped the key chain seeing the logo for Witches Preservation Group, a grey cauldron with a drop of water over the deep red coloring coming from the top of the cauldron. The drop symbolized purification. Around the cauldron and in the background were the colors blue, purple, and green. Watts watched me as I looked over the table saying nothing. Five minutes passed before Emerson came back with his consort, who was a few inches shorter than he was. Her soft brown hair had grey streaks running through it. Her body was turning soft with age. She approached us, her head held high.

"What can we do for you?" she asked.

"We're investigating a kidnapping case. Isobel Daring was taken from her home sometime last night," Watts said leaving the statement open ended.

"And?" the consort answered.

"When was the last time you talked to your daughter?" I asked.

"Seven years ago, when she became an abomination along with her spawn," Jemma Brazen's lip curled back at the word spawn.

My eyes narrowed at the language she was using to talk about her blooded daughter and granddaughter.

"Where were you last night?" I asked.

"We were entertaining friends until eleven o'clock last night."

"Who?" Watts questioned. His polite tone was slipping away.

"Friends is all you need to know," Jemma Brazen shot back. Her soft blue eyes narrowed at the human.

"We're going to need those names, Ma'am," Watts replied his normally upbeat voice was more aggressive, so was the smile on his face.

She gave us a measured stare, as if she was trying to decide if we were serious. When we did not say anything, she glanced at her consort.

"Dear, please go get the guest list from the party last night."

"Yes, my dear one," the male walked back the way he came.

"You are wasting your time with us. We have never seen the spawn nor would we touch it if we had seen it."

It! She had called Isobel Daring an "it". That was enough for me.

"Is that what WPG calls hybrid young or is that just what you came up with on your own?" I snapped.

Jemma Brazen's eyes flared at my statement. She turned her stare on me looking as if she wanted to burn me where I stood.

"You call them hybrids. What they are is a defect that should have no place in society. The young, as you keep calling it, should have been put down just as Emma should have been. Of course, you wouldn't know what standards of a race are being what you've mated," she spat at me. I took a step towards her as Watts placed a hand on my shoulder. I placed myself right in the older female's face and spoke through tight lips.

"You do not speak about my mate. Do you understand? Because the next time you try, I will burn your fucking house down! If I find out you had anything to do with this I will make sure you die slowly and very painfully," I spoke slowly and clearly, enunciating each word.

I stayed where I was as Emmerson reappeared with a page in his hand.

"What are you doing? Back away from my consort, you trash!" he yelled as he tried to push me away. As soon as his hand touched me, Meri grabbed the male's wrist twisting the arm behind his back. His face hit the wall a second later.

"You need to think really hard about what comes out of your mouth next because if it's the wrong thing I will break your shit off," Meri growled.

Watts snagged the list from Emerson's hand that was against the wall. As I continued staring at Jemma.

"That thing is better off or will be soon. Now you have what you came for, you need to leave our home."

I didn't like what she said, it made me wonder if she knew where to find Isobel.

"What do you mean by that?" I questioned.

"Just what I said. Now leave my home," she replied sternly.

I saw as her eyes darted away from me, for just a moment, before they returned to my face. It was enough for me to get a read on who she was. She was a bigot but she was also a coward. If she was involved, her role was a minor one. Jemma would not get her hands dirty. She would hire someone to do the dirty work for her.

"Let's go," I said. She smiled as if she had won the battle. The truth was she had won nothing, this was just the start. Jemma and Emerson Brazen would see us again. The question became would they be in one piece the next time when we left. My guess was not a chance.

Chapter Six

The three of us headed for the cars parked on the street. I could feel Meri still fuming from our meeting with the Brazens. Watts was right behind Meri with anger and disbelief written all over his face. I leaned against Meri's car looking at the two of them. The sun was getting lower by the minute as we stood trying to calm ourselves. Watts was the first to break the silence.

"What the hell is wrong with those people?" he asked.

"They're bigots that believe it's their job as witches to keep the bloodlines pure. Every species has them," I replied.

"I wanted to break that "consort" into bite size pieces," Meri added.

"You and me both," Watts replied.

"Fucking asshats," Meri said.

"Pieces of shit's is a better title for them," Watts replied.

I smiled at them seeing how well suited they were as partners. Watts in some ways was a straight arrow. He had been professional to a fault when he started working with us. He had kept all commentary to himself. Two months with Meri and I, he was less of a straight arrow. I wasn't sure in four months what he would be like or if Ryan would want him back. I also wasn't sure I wanted to give him back, either. Watts was beginning to feel like the missing link we hadn't even realized we were missing until he had joined our ranks. I let the abuse of the two bigots continue for another minute before I brought their attention back to the problem at hand. The shit talking was the best way to blow off steam without violence.

"What do you two think? I mean, other than they're disgusting. Do we think they're involved?" I asked.

"I don't know. They're terrible but are they terrible enough to do this?" Watts said.

"People like that would have no problem killing their own blood, if it meant they stayed true to their beliefs?" Meri replied.

"I think they know something but I don't think they would do it themselves. They would get someone to do it for them," I gave my two cents.

"How do you know that Woods?" Watts asked.

"Because when I was up in her face, her eyes shifted away from me. Add in her little statement, I would put money on them knowing something."

"What do we do next?" Meri asked.

"We make a copy of this list and give it over to Ryan and Cain. We do research on all of these individuals and on the Brazens," I answered nodding my head at the house. "I saw an envelope for a medical group on the table, I want to check them out as well."

"If you're right, we should see if Cain can pull financials on them. See if that leads to anywhere," Watts said.

"Agreed. Let's head back to the office, see what we can get done before my mate comes home," I replied.

THIRTY MINUTES LATER we were back at my house and in the basement. Originally, Santiago and I had agreed to turn the basement into a spare bedroom. With the addition of Meri as an employee and now Watts for another four months we made the space my office. Technically, Meri was an apprentice, not just an employee, for the next ten months. I had fudged her paperwork a bit saying she had been with me longer than she had been. She worked as my back up for years, making no money doing so. I figured it was only fair to say she had been an apprentice for some time. Once she passed her test she would become a hunter. Apprentice or not she had her own desk across from me, she had earned it and I valued what she brought to the table. I had worked on my own for years enjoying the solitude. Meri had proven her ability to investigate when she had helped me prove Robert had attacked me. She was good at this job. With time she would be as good as I was. As a team, we worked well together and that made it more enjoyable.

The washer and dryer were still here but we added a wall, giving the machines their own small room. The rest of the space was an office. We added better lighting, removing the track lighting that had been here before and had installed large canister lights instead. Three desks were butted up against one another in the center of the room. The first month, I had filing cabinets lining the wall behind where Meri sat now. The sight of the filing cabinets were a bit ridiculous. On top of that I had to listen to Meri complain about them along with my mate, he hated them as much as she did. I finally gave into their demands. Duncan was in the process of setting up a secure network and scanning my files. One by one, the filing cabinets were disappearing. I had started out with thirteen cabinets and was down to seven. It was the end of an era for me.

We had added two large white boards to the room that sat behind Watts. One, we reserved for keeping track of open cases. Currently, we had no cases outside of Isobel Daring's. We had worked overtime for weeks to close every case we had before my mating ceremony. We had succeeded after working long, grueling hours to close our cases.

The second board was used to either communicate with each other, if we were working on different cases or for notes on open cases. I had always worked through every case in my head, going off memory of what I had seen or heard. Having the board was a way we could all see what we were dealing with. I had always envisioned a set up like this for me. Now it was for the three of us. It was part of the dream I could never see before.

To finish off the office space there was the security feed surrounding the house or one of the feeds. I had a feed set up here for when we were working. I could see what was happening around the outside of the house at any time. We had another set up in Santiago's office down the hall from our room. We also installed a camera at the front door, with a screen near the door, hidden in a cubie. After being attacked in the town house I was taking no chances. Santiago had made the additions to our security in order to make me feel safe in our home. Maybe I had become obsessed with personal security but it was better than the alternative.

I hung the party list on the board and snapped a picture of it through my scan app before I sent it to Cain. I took my seat as I dialed Cain.

"Cain," he answered.

"Hey, it's Woods I just emailed you a list of witches that were with the grandparents on Saturday. Figured you would want to run them down."

"Hold on, Woods," he replied. I could hear voices in the background along with some rustling.

"Lieutenant, I got Woods on the phone," I heard him yell before I heard a door shut.

"Woods, I'm going to put you on speaker. The Lieutenant wants a word with you."

I sat waiting for Ryan to come on the line, while I listened to Cain peck away at the keys on a computer. A minute later Ryan was there and his voice was harsh.

"Woods, what the hell happened with the grandparents?" he snapped.

"They were less than willing to talk to us."

"Well, they called the station to file a complaint about you. So tell me what happened?"

"First off, was the complaint against me or was it all of us?" I asked.

"Just you. Now start talking," he snapped again.

"We knocked on the door and Mr. Brazen answered. Originally, he was not wanting to help until I pointed out he could talk to me or you. He let us in. Mr. Brazen and his consort were both asked the standard questions. They got hostile quickly with us. They gave us a list of individuals who were with them on Saturday night until eleven."

"That's not their story. They called about thirty minutes ago demanding to speak to the detective in charge. They say you forced yourself into their home and began to threaten them."

"Didn't happen," I answered.

"Do you have any proof they're lying?" he questioned.

"I have two witnesses, one of them is Watts."

I looked at the other two who were watching me. I stayed calm as I talked to Ryan.

"Tell Watts to type up a statement and get it over to me. Embers as well. Their complaint says nothing about the other two being there."

"You will have it within the hour," I said.

"Now what did you get from them?"

"They are definitely part of WPG. They had a keychain with the emblem of WPG. Not to mention the way they spew their beliefs so openly. They hate Emma Daring and Isobel even though they have never met the young. Jemma Brazen said something interesting that makes me think she knows something."

"What'd she say?" Ryan continued to question me.

"She said Isobel was better off now or would be soon."

"Cain, I want you to start digging into these people."

"Anyway we can get financials on them?" I asked.

"Not without more on them. Suspicion is not enough to get a warrant for their financials," he answered.

"I also sent the list of witches they say were at their house on Saturday."

"I'll let you know what we find out. I'll see you in the morning Woods."

"Roger that." I disconnected the call and sat looking at Meri and Watts.

"Okay, so you two need to fill out witness statements to what happened with the Brazens. They're claiming I forced my way in and bullied them."

"Shit," Watts breathed.

"Yeah, nothing was said about either of you."

"How long do we have to get them done?" Meri asked.

"One hour."

Both went to work as I sat thinking about the sequence of events that had led to us getting physical with them. We shouldn't have gotten physical with those asshats but they had said just the right thing to push my buttons. It was curious why they had only named me. I had threatened them but Meri had been the one to get physical. So why put it on me? Was it because of who I was? Revenge for hating their bigotry? Or something else?

I wanted to start on the list we had gotten but I would wait until Meri and Watts were done. I turned to researching H&W Clinical Research. I typed in the name and hit search. It took my computer a matter of seconds to pull up an address and a contact number along with their website. I started there. The first thing I saw as the page loaded was the logo, a grey medieval axe with a blue half moon under it with three blue teardrops. They were witch symbols from medieval times. The axe stood for renewal or transition, the half moon was for blessings. Why were medieval witch symbols being used as a logo for a clinical group? I began reading their mission statement. They were a research company whose goal was to improve life for witches throughout the world. They were researching ways to treat the few ailments witches contracted by studying DNA and environment. They were also looking at ways to create pain medication that could work in our bodies. In the background there were smiling faces of individuals in white coats and microscopes. The website had a question section, careers with H&W Clinical Research and how to help with their research. It was a fairly generic website. I headed back to my search page looking for more information on the research company. The internet is the information highway, usually you could find anything and everything there. H&W Clinical Research had somehow avoided the internet. Not one article, good or bad, not any complaints through government agencies, nothing. Something was definitely not right here. There was no way they had never been sued or a complaint filed against them. How was that possible? What were the Brazen's doing with mail from this company? Maybe they were donors? Test subjects? I went back to their webpage and printed the mission statement and the logo. I had no clue why I was doing it but my gut was saying to. I put the page on the far corner of the white board before I took the list of alibis from the board next.

I read through the names on the list recognizing none of them. There were fifteen names in total with phone numbers. I would let Ryan and Cain handle the calls to these hellborns but we would handle some of the background information on them. The cops could get the criminal backgrounds. I split the list three ways and wrote down the names I was taking. Once Meri and Watts were done with their witness statements then we could move on.

The silence in the office allowed my brain to turn over the little information we had. The female was taken between the hours of ten p.m. and nine a.m. No one had seen or heard anything in the neighborhood. You would have thought Isobel would have made some noise. Maybe the female knew her abductor? Maybe he threatened her?

The scent of the female was followed miles away from the home to the most human part of the city before it was lost. Why go there? What was the point? How did the dogs lose the scent? That one really confused me. It made no sense how that could happen.

The grandparents were shady as hell but it could be they were just bigots and nothing more. The comment from Jemma Brazen played through my head. It was a suspicious comment but it didn't mean they knew anything.

How does a young disappear from her bed without anyone knowing? The questions were starting to build up in my head. I hated that I had no answers to any of them. I hated even more that Isobel was going to be spending her first night away from her parents with a predator. Fear for the young's survival was increasing as well. Her chances of survival were becoming smaller and smaller. Soon the search for Isobel would turn into a search for a body.

Watts spoke first, breaking my train of thought.

"What are you thinking about Woods?" he asked.

"Trying to figure out how someone takes a young without two hellborns not being aware a stranger is in the house?"

"Their room is down the hall. Maybe they had their door shut?" Watts speculated.

"Yeah, but Brian Daring should have smelled something or heard something," I said.

"Maybe he's a heavy sleeper. Or Cain could be right. Maybe the parents did kill her."

"I still don't believe they have anything to do with this," I countered.

"Not all parents want their kids," he replied.

"Believe me I know parents can do terrible things to their kids," I said as I stood up and began to pace. "I don't think they fit the mold as killers."

"Like I said maybe the parents were heavy sleepers," Watts repeated.

"Maybe we need to figure out how she was taken," Meri offered.

"We know how she was taken," I snapped.

"No. We know the guy came through the bathroom or at least appears to have. Maybe we need to walk through how the crime actually happened," she explained.

I continued my pacing as I thought about what she was saying. Meri was right; we suspected how the crime happened but we didn't know or have all the facts. Running through scenarios could answer a question maybe two if we were lucky.

"Watts, can you draw a diagram of the Daring house?" I asked.

"Yeah."

"We need a map of the city," I said as I riffled through my drawers. I couldn't find a map and stopped before I drove myself crazy. I knew we had one in the house but the question became where.

"Why do we need a map of the city?" Meri asked.

"If we are going to run scenarios then we need to see the escape path to where the dogs lost the scent." It hit me as I spoke where one was. My mate had one in his office. I ran up the stairs and then hit the second set of stairs that led to the top floor. Hugo had wanted to start expanding his business portfolio again and Santiago had been looking at properties outside The Gallery. I found the map on his desk, snagging it. Normally, I would have asked but this was about a missing young. I knew he would understand. I ran back to the basement with the map in hand. I held it against the other whiteboard we would not need.

"Meri, grab those magnets and help me out," I said.

She did as she was asked as Watts drew a diagram of the house. Once the map was up, I grabbed three markers from my desk: red, blue, and green.

"Are you two done with your statements? I don't want Ryan calling and bitching at me," I said.

"Yeah," they answered in unison.

"Okay. Let's run through all the possibilities."

We looked at the diagram, studying it.

"So we think the perp came through the bathroom window, grabbed Isobel from her room, walked back and exited through this window," I said using my red marker to draw the path.

"The guy could be in and out with Isobel in minutes," Meri said.

"True. What's another possibility?" I asked.

"What if the perp was already in the kid's room when they returned home? The perp could have gone in through the window and waited for everyone to go to sleep," Watts asked.

"Not possible. Brian would have smelled our guy," Meri pointed out.

The room went silent again as we all looked at the map.

"Okay, the perp would have had to time the abduction just right. Which means he would have had to have been watching the house, right?" I asked the room.

"It would be the only way to lower the risk of not being caught," Watts added.

"Okay so... the perp stations themselves outside the house somewhere and waits. How long would you wait?" I questioned.

"Three hours," Meri answered.

"Why three hours?" I asked.

"The parents checked on her at ten, so they probably went to bed after that. Let's say they had sex and then went to bed. Three hours would give them time to get into a deep sleep, less likely to notice anything," she explained. In that moment as she spoke I was proud of all she had learned.

"Makes sense, let go on the assumption Brian Daring doesn't notice the change of scent in the house. Our perp climbs through the bathroom window and heads to Isobel's room grabs the young and leaves the way he came in? I don't think so. It would be difficult to climb out of the bathroom window with a young in your arms," I said.

"That could mean there were two of them," Watts said.

"One outside to take the young from the other," I finished his thought.

I still didn't think that was the answer. It didn't feel right.

"I think our first assumption that the front door was the exit is right on," Meri said.

"Agreed," I answered.

We stood in silence once more.

"What if the bathroom window was staged?" Watts asked.

"What do you mean?" Meri questioned.

"What if the perp comes in through the front door and leaves through the front door?" Watts explained. "Neither parent could remember the door being locked. The distance between the door and the girl's room isn't that far so it would still take minutes."

I thought about what he was saying it was possible but why go to the trouble of staging the entrance.

"I'm going to sound like Ryan for a moment but please go with it. What makes you say it was staged?" I questioned.

"That window from the outside sits almost six feet off the ground. It is bigger than most bathroom windows but it's not large like the other windows in the house. It would take someone small to get in through that window. So what if our guy set the window to look like he went in through there just to add a distraction?" Watts explained.

"Why the need for a distraction?" I asked.

He seemed to stop to think about the why.

"You said the cops would focus on the parents. Ryan and Cain seem to be staying on them as you said they would. Why?" Meri asked.

"Parents harming their kids and pretending they're missing is more common than actual stranger abduction," Watts explained.

"There's the why," I replied.

"What?" Watts said.

"Our guy knows law enforcement procedure. If the bathroom was staged, they did it because it would make the cops question the parents," I theorized.

I took each of the markers making a different path through the diagram of the house. The more I thought about it, the more it made sense the bathroom was a distraction. And we all fell for it.

"Maybe the intersection was a distraction as well," Watts offered.

"Yeah it could be," I replied.

"Where did they track the scent of Isobel to?" Meri asked. Her focus had shifted over to the map of the city.

"Maker and Milton," Watts answered.

"Let me see one of those markers, Savannah?"

I handed her the red marker as she found the intersection and placed a big red dot on the map. She then traced the map with her finger looking closely at the streets and made another mark on the map. She took a second marker from my hand, the blue one, and made a third dot toward the south part of the city. The parents' home.

"The grandparents house is ten miles or so from where the dogs lost her scent," Meri pointed out.

"Interesting," I said.

"Or coincidence," Watts replied.

"Well, I don't believe in coincidences when it comes to crimes," I answered back.

"Or our guy knew about the grandparents?" Meri offered.

"They would have to know an awful lot about the Darings," I said.

"Still leaves the question of how didn't Brian Daring not know someone was in their house?" Meri added.

She was right, it did leave that question. The three of us stood there staring at the map of the city with no additional answers coming to us. The perp would have had to know the family to be able to enter into the house so confidently through the front door. If the drive to that intersection was a coincidence, then the perp had to know the grandparents were bigots. It would force us to look at the grandparents as well. It would slow everything down allowing them time to get away with Isobel. I was beginning to think this was not just a pedophile but someone who liked to hold his victims. Was he already out of the city? Or was he a local? Either way our perp was smart enough to know police procedures. That thought didn't make any of this any better.

Chapter Seven

We worked for another two hours trying to piece together the little information we had with our theory. I was beginning to suspect we were on the right track in terms of the bathroom window. The only way we could know for sure was to go take some measurements and for us to reenact the kidnapping. I also realized I needed to talk with Darings once more. I wanted them to go into greater detail with me, than they had previously. I was sure they had already been over the story with the police a dozen times but I would have to ask for them to go through it once more with me. I had a feeling a cognitive interview would be the way to go. The information they had given us so far had been first reaction responses, they were scared and traumatized and were forgetful of the small details. A cognitive interview would be the best way to get to those details.

Cain had sent a copy of the Brian and Emma's financial statements over. We each glanced over them but nothing more. I would dive into them if I had time before the press conference the next morning. From what I saw they had little in terms of money or credit. I had little hope of finding anything that would be helpful.

I said my goodbyes to my team and headed for the shower. Santiago was not home yet and I wanted to wash off the crap of the day. The day had started out with the stress I was feeling about my mating ceremony, that was happening in seven days. It ended with me replaying every piece of information we had on this case. I tried to stop the reel of the events as the water from the multiple shower heads hit my body with jets of hot water. It worked long enough to realize I still had things to do for the ceremony. I still had jewelry to buy, confirmation calls for delivery times of flowers, food, music, and so on and a final walk through of the venue. I started to wonder how I was going to handle all of it while I worked this case. The panic I had felt turned into guilt, I was worrying about some dumb ceremony instead of focusing every bit of brain power on Isobel Daring. I gave up on my shower after that. I needed a release valve for my mind, maybe a good run would do the trick.

I was wrapped in a towel and wringing my hair out when Santiago arrived home. I watched as he hung his jacket and tie up before he came into the bathroom to greet me. He smiled at the sight of me in the towel before he walked slowly towards me. Our lips met as he pulled me in against his body. It was all my body needed as an invitation. The quick kiss he had planned was turning into much more as I leaned as close as I could into his body. Santiago growled with anticipation as we kissed. His large hand found the back of my neck holding me in place. I went for the buttons on his shirt when he pulled back enough to look at me. His dark brown eyes were heavy with arousal as he looked into my eyes.

"It appears I came home at the right moment," he smiled.

"Yes, you did."

"How are you doing, Mi Amor?"

"I am wishing I had answers."

"Is there anything I can do to help?" he asked.

I had talked enough about the case. Right at this moment I needed to feel something that wasn't about a missing seven year old. It made me feel guilty for being so willing to drown myself in my mate but he was my home, my reset. I needed him in that moment. I needed to clear my head.

"There is definitely something you can do," I said with a smile as I took a step back and freed the towel from my body.

Santiago stood there taking in the sight of my naked body, still damp from the shower before his arm reached out for me, pulling me hard against his body. He kissed me as if he needed me for his survival. The need he was feeling was in the kiss. His other hand caressed down my shoulder to my breast where he brushed across my nipple, a moan escaped my lips as I began to unbutton his shirt again. We started a slow progression towards the bedroom but I was confident we would never make it. I pulled his shirt free from his body, dropping it to the floor. I went for his slacks next, sliding the zipper down freeing his erection. I grabbed onto his cock and began stroking up and down. He broke our kiss throwing his head back as I stroked him. Santiago's hips began to pump with the rhythm of my movement. I watched as my mate became lost in the sensation. Watching him made my own desire grow. My scent must have changed because the next thing I knew I was against the bathroom wall. I released him as I hit the wall. Santiago's hands found my ass and lifted me up. Instinct took over as I wrapped my legs around his body, my arms went around his neck. One moment I felt the head of his erection against my wet sex and the next he was pushing inside of me with a great thrust. The thrust was harsh but in a good way. Santiago moved in and out of me with such force that he drew a sharp intake of breath from me. The feel of him as he worked himself in and out of my body was the most wonderful feeling ever. I tried to keep my eyes on his as we continued to move but it became too much for me and I lost my focus. I orgasmed hard around him as he continued his unrelenting thrusts. His hips were finding a faster pace. I felt as he moved his face into my neck. The feel of his fangs as he dragged them down my flesh made my body tighten with anticipation. Just as the sex had not been gentle, neither was his fangs as they sank into my vein. I cried out as he sucked on my neck and his hard cock pounding in and out of me. I looked in the mirror across the bathroom watching as his hips moved. The sight of our bodies intertwined pushed me over the edge yet again, as my sex spasmed around him he came as well. He released my vein keeping us against the bathroom wall. We both were breathing heavily as his eyes met mine. Santiago slowly pulled his cock from me, sending a shiver down my spine before allowing me to stand. I watched as he pulled his slacks back in place, taking in every inch of his glorious body. Damn my mate was hot. His eyes found mine and he could tell I wanted more of him. He retrieved his shirt next.

"Are you sure you want to get dressed again?" I asked, still leaning against the wall.

"I brought us dinner and there is no possible way I will be able to eat if we stay naked."

"Well we could skip dinner for now and have a repeat of what we just did," I said as I moved towards him.

"Before I take you again, you will need to eat." His hand brushed one of my nipples, causing me to gasp. He leaned in, placing his mouth close to my neck. "I will see you in the dining room, Mi Amor," Santiago whispered against my skin before he walked away from me.

My body flared at his words. Damn! He was good.

I PULLED ON A PAIR of yoga pants and a tank top and headed down the stairs. The dining room was cream colored with a long, heavy barn table. The tabletop was smooth and polished in a dark walnut finish. Each side of the table were carved with intricate Moorish and Spanish designs. The legs were smoothly curved. The table sat eight, with chairs that matched. The table and chairs had been built by Santiago, himself. He had been working on the project for months before we bought the house. From what I understood he had started it when we had gotten together. It was one of my favorite pieces of furniture in our home.

By the time I reached the dining room, Santiago already had the table set with square plates that were red on the inside and black on the rim. Heavy silverware was placed to the right of both plates that were sitting side by side. The food was on the table. Tonight's dinner was salad, chicken and steamed zucchini. As the smell of the food hit my senses, my stomach let out a growl. I hadn't felt hungry until I saw and smelled the food making me realize I had skipped every meal today. Santiago carried in one hand two tall wine glasses and a bottle of wine in the other hand. The cork had already been removed. He set everything down onto the table.

"Allow me get your chair for you?" he said coming over and pulling it back from the table. I sat down as he scooted the chair in for me. Santiago handed me a plate with chicken on it before he left the room once more. He was back a minute later with a small plate of bread.

He took his seat next to me. We both filled our plates before we began talking. I took a bite of the moist meat and groaned at the taste of garlic, lemon and something else I couldn't name as it filled my taste buds.

"My guess is you have not eaten much today," Santiago said as I ate.

"No, I didn't. Thank you for dinner."

"It is my pleasure. Ms. Radmaker called me today, I have the final fitting for my suit tomorrow."

"At least I accomplished getting that done for Saturday," I replied. All the stress I had been able to let go came tumbling back.

"What else needs to be done?"

"I still need to get a necklace and earrings according to Ms. Radmaker. I also need to confirm the time for the caterers and the venue, along with making sure they know how everything is to be set up. I need to make a few other calls."

"I will take care of it all for you," he said simply.

"What?"

"Finding Isobel is the priority. You will be working day and night. I can handle what needs to be done for our ceremony."

"But you already have done more than half of the work for this. It's not fair to you. Besides, how are you going to take care of the jewelry?" I asked.

Santiago had made most of the calls for the venue, the food, and even Ms. Radmaker. He had taken care of the invitations, the announcement, even the decorator. I felt all I had done was give him names for the guest list and pick a dress. Now he was willing to pick up the slack while I worked.

"You have done plenty for our mating ceremony. I am more than happy to take care of the remaining details. I am more concerned with you being able to do your job. As for the jewelry I can call Ms. Radmaker myself and find out what you were instructed to buy."

I leaned toward him, placing a hand on his cheek as I captured his lips. It was a quick kiss but it was all I could allow myself without a repeat from what had happened upstairs.

"Thank you."

"Whatever for?" he asked.

"For being understanding."

"Thank you for taking this case," he kissed me once more. "Now please eat your dinner, you will need the energy." His words made me smile as I returned to my food. "Did you have the opportunity to speak with Lieutenant Ryan about the reward money?"

"He is having a press conference tomorrow morning and wants you there along with my team."

"What time?" he asked.

"Eight in the morning."

"I will have to draft a statement tonight then," Santiago's voice held sadness in it. The Darings were part of his family. They were his people.

"Oh and I will have to buy you a new map of the city."

"Why?"

"I needed a map and I kind of took yours. I'm sorry about that," I apologized.

"It is fine, Mi Amor. Whatever you need to get the young back, you will have," he replied.

God! I loved him.

"Do you have any leads as of yet?" he asked.

"No. The grandparents are suspicious but it could just be because they're bigots that make me question them."

Santiago grabbed my hand and squeezed it.

"I learned years ago with you. If you suspect someone of doing wrong, you are usually right."

I thought about his words as I kept eating. Santiago was right, I was right more times than I was wrong when it came to individuals. It made me want to take another go at the Brazens. The problem was I didn't like them not just because I suspected them of wrongdoing, but because of the trash they had said to me. There was also the fact that they had filed a complaint with the department against me. I needed to see what the police department was going to do. I was fearful they would pull me from the case. If they did, what was I going to do then? There was no way I could walk away from this now. The need to find Isobel was too great for me.

"Are you alright?" Santiago asked.

"I'm fine."

"No, you are worried. Is there a way I may aid you in finding Isobel?"

"Unfortunately, no there isn't. The reward money is going to be helpful but outside of that no."

"If there is, please ask," Santiago said.

"I will."

We spent the rest of dinner talking about Saturday and other distracting topics. I cleared the table while Santiago headed to his office. He needed to call Hugo and let him know about the press conference. I stood in our kitchen loading the dishwasher and packing away the food we hadn't finished. I had hoped the dishes would be a distraction from everything around me. The problem was it was a mind numbing task, which meant my brain went right back to work. The department was working around the clock to find Isobel. There were officers searching the streets. Ryan and Cain were digging into every person that had had contact with Isobel. I kept going back to the little we knew so far. I needed to check in with Ryan once more before I went to bed. Maybe Ryan had found a lead and hadn't called. There was no way a young could disappear so easily with no trace. I got the dishwasher going before I leaned my butt against it and pulled up Ryan's contact information in my phone.

"Ryan," he answered quickly. I could hear the chatter in the background as detectives and officers worked.

"It's Woods, anything new?"

"We are still going through footage from that intersection. Past that, nothing as of yet."

"Do you need any help with the videos?" I offered.

"No. I have the techs working on them. If we find anything I will call you."

I nodded my head even though Ryan couldn't see me.

"What is the department going to do about the Brazens?"

"I don't know. I'll have an answer for you in the morning. From what I can tell, you did nothing wrong. Chances are good the department will just say sorry to the Brazens and keep you on the case. You won't be able to go anywhere near them. So if you're right about them, we will have to either get another hunter or pick them up ourselves."

"Why apologize if I did nothing wrong?" I questioned.

"Because sometimes it's easier to say sorry to a barking dog than ignore them." It was bullshit is what it was. Apologizing to those assholes just angered me more. "Is your mate coming to the press conference?" Ryan asked.

"Yeah. He's working on a statement from the Clan as we speak."

"I'll call you if we find anything."

"Thanks Ryan. Oh and I am going to talk with the Darings in the morning after the press conference."

"Why?"

"My team has a working theory but I need to talk with them first. If we're right I'll let you know."

"Fine," he said with finality.

"See you in the morning," I said.

"Yeah," was all he said before the call disconnected.

I wanted to go out looking for Isobel Daring because I wanted to feel like I was doing something, anything other than sitting on my ass. The problem was where would I start? If my team was right, the area the dogs tracked the girl to was nothing more than a diversion. We knew Isobel had been kept out of The Gallery. Where would I go if I did go out searching? The answer was simple: I didn't. I hated feeling useless and right now I was feeling pretty fucking useless as I stood in my kitchen. I took a few deep breaths finding they did nothing to loosen the tightness of my shoulders. I gave up and headed for the stairs. Santiago would be done soon enough and maybe I could find distraction in my mate again.

Chapter Eight
Six Days before the Mating Ceremony

The next morning came earlier than I wanted. Santiago and I both dressed for the news conference. Normally I worked in either my hunter clothes or a pair of jeans. Today a pair of black slacks and a hunter green blouse. A jacket that matched the pants and a pair of black pumps would finish it off. I had owned the suit for two months and had only worn it once. I had bought the suit because of Santiago. He had asked me to attend a business lunch with him and I had had no suitable clothes for the occasion. Now as I stood in front of the mirror I was grateful I had made the purchase.

Santiago as always was in one of his custom suits. Black on black was his choice with a black tie. I watched as he adjusted his tie. His hair was shorter than it had been almost a year ago, he wore it cut short off of his neck with it brushed back from his brow. When we met he had worn it longer. As much as I loved the soft locks, I liked his hair as he wore it now. I watched as he slid into his jacket, buttoning it into place.

"Are you finished watching me dress, Mi Amor?" Santiago asked, smiling as he faced me.

"What can I say I like watching you move. Mind you, I prefer watching you undress but I will take this view too," I walked over placing my hands on his chest as his arm wrapped around me.

"You look spectacular."

"Thank you. Do you want to drive together?" I asked.

"How will you get around today? Unless you are planning on taking me to work?"

"I'll let one of the other two drive today. I figured it would be best if we arrived together. Show we are a united front in the effort to get Isobel back."

"Are you sure?" he asked.

I liked driving myself and Santiago knew it. It was one of the control issues I had. The only exception I made was if we were going out together. Today, I was not going as just a hunter but also as Santiago's mate. Santiago was the male who would be speaking for the clan and I needed to be at his side. I hate politics but they were a part of life. Being mated to the second in command of the Black Grove Clan meant I would have to play the game with Santiago. Arriving together, showed the city Santiago had made a good choice in mates.

"Yes," I answered.

He gave me the look he had given me so many times in the past. The look said he wanted me. I felt as he grew hard, pressed against me. I glanced at the clock, seeing we didn't have time to take care of our sexual needs. We needed to arrive before the press conference started. I was tempted to say screw it, let's be late but I thought of Isobel being gone one more day, forcing me to step away from him and rest my hand in his.

We headed down the stairs hand in hand.

"Let me just grab my bag from my car. We can take yours," I said to Santiago as he set the alarm and locked the door.

We had a two car garage, perfect for both of our vehicles. My SUV was on the bigger side with plenty of seats and a large trunk space. I drove a black Suburban. The inside was tan only because they didn't offer it in black as I had wanted. The SUV was an eight cylinder and offered plenty of space for my hunter and crime scene bags and passengers or in some cases prisoners.

My mate drove a black Porsche Panamera. It was the one area in our life where we differed. I needed a bigger vehicle for not just my bags I carried but because you never knew if I was going to have drive a hellborn for booking. Santiago liked luxury when it came to what he drove. The way I saw it, we had the best of both worlds.

He opened the trunk for me as I placed my go bag inside along with my crime scene bag. Meri already had a bag in her car for hunting, so at least I didn't need the other bag. Meri had been dragging her feet on making a crime scene bag, which had driven me crazy, I would have to bring both bags. In a matter of months she would have her hunters license and she needed her own crap.

Santiago went around to the passenger side of the car opening the door for me. I slid into the all leather interior enjoying the scent of it. The seats were bucket racing seats, that were a smooth black top grain leather. All of the leather was hand sewn and made for this car. The overhead liner was a black leather that felt more like velvet. Santiago climbed into the driver's seat and within minutes we were off. The engine sounded like a V8 should sound. A smooth deep rumble filled the air as we drove down the lane from our home. The Panamera was made for speed with its four driving settings, each one giving more control to the driver in terms of handling. The stopwatch on the dashboard was for you to have the capability to time your lap speed. The car was a beautiful piece of machinery.

"I would like to speak to the Darings after the press conference and I would prefer you to be by my side when I do so," Santiago said as he drove us.

Today we would be playing on both sides of our jobs. I would have to play hunter for most of the day but this morning I was Santiago's mate and part of the clan. This was where our lives became complicated. It was a fine line we would have to walk. I had to be detached to do my job as a hunter but I also had to be there for the Darings as a leader. There were days I felt like I had too many roles to play. There was no way I could stay completely detached from this case while still being part of the clan.

"I can do that," I answered.

"Thank you," he gave my hand a quick squeeze before his hand returned to the gear shift.

WE ARRIVED AT THE DARING'S house with fifteen minutes to spare before the news conference began. The road blocks were down and the press was beginning to assemble in the street. I made out the tall figure of Ryan, he was talking with uniformed officers, giving them instructions if his hand movements were any indication as he pointed his finger to the growing crowd. Meri and Watts were also present, they were standing in the narrow driveway of the Daring's home. Meri was dressed in a suit just as I was. The difference was her's was more expensive than my own and she had a loose cream colored blouse on. Watts had one of his suits that he wore to work when he was working with the police department. His grey suit paired with a crisp white shirt was pressed and clean. He fiddled with the grey tie as he stood chatting with Meri as if he was uncomfortable in the suit. I was ready to climb from the car, hand on the release, when I stopped myself. I needed to be patient enough to allow Santiago to open my door. I waited as he came around the car. The media had seen the arrival and were beginning to move as one towards us. He opened the door and extended a hand to me. I stepped from the car as Ryan sent four uniformed officers to push the press back. I kept a hold of my mate's hand as we moved, the reporters throwing out questions at us. I could hear cameras as they snapped photos of the two of us. We moved towards the house, Ryan meeting us halfway.

"You know I remember the days when you would show up to these things and the press was less interested in you," he said as he approached.

"The press has always been interested in me. I'm a hellborn who hunts hellborns. The story practically writes itself," I replied sarcastically.

"Yeah." Ryan turned his attention to Santiago. "Mr. De los Rios good to see you again," Ryan extended his hand. My mate, always the gentleman, took the cop's hand shaking it.

"Good to see you as well, Lieutenant."

"I wanted to thank you for offering the reward money."

"The Darings are part of our clan. We will help in any way we can."

Ryan nodded his head. "I am going to go get the Darings so we can start."

He walked away from us as my team approached.

"Look at you?" Meri said with raised eyebrows and a small smile.

"Yeah, I know."

"Who knew you could dress so nice? This must be all Santiago's doing, right?" Meri probed.

"Actually, Savannah did this, not I," Santiago came to my defense.

"See, I can dress nice when needed."

I watched as Watts fiddled with his tie some more.

"You okay there, Watts?"

"It feels like I haven't worn a suit in years. I've gotten used to wearing my jeans to work."

"Oh man! Is Watts thinking about crossing over to our side?" my voice was heavy with sarcasm.

"I told you we would grow on him," Meri added smiling.

"I like being a cop. I'm just out of the habit of wearing suits is all," he said, a little uncertainty in his voice.

"We'll see at the end of the next four months," I replied.

"It wouldn't be hard to make this a permanent thing," Meri offered.

He shook his head at the two of us as we stood there, a smile on his face that I couldn't decipher if he liked the idea of staying with our team or going back to the other side. As we stood there, the Darings exited the house with Ryan and Cain. Emma Daring still looked as if she was barely conscious as her husband moved her down the lawn. We took our places behind Ryan and the Darings as the media moved to stand in front of us. It took a few minutes for the crowd's chatter to settle down.

"Good morning. Yesterday at nine a.m. Isobel Daring was reported missing. As you all know we have been working tirelessly to find Isobel. She is a hybrid female, age seven, with brown hair and dark blue eyes. She was last known to be wearing a pink shirt with a rainbow unicorn on it and black pants. Isobe attended the Sweetclover Fair on Saturday with her parents until approximately seven-thirty p.m. at which time she returned home with her parents. Isobel Daring was last seen in her bed at ten p.m. on Saturday night. The next morning her parents discovered her missing. If anyone has any information we urge you to contact the Sweetclover Police Department. At this time we have no suspects or persons of interest," Ryan said as he held up the photo of Isobel that had been released to the media the day before. There was a pause as questions began to be hurled at Ryan. He began talking again forcing them to quiet down once more. "There will be time for questions in a moment.

Right now, I will be turning this press conference over to Santiago De los Rios and his mate of the Black Grove Clan."

Ryan stepped to the left as Santiago and I moved forward.

"Thank you, Lieutenant Ryan," Santiago slightly inclined his head to Ryan before turning his attention back to the press. "I have a short statement I would like to read. As the second in the Black Grove Clan I am here to offer a cash reward to any human or hellborn with information, which will lead to the safe return of Isobel Daring. The Darings are part of our family and the community. We want nothing more than to find Isobel. The cash reward is set at ten-thousand dollars. If you have seen this young, we urge you to contact the police. We will be working closely with the Sweetclover Police Department until Isobel is found. We will not rest until she is safely back with her parents," Santiago stated giving the cameras a serious look. Santiago and I stepped back away from the crowd allowing Ryan to move up once more. The transition allowed for reporters to start asking questions.

Ryan took questions from the press for five minutes before he ended things. Many of the questions provided no further information to the public than they already knew. My role as the hunter on this case and Santiago's mate was questioned, which Ryan handled well. The reporters were unsure if I could handle being objective. Ryan's answer was simple, he referred to my record with the police department and stated they had confidence in me as a hunter to do my job. I hated the fact that it was asked but it wasn't surprising either. I kept my head held up and listened as the reporters pressed on, not reacting to their ridiculous question. The Darings had no wish to speak to the media, they had been present so everyone could see they were cooperating with the police.

"We will be providing updates as they come in. We urge anyone with any information to please call our hotline that has been set up. Thank You," Ryan finished the press conference.

The Darings were escorted back into their house as uniformed officers stepped up stopping the media from going after them. My team followed inside. Watts was the last one through the door, which he closed behind him. Ryan, Cain, Meri and Watts hung back near the door as Santiago and I moved towards Isobel's parents. The press conference seemed to have broken the dam for Emma as she began to sob, her husband pulling her into a tight embrace trying to console her.

"Emma, I am so very sorry for all of this," Santiago said, placing a hand on her arm as she cried. He kneeled down in front of them with me at his back.

"Thank you for offering the reward. You didn't have to do this for us," Brian said.

"Of course, we did. You are part of our clan and that is what we do for our people. Savannah and I are honored to offer the reward if it means bringing Isobel home safely."

"We will repay you somehow for this act of kindness," Brian replied, his voice a little on the hollow side.

"There is no need. We are happy to do it," I reassured Brian.

"If you need anything else please either speak with my mate or call me directly. I swear to you we will do everything we can to bring back your young back alive. I give you my oath if she is not found alive we will find the individuals who harmed her and they will pay for their crimes," Santiago vowed.

They looked at him with a mix of grief and gratitude. Their eyes sliding over to me.

"Whoever did this, I swear will pay for their actions," I added.

Brian nodded his head giving us soft thank you's. Santiago stepped back from the couple as I stepped closer.

"I have a few more questions for you. I want to give you two a moment before I start. Take your time and I will be right back," I said.

Brian nodded as Emma was beginning to drift into silence once more. I motioned to my team to follow me outside while Ryan and Cain moved forward toward the couple. Ryan gave me a look that asked the question: did that just happen. I kept moving, not caring if he liked the vow my mate had just given. Santiago and I were the first out. Some of the reporters were doing their wrap up for the local news as we stood on the porch.

"Meri, you're driving today. I need to put my bags in your car. Before we go in there, Watts I want you to measure how high the bathroom window sits and its width. While I'm talking to the Darings, I want you two to see how easy it would be to get in and out of the window," I ordered.

Santiago's vow had lit a fire under me, so to speak. I was already determined to find Isobel, now that determination was different in some way I couldn't put words to it. The Darings were our people and someone had harmed them. This was not something that would be forgiven. No, whoever did this would die slow and painful.

"Got it. I'll see if the Lieutenant or Cain have a tape measure."

"No need, I have one in my bag. When we're done here I want to go to the intersection where the dogs tracked her scent. We should go see WPG while we are out today."

"Should we offer to help with the phones? Everyone and their mother is going to be calling?" Watts asked.

"No, the cops can do that. If they get anything, Ryan will call us. The best thing we can do is continue our search on the streets. Someone has to know or has seen something," I answered.

"With that Mi Amor, I am going to go to work," Santiago said. "I'll walk you to your car."

Meri and Watts headed to Meri's car while Santiago and I moved to his. I slid my hand into his as we moved, feeling the comfort of his touch. My soul hurt in so many ways for the Darings.

Last night, I felt utterly useless and I would not feel that way again. We needed to find a clue, or a sighting, something that told us she was alive today.

We reached the car as Santiago hit the trunk release. I was on the verge of reaching for my bags when he stopped me. We faced each other as his hand cupped my face. I kissed him quickly.

"Please be careful today?" his voice, softly pleading.

"I will," I tried to reassure him.

"I do not like you going to WPG."

"I don't either but my gut is saying I need to."

"I do not trust these hellborns, they are the worst of our kind. I do not have a good feeling about this," Santiago warned me.

"I have the same feeling. I will have Watts and Meri with me so please don't worry too much."

"If you need any other back up, call me and I will be there."

"I will, I swear," I reassured Santiago.

"Will I see you tonight at home?" he asked.

"Of course."

He gave me one more kiss before he helped me pull my bags from the trunk. I took both bags, one on each shoulder, before I squeezed his hand once more. He left as I headed to Meri's vehicle. I watched as he drove off before I dumped my bags in Meri's car. I searched my crime scene bag for my tape measure before I said anything to the other two. Going through my head what we would be dealing with today. I still needed to talk to Ryan before we left for WPG. I found the tape measure, handing it to Watts. He headed to the house as Meri and I stood there.

"You okay?" she asked.

"No. I feel useless because we haven't found anything."

"I thought it was just me feeling that way," Meri answered.

"Not in the least," I replied. "We need to talk with the Darings again. There is something we're missing. I don't know what but there has to be," I said.

"Agreed. I kept thinking about Brian Daring not knowing someone had entered the house. It doesn't add up," Meri said, agreeing with me.

"No, it doesn't."

"Even if we solve that part of the mystery, do you think it will lead us anywhere?" she asked.

"I don't know. There is a chance it could. There's a bigger chance it will just be a piece of the puzzle that will go nowhere," I said as I started to move back toward the house. Meri shut the trunk and followed.

"I brought work clothes and so did Watts," Meri said switching topics.

"Good. Let's go back in there and talk to them and then Ryan. As soon as we do that we can head out."

We headed back towards the house. Watts was coming back from the side of the house.

"What do you have?" I asked.

"It's five feet and ten inches from the ground. The width is twenty-four and a half wide."

"Which would mean the glass itself is about twenty-three inches."

"Yeah," he confirmed.

"Any marks or footprints in the dirt?" I asked.

"None."

"I think Watts was right, the window wasn't used," Meri chimed in.

"Agreed. So that leaves us with the front door," I stated.

"Did anyone check out the other doors or windows?" Watts asked.

"I don't know," I answered honestly.

"Why don't Meri and I not only run drills at the bathroom window but also check the other windows while you talk to the Darings," Watts offered.

"Good idea."

I headed for the front door while they went to the side of the house. Ryan and Cain were standing over the Darings when I entered. Ryan looked up as I shut the door and headed to me.

"My team is checking out the remaining doors and windows of the house. While they're doing that I want to talk with them," I said nodding my head towards the Darings. "Then, can you and I have a conversation?" I asked.

"Yeah."

I nodded as I headed for the Darings. I grabbed the chair from the desk in the far corner, as I had done the day before. I placed it in front of them.

"I am sorry to have to do this but I need to ask you some additional questions," I informed them as gently as I could. We heard the bathroom window slide open. They both jumped. "I am having my team check your other windows and doors out, so it's just them you're hearing.

"Okay," Brian nodded.

"I want you to take me through your entire night from the moment you left the fair until the next morning can you do that?" I asked.

"We have already been over this multiple times," frustration was in Brian's voice.

"I know you have but I think there is something we're missing. It may be something so small you never even realized it happened or that it was important. I am not asking you this to upset you. I am just trying to piece everything together. The more we know the better chance we have of finding your daughter," I leaned forward placing my arms on my knees as I spoke.

"Okay. We left the fair about seven-thirty on Saturday night. We had been there all day and Isobel was tired."

"Did anyone approach you or did you notice anything when you got to the car?" I asked.

"No."

"Okay. What route did you take home?" I asked.

"Uhm...Uhm... we took Barnes to South Road and then turned on Stears. We wanted to avoid The Gallery traffic and give Isobel a little longer to sleep before we moved her."

"Okay, good. When you got home did everything seem normal?"

"Yes. Emma opened the door while I got Isobel out of the back seat. I carried her in and put her in bed. I pulled her shoes off and placed them at the foot of her bed on the floor. Then I shut the door and came in here."

I didn't remember seeing any shoes at the foot of the bed. It was one more thing to check. I could hear Meri and Watts as they worked.

"What did you do then?" I questioned.

"We were both tired, it had been a long day," he answered. I watched as his eyes lost focus as he reviewed as the events of the worst night of his life played over in his head. "Uhm... Emma made us some tea and we watched some television. We fell asleep on the couch,"

"I know this is going to sound weird but what kind of tea?" The tea could be laced with something. Or maybe it was just tea. Maybe I was reaching.

"Its blackberry tea, a neighbor gave to us. She and Emma became friends about three or four months ago. She gave it to us as a farewell gift before she moved."

"Which house did this friend live in?" I asked.

"She lived on the next block right behind us. We met her when Isobel lost a ball over the fence."

"What's her name?"

"Bree Miller," he replied confused about where I was going with this. "I don't see how this has anything to do with Isobel?"

"I am just trying to get all the information," I tried to reassure him. I wasn't sure this neighbor was important but it was another piece to their lives we didn't know about. "What can you tell me about Bree Miller?" I asked.

"She's a human, who was working as a consultant for a few businesses here," Brian answered, still confused.

A human living in The Gallery?

"Do you know why she was living in a hellborn neighborhood?"

"She said one of her clients offered her the house while she was here. She only lived there for a few months," Brian explained.

Now I was curious about Bree Miller. It wasn't like there were no humans who lived in the Gallery but there were very few. Most didn't want to live next door to one of us. I moved on filing the information away.

"Let's go back to that night. So you two had tea, what happened next?"

"Emma woke me up and I went to bed, it was ten o'clock. Emma said she was going to check on Isobel. A few minutes later she joined me in the bedroom and we both went back to sleep."

"What time did you get up on Sunday?" I questioned.

"We woke up later than normal. Isobel is an early riser so she usually is up by seven. Emma gets up before that on Sundays to make breakfast. We didn't wake up until almost nine."

They had slept later than normal. Emma had an internal clock that normally got her up early on Sunday mornings, except the morning when their young went missing. It seemed odd. Maybe they had just been exhausted and that could explain the over sleeping? Or maybe it was something else?

"Did you feel okay when you woke up?"

"What do you mean?" he asked.

"I mean did you feel woozy or little headed. Anything like that?"

Brian said nothing for a long moment as he thought about what I was asking.

"Emma said her head hurt."

Emma had overslept and woke with a headache. Brian Daring had smelled nothing nor heard anything as someone entered their home. I would say they had been drugged but drugs didn't work on hellborns, like they did on humans.

"Thank you for the information Brian."

"Did that help?" he asked.

"Yes, it did."

I got up, placing the chair back in the corner and headed back outside with Ryan and Cain on my heels.

"What was that all about Woods?" Ryan asked.

"We think our kidnapper didn't come through the bathroom window."

"What... No way the window was open and wiped down. Why do all that for nothing? It's a waste of time for the kidnappers to do that." Cain asked.

"To misdirect us," Ryan answered looking at me.

"Yeah. The question I have is how did Brian Daring not know someone was in the house?" I questioned.

At that moment Watts and Meri were back from the far side of the house. She was carrying a clear hose or a piece of one. It was only a couple inches long.

"I can answer that or well we can actually," Meri said.

"We found this under the living room window in a bush," Watts said.

"And it smells like lilacs," Meri added.

Cain pulled gloves from his jacket pocket taking the tubing from them.

"Why would it smell like lilacs?" Ryan asked.

"My guess it was some type of charm that was turned into a gas. It would explain why they fell asleep and didn't hear anything," I answered.

"But the girl was there at ten so the perp gasses them and then waits two hours?" Ryan asked.

"I don't know, maybe. Or they have the time wrong."

"It doesn't make sense, Woods. You wouldn't wait around," Cain chimed in.

"I wouldn't but that doesn't mean anything. Let me do some research on charms that smell like lilacs."

"Cain, I want you to log that and get it to the lab. See if they can help narrow it down. I also want a team out here and dusting that window for prints," Ryan ordered.

"You got it, Lieutenant."

Cain took off with the only piece of evidence we had.

"Good find, guys," Ryan said to the other two.

"What did you two find out about the bathroom window?" I asked.

"Watts couldn't get in easily without making a lot of noise. Myself, I can but not easily. There is no way I could have gotten out without making an imprint in the dirt. Getting out with a young would mean I would have to have a partner to hand the young off to," Meri explained.

I nodded at her assessment of the situation. We were either dealing with two people taking Isobel and we were wrong about the bathroom window. Or we were right and the window was a distraction. I turned my attention back to Ryan.

"Now what did the higher ups say about the complaint?" I questioned.

"They feel you did everything right but you are to not go near them without law enforcement with you from here on out."

"I figured that would be the case," I replied irritated.

"Sorry, Woods."

"It's fine. Did your CSU guys find anything on the security footage?"

"Nothing yet but they are still combining through them. We pulled in a few individuals from the area who had a record. We haven't gotten anywhere with them."

"What kind of individuals?" Meri asked.

"Sex offenders," Watts answered.

"Yeah," Ryan confirmed.

"Any prospects?" I asked.

"Not really. But I have a few guys sitting on them to see if anything happens."

"Let us know," I nodded.

"Will do."

"What about Isobel's school?" Watts asked.

"We talked to everyone and did background on the staff. No one looks suspicious. They all say how sweet Isobel is. She has had no behavior problems at school."

"And the people running the carnival?" I asked.

"There were a few employees for the vendor of the rides that have a criminal past, mostly drugs or drinking, nothing as serious as this," Ryan answered.

No criminal past didn't mean one of them wasn't our guy. It also didn't mean that they were either. I doubted the carnival workers had anything to do with this. A teacher or a staff member at the school was a better suspect. It would explain why Isobel didn't scream or fight. Could she have slept through the abductions? It was possible, especially if a charm was used.

"We're going to go check out the intersection where Isobel's scent was found and WPG," I informed Ryan.

"You think going to WPG is a good idea?"

"Why wouldn't it be?" I challenged him.

"After what happened with the Brazen's. They could cause trouble for all of us."

"Maybe but do you really think I should not go just because they could cause problems?"

He shook his head and sighed.

"Be careful and try not to antagonize them," he warned me.

I nodded my head. We headed out from the Darings. I needed food and a change of clothes. I didn't think I could go another day without food in my stomach again.

"Let's head to Delilah's," I suggested.

"Don't you want to get started," Watts asked.

"I do, more than you know but I want out of these clothes and I don't think any of us should go without food, like we did yesterday."

"Agreed," Meri said.

"Alright then," Watts replied, sounding disappointed.

We all climbed into Meri's Range Rover. She had gotten the car last year when Duncan had bought it for her birthday. At the time, I thought it was ridiculous for her to own an SUV. Now I was grateful she did. The outside of the vehicle was dark silver while the inside was tan leather. As I took the front I realized I hadn't seen Watts' car.

"Watts, where's your car?" I asked.

"I drove to Meri's this morning, that way we would have less vehicles to worry about."

"And a go bag?" I asked.

"Back here with me."

"Good man."

Chapter Nine

Our visit to Delilah's was short. We all changed into our usual work clothes and I ordered us food to go. It would have been better to sit and eat but we were all feeling the need to be of some use today. We could eat in the car, which got some dirty looks from Meri at the idea. She still hadn't learned sometimes you had to eat on the go. She would learn that lesson the longer she did this job.

Our first stop needed to be at the intersection of Makers Drive and Milton Boulevard. The police had already canvassed the area but I wanted to see the area first hand. The police had already canvassed the area, which meant they had talked to the business owners in the area, those who were viewed as upstanding citizens. The problem with only talking to the business owners, human or hellborn, they are not usually the ones who saw the criminal behavior. The reason was simple; criminals and cops notice criminal behavior. Cops notice suspicious behavior because it was what they were trained for. It was the same for those who lived on the streets. For criminals, it was a means of survival, you had to be aware of your surroundings and the players in the area. Criminal life brought heavy consequences. Prison or death were their only options.

For homeless individuals they were part of this secluded group, the police usually counted them in the criminal category. I didn't because most were individuals who fell on hard times or were ill. Homeless individuals noticed criminal acts because it was part of their survival, you saw suspicious behavior you made yourself invisible. For homeless individuals it was easy to not be seen because most didn't see them. Society could see a homeless individual and look right past them. The homeless saw and knew more than any business owner or resident would. There wasn't much in terms of homelessness for the area but there would be a few. I was hoping we could find someone who had seen something that night.

The area we were heading to was predominantly a human area made up of mostly businesses. There were surrounding neighborhoods that were filled with homes. We parked in a long lot that held eight store fronts. All were small businesses that would have limited funds for security. We sat in the car, eating as I watched the street. Most of the small businesses didn't open for another hour. The bigger franchises were in full swing and had been for hours. McDonald's was on the corner diagonally from where we were parked, was a twenty-four establishment. Many of the homeless would angle for the place, especially on colder evenings and mornings. Any loose change they may have been given would allow them to at least get a cup of coffee or an apple pie. I looked at the other businesses in the area. A small mom and pop breakfast place was on the opposite corner. The small restaurant would be more willing to give food to the homeless for free than a big franchise. If there were any in the area they would be on one of those two corners. Just as the thought crossed my mind, a man came out of the mom and pop restaurant. There was a cart parked on the side of the building, which he retrieved. His cart was full of junk as he wheeled it to the corner. Chances were good he stayed in this area begging for change and food. I sat watching the man wanting to know where he was going.

"Is there a reason we're here?" Meri asked.

"Yeah, there is."

"Are you going to tell us or do we need to play twenty questions with you?" she asked.

"Just give me a minute," I said as I watched the homeless guy cross the street. Watts saw me watching the guy.

"You want to talk to the homeless guy don't you?" he surmised.

"See that's why I like you, Watts. You know how to put two and two together."

"Didn't the cops already talk to the people in the area?" Meri asked.

"They did," I said as the man worked to get his cart onto the sidewalk.

"Chances are they didn't talk to the homeless people, only store owners. Homeless people aren't seen as a reliable source of information," Watts explained.

"The problem is that they have the most information about a neighborhood. Because they don't have an address and live on the streets, they are seen as unreliable to most citizens." I climbed from the car as the man turned to the right moving down the street. "Excuse me sir," I called as I ran after him.

He gave me a fleeting look before he kept moving, picking up his pace. I stepped in front of his cart stopping him from going any further. He wore an army green skull cap that was closer to brown than green. His pants were dirty with holes in them, just as the hat was closer to brown so were the pants. His large T-Shirt was about three sizes too big on his thin body. His tennis shoes were beat up and on their last leg of life. I could see the toe of his shoes were worn down to almost nothing. Winter was coming and he would be at risk for frostbite if he didn't find better shoes.

"I don't want any trouble," his voice was gravelly as he spoke to me.

"Neither do I. I just want to ask you some questions," I replied.
"About what?"
"Saturday night, early Sunday morning," I answered.
"What about it?"
"What's your name," I asked.
"John."
"I'm Savannah," I introduced myself

"Now what do you want from me?" he demanded.

"Were you in the area on Saturday night and Sunday morning?"

"Maybe," he gave me a toothless grin.

I reached into the back pocket of my jeans and pulled two twenties for him to see.

"You tell me the truth and the money is yours, John," I said. I eyed him as he tried to see if I was telling the truth.

"Yeah, I was here," he finally said.

"Did you see anything out of the norm?"

"Like what?"

"Like a suspicious car, a little girl, anyone who you've not seen before late at night?"

"I saw a car pull into the lot here. It went to the back of the building?"

"Do you know what type of car?" I asked.

"Do I look like Henry Ford?" he gestured to his clothes.

"There wasn't a name on the back of it or an emblem on it?" I asked.

He didn't answer as he thought about what I was asking.

"You hold back from me and I'll know. You won't get any cash from me," I threatened.

"Fine...it had a circle on it like..." he looked around the street finding a car at the light, a blue Toyota. "Like that one but the car was smaller."

"What color?"

"Blue. Now give me my money."

"Not yet. Did you see who was driving it?" I asked.

"No, the windows were tinted and it was dark."

"You see anything else?"

"Little later another car came through but from that end and headed that way?" he said pointing south.

"What did the car look like?"

"It had an H on the front and it was grey."

"What time was this?" I asked.

"Do I look like I wear a watch lady?"

I smiled at his sarcasm.

"Was it early in the evening or late?"

"It was late. McDonald's had just shut the dining room down for the night."

"Thanks for the help, John," I replied, handing him the cash and stepping out of his way.

He pushed past me sliding the money into the jacket he was wearing. I waited until he was out of earshot before I spoke.

"Now we can narrow down the car."

"It could have been one of the residents in the neighborhood, Woods. Their garages open into the alley there," Watts pointed to the back of the building.

"Maybe but it's still a possible lead," I replied.

"What time do they close the dining room?" Meri asked.

"Ten during the fall and winter. Summertime not until midnight" Watts answered.

"That would mean the perp grabbed the girl before ten if it was our guy," Meri said.

"It means the entire timeline is off," I pointed out.

"Why did the mom say she checked on her at ten?" Watts asked.

"I don't know."

"Maybe we've been wrong and Mom killed her?" Watts offered.

"Maybe it had something to do with the smell of lilacs," Meri countered.

I still didn't believe either of the Darings had anything to do with this. I could be wrong but it didn't feel that way. What had been in that tube? We needed to get back to the house and start going through spell books. See if we could figure out what had been used. First we had one more stop and I needed to call Ryan. I also wanted to check the neighborhood.

"Let's walk around the neighborhood that meets up with this alley," I said looking around at the street.

I glanced at the mom and pop restaurant and caught a look at a large male with a bald head. I did a quick double take at the restaurant. Whoever had been there a moment before was gone. The thought of Matthew came to mind. I scanned the street once more before shaking it off. Matthew had been silent since he had sent me Robert's head to my new home. I had enjoyed the silence but in the last few weeks I had become more cautious. I knew he was out there somewhere keeping tabs on me. With my mating ceremony coming, it would be only a matter of time before he sent me another present or called me. As much as I tried to not think of the male I couldn't help it. He had made a promise he would come for me again. The thought scared me in more ways than one.

"Woods, you okay?" Watts said bringing me back to reality.

I shook my head clearing it before I answered.

"Yeah I'm good. Uhm...Let's go see what we can find.

WE KNOCKED ON DOORS for an hour. Most of the residents were not home. The ones that were home, gave little help. We had no luck finding the car we were looking for. I wasn't sure if it was an actual lead. The car could have been just driving through. It could belong to one of the residents who were not home. Either way I wanted Ryan to know. Maybe one of the cameras caught the vehicle on camera. If it turned out to be nothing then we could move on. We climbed back into Meri's car as I dialed Ryan's number.

"Ryan," he answered, his voice rushed. I could hear as the phones at the precinct were going crazy.

"I have something for you," I said.

"Hold on," he demanded.

I waited as he moved. I could hear him as he talked to officers, giving orders to pass a call to someone else. It took him a few minutes to get to his office. I could tell when the door was shut because all the background noise died down.

"What did you say, Woods?" he asked.

"I said I may have something. Tell the CSU guys to find a small blue Toyota on the security footage, it should be from the lot with the small businesses on Marker. And then look for a grey Honda or Hyundai. It would be between nine p.m. and ten p.m."

"The mother said she checked on the girl at ten."

"I think she has the time wrong."

"Or she's lying," Ryan offered.

"Let's see what we find first. Anything from the tip lines?" I asked.

"Nothing I've seen at this point but we have thirty officers taking calls. I'll call you if we get anything."

"I'll do the same. Hey, Ryan don't go at the parents again until I can figure out what was in the tube."

"I can't promise that," he answered.

"I know. Just...try to wait until we have more."

"Yeah."

The call ended. I sat there looking at my phone for a moment. If he went at the parents and accused them of anything they would shut down or at least Brian Daring would. Emma Daring was already gone emotionally. If we didn't get her daughter back alive she would be gone physically soon enough, as well.

Chapter Ten

We drove to Witch Preservation Group. WPG had placed their headquarters outside The Gallery near the police station that housed the HCU. They were smart to do so. WPG was not just against hybrids and mixing of the species they were also against selling any form of magic or making money from magic. The group promoted witches staying with witches. They were not to be friends, lovers, or mates to anyone who was outside the species. They had gone as far as trying to build a neighborhood for just witches. Their proposal to the city didn't get far because there were more witches who felt they were not better than humans, who hated us for being hellborns. The group had enough support that it had spread throughout the country. In larger cities, the group had almost succeed in getting its own gated communities until other hellborns sued for discrimination. Being inside The Gallery could put their group in danger. Setting up shop near law enforcement wouldn't necessarily stop someone from retaliation but they would think twice about it.

Going to WPG headquarters was going to be interesting. Personally, I broke all of their rules. I was mated to a vampire. I was friends with wolves, vampires, and humans. And to add a cherry on top of the sundae, I was about to become a hybrid. I was confident if they could, they would set me on fire as soon as I arrived. They were really going to want me dead when I walked in with a vampire, who was protective over me, and a human who didn't have patience for bigots. This was going to be fun.

The building they used had been an old church, painted bright white on the outside. All the stained glass had been removed and replaced with regular windows. The cross that had been at the top of the steeple was long gone as if it had never been there. We parked on the street outside of the building. We all stood looking at the place like it was filled with evil. In some ways, I guess we were right. The witches in there were a special kind of evil. Unfortunately, they seemed to get more attention than they deserved. Hatred always did.

I took the first step towards the building as the other two fell into step one on either side of me. I pulled the heavy wooden door open and walked in smelling sulfur. The smell was so strong, I coughed as I tried to breathe around it. The sulfur was used in a cleansing ceremony for earth witches. I was confident once we left the smell would intensify. The inside was all red carpet with wooden pews. They hadn't got rid of those. I guess it was probably cheaper to keep them instead of replacing all of them. People were moving around at the far end of the room where the stage was set. I could see witches moving around, hanging decorations and chatting. We moved down the center of the isle watching them. I waited until I was six feet from the stage before I said anything.

"Excuse me," I spoke loudly. My voice was no more pleasant than it needed to be.

The first one to notice our presence was a male witch who had been handing another male a hammer standing on a ladder. From there it was a domino effect as slowly all the heads turned to face us. The cheerfulness the witches had been feeling evaporated in thin air. Their faces turning cold as they took us in. The one with the hammer hopped down from the stage. There was nothing spectacular about the male from his small stature to his brown hair that was parted on the side, to his soft color polo shirt and khakis.

"Only members are allowed on the premises," he spoke.

"Who's in charge here?" I asked.

"Did you hear what I said, defect? We don't allow.." that was as far as he got before I turned a cold look on him.

"Isn't it cute how they all use the exact same names," I said to Meri.

"It's as if they don't have a mind of their own."

"They don't," Watts said dryly.

I pulled my I.D. out from under my shirt, flashing it at the kid. Calling him a male was too nice.

"I am here on official police business. Now let's try this again. Who's in charge?" I said putting more emphasis than I needed to on the last sentence.

"You need to leave," our little spokesman had found an ounce of courage again.

His courage started to slip as Meri sauntered over to him. I'll give him credit, he didn't step back as she approached him. He stood his ground. Meri left an inch between their bodies as she met his eyes. I watched as those eyes lost focus.

"Look at how sweet you are. We just need to speak to whoever runs the show around here. Could you show me where to find him?" She said the last part as she leaned forward placing her lips near his ear. Normally, I would have stopped her but screw it, this was so much easier than all the defect talk.

"Mr. Salazar's... office...," he whispered back to Meri.

"Billy!" chimed in one of the witches on the stage.

"What are you doing?" Another yelled.

"Don't help them!" A female demanded.

Their voices fell on deaf ears. Billy's thoughts were only for Meri or at least her power. He was on the edge of telling us where to find their leader, when a male with rich brown, medium length hair came around the stage. His blue eyes were almost purple as they flashed on the scene playing out in front of everyone. He had a medium build, he almost swaggered into the room. A blond female with hair so fair it was almost white followed behind him. Her soft green eyes held an innocence as Bambi.

"That is enough," he said with a stern voice.

Meri stroked Billy's cheek before she released him from his trance. Billy came back on line and looked around seeing his fearless leader as he approached us. His head dropped in shame at his own weakness to Meri. I moved up joining Meri, with Watts right behind me. She stood there with one hip cocked out a hand on her hip as he stepped up.

"I'm Troy Salazar, I am the president of this chapter of WPG. What is it that we can do for you?" he said. He smiled a pleasant enough smile. I noticed the muscles around his face were tight as he looked at the three of us. The smile he wore didn't reach his eyes. He hated the fact that we were there.

"We are investigating the disappearance of Isobel Daring. We would like to ask you a few questions about your group and its members," Watts said.

"Oh, the young that was taken from her bed," he replied nonchalantly.

"Yes," Watts answered.

"We do not believe in hybrids or their existence. So why would we know anything about that young?"

"Because she is the granddaughter of two of your members. Jemma and Emerson Brazen," I pointed out.

I saw his eyes dropped away from us for just a half a second.

"I'm sorry but we have over a hundred and seventy members. I don't know everyone personally."

Yeah, right! As soon as we said the name he knew exactly who we were talking about.

"That's a lot of members for a city our size?" I said.

"Our members come from more than our fair city. But also Dunnin and Bearstone," he informed us.

Both of those were more towns than cities. They were small and only about an hour drive from us. There was no way that was the only area they had recruited from.

"Did you know two of your members had a daughter and a grandchild who were hybrids?" I asked.

There went his eyes again darting away as his muscles grew tight around his eyes.

"No, but it doesn't shock me. We cannot control what others do. All we can do is spread the word about how witches should be living instead of how they are currently. Too many witches have forgotten the values of our species."

"How are they supposed to live? What makes you the hellborn who decides that?" I asked.

"I was chosen by the members of my congregation of witches who feel as I do. If we do not preserve the witches bloodlines then it will die out. Then what will happen? Our young become contaminated with diseases as humans or will they be weakened by other hellborn's DNA. Our magic could die out because we have allowed for the mixing with other hellborns and humans," he preached.

What a joke! Weakening the species DNA was their argument. It was disgusting to think hellborns could actually have bigotry towards their own. We got plenty of it from humans for years and now here it was in my face, my own kind saying I was killing the species.

"Now if you have nothing further, I will have to ask you to leave. This is our sacred space."

Like I was contaminating it with my presence.

"Thank you for your time," Watts said. Meri and Watts began to make their way back to the door as I stood there. I don't know what made me do it but a question slipped out of my mouth.

"Do you know of a group called H&W Clinical Group?"

There was a twitch at the corner of his eye with the name of the group. It was a tell he knew who I was talking about.

"They donate to our cause," he answered. It took his eyes a second to meet my stare.

"Is that all they are?" I asked.

His head twitched back and forth a fraction of an inch for a moment before he answered.

"Yes."

With that I turned and walked away from the bigot.

"You know, Ms. Woods, it's not too late to save yourself," he said as I walked away. It was enough to stop me. I turned and retraced my steps this time coming within inches of the male.

"Your little cause as you call it, is nothing more than bullshit. I don't need saving. I know you're lying. I think you know more than you're saying. I will find out the truth and when I do, we will be back except next time I'm betting I will be less than nice."

"You have forgotten you are a witch and your mate as you refer to him is called a consort. This is what we speak of. Our ways are being lost as witches. You defile yourself with scum like..."

I took a step closer to the male before I spoke in a whisper. I wanted to grab him by the throat and beat the living shit out of him but I didn't. I didn't need another complaint. I should have gotten a medal for not beating him.

"You need to understand I know exactly who I am and if I were you, I would watch what you say about my mate. Or you can keep running your mouth and I'll show you what this witch can do," I growled in a whisper.

He looked down at me with a smile on his face.

"Are you threatening me?" he asked.

"No, I'm making a promise. I promise you I will be back for you personally."

"Please leave defect, you are not welcomed here. Your presence is offensive. Oh and I have no intentions of filing a complaint as Jemma has done."

"See, there is that word defect again," I replied, wagging my finger at him. "I'll leave for now. Just remember what I said." I replied as I walked away.

I reached my team as they stood at the door at the top of the isle watching the scene playout. We walked out and headed for the car before anyone spoke again. I had pushed just enough for him to rise to the occasion. I didn't know if the Brazens or Troy Salazar were involved in Isobel's disappearance but there was something fishy about all three of them. They were on my radar now and I was going to find out everything I could about them and H&W Clinical.

Chapter Eleven

We headed back to our office and went straight to work. I had called Ryan and gave him Troy Salazar's name. He would run a background check on him and get back to me. My team split up the names from the list the Brazens gave us. I added Troy's name to my list. I wanted Salazar for myself but the other two argued against it saying I should be the one to do the research on the lilac smell. I argued back saying one of them should because it was a teachable moment for them. The arguing got us nowhere, I finally said we would all do it once we tackled our list of individuals.

The office was quiet as we all worked. I went through the names one by one, finding nothing of use on any of the witches on my list. Most of them had little in terms of social media presence, but one female named Sue, who was ninety years old, was like a teenager. She posted about everything including her Saturday night at her friend's house. From the photos, it appeared the dinner wasn't just a dinner party, it was a fundraiser. Troy Salazar was present and there were photos of him speaking to the crowd. Sue even took a selfie with him. How special for her. I hit print. It was interesting the Brazens never said anything about Troy being at their dinner party. He lied saying he didn't know them. What were these three hiding? Was it tied to Isobel? Maybe or maybe it was something else.

I continued to go through Sue's page finding more photos of her at other events for WPG. It appeared they had fundraisers, luncheons, even small carnivals. When I say carnivals there were no rides just games for the young and adults alike with food and prizes. I scanned through multiple posts and photos seeing nothing of value at first. I was about to leave her page when I saw two things on a post dating back seven months. The first thing I saw was a photo of Troy with the blond who had been with him earlier. They were standing side by side with his arm around her waist both slightly turned facing each other. She was looking down, a soft blush to her face. I printed the photo and looked at all the individuals who were tagged in the photo. Everyone but Troy and the blond were. It made me wonder who she was. She was pretty, petite and young. As witches our aging slows down around twenty one. She could be older than she looked but there was something about the girl. I didn't know what it was. The second thing I noticed in the same post on another picture was a sign in the background on a table. It was blurry and partially obscured by a male's arm but from what I could see it looked like a banner for H&W Clinical Group. I saved the image to my computer and hit print one more time. Troy had said they were supporters of WPG. Why would a medical research group be a supporter of a hate group? From their website it had said they were doing testing for drugs that would help witches. What else did they do at their lab?

"Hey Watts, you have any friends in the CSU?" I asked.

"One of the fingerprint techs, why?"

"I need a photo cleaned up. I can do small stuff but they have better programs than I do."

"Sorry, Cain is the guy to call for that. People always own him."

It was true, Cain knew how to get people to own him favors, I was one of those individuals. He had been the one who helped me nail Robert for attacking me. Without Cain, I would never have known about two additional victims who hadn't been as lucky as me. Now I was on his list of people who owed him and in a big way.

"Yeah, I thought you were going to say that," I replied.

"Did you find anything?" Watts asked.

"Yeah... well...maybe," I hedged.

"What does that mean?" Meri asked.

"I found a photo from Saturday night of the dinner party the Brazens had and guess who was there?" I answered, passing the photo to Meri first.

"I thought he didn't know them," she said before passing it to Watts.

"We knew he lied with his comment about not filing a complaint against me. But this is just proof. Also it wasn't just a dinner party, it was a fundraiser," I added.

"For what?" Watts asked.

"The post didn't say. All it said was WPG's fundraiser."

"So what do you need a photo cleaned up for? This one looks fine," Watts pointed out as he handed me the photo back.

"For this one," I handed the photo to Meri first. She looked at it then handed it over to Watts.

"What are we missing because I didn't see anything wrong with the photo?" Meri asked.

I pulled out the mission statement from the H&W Clinical Group from my drawer, handing it to Meri.

"The Brazen's had mail from this research group, whose focus is supposedly on witches' health," I informed them.

"What's the big deal?" Watts said.

"Why didn't you ask Troy about this company?" Meri asked.

"I did."

"Again, what's the big deal about this medical group?" Watt questioned.

"Witches generally don't go to modern medicine for medical help, they go to other witches or their own concoctions. Our bodies metabolize human drugs quickly. So that is suspicious to me. There is also the fact that they are supporters of WPG."

"Okay how does it connect to Isobel?" Watts asked.

"I don't know if it does but something is fishy about the Brazen's, Troy Salazar, and this group."

"Woods we need to..." Watts began to say.

"I know, but this group keeps popping up," I held up a hand stopping him. "I don't know what it is but my gut says we need to see what else we can find out about them."

"What if it doesn't lead to anything?" Meri asked.

"Then it doesn't but I would rather eliminate all three than not." I finished speaking as my phone rang.

I looked at the screen seeing Ryan's name.

"Woods," I answered.

"We just got a tip about Isobel being at a motel called The Golden Mirror. You know where it's at?" he asked.

I knew where and what The Golden Mirror was. My old informate stayed there a time or two. It was located in the southern part of the city. It was mostly known for its hourly rates. The fact Isobel had been spotted at The Golden Mirror scared the hell out of me. I was at least forty-five minutes from the place.

"Yeah, I know where it's at. We'll meet you there."

I hung up with Ryan and looked at my team.

"Isobel was possibly spotted at The Golden Mirror."

There was a collective breath taken before everyone went into high gear. Taking the stairs as quickly as we could. I said a silent prayer, she was okay as we piled into Meri's SUV.

Chapter Twelve

M eri drove like a bat out of hell as she weaved in and out of traffic. This was one of the times I wished the police would let me have a siren. It would have made it easier to get through traffic. There were a few close calls as we made our way south. I cursed at every one of them. I was starting to wish I had driven until we got to the motel fifteen minutes before I had anticipated.

The small ten space parking lot was flooded with police cars, lights were flashing red and blue. We were forced to park on the street as one of the marked cars was blocking the driveway. I pulled my crime scene bag out of the back, grabbing gloves for all of us, before we approached the police tape. We stopped at the yellow tape finding my favorite uniformed officer doing the check in.

"Houston, long time no see," I said sarcastically.

"What are you doing here?" he grumbled.

"Oh, you know the job you can't do."

"I see you have expanded Freaks Incorporated. Watts, I should have known you would be a traitor to your own kind."

"Officer, I would like to remind you who you are speaking to. I may be on leave but I am still a higher ranking officer than you. Now give me that clip board and let us do our job," Watts said, staring down the shorter man. He snatched the clipboard away from Houston's pudgy hands and signed in with his badge number and name. He then handed it to me. I did the same before I handed it over to Meri. She smiled as she handed it back to him. The smile said please say something. I guess Houston wasn't as stupid as he looked because he kept his trap shut. Watts held the tape up for the two of us before he crossed himself.

"This is your one warning, you ever speak to these females that way again. I will make sure your watch commander writes you up and sticks you behind a desk. Do we have an understanding?"

"Yes, sir," he said with force.

We walked on and I smiled at Watts. The enjoyment I was feeling at Houston's expense was petty but so satisfying.

The motel had two floors with eight rooms on each floor. The door stood open in the middle of the line of doors on the ground floor. We each snapped on a pair of gloves as we moved. I stopped pulling on my paper booties before I entered the room. Watts and Meri did the same. I stepped in first looking at the room. There were junk food wrappers and fast food bags in the small trash can and on the floor around it. Two full size beds with blankets and sheets thrown back haphazardly. Ryan was coming out of the small bathroom writing in his notepad.

"Please tell me you have her?" I impolored.

"No, the woman left about five minutes before we got here. The maid tried to stall her but it didn't work. The maid is the one who called."

"Dammit."

"Cain is at the front desk seeing what we can get from the clerk now," Ryan informed us. I dropped my bag and moved towards Ryan as Meri began to move deeper in the room towards the bed. Watts stood still taking in everything. "I've set up check points on the highways leading out of the city. If this woman is trying to flee the city she will find it difficult."

"It's a female?"

"Yeah."

"Wait... you said woman. Was it a human or a hellborn?" Watts asked.

"We believe she's human."

A female had taken Isobel. I didn't know if that was a good thing or not. I guess it meant a male wasn't doing indescribable things to her but it was of little comfort. To top it all off she was possibly a human. It didn't make sense. Maybe she didn't know Isobel was a hybrid? Or she didn't care what Isobel was?

"Look what was left behind," Meri pulled from in between the pillows a small orange stuffed animal.

"Fuck," I said. Ryan had been five minutes too late. He had one of the CSU guys take the stuffed animal from Meri. She was still standing in between the beds as we talked.

"Which way did she go?" I asked Ryan.

"She made a left out of the motel. I have officers looking for camera footage."

"Good luck finding any down here," Watts said.

"Yeah, I know," Ryan replied.

"Can we get everyone out of here?" Meri inquired.

"Why?" Ryan questioned.

"Because I think I smell something but there are too many humans for me to be sure," she explained.

Ryan let the CSU guys finish with processing of the scene. The trash was taken and would be tested for DNA. The bedding was next and pillows. Meri watched as they worked and I watched her, I could see her wheels turning. Once they were done and out of the room she began to walk around. The fingerprint guys still needed to do their thing but they could wait. Meri moved to the bathroom saying nothing just taking in the scents of the room.

"The Darings said the place smelled like lilacs?" she asked.

"Yeah." I answered.

"The scent in here is like a fruity smell and tobacco. It's strongest in the bathroom but that could be because less humans have been in there. How many other than you have been in the bathroom, Lieutenant?" she asked.

"None. CSU still has to process it."

"The bed smells like lemons and a female, human," she added.

"It could be from the maid," Ryan offered.

"Or a previous working girl," Watts suggested.

"How many hookers do you know that smell like lemons? Go talk to the maid," I ordered Meri and Watts.

Meri and Watts went outside as I retrieved my bag from where I dropped it. Ryan waited for me. As soon as I was out of the room CSU took over once more.

"What do you think, Woods?"

"I have no clue at this point."

"I hate when you say that," he replied.

"I don't like it any better than you."

"We haven't found anything on the grandparents."

"I figured. Can you check out a medical company for me?"

"How does a medical group tie into this?" he questioned me.

"I don't know that they do. What I do know is that they are tied to the grandparents and to Troy Salazar," I answered.

"We can't go chasing down crap like that Woods."

"Listen I know it's a long shot. Chances are good it doesn't lead to anything but what if it does."

He said nothing as we stood outside the door as Ryan tried to decide if it was worth his time. He was right, we didn't have a lot of time and chasing down every potential lead could cause problems. But what other options did we have though?

"Look, I'll see if I can get a boot to do it. It's the best I can do."

"Thanks."

Cain came running over from the office with a paper in hand.

"The place has one camera but I have the print out from the information she gave along with the driver's license," he said.

"When did places like this start taking copies of licenses?" I asked.

"When the state forced them to. It was the governor's way of trying to curb illicit acts. All they end up doing is renting the room in the girls name and she then has a place to go with her johns for however long they rent the room for," Ryan explained.

"Amazing. If there's a will there's a way, I guess."

Ryan looked at the pages before handing them to me. The room was rented to a Lucy Cordova from Arizona. She had been driving a Honda according to the paperwork. I thought back to my homeless man and what he said.

"Did the CSU guys find any Hondas on the tapes?" I asked.

"I don't know, why?" Ryan asked.

"Because according to this she's driving a Honda Accord."

"Cain call the guys working on the surveillance videos to see if they have anything, then run down this plate number."

"On it, Lieutenant," he replied as he took down the information.

"We need to go see the Darings and see if they know this Lucy Cordova," I replied.

"Why doesn't your team take that?" he replied in a hollow voice.

I looked at Ryan seeing that he wasn't looking at me.

"What happened?" I asked suspiciously.

"I questioned them after we spoke earlier about their timeline."

"When did you speak to them?" I asked, feeling my anger rising.

"About an hour ago. It didn't go well."

"What is that supposed to mean?"

"It means they may be less willing to help us."

"What did I ask you to not do earlier?" I demanded.

"I had to ask them. I needed to know if we're chasing our tails or not, Woods. You know when we get conflicting information we have to do a follow up."

"You better hope I can make this right. My team and I are going to head out and I'll call you when I'm done with them. I'll let you know what I find out." I snapped my gloves off along with the booties finding the bag not far from the door. I took a photo of the picture before I handed it back to him.

Watts and Meri were finishing with the maid as I approached them. We began our walk back to the car.

"What did the maid give you?" I asked.

"The woman had blond hair with hazel eyes. She said they were almost a yellow color. The girl was asleep when she saw the woman carrying the girl out. She recognized the girl from the news.

"Did the lemon scent come from the maid?" I asked.

"No."

"Okay. We need to go see the Darings now. I need to call Santiago see if he can meet us there."

"Why?" Meri asked.

"Ryan questioned them about their timeline."

"Let me guess they got upset," Watts asked.

"Yeah."

"Shit!" Meri cursed.

It was exactly how I was feeling as we did our sign out from the scene. We needed the Darings on our side. If they were unwilling to help us it would make finding Isobel even more difficult. As we ducked under the tape I scanned the crowd that were gawking at the scene. Most were from the motel itself. Others were from the neighborhood. The hairs on the back of my neck stood on end, as if I was being watched. None of the faces registered any recognition but the feeling lingered. I continued moving towards the car as I pulled my phone free of my pocket.

As soon as we were back in the car I dialed Santiago.

"Mi Amor," he shouted. I could hear the music of the club, he was on the floor at Obsidian.

"I need your help!" I yelled.

"Give me a moment," he yelled back.

The music played for several minutes. I waited for him to find a quiet place to talk as Meri drove.

"I am sorry you called as I was dealing with a problem at the bar."

"It's okay. I need your help," I replied.

"Is this about the Darings?" he asked.

"It is. Can you meet me at their house in fifteen minutes?" I asked.

"I am on my way."

"Thank you."

"It is my pleasure. I will see you soon, Mi Amor."

"See you soon."

I wasn't sure if they would open the door for me without Santiago at my side. I was his mate and was given the same level of respect Santiago was given, but I was also a hunter who worked with the human police. The humans had accused them of lying about their missing daughter. I had also given my word Ryan was the best and he could be trusted. The trust we had built with them may have disappeared with the little trust they had in the humans by being called liars. I wasn't sure I would be able to repair the damage. Why couldn't Ryan have waited for me?

Chapter Thirteen

We arrived in front of the Darings before my mate had. I sat in the car thinking about the fact that a human had possibly taken Isobel Daring. Why would a human do that? Was I looking at the wrong hate group? Maybe I was but that led to what they wanted with a child. It made no sense. My head was pounding as the thoughts spun around and around. There were no clear answers to the questions I had.

Santiago arrived five minutes later, pulling in behind us. We all climbed from the car. The other two moved to the front of Meri's car while I met my mate at his car. His arms encircled me as I fell into them. It eased the pain in my head along with frustration I was feeling to be in his arms. This was what I needed before we went inside. I needed him with his arms around me.

"What has happened, Mi Amor?" he said in my ear.

"We almost had her. Ryan missed the kidnapper and Isobel by five minutes. They are looking for the woman and the car she was driving," I answered, stepping away from him taking his hand in mine.

"Woman! As in human?" He pulled back looking at me.

"Yeah, it looks like it."

"Why did you ask me to come?" he questioned me.

"Because there is a chance their timeline is wrong and Ryan questioned them about it."

"And now they do not wish to speak with the humans," Santiago almost spat the words. I felt the disgust he was feeling at the situation.

"Correct. I have a photo I need to show them."

"Let us see if we can persuade them to help."

We walked up to the door with Watts and Meri behind us. I let Santiago take the lead. He knocked as we stood waiting. It took a moment for Brian Daring to answer the door. When he did the look on his face said he wasn't happy with our presence. His brown eyes were hard as he took us in.

"May we come in Brian?" Santiago asked.

"I am not sure that's a good idea."

"I am sorry for how you and your mate were treated earlier but there has been a development and we need you to look at a photograph," Santiago explained.

"According to Lieutenant Ryan she was the one who made him question us," Brian shot back indicating me.

Crap! Ryan had thrown me under the bus.

"There is a chance your timeline could be wrong because someone may have drugged you and your mate or may have hit you with a spell. Lieutenant Ryan had to ask the questions he did to ensure there were no questions later if we did our due diligence. Please Mr. Daring. I need to know if you know a woman named Lucy Cordova."

"No, we don't," he said, beginning to shut the door. Santiago put his hand out to stop the door from closing. I pulled my phone out showing him the photo of the woman.

"That's Bree!" he said shocked. He looked at the phone stunned, not sure what to make of the photo.

"The neighbor your wife made friends with?" I asked.

"Yes. She took Isobel?" disbelief in his voice.

"May we please come in Mr. Daring?" I asked again.

Any anger he had been feeling evaporated as reality hit him. The kidnapper was a friend of the family. I was confident his anger towards us had turned into guilt at himself. We walked into the living room. Emma Daring was nowhere in sight. I could guess she was lying down, still lost to the world. If we didn't get Isobel back

I wasn't sure Brian would get Emma back either. In one fell swoop he would lose both his females. My heart ached for them.

I waited for Brian to say something, anything as he stood in the middle of the living room, still clinging to my phone as he stared at the image.

"Tell me about Bree," I spoke gently.

"She lived directly on the other side of the fence. We met her when Isobel lost a ball in her backyard, like I told you. She was so nice to us. She became friends with Emma. Bree was always willing to play with Isobel," the back of his legs hit the couch, as he collapsed onto it.

"What else can you tell us?" I asked.

"Uhm... She ate dinner with us regularly. She and Emma used to go out once a week. Bree is the one that got Emma to like tea. I can't believe this is happening," shock was taking over as he tried to answer my questions. I took a seat on the sofa next to him and forced him to turn to face me.

"Did she ever say which company she worked for?"

"Uhm... Not... not that I can remember."

"Did she say where she was from?" I asked.

"Yeah... Uhm... she said she's from Fairetree."

Fairetree was a two hours drive south of Sweetclover. Was that why she was at The Golden Mirror? Why hadn't she left town yet?

"How long did she live in the neighborhood?" I asked.

"I don't know, three maybe four months," he answered uncertainly.

"You said earlier she gave your wife a gift?" Meri asked.

"Yeah... she gave her tea. They would have tea together and... Bree wanted her to have something to remember her by."

"Do you know the brand?"

"I don't. It's a lavender tea."

"May we see the tea?" I asked.

"Yes... of course. Let me go and get it," he began to rise and I placed a hand on his arm.

"Why don't you let my people get it?" I suggested.

"Okay." he nodded. "It's in the cupboard by the sink," Brian instructed.

I looked at Watts and nodded. He gave me a silent nod and headed for the kitchen. I turned my attention back to Brian and slipped my phone from his grasp. He was sitting still looking at nothing that was in front of him.

He finally spoke softly. "Why would Bree do this?" he asked tears in his eyes.

"I don't know but we are doing everything we can to find her. Now Mr. Daring do you know Bree's full name?" I asked.

"Bree Miller is the name she gave us."

"Is there anything else you can tell me about her?"

"She seemed so nice. She used to take care of Isobel so we could go to dinner. She... uhm... she was so good with Isobel."

If he did know anything else about this woman, he was too far gone at the moment to tell me. I moved on.

"Do you have any pictures of the two of them together?"

"Yes, my wife got a picture of them in the backyard playing. Isobel was having a tea party and she invited Bree to it. She came over and played with Isobel. Bree never liked having her picture taken," he said absentmindedly.

"Can you get it for me? Please."

He got up leaving us alone and headed down the hall. Watts came out with the canister of tea in his gloved hand. I had no clue where the gloves had come from but I was grateful he had them.

"I found it," he said.

"Go bag it and call Ryan. Make sure you take a bit for us as well. We can take it to some shops, maybe a local witch can help us with it. Oh and take a photo of the canister."

"You got it."

"I'll go with him," Meri said.

I nodded at her as they both left. A few minutes passed before Brian was back. He handed me a picture of the woman with his young. She was sitting across from Isobel with her pinkie in the air and a small cup in her hand. It was a profile of the woman but it would do.

"Thank you for your help," I said. "Currently the police are searching any vehicles trying to leave the city. Chances are good she is still within the city limits. Do not lose hope," I tried to reassure him.

He nodded at me, unable to say anything else. As I moved towards the door he grabbed my hand.

"I am sorry for how I acted when you got here," he apologized. "Please find my daughter."

"I will do my utmost to find her. I promise."

He released my hand. Santiago fell into step behind me, placing a hand on the males shoulder before we left. I stopped to watch as my mate leaned into the male whispering in his ear. Whatever was said they eyed each other before they shook hands. We took our leave, shutting the door behind us. I waited until we were almost to the car when I spoke.

"What did you say to him?" I asked.

"I vowed that this woman would pay for what she has done. We cannot allow an outsider to do this to our people, Savannah," Santiago snapped. "If the young does not survive this, she must suffer greatly or other humans will try to harm our people."

"I agree but humans have different rules than we do," I tried to reason with my mate.

"She conned this family into trusting her. We cannot do nothing. Human law should not apply here. Clan law should."

"Human law shouldn't apply to her but it does Santiago," I answered.

"This is one of those moments you may have to choose which side you are on. You are part of the Black Grove Clan and this human has harmed one of our own."

"Please don't go there," I answered.

"I love you and would do anything for you but we cannot turn from this. Someone needs to pay for this."

I took a deep breath staring at the hard lines of my mate's face. The anger he felt was making his eyes appear more black than brown.

"Look, we aren't there yet. Isobel is still alive, which means this woman has other plans for her. Let me do my job. I'm not saying I won't kill her if I'm given the chance. Just... let me do my job. Okay?"

"For now, Mi Amor," he pulled me into him, kissing me quickly before releasing me.

This was one of those times Ryan had been worried about. If Isobel didn't survive this, I would have to make a choice when I caught the human who stole her. What was I going to do? Santiago and I had only been mated three months, my job and our positions in the clan were making things complicated with this case. This wouldn't be the last time it would happen. What the hell was I going to do when things became more difficult? Right now, I was praying when I found the human she tried something stupid. It would give me a reason to kill her and give Santiago what he wanted along with the rest of the clan. Could I be that lucky? I didn't think so.

"I must return to work. I will see you at home."

"Yes," I answered. I went to turn away and stopped myself. "I would do anything for you too. You know that right?"

"I do."

"I will do what I can if this ends badly but you have to let me do what I do and believe me when I say I'm going to do everything I can to save Isobel."

"I know you will. Be safe," he kissed me quickly before he climbed into his car and drove off. The anger was there in the kiss and his body.

I heard the words he said but it didn't feel like I had said enough to calm the situation. Or maybe he hadn't. Maybe both of us had failed in that department. I wasn't sure if there were words that would do the job. The only way to calm the situation was to find Isobel. With this new development the entire hellborn community would be up in arms soon enough.

I walked to the back of the car to join the other two. Watts was still on the phone as I approached.

"Ryan says they found the car about five miles from the motel, just inside The Gallery."

"What about the female?"

"It was abandoned. No sign of Isobel," he replied.

"Shit."

"Ryan says they are bringing in the search dogs again."

"Give me the phone," I said, taking the phone from Watts. "Ryan, do you want us to come help with the search?"

"No, we have enough cops down here, I don't need you three down here too."

"Look we have the tea the Darings were given. What street are you on? We can do the hand off," I offered.

"We're not far from Bloody Nights."

"Okay," I replied. I waited a moment before I tried again. "Look I know you said no but we can't just sit around and do nothing. If any hellborn saw anything they will be more willing to talk to me and Meri. Let us help. We will stay back when the dogs get there."

He was silent for a moment.

"Fine," Ryan finally answered.

"We're on the way."

I hung up and handed the phone back to Watts. I took the bag from my kit and smelled the stuff. Lavender and a musty scent.

"It's what I smelled at the motel," Meri said.

I sniffed one more time. I knew the scent. It took my brain a moment for it to click.

"Mandrake and lavender."

"Isn't that poisonous?" Meri asked.

"Mandrake can be if you ingest too much but in small amounts and being brewed into a tea, it's safe."

"What is it used for?" Watts asked.

"Both herbs are used for sleep problems. You generally don't combine them. Lavender is for relaxation. Mandrake sleep," I explained.

"Do you think Emma knew?" Watts asked.

"I would have to say yes. She was a witch first, hybrid second. Maybe she just thought it was a nice gift? She could have had trouble sleeping," I answered.

"So was this a gift or was there a purpose behind it?" Meri added.

I thought I knew where she was going with it.

"What do you mean?" I asked with a smirk.

"You sound like Ryan when we go to a scene."

"I know but explain anyway," I replied.

Meri sighed. "You said the tea would be used to help with sleep but not usually together."

I waved her on.

"What if the tea was given to Emma on purpose? This human had to be planning this for months. She would have to think about how to get around their sense of smell. So what if the tea and whatever was in the tube was used to not only camouflage her scent but to keep them asleep," Meri explained.

I smiled at the explanation. I believed Meri was on the right track.

"It would also explain why no one saw anything weird. The neighbors would have seen Bree and Emma together regularly," Watts added.

"The only thing that doesn't add up is how she knew they would have tea. There was no guarantee that Emma would make tea that night," Meri asked.

I thought about it. She was right there was no guarantee that Emma would have tea or that Brian would.

"What if we are right about the timeline?" I asked.

"Okay, what if we are?" Watts said.

"This woman knows these people. She spent three months getting to know them. So maybe Emma is known for making tea at night or maybe she has sleeping problems. Bree gives Emma the tea and hopes she uses it but whatever the lilac smell is more than likely to ensure they are asleep, so she can grab Isobel."

"The parents are double dosed though, so they shouldn't have woken up. Right?" Watts speculated.

"Maybe because Emma's a hybrid it didn't last as long. Or Bree Miller went light on the other substance in the tube. Either way, Emma is still more than likely loopy. She wakes Brian he goes to bed and she checks on Isobel or maybe she thought she did and instead goes to bed," I theorized.

"Why would the tea and the gas work differently on a hybrid?" Watts asked.

"Because as hellborns we metabolise drugs and alcohol faster than humans. Maybe hybrid bodies work even faster than a normal hellborn," Meri replied.

"Let's get over to Ryan, see if we can help in the search. After we're done, I want to go check out the house she stayed in."

I needed to find the substance that was in the tube. I was confident once we had the answer to that, other pieces would fall into place. Hopefully it would all lead to finding Isobel alive.

Chapter Fourteen
Five Days till the Ceremony

We searched for Isobel for four hours. No one saw the woman or the young and there had been no signs of her in The Gallery. The good news was that CSU had found the Honda on the footage from the night Isobel went missing. It confirmed our theory that the timeline was off. It was not the car that was used to drive Isobel away from her home. The Toyota in question had also been found on the tapes. We had a plate number and an APB out on it. The cops were now collecting tapes from businesses within The Gallery. We had almost an exact time for when they would have entered The Gallery. It would take time to search all of the footage but we were confident we would find where they went next. We did a drive by of the property the woman had lived in before she kidnapped Isobel. The place was already rented out. I added it to my list of things to look into.

As we searched The Gallery it felt as if eyes were on me. I could feel the tension between my shoulders as we talked to humans and hellborns within the area. I wasn't sure if the feeling was from actually being watched or if it was my nerves as they grew tight with the stress of not finding Isobel.

By the time we called the search off everyone including the dogs were done for. I dragged myself home finding my mate in bed. I stripped my clothes off leaving my weapons and clothes on the floor and climbed into bed next to him, moving in close. He felt my presence and wrapped his arms around me. Sleep took no time to claim me as I lay with Santiago. The sleep I got wasn't the most restful but it was better than nothing. My brain was still trying to work out the problems with this case as I slept. By morning, my head hurt and I had no desire to leave my bed. Santiago was next to me looking at me as I woke.

"You were tossing and turning last night," he said.

"My brain was working overtime. This case is confusing in so many ways," as I readjusted myself slightly turning towards him. "Everytime I get one question answered, three more questions pop up. I just...arrrggg...I feel like I can't find the answers and the more I fail to get the answers the farther she gets from us."

"I am guessing our talk last night did not help matters either?" his dark eyes held a guilty look.

"To be honest, not really. If I don't find her alive and I give the human to you or kill her myself it could cost me my business. But if I don't then you and every vampire will question where my loyalty lies. It's a lose-lose for me," I said, not meeting his gaze.

"I should not have put this on you. I am sorry. Whichever you decide to do when the time comes I will support you," he said stroking my hair away from my face.

"I love you for that but it could cost you if I make the wrong decision. And I don't want you hating me for the fallout."

"Listen to me," Santiago said, forcing me to look at him. "I could never hate you no matter what you do. Do you understand? I told you three months ago I will not leave you, ever. I was wrong for what I said to you. I was angry and I took out my anger on you. There is no justification for my behavior. I have every confidence you will find her."

"I hope you're right."

"I am," he said, lowering his lips to mine.

The feel of his bare chest against mine made me lean into the feel of him. I needed to get to work but I also needed this, too. I placed one hand on his chest while my other slid into his hair. Santiago understood what I wanted and rolled onto his back bringing me with him. I could feel his erection as I climbed on top of him. Just as things were about to get so much better, the doorbell rang. We both stopped and looked at each other before it sounded again. I looked at the clock on the bedside table. It was only eight I still had an hour before my team would arrive. Who the hell was at my door? I was willing to ignore the door if he was. I leaned down kissing my mate as the doorbell sounded again. This time the individual was pushing the button every few seconds.

"I think we are going to have to answer the door," Santiago said.

"Dammit!" I yelled.

Santiago laughed heartily at my frustration. I climbed off of my mate finding my clothes and throwing them on. I ran down the stairs with my gun in my hand. Whoever was at the damn door had better have a good reason to be there. If they didn't I was going to shoot them.

"What ca...." my words died in my throat when I saw my guest as I threw the door open.

"Hello dear," my mother said as if we were old friends.

I looked enough like the female for others to know we were related. Her red hair was a shade or two darker than my own. She had it pulled back in a bun at the back of her head. Her eyes were soft grey as she took in my appearance. She wore an ivory colored suit with a bag to match. She must have either married well or robbed a very wealthy human to be dressed as she was. Her makeup softly highlighted her features.

"What the hell are you doing here?" I growled.

"Well I heard you had gotten mated and were having a ceremony. I figured my invitation must have gotten lost in the mail."

Only this female would think that. The feel of my gun in my hand felt amazing enough for me to think about shooting her right where she stood. I heard footsteps on the stairs right behind me. I glanced seeing my mate half dressed in slacks and a black dress shirt. He was finishing tucking the tail of the shirt into his pants as he reached the door.

"This must be "the" mate. I have to say he is quite attractive for a vampire," she made a move to try and walk in. I threw up my arm blocking her path.

"The invitation didn't get lost in the mail, you weren't invited," I snapped.

"I'm sorry," She acted as if she didn't hear me.

"Don't play dumb, you were never good at that."

"You are my only child and I want..."

"I'm going to stop you right there. I am no longer your child and haven't been for almost twenty years. So what are you doing here?" I interrupted her.

"I told you dear. I am here for your ceremony."

"Don't call me dear. My name is Savannah. Now, why don't you turn yourself around and go back to where you came from."

"Please can't we just put it all behind us," she whined. Her left hand came up against her chest as if her heart was breaking. She would have to have a heart for it to be breaking. That was when I saw the big rock on her hand. She had married up. Poor fool of a male. Those grey eyes that were almost blue stared at me with determination. This had nothing to do with my ceremony, she was after something.

"Mi Amor perhaps we should let her in," Santiago whispered.

"No! She isn't welcomed in our home," I snapped without taking my eyes off of my mother. "Where are you staying?" I asked coldly.

"At the Hilton."

"Fine, I will meet you there in thirty minutes. In the lobby."

I shut the door in her face before she could argue with me. I turned the locks and threw my back against it as if it would hold her off. My head dropped as this new complication to my life, increased the pain I had woken up with.

"I take it the female is your mother?" he asked.

"More like incubator. Mother would mean she actually gave me love. She is the last thing I need right now."

"Would you like me to come with you?" he offered. His hands began to caress my arms.

"No, I got this."

"I do not mind?" Santiago offered once more.

"She is up to something and I will have a better opportunity to find out what it is on my own. If you're there she will put on a show. With me she'll have a more difficult time acting innocent."

Santiago said nothing for a moment as he continued to caress my arm.

"It will be fine," he pulled me into an embrace.

"Yeah," I wanted to go back upstairs and finish what we started. Instead I was heading to a hotel to meet my mother.

I CALLED MERI TO LET her know I would be late and why. She offered to join me just as Santiago had. Her reasoning was one I could get behind. Santiago had offered to come for support, Meri offered in hopes we could scare the witch out of our city. I also suspected she wanted a chance to kick her ass. Now that was family. One to support you, the other for the more crazy ideas. It was clear who was the more reasonable out of the two. I thanked her and told her no. I needed to deal with this little problem on my own. Meri and Watts could still start working on research while I was dealing with Chloe.

I valeted my car and headed inside. It took my eyes a moment to adjust to the inside lighting. To the left was a sitting area with chairs arranged in pairs. I found Chloe sitting in the far corner. I took a seat and gave her a hard stare.

"You know dear you should scowl less, it would help to prevent lines," she said with a smile.

"I only scowl when a piece of crap like you ends up at my door. So why don't you come clean about why are you here? Is it to see what I have? Or is it to con humans out of their money? Oh, I know you wanted to see if my mate was foolish enough to fall for your game?"

"I told you I wanted to be here for you."

"Bullshit! Look whatever game you're playing ends now. I am too busy working to deal with you. Go home and don't ever come back."

"Are you working on that missing hybrid case?" she asked. She said hybrid as if it was a dirty word.

"Why?"

"I just thought maybe I could help."

"How could you help?" I demanded, confused.

"As you recall I am a spirit talker, maybe the dead..."

"Stop right there. No."

"I am just offering my services."

"And I am saying no," I spoke slowly emphasizing the no as I leaned towards her.

We stared at each other for a long time until a male with a wide gut and big belt buckle came over to join us. He wore jeans, a white button down shirt with a beige coat. His brown cowboy boots completed the outfit.

"Sorry, I'm late. You must be Savannah. Your mama has told me all about you," he said sticking out his hand.

"You are?" I stared at him.

"Beau Nichols. Your mama's consort."

"First off, she isn't my mother, hasn't been since she disowned me," I said with a smile giving my mother a fleeting glance before turning my attention back to the male. "Secondly, why don't you take your new bride and head back home. There's nothin here for her," I replied with a cruel smile.

He gave me a grin that didn't meet his eyes.

"She is a spitfire isn't she," he said to Chloe.

"I warned you she was."

"Listen, I want you gone by tonight. Do not come to my home or go looking for my mate or anything else. Do you understand me?" I stood up and turned away.

There was a sharp intake of breath as I gave her my back. I turned back around looking at the look on her face. Beau had that grin still in place but his eyes were sizing me up.

"You have already become one of them?" she said.

"If you mean part of the clan. Yeah, I have."

"I was hoping you would have waited to do this. But as always, anything to shame me."

"To shame you?" I demanded with a harsh laugh. Unbelievable!

"Savannah you are a witch who should..."

"Watch what you say next," I held up one finger stopping her. "If the next words are anything disparaging about my mate you will see an entirely different side of me," I warned.

"You need to watch your tongue," Beau warned.

It was my turn to size him up.

"No. I think you need to watch hers," I said nodding my head at Chloe.

"We all need to be concerned about what is happening to our bloodlines dear."

"I take it you are part of WPG then?"

She said nothing just looked uncomfortable.

"Why am I not surprised? I will say it again, leave and leave now."

I turned my back on the two of them and moved towards the exit. I handed the valet my ticket as my phone rang. I answered without paying any attention to who was calling me.

"Woods," I snapped.

"It's Ryan. Are you okay?"

"Fine. What do you need?" I knew my tone was less than friendly but it was the best I could do in that moment.

"I need your team here now."

I groaned as I started to rub my head.

"What's going on?"

"An FBI agent just showed up. It appears Isobel isn't the first hybrid to go missing."

Fucking hell!

"Alright, we'll be there in thirty," I said as I rubbed my head. The guy pulled up with my car. I handed him a ten and jumped into the Suburban.

"See you soon," Ryan replied back.

"Yeah," I replied. I put the SUV in gear, then dialed Meri. She answered on the first ring.

"Are you guys at the office?" I asked.

"We're about to leave my house. Why?"

I was grateful they hadn't left Meri's house yet. Her house was closer to the station, which meant I wouldn't have to backtrack.

"I'm on my way to pick you guys up."

"What's going on?" she asked.

"The FBI."

"Shit!"

"Yeah. As soon as I pull up, be ready to go."

"Got it."

I hung up and let it sink in the fact that the FBI was now involved. I had enough issues with this case now I would have to deal with the FBI. The fact that Isobel wasn't our only victim had been a bit of a shock. If that was the case why hadn't they shown up sooner. I was worried they would take the case from us now that they were here. The last thing I wanted was some fed screwing up the entire thing and we would never find Isobel. Dammit! This was supposed to be an easy week. Finish up final details for the ceremony and then be mated one more time. Now I was hunting a human who had stolen a hybrid young. To top things off my 'mommy dearest' popping in for a visit and was part of WPG. This week was getting better and better by the minute.

Chapter Fifteen

We reached the station a few minutes after ten a.m. I waved a hand at the desk sergeant as we entered, she buzzed us in. I had been working with the department long enough to know every human who worked the front desk. They were now getting to know Meri, which made all of our lives easier.

We walked into the squad room filled with detectives and uniformed officers answering phones from the tipline. There was no lull in the noise and activity in the room. The photo of Bree Miller/ Lucy Cordova had been released to the media the night before. The phones would continue this steady pace of calls coming in until we found her or Isobel. We moved across the room to the back of the squad room where Ryan's office was located. He sat behind his desk looking tired. Ryan had his jacket off, his tie was gone as well, with his shirt sleeves rolled up. He leaned back in his chair as he pressed a pen down on his desk before he flipped it on its end repeating the move. Cain stood in the corner arms crossed over his chest looking less than happy about whatever was happening. I could see a man sitting across from Ryan, his brown hair was dull in color. He had on a jacket that had F.B.I. stamped on the back. Ryan saw our approach as we reached the door and waved us in.

"Woods," Ryan said as we entered. "This is SSA Eric Illingworth," Ryan said, indicating the man.

I got my first look at the agent. He had green eyes and an easy smile. I didn't trust anyone who could smile at a time like this. His dark brown hair was combed to the side. He wore a white dress shirt and dark pants. His loafers were well worn from the look of them, the black leather was dull in color.

"Hello," he greeted as he stood and held his hand out to me.

"I'm Savannah Woods," I replied as I shook his hand. "This is Meri Embers and Antoine Watts, my associates."

"Nice to meet you," he shook each of their hands.

I will give him credit for shaking our hands. I wasn't sure how much the F.B.I. actually interacted with hellborns but most humans were nervous about even touching us.

"So what can we do for you SSA Illingworth?" I asked.

"The Isobel Daring's case. I have eight open cases of hybrid children who have gone missing over the last several years. I believe that your case or Lieutenant Ryan's case actually is connected."

I liked how he tried to be sly with the dig of whose case this was. This was going to be fun.

"Before you go any further. Are you planning on taking this case from us?" Watts asked.

"No. I tried to get my boss to send a team with me but my request was denied. The best I could do was come on my own and ask for the department to work with me."

There it was again. It wasn't missed that he had said the department, not all of us. I wanted the guy's information but I had a feeling he planned on trying to push us out. I wasn't going to allow that.

"The Lieutenant has agreed to include me in the investigation and asked that I wait for you all to arrive before I briefed him on my other cases."

"Then let's get to it," I prompted.

"I have us set up in the conference room down the hall," Ryan said to the room. "I need a moment with Woods. The rest of you head down."

I stood with my arms crossed over my chest as everyone filed out. Illingworth had to slide past me as he left, so did Cain. Cain was the last one to leave, shutting the door behind him.

"Let me guess he wants us out of it."

Ryan nodded his head as his pen continued its end over, end routine.

"I told him no and you would continue to be a part of this investigation until we find Isobel."

"Thanks, Ryan."

It was nice to know who your friends were.

"He's arrogant and it shows when he speaks. I've just spent the last hour with the man and I'm ready for him to leave. He wants to be the hero on this."

"Those are the guys that get others killed," I pointed out.

"Yeah, they are. When we go in there, we let him do his thing, get his information and put him on a short leash. I want him with Cain and me. I don't want him anywhere near your team. I don't trust him," he said.

"What do you want from me?"

"Be on your best behavior. Do you understand me?" he asked. I gave Ryan a short nod while I rolled my eyes.

"Yeah I got it."

"Let's go."

We walked out of the office and headed down a long hall to the left of Ryan's office. The little respect I had for our SSA Illingworth was gone.

The conference room was large with a long table taking up most of the room. There were six chairs placed along both sides. The white walls had nothing on them but a large whiteboard, like I had in my office but larger. Cain and my team took the side of the table facing the board. Along the opposite wall was a brown cabinet with a small countertop that held a coffee carafe and mugs. I walked around leaning my ass against the cabinet. Ryan took a seat close to the whiteboard spinning the chair around angling it so it was closer to the end of the table. I watched Mr. F.B.I. placed pictures up on the board. The room was silent as the pictures went up one by one. These young looked to be around the same age as Isobel. There were boys and girls, black, white, and hispanic. He wrote the date they went missing under each of the pictures with their names and ages. He also included the city and state they went missing from. Isobel was number nine in this line. Were there more? How could no one be looking for them? I knew the answer to that last one.

"As you can see Andrew Corker went missing in 2008. He lived with his grandmother in California. Two years later, Marissa Jefferies and Denise Clark were abducted within eight months of each other. They lived in Georgia but in two different cities," he said pointing at the young faces. "Faith Holden was taken a year later from her home in Montana. Ian Brice, Jay Guzman, and Grayson Mathis all abducted three years later from three different states but right around the same time. Ian Brice was from New York, Jay Guzman, California and Grayson Mathis, Oregon."

He looked at us to make sure we were paying attention before he carried on. "Callie Rider was abducted a year later from Nevada. Then two years later Meg Travers was abducted in New York."

"All hybrids?" Cain asked.

"Yes."

"How many were taken from their homes?" Meri asked.

"Denise Clark, Faith Holden, Greyson Mathis, and Meg Travers."

"What about the others?" Watts questioned.

"Andrew was taken on his way home from school. He was supposed to be walking with an older sibling and ended up on his own. Marissa was taken while at the store with her father. Surveillance tapes show him walking to the restroom and then nothing after that. Jay was with his grandparents at a fair when he was taken. Ian was on his way to school, another kid saw him approach a green van and climb in. Callie was taken while she was playing outside her home in the front yard."

"How do we know they're connected?" Ryan asked.

"The only thing that connects them is their species," Cain pointed out.

"In the home abductions, did anyone smell lilacs?" I questioned.

"Faith Holden and Greyson Mathis' family did," He turned to Ryan. "To answer your question, I think they're connected because one, their species. There is also the age bracket they all fall into," he answered our questions.

"Anyone have a relative or neighbor connected to WPG?" I asked.

"I don't know," he replied as he began to go through the digital file. "Doesn't look like it. Why?"

"Because Isobel Daring's grandparents are and I want to see if that's the connection."

"Nothing in the files."

"Do you think anyone thought to ask?" Watts questioned.

"It's possible it was missed," Illingworth answered tightly.

It didn't shock me if it was. They would have looked hard at all the people connected to the young. WPG would not have been on their radar. This was the problem when humans didn't know the right questions to ask in the Hellborn world.

"Do you have any other information?" Ryan asked.

"All of the families come from different backgrounds."

"Any working theories?" Watts inquired.

"Traffickers. It would explain the differences in the children. It would also explain why they are missing from all over the country."

The room fell quiet as we all looked at the young faces on the board.

"Okay," Ryan said, getting to his feet. "SSA Illingworth you will be working with Sergeant Cain. We will take the trafficker angle. Woods, I want your team to work on the WPG angle."

"Lieutenant, I was thinking maybe we should wait to bring in the hunters while we run down leads," Illingworth suggested.

"Woods knows how to talk to hellborns and get information. She has been working with us for over ten years. She will continue to be part of this investigation. Any other questions?" Ryan's voice held a tone of finality.

There was a pause in the room as the two men stared at one another gauging mettle.

"Fine," Illingworth finally answered.

"Do you need anything Woods?" Ryan asked.

"Contact information for the families of these young."

"Can you give Woods the information?" Ryan asked.

"Yeah," Illingworth said grudgingly.

"One more thing before we break up this party. We did a background search on Bree Miller and Lucy Cordova. Both names are aliases. CSU did get a few partial prints in the motel. They're being run through the system now," Cain informed us.

"I could send them to the FBI lab for analysis," Illingworth offered.

"We can get you a copy of the prints," Ryan said. "Okay let's get to work."

I leaned down to Meri and Watts speaking softly. "You two get photos of each of those young. I'll get the numbers for the families."

Meri took one end of the board while Watts took the other side. I approached Illingworth.

"What makes you think this witch group is involved?" he questioned.

"You guys have no hellborns working for you do you?"

"Why would you say that?"

"Well first, WPG isn't some witch group. They're a hate group like Human Alliance or the KKK. The difference is they hate other hellborns and any witch who doesn't follow in their beliefs. Second you showed up in loafers. You can't chase a hellborn in loafers."

"Lieutenant Ryan and Sergeant Cain are wearing dress shoes."

"For here in the office, yes they are but if we have to raid a location or serve a search warrant they will have different footwear. Besides, chasing hellborns is more part of my job than their job."

"Which is why I don't understand what you're doing here for this part of the investigation."

"Again another sign you have no clue how to deal with hellborns. Hellborns are not going to talk to you because you're human. There's too long of a history of hellborns being mistreated and discriminated against by humans. They will talk to me or Meri Embers because we're one of them."

"Discrimination doesn't happen anymore and hasn't in years," he replied.

"Really. Look at what happened in L.A. Watch the news, you see it all the time. Better yet look at those eight young and the response from the F.B.I.," Illingworth looked away from me as I spoke. "If Isobel Daring was a human and these other young were, the F.B.I would have sent an entire team. You guys would have swooped in here and taken over the case. These young would be considered more of a priority. As far as society has come, we haven't changed all that much, Illingworth. The fact that you're looking away from me means you know it just as well as I do," I pointed out.

"So is it all humans that are the problem?"

"No, it's not all humans. I'm friends with the three humans in this room. The problem is there are enough to give a bad name to the rest of you."

"Are you going to answer my first question?" he met my stare evenly.

"It was something Isobel Daring's grandparents said and the behavior of the chapter leader when I went to see him. Call it a hunch. Now are you going to give me the numbers for the families?"

"Yeah."

He pulled up the contact names and numbers on each of the kids. I took Watts notepad and recorded the information down.

"Thank you," I said as I finished.

"You know if we find these traffickers or whatever they are, you may not be part of the take down?" he pointed out.

"We'll see about that."

"Are you always so confident?"

"In this, I am."

I could feel his eyes on me as I moved to say my goodbyes to Ryan and Cain. Ryan was right, he was arrogant but I also believed he was smart. I could see how he believed the cases were all connected. They'd all been taken fairly close together over the last ten years. He was wrong in thinking traffickers had taken these young. I didn't know how the woman who took Isobel fit into this but I would put money on it that witches were behind all of this.

My team was about to take their leave when a uniformed officer entered the conference room.

"Lieutenant! I have a man on the phone who says he rented a house over on Billings Road to our suspect."

"What line?" Ryan asked.

"Seven."

Ryan put the phone on speaker as he answered.

"This is Lieutenant Ryan. Who am I speaking with?"

"Henry Vanwell."

"Mr. Vanwell, I understand you have information on our suspect?" Ryan asked.

We all circled around the phone waiting to hear if this was a legitimate tip or a hoax.

"She rented one of my rental properties two months ago. A month to month lease."

"Can you give me the address?"

"3550 Billings Road. The name she had the lease under was Paula Anders," he answered.

"Do you have all of the paperwork?"

"Of course, I do."

"Is she still leasing the property?" Ryan asked.

"No, she called me three weeks ago. Her last day in the house was Monday. She never showed for the final inspection or gave me a forwarding address to send her security deposit."

"Mr. Vanwell, would it be alright if we came to search the property?"

"I guess."

"Great. I'm sending uniformed officers over to secure the property now. If you can meet us there with the lease and the information you have? We would greatly appreciate it."

"I can be there in a half an hour."

"Thank you, Mr. Vanwell."

"Anything I can do to help."

The call ended and we all took a moment before the rush kicked in. Ryan was instructing Cain to get a warrant to cover our asses. He then started yelling out the door to get two uniforms to the address now. My team waited long enough for him to finish giving orders before we headed to the house in question.

Chapter Sixteen

The drive from the station to the house in question took fifteen minutes. I drove behind Ryan and the other units with their lights flashing in order to make it to the house without any issues. The house was located a block from where the dogs had lost Isobel's scent. Its garage opened in the alley behind the businesses. The neighborhood was nice enough, it was a lower middle class, made up of working families. The house itself was a single story with light blue paint and white trim. The lawn was well maintained with no flowers in the flower bed. We stood with officers outside the perimeter as two uniformed officers ran yellow tape around the perimeter of the property. Ryan stood waiting for the landlord as he turned his head left to right looking for approaching cars. I could see the tension tightened his body as his head swung back and forth. Every once in a while he would call out a command to an officer. Illingworth was beside him pacing from the tape to the car and back. Ryan's phone rang as we stood waiting to go in. There was a lot of yeahs and great followed by a good job.

"Cain got the warrant. He's on the way."

I pulled out gloves and booties for each of my team members as we went back to the waiting game. It felt like years by the time Mr. Vanwell arrived. He pulled up to the property with wide eyes at the amount of police presence. Mr. Vanwell was no taller than myself but with a round protruding belly. His brown hair was growing thin on his head, leaving a ring of hair around it. He climbed from his car as Cain arrived with a warrant in hand.

"Here's the application and her credit report. There is also a copy of the social security card and her license," he handed the folder to Ryan.

"Thank you Mr. Vanwell. May we have the keys?" Ryan asked.

"Sure. Here they are," he handed two keys over.

We approached the property as one large group. I slid into my gloves as I crossed the police tape. Booties came next as soon as I was close to the porch. Ryan opened the place up, entering first. The door opened to a large open living room with plush tan carpet. The walls were your standard white. To the left was the kitchen, which also had white walls with white cabinets. The kitchen floor was red linoleum.

"Illingworth, you take the kitchen. Woods, you and your team take the garage. Cain, I want you and a couple officers to take the bedrooms," Ryan ordered.

We all nodded as we moved to our assigned rooms. The garage was off the back of the kitchen attached to the house. At least we wouldn't need two warrants, that was a plus. The garage was like any other garage, there was a washer and dryer near the door, along with wood shelving in the back of the garage. Sitting inside, was the car our homeless guy had identified. A blue hatchback Civic sat in the garage.

"Meri, get Ryan and tell him we have the car she left in from the Daring's house."

Meri turned and ran back through the house. I checked the passenger side door finding it unlocked. I popped the glove box, the registration said Bree Miller lived in Texas. I placed the paperwork back in scanning the front seat, while Watts popped the trunk and searched it.

"Anything back there?" I asked.

"Nothing."

CSU would take the car back to the lab and vacuum the interior and then take the car apart. Chances were good we would get at least some hairs, if nothing else. I glanced in the back seat, seeing nothing back there. As I climbed out of the car, the crime scene techs came in and started demanding access to the car. Watts and I stepped back allowing them to do their job. We headed back inside. Illingworth had opened all of the cabinets leaving the doors open as he moved from cabinet to cabinet.

"Anything?" I asked.

"No. Nothing in the fridge or cabinets."

"This was a backup for her," Watts said.

"Yeah," I agreed.

"You guys found a car?" Illingworth asked.

"Yeah. It's the one she used to take Isobel," I answered.

"Did she leave anything behind?"

"No, just the registration that says Bree Miller."

I walked into the living room looking at the carpet. There were no indents in the carpet or any marks on the walls. This had been a safe house nothing more. I doubted she stayed for more than a night, maybe two in this place. I had to give the woman credit, she was damn good at being a ghost. Meri came from down the hallway to the right of the living room.

"Cain find anything?" I asked.

"Nothing."

"Let's head out. There's nothing to learn here," I said.

"Agreed," Meri replied with irritation.

"Watts, let's go," I called out.

Watts came out of the kitchen with a question on his face.

"The CSU guys will take a day or two before they have anything. I doubt they will find anything," I explained.

"That's what Illingworth was saying."

"He has that part right," I said as the F.B.I. agent walked out of the kitchen. I gave him a wave as we headed for the exit. Ryan was still talking to the landlord. As I peeled my gloves off, my team followed suit. We dumped them with the booties into the trash bag as we approached Ryan.

"Give me a moment, sir," Ryan said.

He approached us with his hands on his hips.

"Nothing in the house?" he asked.

"No, just the car in the garage."

"Fuck!"

"Maybe we'll get lucky and the CSU will find something inside the car," I offered.

"Maybe."

"Have Cain send me a copy of the paperwork, would you?" I asked.

"Yeah. Where are you heading?"

"To The Gallery. I think I have a few contacts that may be able to help us with whatever

charms was used on the Darings."

"Let me know," he ordered.

"I will."

We took our leave from the vacant house. I don't know why we all were so disappointed in the lack of evidence in the house. This woman had already proven that she was good and understood police procedure. Yet we still all had some hope that we would find something that would lead to Isobel. The let down was harsh but in reality not unexpected.

Chapter Seventeen

We headed to the Gallery. Meri and I each had a copy of the photos of the suspect and the tea she had given to Emma Daring. I parked in one of the lots, paying the fifteen dollar all day fee. There were three shops I knew would help us. Meri would take one of the shops called Earth Solutions. The owner of the shop was a small male witch who had a thing for her. He would be more than willing to help her if she asked for it. It would also take a while to get anything from him. He enjoyed flirting with her and Meri tended to play along. Watts and I would take Bally's Magic and Earth's Apothecary Shop while Meri worked her own magic.

As we walked down the street Watts spoke.

"What do you think of the F.B.I. guy's theory?"

"I think it's too easy to go that way."

"Maybe but it could be that these kids are being auctioned off online. It happens," he offered.

"Watts do you know what happens when hybrid children grow up?"

"No."

"They grow like any other kid until they hit their mid twenties. That's when things change for them. They stop ageing. They become physically stronger, harder to kill. The vampire side becomes stronger. It's like their transition stalls out or they have a second transition. Prior to that they have their magic that makes them strong. Think about that for a minute. Why would a trafficker take a hellborn in the first place, let alone a hybrid? There is something else happening here," I explained.

"I don't know Woods. Maybe there's a market for them in the pedaphile world."

"I'm sure there is but it still doesn't fit. There's also the fact that some hybrids require feedings like vampires do. One of those kids could easily kill their kidnapper."

We walked into Bally's Magic first. There were a handful of witches doing their shopping who looked up seeing us as we approached the counter. Bally, the store owner, was behind the counter. He was as big as a wall with wide shoulders and hips and was taller than Watts. He offered me a wide smile. Bally always seemed happy, which made me nervous, no one could ever be that happy all the time.

"Savannah, where have you been lately? It's been weeks since I've seen you. Do you not need your old friend Bally anymore?" he asked.

"Bally, I always need you. You should know that by now. I haven't been by because witches in the city have been taking a break from a life of crime."

"Hey, what's with the human with you?" he asked, signally to Watts with his thumb.

"This is Antione Watts, he's training with me. He's a good guy, don't be too hard on him just because he's human," I smiled.

"We all have our flaws," Bally agreed with a smile of his own.

"That we do." Watts took all this with a smile of his own.

"So what can I do for you on this fine day?"

"We're working the Isobel Daring case and we believe the kidnapper may have drugged the parents with this and another substance."

"Man that case has been all over the news. Took her from her bed and you think the parents were drugged. What is wrong with this world?"

"Got me."

"Let me see what you have."

Watts handed him the bag of the tea. He smelled it and placed a large meaty hand inside the bag feeling the ingredients.

"This looks like a lavender tea I sell for sleep but it has mandrake added to it. I would never add mandrake to lavender, it would make the tea too strong."

"Can we see the tea?" I asked.

"For you, no problem."

He headed to the back room. I watched as he ducked to walk through the door. He was back a minute later with a dark blue canister in his hand. The canister had a green planet with stars above. Peace and relaxation was written at the top of the thin canister. It was the same as the one from the Darings house. I made to pop the can open when Bally stopped me.

"You know I love you Savannah but if you open it you have to buy it," he informed me with his meaty hand over mine.

"Really, Bally?"

"Yes, ma'am. If you open it I can't sell it."

"Fine. How much?" I asked.

"Eight dollars and fifty-six cents."

I pulled out my card handing it to Bally for him to run it. I opened up the canister and smelled the tea. It had a nice aroma without the mandrake in it.

"By adding the mandrake what happens exactly?" Watts inquired.

"The tea as it is strong. It helps one relax enough to sleep. Mostly, I get insomniacs who buy it. With the mandrake it doesn't just relax you it actually puts you to sleep. If you get too much of the mandrake in the brew you could poison yourself," he answered as he handed me back my card.

"So you would have to know exactly how much to add to it so you didn't kill yourself or someone else?" Watts asked.

"Yes."

"How many other shops sell this?" Watts asked.

"None I know of in The Gallery. I get this from my cousin. He makes the tea and sells it wholesale to shops in Hawaii."

"Do humans buy it?" I asked.

"I get a few regulars but it's mostly other hellborns."

"How about her?" I placed the photo of the woman on the counter.

"I don't remember her. What's her name?"

"She has three alaises Bree Miller, Lucy Cordova, or Paula Anders."

"Doesn't ring any bells."

"Does your cousin sell these to individual buyers?" Watts asked.

"No."

"Is there any way you can get me connected with your cousin?" I asked.

"I can make that happen. Give me a few hours and I'll call you."

"You're the best Bally," I leaned across the counter giving him a hug.

"Anything to help that little one."

"I have one more question. Do you know of any potion or spell that would smell like lilacs that could be turned into a vapor?"

He looked up at the ceiling as he thought about it.

"Not off the top of my head but I'll ask around."

"Thanks, Bally," I replied as we headed for the door.

"Anything for you, Savannah."

Watts looked at me as we headed down to the next shop.

"He's interesting?" Watts said.

"Bally is a good male," I said with a chuckle.

"How did you win him over?"

"Seven months ago, I was working a petty thief case. These males were going into stores like Bally's and grabbing whatever they could get their hands on and running out. They were juvenile wolves who thought they could do what they wanted then make some money off the stolen goods. They went into his store and tried to steal from him."

"That's bold of them."

"Right! Anyway, I get to Bally's store, it's a mess. He caught two of the wolves and held them. I get the two booked and start demanding where the rest of the males they were. I end up getting the other three wolves and all of Bally's stuff back along with a few other stores. His shop isn't one of the more popular ones down here so it was going to cost him a good chunk of change to fix the damage that was done. I was able to get the pack to cover his damages. Ever since he's adored me," I explained.

"How much was it in damages?" Watts asked.

"About three thousand dollars."

"So is that the secret to getting hellborns to trust you."

"For some, yes. They want respect like humans do. For others it takes proving that you aren't like the others doing this job. I work for the human police and hunt down my own kind. Many see me as one of you. Some I will never win over. Mating Santiago has made things easier and others more difficult."

"Because of the fact he's a vampire and you're a witch?"

"Yeah and the fact of what each of us do within the community."

"It's a fine line you walk, Woods," he pointed out.

"You have no clue how fine the line is."

We walked into the next store, Earth's Apothecary. The shop was made up of mostly charms and ingredients. There were satchels of different colors, reusable tea bags, and candles everywhere. The smell that filled the shop was a peaceful scent, almost a sandalwood smell but something more. I approached the counter finding the owner of the shop, a small white haired woman with a raspy voice.

She was busy scribbling in a book. She didn't look up when she spoke, she just kept going with her notetations.

"I knew you would be here soon enough," she replied.

"Hey, Ruth. How's it going?"

"Cut the small talk. What do you need?"

"Do you know of any charm or potion that could be turned into a gas?"

"A few. What did it smell like?"

"Lilacs," I replied.

She said nothing as she kept writing in her book. She paused for a moment before she went back to writing. She looked at me finally over small red framed glasses.

"There's a charm, the sleep of the dead. It was used centuries ago. Witches were using it to hide from the humans during the witch trials. They would dose themselves just as the church would come to take them. As they lost consciousness they would point the finger at a human. The humans would go after the one who they believed to be a witch."

"How long did the affects last?" I asked.

"Generally a couple of hours at most. Just long enough for the humans to be distracted with their next victim and for the witch to get away from the mob. Many times they changed their name. Made it easier for them to disappear in a new town."

"Do you know how to make the charm?"

"I may have a book on it. It hasn't been used in ages. The second part of your question, I don't know if it could be turned into a vapor," she stated.

"If I asked you nicely enough to look into the charm, would you?"

"Would I have the chance at that ten thousand you and your mate are offering?"

"No. The money is for leads that will lead us to the young, not for what I'm asking."

"What will it get me?" she asked shrewdly.

"It will get you a get out of jail free card the next time I find out you're selling colored sugar water as a charm to humans."

She stared at me shrewdly to see if I was telling the truth.

"I'll let you know what I find."

"Thanks, Ruth," I said as I started for the door. "Oh and one more thing this offer has a time limit. If I don't hear from you in the next eight hours it expires."

"You can't do that!"

"Yes, I can. You and I have done this before. You drag your feet to get the information and still want me to fulfill my end of the deal in a timely manner. Not this time," I said, shaking my head at her. "You will do what I need in the next eight hours or I will terminate the deal."

"Fine, I will have it for you in the next eight hours."

"Talk to you soon, Ruth," I waved as we walked out.

Watts looked at me as if he couldn't believe what had just happened.

"What?"

"You are going to give her a pass for breaking the law?"

"Sometimes it's a necessary evil," I answered.

"But if she is scamming humans."

"Look what she does is harmless. Yes, it's a crime but it's barely a misdemeanor."

"Woods, she is still a criminal," he pointed out.

"Maybe but she knows more about history and spells that were used than anyone I know. If she is right, it will explain why the Darings got the timeline wrong."

He shook his head at me.

"You never made a deal with a guy who had a minor offense to get a bigger fish?" I asked.

"Yeah, when I worked in other departments but not so willingly."

"It's the same thing Watts. This is one of the areas in life, humans and hellborns are very much the same. In this world no matter what side you're on information is a commodity."

We walked back to the car chatting about what was next. It took us ten minutes to make it back where Meri was leaning against the passenger side of the Suburban.

"Did you get anything?" she asked.

"Yeah, we did," Watts answered.

"Good because Ernie had nothing to offer me other than himself," she replied with disgust. "What did you find out?"

"We'll talk in the car on the way back to the office."

We left The Gallery behind as we made the trek back to our office. I was hoping this would lead us closer to Isobel and with any luck the other young that were missing as well.

Chapter Eighteen

Watts and I explained everything we had learned from Bally and Ruth to Meri. The information from Bally was helpful because it could explain why they had fallen asleep in the living room. I didn't know why Emma Daring had woken up but I was willing to bet it had to do with her hybrid DNA. Ruth's information made me believe it had been later than ten o'clock when they had woken. I needed to ask why they thought it was ten p.m.

At least we were finally getting answers to some of our questions, now we needed to find something that would lead us to find Isobel. The information we had gave us an idea of what we were dealing with. The human who took her was a professional, which told me she had probably been hired to take Isobel. The question became for whom? Why would someone hire a professional? Most traffickers had people on the payroll for that, they didn't outsource nor were traffickers this good. Traffickers either did snatch and grabs or they lured their victims. There were some snatch and grabs in the group of young, who were missing but this was more organized. I doubted our abductor worked for one employer. There was more money to be had working for multiple sources.

As we pulled into the driveway I noticed my front door looked open. Normally, I would have pulled into the garage but something wasn't right. I pulled my gun and also grabbed onto the nearest line with my metaphysical hand. The energy flooded my system. I heard Watts curse as he pulled his own weapon. The door was slightly ajar, as if someone wanted a silent escape. I went in first slowly opening the door moving with it as I raised my gun to chest level. Watts moved to the left and Meri stood in the entryway sniffing the air. She mouthed the word witch and pointed towards the kitchen.

I went first, clearing the dining room. Watts walked around the other side of the table pushing the kitchen door open silently as he scanned the room. Meri pointed down to the basement. Someone was in our office. I went down the stairs sweeping the room. Standing looking at the whiteboard was my mother. Obviously, she didn't get the hint from earlier in the morning. I put my gun away and approached her grabbing a hold of her arm swinging her around.

"What the fuck are you doing here!?" I demanded.

"Your mate let me in," she met my fury with calmness.

"Try again. My mate would have never allowed you in our home let alone my office."

"Well he did. He said..." she got no farther as I pushed her into a wall, spinning her so her face was against the wall.

"You're here for something and I'm going to find out what it is."

I snatched her Gucci purse from her hand and tossed it to Meri. "Search that."

I kicked her feet apart and began to pat her down. She tried to push against me as I searched her. Watts came up placing his gun next to her head.

"Don't move," was all he said, Watts' deep voice sounding menacing.

Her body was clean of any weapons.

"Savannah, look at this," Meri said from behind me.

"Watts make sure she doesn't move."

"You got it."

"Like a human could stop me from doing anything," Chloe said.

"He could," I warned.

I walked over to my desk looking at the contents of her purse. Most of the contents were what you would expect. Some cash, lipstick, mints. Sitting in her wallet was a card for Troy Salazar. Well that was interesting.

"Did you think you were going to come here and get information for Troy Salazar," I said walking back over to her.

"I don't know what you're talking about."

"Really? Because his card is in your wallet," Meri said.

I spun her around meeting her eyes. Those eyes were blazing as I stared at her. She was pissed at being caught.

"So what does WPG have to do with Isobel Daring's kidnapping?" I asked.

"Nothing," she answered quickly, almost too quick.

"She's lying," Meri said.

"Yeah, she is."

"I am not. You are my only child Savannah. We should be able to work this out," she tried to sound upset but there was too much of a hard tone to her voice. The sympathy card was a nice go to for someone else, not her.

"There is nothing to work out," I snapped as I pushed closer to her. "I will ask again what does WPG have to do with Isobel Daring?"

"And I have already...."

"You're lying. You have no plans on being honest, no matter what happens next," I cut her off.

She gave up the charade and she smirked at me.

"Why don't you let me try?" Meri offered.

"Don't touch me," she pointed a finger at Meri.

I was tempted to let Meri have her way with Chloe but I had a feeling she was just taking orders on this one. No, the smarter play was to see where she led us.

"Watts, walk her out the front door."

"You got it," he put his gun away taking Chloe by the arm, guiding her to the stairs.

She snatched her arm away from Watts and walked around him, snatching her purse and all her contents from my desk before turning towards the stairs. She kept her head up as she went up the stairs. Why had she been here? If anything she just reaffirmed that the WPG was somehow involved. I turned to my desk and began to open drawers. Meri followed suit checking her desk.

"Nothing is missing from my desk," Meri informed me as I closed my final drawer.

I looked at the top of my desk taking in everything, when I saw the sticky pad was not where I had left it. I was so much of a control freak everything had its place on my desk. Normally, the sticky pad would be to the left of the pens instead it was in front of my pens as if it had been thrown lazily on the desk. I looked at the pad trying to remember what had been on the note when Watts came back down.

"She's gone. A white Cadillac pulled up as soon as we got to the door."

"Probably the new husband," I answered.

"What did she want?" Meri questioned.

"My guess to see what we have. She took a note I had written" I replied waving the pad.

"What was on it?" Watts asked.

"That is what I am trying to recall."

"How did she get past the security system?" Meri wondered.

"That is another good question. I need to call Santiago."

I hit his name on my contact list and waited for the call to connect.

"Hello, Mi Amor. Did you resolve the situation with your mother?"

"Not even close. What time did you leave for work?" I asked.

"Approximately eleven o'clock. Why?" he asked me curiously

"Did you set the alarm?"

"Of course, I did. Why are you asking me these questions?" I could hear as irritation entered Santiago's voice.

"We had a visitor. My mother was in my office when we got here."

"I am on my way home."

"She is gone but..." I tried to stop him from rushing home.

"Savannah, I am leaving now," his voice was harsh as it had been the night before.

He hung up before I could argue with him any further. Ever since I had been attacked, Santiago had made it his personal mission to keep me safe. It had been a vow he had made to me the night we mated. I loved him for his dedication. Finding out someone had breached our security system put him on edge. What he did next would all depend on his mood when he got here.

The headache I had been fighting all day was bearing down on me. I squeezed the bridge of my nose as I planned what my next step would be. The headache was getting worse with each obstacle that came along.

"Okay, we need to focus on finding these young," I said as I slid my phone back into my front pocket. "Watts, I want you to start digging into Beau Nichols. Meri and I will take the families of the missing kids."

"Who is Beau Nichols?" he asked.

"My mother's new mate. Also, see if you can get Cain to pull info on him."

"You think your mother and her husband could be involved?" he questioned.

"There's a chance she is. She knows Troy Salazar and that's enough for me to wonder where she fits into this."

"What about when Santiago gets home?" Meri inquired.

"I will let him handle the security system."

"Really?" disbelief filled her voice.

I could understand her disbelief. Three months ago, I would have insisted on handling it myself. Now I was willing to step back and give Santiago the reins. If being mated had taught me anything, it had taught me how to prioritize and allow someone else to help you. See I was growing.

"Yes. We need to focus on finding these young. If I try to deal with the security threat then my attention will get diverted. Isobel's case needs my full attention," I answered.

We all sat down at our desks and got to work. The first two families I spoke with gave me a little help. Their children had been taken in broad daylight. The sound of the grief they felt made it hard to ask questions. With every question their voices became heavier. I asked if they knew anyone connected with WPG. Both answered with a resounding no. The third number I called was Denise Clark's family. There was no answer. I left a message and was unsure they would get back to me. I was about to dial the next number when I heard the rushing feet of my mate. I looked at the time, seeing it had taken him only twenty-five minutes to arrive home. I met him at the bottom of the stairs. His warm embrace pushed the headache back, dulling the pain. Santiago pulled back enough to look at me, placing his hands on my neck. I could see the worry on his face.

"You made good time."

"It is the benefit of owning the vehicle I do."

One of the selling points for Santiago when he got the Porsche, was the fact it went from zero to sixty in less than five seconds and topped out at a hundred sixty-five miles per hour.

"Have you called the security company yet?"

"No, I haven't. I need to focus on Isobel."

"I will take care of it. This will not happen again."

"I know because you won't allow it, and the next time I'll just shoot her," I said with a

smile.

"I assure you this will not happen ever again."

"As soon as you know how she got in, let me know."

"I will," he gave me a quick kiss before going back up stairs.

I watched as he headed back up wishing I could follow. Instead, I turned away and

headed back to my desk. I dialed the last number. A woman answered after a few rings.

"Hello, this is Savannah Woods. I am a hunter with the Sweetclover police department and..."

"Is this about my Faith?" she asked before I finished.

"Yes, it is actually Mrs. Holden."

"Have you found her?"

"No, but I am working on a case that is similar to your daughters. I was wondering if you would be willing to answer a few questions for me."

"Oh...yes...how can I help you?" Her disappointment was heavy.

"Your daughter was taken from her bed. When you realized she was missing, did you notice anything different?"

"Like what?"

"A smell or anything that was out of place?"

"Uhm...I smelled lilacs but it was summertime and we had a bush outside the window. It was the window we had left open. That was how they got in," she said.

I wondered if that was really how they got in.

"I know this will sound like an odd question but did you know anyone connected to WPG?" I asked.

"No...not that I know of. They did send someone to our house, about a month after Faith had been gone. They wanted to give their condolences and offer me a chance to leave my mate. They had the nerve to offer to pay for the divorce."

"Mrs. Holden, are you a hybrid as well?" I asked.

"No. We got lucky when we got pregnant. Just Faith."

For a vampire and witch to get pregnant was somewhat a miracle. It wasn't something that happened often. No one knew exactly why the pregnancy usually failed but the working theory was that the two DNA's tended to reject each other. It was like when a witch became a hybrid you never knew what the outcome would be. There were vampires that could reproduce, it didn't happen often, but it did. More times than not when vampires went through the transition their ability to reproduce ended. In many ways witches and vampires were connected to humans in the genetic sense. The vampires who could reproduce, gave birth to a vampire that grew into a vampire adult. Vampire offspring stopped ageing around the same time as hybrids. I knew little about vampire children because there were so few out there.

"Before your daughter was taken did you meet anyone new or make any new friends?" I asked.

She was silent for a long time before she spoke.

"I did about six months before Faith disappeared. We had a new neighbor and I became friendly with her until she moved."

"What species was she?"

"She was human. We lived in a neighborhood that was mostly human."

"What was her name?" I asked.

"Uhm...Lauren, Laura, something like that. I don't remember her name. Why?"

"Could I send you a photo?"

"Yes," she answered.

"Give me a moment."

I sent the photo through text message and waited until I knew she had it.

"Was the woman you made friends with look like the photo I just sent you."

I could hear as I was placed on speaker. It took her a long moment before she replied.

"She looks like her, but the woman I knew had dark hair. It could be her. It's been a while since I've seen her. What does this woman have to do with my Faith?"

"She's a suspect in a missing young case here in Sweetclover. I don't know if she is connected to your young. I am just trying to get an idea of what happened."

"The police here searched for a few days before they began to give up. I feel like they spent more time focusing on my mate and I than they did anyone else," she explained.

"Thank you for your time Ms. Holden," I said.

"May I ask you something?" she asked.

"Yes."

"Is there still a chance my Faith will ever be found?"

Damn of all the questions she could ask. Chances were good her daughter was dead and had been for some time. I didn't want to tell her that. It seemed cruel to say her young was dead but to give her hope seemed just as cruel. Sometimes hope could be more cruel than the devastation of the truth.

"There is always a chance she is still alive..."

"But not much of a chance," she interrupted me.

"Yes."

"Thank you."

The call ended. I placed my phone down and covered my face. There were days I hated my job, this was one of them. These young had been taken and no one cared enough because of their species. It made me sick.

"Two of the young on my list had a connection to WPG. The first one was Ian Brice. Their neighbor is a member of the local chapter. From what I understand he was happy to see the young gone. From what I gathered the cops couldn't find any evidence the neighbor was involved in Ian's disappearance," Meri said. I sat back in my chair and looked at her.

"They also couldn't prove he wasn't," I said.

"Yeah. The other was Meg Travers, she had an uncle who was less than happy about the young being a hybrid. He is also a member of the WPG."

"So we have three out of the nine kids who have a connection to the group. Faith Holden's mother said they came two months after Faith was taken with condolences and offering to give her a second chance at having kids with a witch. Even offered to pay for the divorce."

"Disgusting," Meri cringed.

"Yeah. But she did smell lilacs and thought it was from the bush she had outside the window. There was also a woman she made friends with six months before Faith went missing."

"Could she I.D. our human?" Watts asked.

"No. She said they looked similar but she couldn't say for sure."

"Did she give the name of this friend?" Meri inquired.

"She couldn't remember the name. Lauren or Laura was all she could recall."

"Do you think Ruth will come through for you?" Meri asked.

"I do. She wants that get out of jail free card."

"Watts, do you have anything?" Meri asked.

"Almost."

"What does almost mean?" I asked.

"It means I need more time," he snapped.

I sat back as we waited for Watts to finish whatever he was working on. Chloe breaking into my home was unbelievable. The fact that she and her new mate were working for or with WPG, wasn't at all shocking. It made perfect sense she would. What I didn't understand was why they thought Chloe would be the person to send? The only reason I could see was they thought I wouldn't kill her or maim her. Her mate and Troy would be wrong on that one. They had to think I was close to something. Maybe because we now had a face of the woman who took Isobel. Maybe there was something I just wasn't seeing. Chloe wanted to see what we had. She tried playing I'm your mother card but that failed. She had to know it wouldn't work. Maybe she had warned them that it wouldn't and they insisted. When the attempt to win me over had failed she was sent to break into my home. There was no way she could have known when I would come home. It made sense to a point.

The only thing I couldn't figure out is how she got around our security system. The fact that she got around the system was a reason to pause. I had lost the feeling of safety once, I didn't want to lose the feeling of safety again. Especially when it came to this place. I loved our home, it was where we found healing when we both needed it so desperately. I thought back to the night we had consummated our mating. It had been a night of more than healing; it had been the start of a new life we would live together. It was as if Santigo had sensed my thoughts, my mate descended the stairs.

"Mi Amor, do you have a moment to spare?"

"For you, I do," I said getting up. "I'll be back in a bit guys."

Watts gave me a wave as Meri gave me a smirk, as if she knew what we would be doing. I followed my mate up the stairs, enjoying the view I was being given.

"I need you up in my office. I spoke with the security company and they feel nothing has been breached. On their end. The video footage I have shows differently. I have Duncan coming over to explain to us what we are looking at," he said as we hit the top of the stairs. Santiago stepped to the side allowing me to take the lead up to the next set of stairs.

"I take it you found something on the video?" I asked.

"Yes."

"Should we be concerned about more breaches?" I asked as we reached the hallway.

Santiago grabbed my hand, stopping my progress down the hall. He looked down at me studying my face.

"Duncan and I will ensure it will not happen again. I swore I would keep you safe and I will do just that."

"I have told you before it is not just on you, it's on me too."

"I am your mate so it is my responsibility to ensure you are safe. It is my role as your mate to ensure you are taken care of in every way possible."

I gave him a weak smile. I had never been good at letting anyone take care of me, that still hadn't changed.

"I know you detest the thought of me taking care of this," he replied.

"I don't hate it, I just don't like it."

"If you would like I will step back and let you handle this."

I looked at him, seeing how hard he was trying to hide his feelings on the matter. I really wanted to be the one who took care of the security issue but I also had a case I was trying to solve before our ceremony. I took a deep breath and shook my head.

"No, I can't do what's needed for the security problems. I need to focus on Isobel and the other young that are missing. I want you to take care of it. I trust you," I said, feeling my inner voice scream no. I told the voice to shut up this was a good thing. Sometimes I really hated my internal monologue.

"Then I will take care of it." We continued down the hall hand in hand. "Did you say other young?" he stopped again.

"Yeah, I did. It seems there are eight other hybrids who have gone missing over the last ten years."

"How is this possible?"

"What do you mean?" I asked.

"If there are eight other hybrid young missing, how have none of the clans known about this? When I ran a background on the Darings, I also made a few calls, no clan spoke of any hybrids missing from their region," he answered.

"I can answer for the human front and probably the hellborn side too. The short answer is, they're hybrids, so they aren't witches or vampires, no one cares. If they were human, they would have gotten more attention."

"It is sad no one has cared until now," he replied.

"I agree."

"Are they connected to Isobel?"

"The F.B.I. agent that showed up this morning, believes they are but so far only three have anything similar to Isobel's case. I mean they could all be connected. At this point I don't know," I answered honestly.

Santiago paused at the door allowing me to enter the room first. I walked around the desk, seeing the footage from the front door that had been paused on the computer. I took a seat in his big leather chair as Santiago leaned down and hit play. I watched as my mother knocked and looked around. She stood there taking stock of who or what was around. She turned around and a second body came into view of the camera. A dull looking male who was maybe eighteen. Billy, from WPG. He had a device that appeared to be a keypad similar to what we had inside the house and a laptop. I watched as the kid worked on the computer. He was at it for ten minutes when he nodded to her. The next thing I saw was her picking the lock and waltzing into my home. There was a knock on the front door, I backed up the video and watched it again. Santiago headed down stairs to answer the door. I sat back in the chair taking it all in. It was one more nail in the coffin of WPG. Whether they were involved in the kidnappings or not it didn't matter. What was my next move?

"Hey, Savannah. Do you mind if I take a look?" asked Duncan. He was standing next to Santiago's desk. I hadn't even noticed when he entered the room. He was standing there with a tablet in hand, in a pair of jeans, black lace up boots, and T-shirt. He was at ease as he watched my brain register he was waiting for me to move.

"Sorry...Yeah... can you send that video to this email address?" I replied as I started opening my mate's desk drawers looking for a paper and pen.

"I can do that."

Santiago came around pulling the small drawer to the left open handing me a pen and yellow sticky pad. I scribbled down Cain's email with his name. I hadn't planned to report the break in but as I sat watching Chloe pick my lock, I knew the weak link in this equation would be Billy. I kissed Santiago when I stood and gave a pat to Duncan's shoulder as I passed him.

"Let me know what you find out and what we do to stop it from happening again," I said.

"I can already tell you how they got in," Duncan answered. He took the chair I had just vacated and started working.

"How?" I asked.

"The kid found the system you were using. All he did was get into the system and repeat the code back to the system, like a mirror, all the security system saw was that everything was secure. From there they can open the front door and walk in."

"How can we stop this from happening again?" Santiago asked.

"I'm going to give you a few upgrades on your system. I was already working on building a more secure network for you guys so it won't be hard to add to your security system. It'll take me a couple hours but that kid won't be able to do it again. I also need to call your security company. We'll be switching you guys over to my company."

Duncan had a few businesses he owned. Home security was just one of them. Duncan was a male who always had ten things going on in his head, where most individuals only had one or two. He was always inventing or learning something new. It was like his brain could never rest. It always had to have something new to learn, create, or build.

"Thanks, Duncan," I said as I left.

"I already sent the email," he said.

I waved as I left with my head down, looking at my phone. I dialed Cain and waited for him to answer.

"Cain," he answered.

"Hey, it's Woods. I sent you a video of two witches breaking into my house a minute ago."

"What? Hold on, I'm putting you on speaker," he said. "Lieutenant, it's Woods. Say that again Woods."

"Approximately two hours ago, two witches from WPG broke into my house. They hacked into my security system to bypass it."

"How do you know they're with WPG?" Ryan asked.

"Because the woman who entered my home I know personally and the kid who did the hacking I met when we went to WPG. His name is Billy."

"Who's the woman?" Cain asked.

"My mother, Chloe Woods or Nichols, I guess is her last name now."

"Wait! Your mother?" Ryan sounded astonished.

"Yeah, she showed up at my door this morning. I told her to leave town and stay gone. It seems my warning fell on deaf ears."

"I have to ask this Woods. Did you know your mother was part of WPG?" Ryan asked.

"No, I didn't. Not until we searched her when we found her in our office."

"How could you not know?" asked another voice.

"Who's that?"

"Agent Illingworth."

"Agent Illingworth, hello," I tried to sound upbeat but all that came out was sarcasm. "To answer that question I didn't know because she and I aren't family. I haven't seen or spoken to her in almost twenty years, when she disowned me. This was the first time I had any interaction with her."

"Do I need to find another hunter for this one?" Ryan asked.

"No. I got this. If anything, the breaking and entering just sold me on the idea that WPG is connected to this somehow."

"Excuse me, you want us to believe you can separate yourself from the fact your mother could be involved? There is no way any person can do that?" Illingworth replied.

"Maybe a human couldn't but I'm a hellborn and all that woman has ever been is an incubator. So yes, I can distance myself."

"What if you have to hunt your mother?" he asked.

Illingworth didn't know me. He had no clue how easy it was for me to distance myself. I could understand his uncertainty in my skills. Most people would not be able to do it. I wasn't most people or hellborn. There was no love lost between Chloe and myself. Taking her out would just be another day at the office.

"Then I will. Hell, I may actually enjoy this one more than I should."

"I don't..."

"If I see any signs you can't handle this one I'm pulling you off. Do you understand me?" Ryan asked forestalling Illingworth.

"You got it."

"Now, do you want us to pick her up?" Ryan asked.

"Not yet. The kid with the computer is who I want arrested."

"Why him?" Cain asked.

"If I'm right, which I am, he's the one who will break."

"Do you have a last name on this Billy?"

"No."

"Cain get on the computer and find information on this kid. See if we can find out who he is. Then send out a unit to arrest him for breaking and entering."

"I'm on it."

"Woods, do you have anything that connects WPG to this?" Ryan asked.

"I'm working on it. Meri and I did find out that one kid had an uncle who was not happy his niece was a hybrid. Another one of the missing young had a neighbor that was part of WPG, as well. Faith Holden's mother was paid a visit by the group. They offered their condolences and offered to pay for a divorce from her vampire mate."

"Anything else?"

"Faith Holden's mother smelled lilacs and thought it was a plant she had under a window she had left open. There is also the fact that a woman befriended her six months before her daughter was taken."

"Do we have an ID on this woman?" Ryan asked.

"Not a positive one but she said Bree Miller looked like the woman she was friends with."

"Do we have a name?"

"No, she said it was Laura or Lauren but couldn't remember anything more."

"Do we have any idea why they are smelling lilacs?" Illingworth asked.

"I may have a lead on that soon but I need a few more hours before I can say for sure," I replied.

"Write up the report on the phone calls and a statement for the break in," Ryan ordered.

"I'll take care of that right now."

"Call us if you get any more," Ryan said.

"Will do."

The call ended and I headed back down stairs. It didn't feel like we were making progress but we were. I wished it could be faster than it was. Isobel had still not been seen since the night before, but the woman who had been known as Bree was all over the news. I was confident she was still in the city. The question was where? The fact no one had seen her or Isobel meant she was getting help hiding. The fear she would hurt Isobel in order to get away was becoming more of a possibility by the hour. This woman was a professional, which means her survival would become a priority. Killing a young was not out of the realm of possibilities to ensure her survival.

Chapter Nineteen

Watts was still working as I entered our office. He was focused on the screen in front of him. The only one taking notice of my presence was Meri. She looked up at me as I made it down the stairs.

"What's going on?" she asked.

"Your mate is helping my mate right now to prevent another security breach."

"Maybe I should go up and see my mate?" she said with a sly smile.

"First, I need you to type up a report on the calls you have made, while I do the same," I smiled at her. "We need to also type up reports for the last few days. We've fallen behind in our paperwork. That goes for you to Watts?"

Watts kept working, not hearing anything that was being said.

"How did she get in?" Meri asked.

"Looks like our little friend, Billy, is good with a computer. He hacked into the system, made it believe everything was secure while she walked in through the front door," I explained.

"That explains why Duncan is here."

"Cain is going to pick up Billy for the break in."

"What about Chloe?" Meri asked.

"Not yet. I want her to think she's in the clear."

"That's why we need to get caught up?" Meri replied.

"Yeah."

With that we got to work. We had all been working night and day to find Isobel. We had ignored the paperwork that came with the case because of the search, it was understandable why we had. We still had no clue where Isobel was but I was starting to think we may actually be close to finding a lead. If we were close to finding Isobel we would need all of our paperwork in order for any arrest or death warrants we may need.

Meri and I worked on the reports, while Watts worked on his research. I was beginning to get curious as to what he was working on. It should have been a quick background search on Chloe and her mate. I was hoping it meant he had something good. I tried to ignore my curiosity as I filled in my forms for the work we had done so far.

TWO HOURS PASSED AS we sat in silence, working. Duncan and Santiago were still upstairs working hard. Meri had disappeared for an hour at some point to go see her mate. I was confident I would have to straighten up one of the guest rooms at some point tonight. I wanted to be mad at her but I couldn't blame her. This case was taking over every inch of our lives and a pick me up was going to be required at some point. As I finished up a report about the phone call with Ian Brice's parents, my phone rang. I looked at the caller I.D. seeing it was Ruth and smiled.

"Ruth, it's so nice you could call. I take it you have something for me?" I said.

"Are you going to hold up your end of the deal?"

"Don't I always?"

"Fine, the charm is called the Drought of Death. It slows the heart rate and breathing down enough to appear as if the individual is dead. It requires only a handful of ingredients."

"Could it be turned into a gas?" I asked.

"Yeah, it could easily enough. Normally the lilacs are used to hide the smell of tobacco particularly when it's brewed. They probably just added more lilacs into the mix you're talking about."

"How do you turn it into a gas?"

"The charm was probably already cooked, so all they did was take a small container of it and heated it with a flame," she explained.

How could they use a flame in a neighborhood? Lighter? Magic? If it was magic, that led me back to having two kidnapers. So far we only knew of one. A lighter seemed like too small of a flame for what she would need. The lighter would also grow too hot the longer it was used. Maybe one of those long candle lighters? Or a torch for cooking could work possibly.

"Has anyone come through your shop looking for the ingredients for this particular charm?

"Not through my shop."

"Could the charm be stored for later use?"

"Of course, it could but it would have a shelf life," she answered.

"How long?"

"A month at the most."

Bree Miller could have become friends with the Darings. Took her time to get to know them and Isobel. Once she was sure the child was a hybrid, she set a plan in motion. How did she get the charm? Bree Miller was a human, she couldn't have made the charm. Isobel's grandparents could have. That led me back to the question of why they would want her? Maybe WPG was killing the young? Or maybe they were selling them? What would WPG want with young they considered an abomination?

"How effective would it be on a hybrid?"

"Back in the day there weren't many hybrids so I don't know how effective it would be. It doesn't say."

"Can you take a guess? Give me something," I demanded.

"From the way it reads it was designed for witches, maybe even humans. Vampires and wolves have a higher metabolism when it comes to substances. Hybrids would too because they carry both vampire and witch D.N.A."

Between the charm and the tea she probably thought the Darings were down for the count. The Darings having tea had been a luck of the draw. The problem was she was human and didn't know enough about the charm she was using. The charm would only work for so long on them.

"Make me a copy of the recipe for that charm. I'll come by and get it tomorrow morning."

"I already made the copy for you."

"See Ruth this is why I like working with you. You always anticipate what I'm going to need from you. Thanks for your help. The next time you're in trouble, give me a call."

"You bet I will. Until then, Savannah," she replied before she hung up.

I placed my phone on my desk as I thought through what I had just learned. Where did the human get the charm? If I could find the answer to that question it could answer a few of my other questions. Maybe this would be enough to get financials on the grandparents. It was doubtful. We needed more connecting them and WPG before we could get a warrant for financial records. Right now all we had were suspicions but that wasn't enough. I turned to the computer and began my report about the information Ruth had given me.

As I worked on my report, new questions began to form in my head. How did the human avoid dosing herself with the charm? She would need some form of a mask or breathing apparatus. It would be the only way to prevent the vapor of the charm from being inhaled. If she had a partner, the partner could have taken care of drugging the parents while she entered. The partner leaves once their job is done. It was the only way I could see a partner could work. If Isobel woke up during the kidnapping seeing a familiar face would keep the child calm. I didn't believe this human had a partner, this looked like a one man job. The less who knew what you were doing, the better chance you had at succeeding. The human was a pro at kidnapping. She knew how to confuse the dogs, had a second location set up, and multiple identities with backgrounds set up. She was damn good at her job. I was guessing she was just hired help for someone or something much bigger than we were speculating. I just needed to figure out what exactly that was.

Chapter Twenty

I worked on reports for another two hours. By the time I was done the feeling of exhaustion was setting in. Paperwork was what made a case, it is what ensured we were able to obtain search warrants, arrest warrants, and death warrants. Without all of our reports we couldn't do much. It was also what made you want to shoot yourself in the head. It took two emails to Ryan and Cain for me to get all of the reports to them. More would come the longer this case dragged on.

I was hoping we were closer to finding Isobel but I wasn't sure we really were. No one had seen her since the night before. There had also been no sightings of Bree Miller. It was like they had fallen into a deep hole. I was sending my final reports to Ryan when Watts sat back in his chair, I heard as the printer turned on.

"I got everything on Beau and Chloe Nichols," he said rubbing his eyes.

"What took so long?" I asked.

"I called in a favor with Cain. He gave me access with his login into the police database."

"Watts called in a favor?" Meri said with a light tone. Watts gave her a dark look.

When Watts began shadowing me, he had told both of us he was working as a civilian not as law enforcement. What he meant was he would not use any of his law enforcement connections to help us with information. I had to respect that. He had wanted to learn about hellborns and how we did our job. The fact he was technically using a law enforcement database with Cain's login meant he was understanding that rules had to be bent from time to time. Part of me was proud he was finally accepting that I would ignore rules from time to time. The other part of me said I had corrupted the poor human.

"So what do you have?" I asked.

"Your mother has a few arrests for fraud in Nevada but none ever went to trial."

"That I know. What do you have that I don't know, Watts?" I replied.

"Beau Nichols has no record, at all. He works for a company called The Wellness Group. It's a survey group who conducts medical surveys. He's a representative for the company. Beau's job is to get doctors and hospitals to work with The Wellness Group. They are based in Fairetree, which is where he and your mother live."

"How long have they lived in Fairetree?" Meri asked.

"Four years from what I can find. They got married and she moved in with him. I have his address and the company address."

There was something about the city of Fairetree that was nagging in the back of my mind. The problem was I couldn't remember what it was. My hand played with the sticky pad that my mother had taken a note off of. Watts continued with his report as I thumbed the corner of the sticky pad.

"According to their site, they work with drug companies looking for individuals who are interested in being test subjects. The Wellness Group works as the third party finding the individuals. They then interview the potential subjects and see if they fit into a clinical trial for the drug companies."

"Do they work with humans or hellborns?" I asked.

"I don't know, the site doesn't say. From what I have seen Beau's financial statements, he's worth a lot of money. His home is worth almost a million dollars. I pulled up The Wellness Group's website and printed their mission statement if you want to have a look at it."

"So she doesn't want money. The new husband has it. We know they're part of WPG, the mate was wearing a pin on his lapel the first time I met him. Why bring Chloe into all of this? They had to know we have no relationship," I said as Watts handed the print out to Meri.

"Maybe they thought she could get to you even if you had a falling out," Watts offered.

"We had more than a falling out, she disowned me. Truthfully, I disowned her long before she did me," I stated.

"Isn't this an earth witch symbol?" Meri asked.

"Let me see," I said, holding out my hand.

She placed the pages in my hand. The print out had a long statement about The Wellness Group written in a script font. I glanced at the text picking out a few sentences. The gist of the statement, showed their goal was to connect individuals with research companies to help overcome chronic illnesses. I looked at the left upper corner and saw the seven point star with a circle in the middle. It was the symbol for magical energy. I went back through, reading the mission statement of the company. Nowhere in the pretty script did it say if they worked with humans or hellborns. Why would they use a symbol earth witches use? What was I missing? I felt like it was right there but I just couldn't see it, at least not yet.

"Yeah, that's the symbol for magical energy. Witches will use it when they need a focal point while working a charm. What else did you find out?" I asked setting the page down.

"Your mother is a chapter leader in Fairetree with the WPG. From their social media pages she has made a name for herself in the group. She has done fundraisers as well as recruitment rallies."

"How come that doesn't surprise me?" I replied sarcastically.

"From what I can tell they have teamed up with the group here for events on a regular basis," Watts said.

"Is the chapter in Fairetree part of the one here?" Meri asked.

"The one here is the head of the region, so yeah," Watts answered.

"So that would explain how she knew I mated Santiago. Troy passed the information on."

"It still leaves us with why did she break in? What do they think we have?" Meri asked.

"The million dollar question," I answered.

There had to be a connection. Fairetree was popping up too many times. Was that where Isobel was? Or was that where Isobel was heading? The question became why? What was in Fairetree? The town was a two hour drive south and it was an even smaller city than Sweetclover. The city itself was a quiet place. There was one mall, which was two stories and was full of stores. The place had a wide food court and a seating area outside that was great for summer days. The seating area even had a play area for kids. The rest of the city had plenty of eateries and other small shopping centers. Humans and hellborns alike travelled to Fairetree from surrounding cities and towns. The more I thought about Fairetree, the more I was seeing the missing pieces. The fact that my mother had been there for four years and I had no clue wasn't shocking. I thought little of the female on any given day. She was connected to WPG in a rather big way and that was shocking. It made me wonder if it was her actual belief or if it was the fact that she had finally landed a rich husband. If all you cared about was what you could make from others, morals and values were easy to sell. There had to be a connection to the city, WPG, and Isobel. The question was what was it? If I could find that piece of the puzzle it could be the start of actually finding Isobel.

My phone went off again. I looked at the screen not recognizing the number. It was an 808 area code.

"Savannah Woods," I answered.

"This is Lono, Bally's cousin."

"Hi. I was wondering if you could help me out?" I said awkwardly.

"Bally told me what you wanted to know. Listen, I don't give out my customer's information..."

"Normally, I wouldn't ask you to but this is about a missing young. All I really need to know is has anyone in Sweetclover or in this region place an order for your tea?"

"Not in Sweetclover, the only one who sells it is my cousin. The area may be a different matter."

I could hear him typing on a keyboard and sat quietly as he went through his database. Minutes passed before he spoke again.

"There was an order for a case of my tea sent to Fairetree."

There was Fairetree again. Now I knew I wasn't crazy.

"Where in Fairetree?" I asked.

"1800 Deeder Avenue," he answered.

As I wrote the address on my sticky pad I knew what I was missing. I knew that address. The note Chloe had taken was the one with H&W Clinical Group address written on it.

"Is the company H&W Clinical Group?"

"How'd you know?"

"Can you email the form to me?" I asked.

"Oh man! I don't know if I should..."

"Look I can get a warrant and force you to turn it over to me or you can give it to me and if I find the young I'm looking for, I'll send you reward money," I cut the bullshit.

"How much?"

"If I find the young because you gave me this now I'll give you five grand," I offered.

"Sending it now. You better be good for it."

"Ask your cousin if I am," I answered. I rambled off my email and hung up.

I went to the whiteboard pulling the papers off that were pinned to the board. The list from the Brazens was there but the information on H&W was gone. She was good. I went back to my desk and hit the computer once more, pulling up the website for the clinical group. Sure enough it was the same as the address Lono had.

"What's the address for the company Beau works for?" I asked.

"1855 Deeder Avenue suite 230. Why?"

"Son of a Bitch! The Wellness Group is connected to H&W Clinical Group, which is connected to WPG," I said.

"Are you sure?" Meri inquired.

"I'm sure," I answered.

"How do we connect them?" Watts asked.

"We can connect WPG to H&W Clinical because the research group are donors to WPG. How we connect the other group, I don't know. But they're connected." I didn't wait for a reply from either Meri or Watts, I picked up my phone and called Ryan.

"Woods, what do you have for me?" he said as he answered impatiently.

"We need to start digging into WPG and H&W Clinical Group?"

"Why?"

"The tea that was given to the Darings is made by a witch in Hawaii, he runs a small tea export business. He sent a case to H&W Clinical Group six months ago. Our human who took Isobel didn't get it from the only shop that sells it here. She had to get it from H&W."

"How do you know she got it from them? I need something more concrete than that?" he pushed.

"They're donors to WPG and the Brazens had a letter from the research group. Troy Salazar confirmed it. There is also a third company called The Wellness Group, Beau Nichols works for. They're a survey group supposedly that connects individuals with medical research programs. They are down the damn street from H&W."

"I don't know if that's enough Woods. I need more?"

"Chloe took the info I had on H&W. It's the only thing missing from the office. She and her mate live in Fairetree where The Wellness Group and H&W is located. She is also the head of the local chapter of WPG."

"Now we're getting somewhere. I don't know if it's enough to get warrants for financials on The Wellness Group but I think I can get one on WPG and H&W. Do you have proof they ordered the tea?"

"Lono is emailing me the order form now."

"Good. Get it to me. Cain is bringing in your boy, Billy Granger, as we speak. He's already lawyered up so we have to wait to question him. Do you want to be here when we do?" he offered.

"I'll send Meri over."

"Remind Embers of where the line is. And keep working on finding more proof these companies are involved somehow. I need a working theory by the end of the day," he ordered.

"I'll see what I can do on my end."

"Good," he replied before the call went dead.

I turned to Meri.

"Meri, I need you to get over to the precinct to handle the questioning of Billy Granger."

"I'll call you as soon as he gives something up."

"Do that. Also, no using your ability on the male. Ryan will not let you get away with that."

"Yeah, yeah. I know," she said as she left sounding disappointed.

"What do you want me to do?" Watts asked.

"You and I are now going to try and connect the dots between the three companies and come up with a theory as to why they would want hybrids."

I had no clue why they would want a hybrid child. Was Agent Illingworth right, all of these kids were connected? If they were, what was this clinical research group doing with them? Was Faith Holden dead and the WPG in Georgia knew? How many hybrid children could they have? So many questions and no answers. If I could find the answers maybe I would find Isobel. What if she was already dead? The thought sent a shiver down my spine. I couldn't think like that, I needed to believe she was alive at least for now.

Chapter Twenty-One

Watts and I worked for hours as we tried to find any connections between the three companies. The problem was we only had access through internet searches, there were times internet searches were great. You could find almost anything as long as you were willing to pay for it. The hard part was not all the information out there was correct. There was little information on The Wellness Group. It was odd to say the least. Watts and I kept working while Meri was at the precinct trying to get Billy Granger talking. I hadn't heard anything, which I was hoping meant he was cracking. The fact that he had lawyered up had me curious about who was paying for it. My guess was WPG, unless he went the public defender route. Most public defenders were overworked, underpaid, and were under prepared to handle most cases. No, Billy's lawyer was not a public defender, I'd put money on that. Troy Salazar did not strike me as a fool. He would try to protect the male at all cost. If that failed he would get the kid to take the fall. The question was how far was Billy willing to go? Was he a fool, willing to be played for a cause or would survival instincts kick in? I had my money on he would break eventually. I was hoping he broke sooner rather than later.

The exhaustion I had been feeling as I had worked on my reports had dissipated at the idea we had were close to an actual lead. The longer we worked the more that exhaustion came back with avengence. I was on the verge of calling Meri and telling her to head home for the night when Santiago and Duncan came down the stairs.

"I take it we're secure once more?" I asked.

"Almost. I'm coming back with my team tomorrow. We're going to add to your existing system."

"What could you add to it? We already have motion detectors, magnetic strips, and cameras," I pointed out.

"I want to add wiring to your system. Which means I want a dedicated phone line for the system that will have an alarm on it. If anyone were to tamper with it, the alarm would trigger immediately. It means you get the best of both worlds, wired and unwired," Duncan informed me.

"Duncan can have the system finished in a matter of hours tomorrow," my mate added.

"Okay."

"If you would like I can have Tony or Liam to come and watch our home tonight," Santiago offered.

"No, we'll be fine."

"Are you sure? I want to ensure our home is safe."

"I love you for that but between your keen senses and my weapons I think we have it covered."

"Agreed," he bent down and kissed me. "While Duncan was working, I was able to finish off the arrangements for the ceremony."

"At least I can cross that off my list of concerns."

"Are you any closer to finding Isobel?" he asked.

"I think we are but I don't know. We need to find a connection between these two companies and WPG. We're striking out at this point."

Duncan was looking around the office.

"Where's my mate?" Duncan asked.

"She's at the precinct handling the questioning of the male who hacked our system," I answered.

"Is she going to be home anytime soon?"

"I will go with yes but I don't know when," I replied.

"On that note I'm out of here," Duncan said.

"Thanks, Duncan for doing this," I said.

"It's not a problem," he replied.

"I will walk you out," Santiago said, ushering Duncan up the stairs.

I sat back in my chair wondering if we were headed in the wrong direction. Maybe it wasn't the wrong direction but the way we were searching. Maybe the question we should start with was; why set up a company who does research in a small city instead of a large city? Wouldn't it be easier to hide? It was something to consider.

The county would require information from the companies when they started up. Between business licenses, the health department licensing, and the state licensing there should be plenty of information. We needed to search county records along with the city and state records. The question was how much information did a small city like Fairetree have online? Most cities had public information online now but smaller cities were less likely to have all their information online accessible due to lack of funding. I was wondering what Illingworth could get for us. Maybe it was time to make nice with the agent.

As I was beginning my search of public records my phone rang. I answered without looking at the screen.

"Woods?"

"Mrs. De los Rios," came a shaky male voice.

It took me a minute to figure out who was on the other end of the line. The only people who referred to me by my mated name were clan members. I hadn't decided as of yet if I would keep my name or take Santiago's. It felt like a mouthful every time I used it or anyone else did.

"Mr. Daring what's going on?" I asked as a loud wail erupted through the phone.

"A witch came to see us. She said ...she said Isobel's...spirit came to her. She is..."

"Mr. Daring..." I said as his own crying started. "Mr. Daring.... Brian listen to me. I am on the way, please try to stay calm. Is the witch still there?" I asked.

"No...she left."

"Okay, I'm on the way." I hung up and looked at Watts.

"What's going on?"

"Someone paid the Darings a visit saying Isobel is dead?"

"Shit! Do you think it's someone connected to this?"

"Yeah and I have a feeling I'm related to her too," I said as we headed up the stairs.

The drive took us longer than I would have liked. The Gallery was in full swing for the night, which meant most of the streets were packed leading to The Gallery, as well. I loved my Suburban but there were times like these that having a car like Santiago's would come in handy. The way his vehicle could maneuver through traffic made me envious at times.

It took us almost an hour to reach the Daring's home. The wailing I had heard over the phone was no longer happening as we approached the house. Brian Daring was waiting at the door, swinging it open for us as we approached. His eyes were red rimmed, tears still running down his face.

"Is she dead?" he questioned his voice filled with pain.

"Why don't we go inside and have a seat and talk? I need you to tell me everything that happened."

"I need to know... is she dead...should we start preparing..." his voice cut off.

I placed a hand on his back, guiding Brian into the house all the way to the living room. He let me guide him to the couch where I took a seat as well. I turned to face him before I spoke.

"I'm going to be honest with you...."

"Oh no!"

"I need you to listen to me right now," I said, my voice firm. "I have no proof your daughter is dead and until I do I am going to believe she is still alive. This woman who took your young did not wish to kill her. If she did Isobel's body would have been found already. This woman wants her alive, which tells me she is more than likely alive."

"This witch showed up saying she was visited by Isobel's soul. She said Isobel is safe now and we should let her go. What if she was telling the truth?"

"What if she wasn't Brian?"

"Why would someone do this? If she was lying?"

"I need to know about this witch. What does she look like? What exactly did she say? I need you to tell me everything that happened. Can you do that?" I asked.

He nodded his head frantically. I waited as he closed his eyes as he tried to breathe normally. His head dropped a fraction of an inch before he spoke.

"Since all of this started the media has been calling us and showing up on our door. Asking us questions, wanting to know if the police have any leads. When I first saw her at the door, I thought she was a reporter. I told her she needed to leave. That's when she said she was a witch, a spirit communicator is what she called herself."

"What time was this?" I asked.

"About eight maybe eight fifteen."

"What made you let her in?"

"She said she could help us find Isobel. I didn't know what else to do so I let her in," panic was setting in again as his voice rose.

"It's okay. I need to know everything. What happened next?"

"She said Isobel came to her this morning. She said ...Isobel was dead and her body would be hard to find. Isobel ...told her, she loved us and she wishes..." There was a long pause before he spoke again. "She wishes she could have stayed longer with us," Brian Daring started crying again.

"Did she say anything else?" I asked.

"The witch said she wanted to help us in letting go of Isobel. If we didn't let go of her, we would be trapping her spirit. Oh God! What if she was telling the truth?"

I had no words for him. I didn't know how to answer him as his head was bent down, tears leaking from his eyes. I pushed forward.

"Brian...Brian? Did she ask for money or anything from you?" I asked.

"No...no she just said she wanted to help Isobel be able to move on."

Well that line was straight out of my past. My mother had used that line a thousand times on clients when I was younger. It was a way to ensure clients would spend more money on her "magic".

"Can you give me a description of this witch?" I asked.

Brian seemed to need another minute before he could answer. I sat patiently as he collected himself enough to answer.

"Uhm...she had... red hair, it was light red. With ...uhm... blue eyes and she had on a suit. White or off white maybe."

"Did she give you her name?" I asked.

"Chloe Nichols."

There it was. A description and a name. Why would she come to them with this story? Was Isobel dead? Or was this just a ploy? Either way, I was going to find my mother and find out the truth, even if I had to beat it out of her. These parents didn't deserve this and neither did Isobel.

"I need to go check on my mate," Brian said, bringing me back to reality.

"Was she the one who was crying when you called me?"

He nodded his head up and down as he rubbed his eyes with the heels of his hands.

"Why don't I go talk to Emma?" I offered.

I had no clue why I had offered. Maybe it was guilt at the fact that my mother was playing a role in all this. Maybe it was me taking a step towards my own role in the clan. Or maybe it was the sadness I felt for them. Either way I felt a need to do this.

"I can't ask you to do that," he replied.

"You aren't. I'm offering. Brian you have been taking care of Emma this entire time. I commend you for it but you need to take a moment for yourself. I will go talk with her and my partner, Antoine Watts, can sit with you. If you need someone to talk to, he is a great listener. If you just need to sit here that's okay too," I said.

"Thank you."

I stood up and headed back down the hall I had travelled down only once before. Isobel's door was closed, no doubt because her room was too hard to look at. The room at the end of the hall was Brian and Emma's room. The door was shut as I approached it. I knocked on the door, waiting for a response, none came. I tried again with the same results. I opened the door finding Emma Daring laying on her side facing the door. The tears had stopped but so had any life in her eyes. It was as if any life that had been left had dissipated with the hope of her daughter being alive. This female was in a new land of Hell. I bent down next to the bed so I was level with Emma's face. I wasn't sure she was seeing me or memories as they flash across her mind.

"Emma?" I said softly. I placed a hand on her shoulder trying to bring her around. "Emma. Brian told me about the witch that came to see you."

She lay there not moving, not even registering my presence. I tried again, putting a little more force in my voice.

"Emma, we have no proof Isobel is dead. That witch was more than likely a con-artist. Nothing more."

Her eyes shifted slightly. At least I knew she was in there somewhere.

"Emma, you have to keep believing she is alive until we have proof otherwise."

"What if..." she whispered.

She didn't need to finish the thought. I took a breath and looked at her.

"We will cross that bridge if we have to. For now we have to believe she is alive. The police and my team are working day and night to find Isobel. I believe we are close to finding her. But I need you to hold onto the thought that she is alive."

"That witch..."

"I know. Some individuals can be opportunists. This female is more than likely nothing more than that."

"I just want my little one home," she sobbed. Her body shook as her eyes squeezed shut.

"I know you do."

I sat with Emma Daring until she stopped crying. It took awhile for her to settle down again. By the time she did, sleep was beginning to claim the poor female. I left finding Watts had taken my place next to Brian. His much bigger figure was sitting next to the vampire male as he tried to pull himself together. A hand on the male's shoulder as he spoke quietly to him. Watts looked at me as I stood watching the two of them. I motioned to him as I was stepping outside. He could take his time with Brian Daring while I made a call to Ryan.

I walked away from the house, placing myself next to my car. Ryan answered quickly.

"Ryan."

"Hey, it's Woods. Is Billy talking yet?"

"No, he's letting his lawyer talk."

"Is the lawyer high priced or public defender?" I inquired.

"High priced."

"Figured. Listen, get the warrant for Chloe Nichols."

"I thought you didn't want us to pick her up?"

"I didn't want to until I got a call from Brian Daring. It looks like she paid a visit to the Darings, claiming Isobel was dead."

"Fuck!"

"Yeah. I think it was a ploy of some kind but I need a warrant to grab her on the breaking and entering," I explained.

"I'll get it."

"Thanks."

"Do you know where to find her?" he questioned.

"She was staying at the Hilton, so I'll start there."

"Roger that. Chances are the girl is already dead," he said sadly.

"I know. For now, let's not think about that," I nodded my head as I spoke.

"Agreed. Are you coming down here to relieve Embers?"

"Not yet."

"Let me know when you have Chloe," he ordered.

"Always do."

The call ended as Watts stepped out of the house. He crossed the small lawn quickly stopping in front of me.

"I hope she wasn't telling them the truth about Isobel," his big form seemed to almost fold in on itself as he stood there. His head hung low. The tension was getting to all of us.

"You and me both. Get in, we need to take a trip to pick up Chloe."

Watts stood up straight at my words.

"I thought you wanted to wait?" he looked confused at my change in mind.

"I did until she pulled her stunt here."

"What about a warrant."

"Ryan's getting one now."

I walked around to the drivers side of the Suburban as I hit the unlock button. Watts didn't hesitate as he climbed in the car. I gave the house one final look before I climbed in. It was as if the despair they were feeling was pouring out of the house. I said a silent prayer to whoever was up above as we drove away. Please let her still be alive. Let me find her!

Chapter Twenty-Two

The drive back through town was just as bad as the first trip. We pulled in front of the hotel, moving quickly out of the car. I didn't even give my keys to the valet. The human teenager stared at me confused. When one of the others tried to stop me from leaving my car, Watts took on a menacing tone stating it was a police matter. I kept moving with a smile on my face as I hit the front desk. A woman with her hair severely pulled back from her face, smiled at me as we approached the counter.

"Welcome to the Hilton," she said pleasantly.

"I need to know what room Chloe Nichols is staying in?"

"I can call up to the room..."

"No." I pulled out my identification as Watts joined me at the counter. "Actually, I just need her room number. I have a warrant for her arrest. I prefer if she doesn't know we're coming."

The woman at the counter looked between Watts and I as we stood there.

"Let me get my manager," she replied.

We stood waiting as she headed for an office behind the counter. A moment later a man in his late forties came out.

"How can I help you?"

"My name is Savannah Woods and this is my associate Antoine Watts. I need to know which room Chloe Nichols is in."

"We are not allowed to give out our client information."

I handed him my I.D. and Watts did the same.

"This is a police matter. I'm a hunter who has an arrest warrant for Chloe Nichols. Now you can give me her room number or I can call the HCU and they will lock your hotel down until we can search every room. If I do that, can you imagine the negative media attention that will follow," I said with a smile.

"Give me one moment, please" He began typing away at the computer. "She and Mr. Nichols checked out this afternoon."

"How about a reservation under Troy Salazar?" I asked.

It took the manager only thirty seconds.

"No. I'm sorry."

"Thank you for your time."

We headed for the door. She was still here in town, the question was where had she gone? I doubted she was at another hotel. No, it would be someplace they could hide in comfort. Hotel would mean a money trail. Where would she go? The better question was where would Beau Nichols go? I had a feeling he was the one pulling the strings. My mother would follow as long as there was money. As soon as she realized her livelihood was in trouble she would bail on the bastard.

"Back to WPG?" Watts asked.

"No, we go to talk to Billy."

We arrived at the station within fifteen minutes. The phones were still ringing but not like they had been. There were fewer cops, which told me the tip lines had slowed down. I wasn't sure if that was a good thing or not. The interview rooms were in the back of the squad room and to the right, not far from the holding cells. The electronic monitoring room was painted a dull white as was most of the building. There were three monitors setup upon a long table, all with views of the interview room. Two speakers were set up around the monitor in the middle. The table had three chairs at the desk. There was a civilian employee parked in one of the hard chairs as Ryan stood behind him watching as Meri and Cain sat across from Billy on a monitor. When we had first met the male he had been arrogant. Now he was scared, he kept his eyes down as Meri stared at him. His lawyer sat next to him in a six hundred dollar suit, addressing Cain. His gold watch flashing as he moved his hands. Ryan had his arms crossed over his chest.

"Where is your suspect?" Ryan asked.

"She's checked out of her hotel."

"So, in the wind?" he queried

"She's still in town, I just have to find her," I answered pausing as I watched the interview. "Let me talk to him."

Ryan looked at me as if I had lost my mind.

"No."

"Why?"

"The kid is already freaked out with Embers in there, you'll only scare him worse," Ryan pointed out.

That was the point, scare the kid into talking. Ryan walked out of the room knocking on the door. I watched as Cain told the attorney to take some time with his client. Meri smiled at Billy before she strutted from the room, Cain behind her. Ryan came in with them.

"That attorney is going to convince the kid to take the fall," Cain said as Ryan shut the door.

"We have enough to charge him for breaking and entering, and a few other things," Ryan answered.

"If Cain's right, it won't matter. The lawyer will plead it down and he'll happily do a few years," Watts said.

Illingworth came in with a laptop in his hand.

"I saw when you came in. I did some digging on that company, The Wellness Group. It is owned by the same corporation as H&W Clinical."

"I take it you're on the same page as the rest of us now?" I questioned crossing my arms over my chest.

"To many coincidences," he answered as he set the laptop down on the desk. "I was able to get financial information on both of them. They are both big donors to WPG chapters all over the country. The corporation that owns them is Witch's Alliance. I'm still trying to find who owns the corporation."

"Do we have anything to prove they have anything to do with this?" Ryan asked.

"Nothing yet," I answered. "What do they research exactly?" I asked Illingworth.

"I have no clue but I have a call into the FDA and the NIH."

"Doesn't the federal government keep tabs on medical research?" Meri piped in.

"Normally yes, the NIH is the one who does that but H&W Clinical Group works only with hellborns. The law does not require government oversight for it."

"Isn't that just peachy," I replied.

"If WPG or these medical research companies have anything to do with this, how do we prove it?" Ryan asked.

"I have a forensic accountant going over their records. Maybe we can find a payment to the woman who took Isobel," Illingworth offered.

"How did you get a warrant for those?" Cain asked.

"We have nine kids missing, it wasn't hard to find a federal judge to sign off," Illingworth answered.

"The problem is we don't know her real name. How are we going to find a payment to her?" Watts pointed out.

"We need to find Chloe," I said.

"She may not know anything," Cain suggested.

"My mother is a lot of things, stupid isn't one of them. If she is involved in any of this she knows everything that is happening. Ryan, let me have a go at the kid?"

"Not yet." He said as he rubbed his chin. "Cain, book the kid on as many counts as possible and put him in with the wolf who was picked up for battery. Let's give him until morning to break. If he doesn't, Woods he's all yours. Agent Illingworth, how long will it take your guy to find anything?"

"Maybe by lunch tomorrow," Illingworth offered.

Ryan nodded as he rubbed his face.

"Everyone, go home for the night. We will go at Billy Granger in the morning again. I want everyone here by eight a.m." Ryan ordered.

I hated the idea of going home. It felt as if we were finally heading in the right direction. Now we were stalled. I wanted to scream. The problem was that it would do no good. We needed something tying WPG to these groups and the woman who kidnapped Isobel. Booking Billy Granger would give him a taste of what was awaiting him if he didn't cooperate. I just hope it was enough to scare him straight.

Chapter Twenty-Three

Ryan sending us all home had been the smart play. We were all running on fumes and we could get a fresh start in the morning. The drive home felt longer than it actually was. Questions continued to fill my head nonstop. Why would they want hybrid children? Were they all dead? Was Isobel? It was an endless cycle of questions I still had no answers to.

By the time I had pulled into the garage, frustration and exhaustion was clogging my mind. I walked into my home, finding my mate waiting for me on the sofa with a plate of food and a glass of whiskey for me on the coffee table. It was definitely a whiskey night. Santiago was still in his clothes from earlier. His tie was gone and so were his socks and shoes, his stiff white collar was open at the neck. I smiled at the sight of him as I pulled my gun and holster from my body and removed my knife from my leg. He was the most beautiful male I had ever known. I needed a release for all the frustrations and dead ends I was hitting, a night to enjoy being with him without any of the other bullshit interfering. I laid my weapons on the coffee table and bent down, finding Santiago's lips. He pulled me down to his body as we kissed. I spread my legs so I was straddling his body. As soon as our bodies met I knew dinner could wait. Any exhaustion I had been feeling left my body as a new energy filled me.

He pulled back a little to smile up at me.

"How are you, Mi Amor?" he asked.

"Better now that I'm home." I kissed him again, putting into the kiss all the need I was feeling. I needed him to wash away the harshness of the day. He was the one male who kept me sane. If it hadn't been for him I wasn't sure if I would have made it through my attack three months ago. Santiago kept me grounded, kept me from shutting down entirely. I loved him for it. In this moment I needed that. My brain was so filled with questions and fears I needed to feel him. It was a reminder of all that was good.

He broke the kiss placing his hand on the side of my face as he looked into my eyes, his thumb stroked my cheek. The look I gave him was all the encouragement he needed to kiss me with a new urgency. I moved my hands down the buttons of his shirt as we kissed. Our kiss broke long enough for him to pull my shirt over my head before his mouth found my skin. Santiago kissed and sucked down my neck as his hands found the clasp for my bra.

"We should take this upstairs," he said in my ear. He ran a fang down my neck bringing a shiver down my spine.

"I'm not sure we'll make it."

His mouth claimed my breast sucking at the nipple. The feel of the pull caused a moan to escape me, followed closely by his name. He released my breast pulling my mouth down to his again. The next thing I knew he was rising up from the couch with me wrapped around his body. He carried me as if I weighed nothing as he moved up the stairs. I pulled at his shirt, freeing it from his body as he moved us down the hall. My lips found his neck sucking and kissing on his skin. It made Santiago stop moving as my mouth started traveling down. I took the pause in his step to climb down from him, forcing him against the wall. I undid his leather belt and then released the button and zipper on his pants. I slid them down as I bent in front of him. His erection sprung free of his pants, hard and ready for the taking. I wanted to rush taking all of his length into my mouth but I forced myself to slow down. Taking him inch by inch with each stroke of my mouth and tongue, sucking him in and out, until I could feel him touch the back of my throat. The taste and feel of him in my mouth was beautiful. His body began to move in perfect timing with my mouth as his hands slid into my hair. I slid my gaze up his body finding his eyes on me, watching as I sucked on him. I grabbed his balls and massaged them. The feel of my hand and mouth was enough to cause him to throw his head back. His body moved faster, pumping in and out of my mouth. His release came fast, as he came into my mouth and down my throat. I took all of him, swallowing. He released my head, pulling me to my feet. His mouth was on mine as he spun us around placing me against the wall. I felt as he grabbed at my pants with force. The seams gave way as he ripped them from my body. Santiago broke the kiss he had started as he lifted me up. My legs wrapped around him once more.

"I need to be in you," his voice was heavy with sexual intensity.

He pushed deep into my wet sex, making cry out. His still hard cock moved in and out of me hard and fast. I felt my own need growing as he moved faster. Santiago's dark eyes never left my face as waves of pleasure washed over me. The feel of those almost black eyes on me heightened my orgasm. I felt as my muscles tightened around him and yet he kept up his unrelenting pumping inside of me until his own release came. We were both breathing heavily as Santiago held me in our hallway.

"I told you we wouldn't make it to the bedroom," I laughingly stated.

He laughed deeply as he carried me the rest of the way down the hall to our bedroom. I looked behind him seeing black fabric scattered all over the wood floors and his forgotten slacks.

"You know those pants were fairly new that you destroyed," I said.

"I will order you several new pairs tomorrow," he smiled.

He sat me on the bed, kissing me again. This kiss was more tender, less of the wild need we had both been feeling.

"We are going to shower and afterwards we can have a late dinner."

He left me lying on the bed as I watched his naked body move to the bathroom. A second later the water was running. I stretched out feeling the slight ache in my legs. I was confident a repeat performance in the shower was on the table. Tomorrow the ache would be worse but completely worth it. Santiago came back in the room to find me stretched out. He extended his hand to me. I slid mine into his and let him lead me to the shower.

WE TOOK OUR TIME IN the shower as round two was less about need and more about worshipping one another. By the time we climbed out of the shower, any tension I had been feeling when I arrived home, had melted away. I slipped into the night gown Hugo had given me as a mating gift while my mate pulled on a pair of silk pajama pants and a robe. He left the robe open, which left his bare chest exposed. We walked down the hall, seeing the mess we had left behind. We took a moment to clean up the hallway. The fabric of my pants went into the trash while his slacks were placed on the bed. We found his shirt on the stairs where I had dropped it. We placed the shirt on the back of a chair with my shirt and bra. My dinner was a large plate of lasagna. It was still sitting on the table next to my gun and knife.

"Let me reheat your dinner," Santiago offered.

"It's fine I can eat it this way."

"No. You need a hot meal."

He took the plate from my hand and carried it to the kitchen. I grabbed both of our glasses from the coffee table and headed to the dining room. I took a sip of the liquor tasting the oak barrel the whiskey had been aged in with a touch of fire. I pulled a chair out for Santiago and then pulled the one next to his for me. Placing my ass on the soft seat made me groan slightly. I rolled my neck, feeling the tension was still there. I drank my whiskey as thoughts of the case came back at me. It was getting harder to believe Isobel was still alive as the days and hours passed by. I had told both of her parents to continue to believe she was alive because I had no proof one way or the other. Now as I sat at my dining room table, I was wondering if hope was as cruel, as the despair they had been feeling tonight. If she was dead the despair would hit an entirely different low, one I was unsure either could come back from.

"Savannah?" Santiago said as he placed a plate in front of me.

I had a feeling he had been trying to get my attention for a few moments. I hadn't even seen him walk in, even though I had been facing the door.

"Sorry."

"Are you okay?" he asked as he took his seat.

"As okay as I can be, I guess."

I turned to my food and began to eat. Santiago placed his napkin on his lap before he began to eat as well.

"I take it you are no closer to finding Isobel?"

"No...Maybe...I...I feel like we are finally on the right track. If I can find Chloe tomorrow, I think I have a good chance of finding Isobel. The question is can we get the male to talk who helped her break into our home, to give her up."

"What does your mother have to do with this?" he asked.

I hadn't told him any of the new developments in regards to Chloe. I kicked myself as I sat there.

"Chloe went to see the Darings tonight."

"Why?" Santiago's voice held an edge to it as it did the other night. I put my fork down and turned to face my mate.

"She is connected to WPG, so is her new mate. She went to see the Darings to tell them Isobel was dead. But I ..."

I got no further than that when Santiago threw his napkin on the table. He turned to face me with a fire in his eyes.

"Isobel is dead! How does she know this? Was she involved in this?" he demanded.

"First off, I need you to calm down."

"Savannah, this is our clan we are talking about. I will not be calm in this. Someone has come to our city to harm our people. We cannot just stand by and do nothing. If your mother is involved in this there will be no clemency for her."

I groaned before I spoke.

"If you will calm down enough for me to speak, you would know I would never ask for clemency for Chloe. Now can I tell you what is happening or would you prefer to continue to rant some more?" I gave my mate a hard look. I had let him have his rant the other night but tonight it was too much. Santiago and I fought very little, if ever. This was because he was usually the calm one between us, making him the more reasonable one. This was different. The clan was a family, our family. Someone had hurt a member of that family and he wanted justice. I understood that. I felt the same way but there was more to all of this than he was aware of. He needed to calm down and have a bit of a reality check about who he was speaking to. Santiago took a deep breath and turned to face me. He placed a hand on the back of my chair returning my stare. I watched as he took a breath. He nodded once for me to continue.

"I believe Chloe was sent to the Darings for another purpose. I don't know if Isobel is dead. So until we know otherwise, we will all continue to believe that she is alive," I spoke with force in my voice. "I have already spoken with the Darings and stayed with them for an hour tonight. They believe Chloe is a con-artist or at least that was what I have told them," I paused and looked at Santiago making sure he was still with me. "We have the male who helped her break in here in custody. He has been booked and will be questioned more tomorrow. Chloe will be found. Outside of Matthew, have I ever failed in finding my prey?" I asked sternly.

"No, you have not."

"Then trust in me to do my job. We have to all believe for now that Isobel is still alive. I won't lie to you, it is becoming less likely that she is but I do believe there is a chance she still is."

"What purpose would Chloe serve in going to see the Darings?" he asked. Santiago's voice was tight but I could see he was calming down.

"I don't know yet. I have been trying to figure that out."

"What is the likelihood you will be able to get this male to talk?"

"WPG is a hate group but for its members it's very much like a cult. They generally recruit young adults because they're the easiest target. They find the loner or the one who feels like an outcast and they bring them in, making them feel like they have someone who cares. The older members are good because they help bring in the younger members into the fold and generally are looking for something in life. Those young members are the hardest to break during an interrogation because they have been made to believe they have nowhere else to go," I explained. "There is a chance he won't break because of that. I will do everything I can to get him to talk."

"There is usually a small piece of these individuals who question what is being said. Could this male be in that category?" Santiago said as he took his seat.

"Maybe. Right now, Ryan has him in a cell with a wolf, so if he is, fear will begin to set in."

"I am sorry for being short with you just now."

"Thank you for that. Now can we eat dinner and enjoy the rest of our night with one another?" I questioned.

"Yes," he leaned forward, giving me a kiss before we both turned back to our food. We were silent for a long time as we ate. I knew Santiago was still upset and so was I. This case was taking its toll on more than my team but also on my mate.

"I need to ask a favor of you?" Santiago spoke, breaking the silence.

"What is it?"

"When you find Isobel, I would like you to call me."

"You want to be the one who delivers the news, if their young is dead, don't you?" I said.

"Yes."

I looked at Santiago seeing the worry in his eyes.

"I can do that."

"Do you believe there is still a chance she is alive?"

"I think the woman that took her is a professional and there was a purpose to taking a hybrid. I think there is a chance she is," I answered.

"What purpose could there be for taking her?" he asked.

Before I spoke, I thought about what to say. How much could I share with Santiago? Technically, I shouldn't share any of the case with him. I had already said too much as it was. This case was different from my other cases. Santiago was involved because of our status within the clan. Even if I had not been called in on the case, I would still be involved for the same reason. I made a decision right then on how to answer his question.

"I have no clue other than I believe it was a medical research group who took her. One ran by what appears to be witches. They have their hands in WPG."

"Are you sure?"

"Yeah."

"Why would they want Isobel."

"I don't know," I answered. "If they took Isobel and the other young, I have a feeling this could end badly for all of them."

"For once I hope you are wrong."

"Me too."

The tension between us seeped away as we ate. Eventually, we talked about other topics. For the most part we stayed away from the topic of kidnapped young. Santiago would be working from home from now until the ceremony. Cristian would handle most of the club business for Santiago, so he could have the time off. It freed him up not just for anything that might arise for the ceremony but also for the Darings if Isobel was found dead. Santiago would continue handling any clan business that came up. Dante had been quiet for some time now but we were both aware he was more than likely working behind the scenes on a new scheme. There had been a few fighting issues that had been creeping up within the clan. We had no idea why but we both suspected Dante was behind it. Cristian stepping in to take care of the businesses would help a great deal right now.

I was grateful Santiago would be here the rest of the week. Duncan and a team of technicians would be back to finish the upgrade to our network and our security system tomorrow. I didn't think Chloe would try breaking into our house again but there was always a chance someone else would.

By the time Santiago and I climbed into bed I was relieved to curl up next to him. I sunk into a deep sleep, letting go of the day with all it's troubles.

Chapter Twenty-Four
Four Days before the Ceremony

The next day came earlier than I was prepared for. I dressed quickly and kissed my mate goodbye. He was still in bed as I slipped from the house. The questions that had filled my head the night before were back again spinning around. There was a piece I was missing and when I found it, I had a feeling it would all come together. For now I tried to push the questions away as I drove to the station. We needed to get Billy Granger talking. I was hoping a night in lock-up would do the trick but I doubted the effectiveness of it. Cult members saw prison sentences as proof they were doing the right thing. If lock up didn't do it for him I was hoping Meri and I could. The longer we went without a lead, meant the farther Isobel got from us. The chances of finding her were growing slimmer each day.

I pulled into the lot at the station seeing Meri and Watts were already there. They were standing outside Meri's Range Rover talking as I pulled into a spot next to them. Both were dressed for a hunt today. Meri was wearing a razor back tank top with tight black pants identical to mine. She had on laced up boots that hit just past the ankle. While I wore my knee high boots. I had chosen a black T-shirt with a round neckline that hit me in the middle of the chest. Watts was in a black shirt and cargo pants with combat boots as if he was planning an assault. He had his gun strapped to his hip just as I did. Meri hadn't gotten behind the idea of carrying a gun. I had got her to start carrying a knife, which she had in a sheath on her hip.

"Look, my own welcome wagon," I said as I set the alarm on my car.

"We aim to please," Meri shot back.

"Everyone get a good night's rest?" I asked, looking at both of them. "I have a feeling it's going to be a long one," I speculated.

"As good as I was going to get," Watts answered.

"Same here," Meri added.

"Let's go see if Billy is ready to talk," I replied, waving my team on. They both fell into step with me, placing me in the middle.

"You know all night I have been trying to figure out why a medical research group would want these hybrids," Watts said as we walked.

"I've been wondering the same thing," I replied.

"What if they're destroying them?" Meri added. Watts and I recoiled at the idea. The problem was that it was a legitimate possibility. Especially with WPG being involved. "What? Are you telling me neither of you have thought about it?"

"I have but I didn't want to say it out loud," Watts answered.

"The thought had crossed my mind but it doesn't feel right. There is more to this, we just don't know what it is yet," I said.

We walked into the station house finding it slightly busier than it had been the night before. As we walked across the squad room I could see Ryan, Cain, and Illingworth in his office. He waved us in as we approached. The small room was already cramped, the three of us made it even tighter.

"Billy is being moved to an interview room. His lawyer is on the way and should be here in the next hour," Ryan informed us.

"An hour? We have to wait an hour?" I asked, irritated at the idea.

"Yeah."

"We need to get in there now. An hour from now could make the difference between finding Isobel today or not at all," I argued.

"The law says we have to wait unless he revokes his right to counsel."

"Technically, I'm not law enforcement and neither is my team," I pointed out.

"Nice try but you're employed by the police department, which means it extends to you," Ryan shot back.

There were days I really hated the law. This was one of those moments. Waiting on a high priced lawyer, who was going to prevent his client from talking in order to protect others was ridiculous. It meant Billy Granger would go down for everything while the others got away. It also meant Isobel would probably never be found. How many more young would have to disappear before we knew what was happening?

"What if we say we are getting a warrant for Troy Salazar?" Watts spoke up.

"That won't get the kid to talk, he'll just shut down even more," Cain pointed out.

"Not if we point out that the lawyer would have a conflict of interest," Watts added.

That had everyone in the room thinking.

"What if Meri and I went in and said nothing to him?" I suggested.

"What do you mean?" Ryan asked.

"We could sit in the room and chat with one another. And when the attorney gets here we can start the questioning. You or Cain could come and state you're getting a warrant for Troy."

"It would be better if I do it. Federal charges are scarier than state charges. Woods, you and I should be in that room together," Illingworth said.

I didn't know how I felt about the F.B.I. agent and I being in a room together with Billy. Meri and I had a shorthand, he and I didn't. There was also the fact that Illingworth didn't think I should be part of this case other than for the clean up. I wasn't sure it would work. Besides, to a hellborn sitting across from two stronger hellborns would be more terrifying than one hellborn and human.

"Let him stew for the next twenty or thirty minutes. Then Woods and Illingworth go in," Ryan ordered. "Do your financial people have anything we can use as leverage?" Ryan asked Illingworth.

"Nothing I've heard but I'll make a call and see if we have anything," Illingworth answered.

Ryan nodded as Illingworth left the room.

"Do we have any idea where Chloe Nichols could be?" Ryan asked.

"Best guess, hiding within the WPG," Watts replied.

"We can't search all of the members' homes. We need to narrow it down."

"Any way we could actually get a warrant on Troy Salazar?" I asked.

"No, we don't have enough on him," Cain answered.

"Have you found anything on the lilac smell the Darings talked about?" Ryan asked.

"Yeah, we have that piece solved. The charm is called the Drought of Death. It was used during the witch trials. It gives the individual the appearance they've died without actually dying," I said.

"Do we have proof its this charm?"

"A local witch has the information waiting for me to pick it up."

"Cain, I want you to go down to The Gallery and get the information."

"Not a problem."

"I'll text you the address. The witch's name is Ruth. I should warn you that she's a real peach," I said with a smile.

"Thanks for the tip, Woods," Cain rolled his eyes as he pushed past me.

I sent the address to Cain and then made a call to Ruth. She wasn't exactly happy a human was coming to collect the information. The way I saw it, she would get over it especially with her get out of jail free card.

Time seemed to crawl as we waited. Thirty minutes turned into three hours of waiting or at least that was the way it felt. Illingworth sat on the phone outside the office, as he talked to whomever on the other end. I could see Ryan's reasoning about him coming into the interview room with me but I still didn't like it. Or maybe it was more that I didn't trust the F.B.I. agent. My first impression of the agent had stuck with me. He had been arrogant, condescending, and dismissive of my team. Illingworth had only been interested in his version of what had happened to these young until I had found proof this was not a simple trafficking case, this was much bigger than that. I was almost grateful for Chloe breaking into my house. How scary was that thought? It spoke volumes of where we were.

Finally, Illingworth hung up his call and came to join us as we stood around.

"H&W Clinical Research has a number of large payouts to five different employees. None of them match the names we have on our human abductor but I'm not surprised."

"How big is big?" Meri asked.

"Between eight and ten grand."

"What are the employees' names?" Ryan questioned.

"Bridget Hernandez, Kelley Norton, Brad Lenstrong, Norma Callaway, and Lucy Whitebar. I have a couple guys looking into the names now."

"My money is on Lucy Whitebar. She's our human who took Isobel," I stated with certainty.

"Why do you say that?" Meri asked.

"Because to sell a lie you have to have some truth in it."

"We have three aliases on the woman, she has no problem with lying," Watts pointed out.

"True, but I bet Lucy Cordova was probably the name she has used the most," I replied.

"I also found out more about what H&W deals with. They have a few trials with some pain relief meds they are trying on witches. The clinic has been doing a blind clinical trial for the last six months. Everything they have reported to the NIH has been on the up and up. Each of the patients they're working with, they have filed patient findings with the NIH. All of the patients have chronic pain. The patients are examined every month to two months to see how they are handling the drug. They're on the verge of going into phase two."

So they were operating as an actual research company, not only were they funded by WPG but they were also getting money from the government as well. I would put money on the treatment they were testing nothing but a placebo.

Ryan looked at his watch as we talked.

"Woods, the lawyer will be here soon, you and Illingworth should head into the interview room. Remember, do not speak to the suspect."

"I got it Ryan," I said with annoyance, like this was my first time doing an interview. Hell, I knew the laws better than most of the cops working here.

Illingworth and I walked out of the office and headed for the interview room. I could feel Illingworth's eyes on me as we moved. I finally looked at him.

"What's up, Illingworth?" I asked.

"You know I checked you out after your Lieutenant insisted on you being part of the investigation."

It didn't surprise me he had researched me. In his position, I would have done the same.

"And?" I said as I stopped outside the interview room.

"You have quite a record. You've hunted in three different states. You have hundreds of arrests under your belt and close to three hundred kills."

"What's your point?"

"Just admiring the work you've done. It's a shame you aren't law enforcement. You would be a great detective."

"Humans don't feel hellborns can work as law enforcement so I guess I'll settle for being a hunter instead. Which suits me fine because I have less restrictions than you or Ryan."

"You don't like me very much do you?" he asked.

"I don't know you, it has nothing to do with liking you. I don't know if you're trustworthy. The F.B.I. has eight open cases and the only one who seems to care is you. It makes me question your motives. Is it a political move? Or are you trying to make a name for yourself in the F.B.I.?"

"Why do my motives matter?"

"Because those motives could cloud your judgement. I believe it already did once. You wanted to believe it was a trafficking case because it was an easy theory."

"No, it's because it made the most sense. My only motive is to find these kids. The parents need closure and I want to give that to them," he answered back. It was a pretty answer, the question was did I believe him?

"I hope that's all it is for these young sakes. Anything else will only get in our way."

"You are an interesting hellborn, Woods," he smiled.

"Not that interesting, trust me. Now are we done wasting our time?"

"After you," he said as he opened the door.

The room was painted grey with a metal table bolted to the floor. Four hard metal chairs were set up two on each side. The room had only one door with no windows. If you were claustrophobic this was not the room for you.

Billy Granger was sitting with his head down on the table. His right hand cuffed to a steel ring set in the center of the table with a flex cuff. The flex cuff had steel in the band that prevented him from using any magic. He looked tired with dark circles under his eyes, his clothes were disheveled and wrinkled from sleeping in them. As soon as I pulled the chair out across from him, Billy sat up straight, looking startled at our entrance. It took him a moment to understand who was in the room with him. The look of disdain and distrust at the sight of me made him try and pull away from the table. Unfortunately for him the cuff made that impossible. I turned my chair sideways so I could lean one elbow on the table and looked at Illingworth.

"Why am I here?" Billy asked.

Illingworth turned his chair to a slight angle so he could see me and the suspect. Neither of us spoke as we sat there.

"What do you want from me?" he whined.

"Mr. Granger, we are waiting on your attorney so we are not allowed to speak to you until he arrives unless you are revoking your right to counsel," Illingworth replied with a stern look.

"Why is that here?" he said pointing at me.

I was now a 'that'. I turned my head to give my own sneer. It was enough to make Billy drop his eyes and look away from both of us. I turned my attention back to Illingworth who did the same.

We sat in silence as the minutes ticked away. Billy fidgeted in his chair.

"When am I getting released?"

"Mr. Granger, I cannot speak to you without your attorney present. He should be here anytime," Illingworth stated once more.

The silence stretched between the three of us. Billy fidgeted as his eyes darted from me to Illingworth and back. I waited five minutes before I spoke.

"When is this attorney getting here?" I asked, bored.

Illingworth looked at his watch.

"He was supposed to be here by now," Illingworth answered.

"I wonder if he's dropping his client, maybe that's why he's late," I said.

"Federal charges are more severe, harder to fight," Illingworth said with a shrug.

"Federal charges. All I did was hack into a security system!" Billy shouted.

We both glanced at the kid as his eyes grew wide.

"Mr. Granger, are you revoking your rights?" Illingworth asked.

"I...I..."

We both turned away from him.

"How long do we have to wait until we have to get this...criminal, a new attorney. I don't have all day to sit around here," I said.

"I'm not a criminal. Do you hear me? I was just trying to..." he trailed off.

I didn't even give the male a look. I just sat back in the metal chair with a bored expression on my face. The time ticked by with another stretch of silence. Billy's discomfort grew as we sat there.

"Let's go try the attorney again," I finally said.

We both got up and headed to the door. I headed out first with Illingworth at my back. We stood in the hall with the door cracked slightly as we spoke to Ryan.

"We need to get this kid arraigned and transferred to federal lock up," Illingworth said.

"We can't do anything until his attorney arrives. I'm sorry Agent Illingworth. You know the law as well as I do.

"Can you call the lawyer again, see when he is getting here? Or get him a public defender?" I said.

"Let me see what I can find out. Worse case you won't be getting him until the end of today," Ryan replied.

"I have to get going on those other warrants, let me know if you need my services for that piece of crap," I said.

"Give me one second," Illingworth said. He opened the door. "Mr. Granger can we get you anything to drink? Maybe a snack, it looks like it's going to be a while longer," Illingworth offered with a smile.

Billy was looking scared now, his eyes were wide open as he sat there. He had heard everything we said, which was the point.

"I'll send an officer in to sit with you," Illingworth shut the door with a hard pull. We stood in the hall. The male was in a panic now. Just as we all stood in the hall, his attorney, a man in his sixties, by my guess, came strolling down the hall.

"Lieutenant, I hope you were not speaking to my client?"

"No, just offering him some food and water," Ryan said.

Illingworth and I stepped aside allowing the attorney to step into the room first. I followed next, Illingworth bringing up the rear.

"Billy, how are you doing?" the attorney asked.

"I...uhm...I'm okay," Billy answered with a shaky voice.

We took our seats as the attorney looked at both of us.

"Where's Lieutenant Ryan?" The attorney questioned.

"This case is being transferred to federal court, which makes it my jurisdiction. Special Agent Illingworth," Illingworth introduced himself.

"F.B.I.?" Billy looked panicked now as his voice went up three octaves.

"This is just a scare tactic, Billy," the attorney replied looking bored.

"No, actually it's not. We have nine missing children and we believe your client is linked to their disappearances," Illingworth explained.

Billy looked between Illingworth and myself. I smiled a cold smile at him.

"What evidence do you have that my client kidnapped anyone?"

"You will get all that information at a later date. Right now, I'm here to ask your client where the children are located. If he helps us, a deal may be on the table. If not, we are going to have to start assuming that they're dead, which is where Ms. Woods comes in."

"Do I need a new Federal license to carry out the warrant or will the license I have be enough?" I asked Illingworth.

"I'll have to check with the U.S. attorney but I'm sure your current one will be fine."

"I didn't take any young. I swear all I did was hack a security system," he begged.

"Billy you need to be quiet," his attorney ordered.

"No...I didn't take any young. I swear."

"Well, here's the problem, Mr. Granger, you committed a felony in order to help your organization cover up another series of federal and state crimes. That means we can charge you with being part of the initial crime," Illingworth explained.

Billy looked at his lawyer who had dropped his head, rubbing his forehead. He looked up trying to see how series we were.

"Let's start with the current case. Isobel Daring, where did your organization take the young?" Illingworth asked.

"Oh, God! Troy said I would be fine. Where is Troy? I need to speak with him," Billy ranted at his lawyer.

"Billy you need to..."

"They are talking about putting me to death. No... Troy asked me to hack the system. He said I would get a year, maybe less. Troy said we had to stop her from coming after us," he yelled, pointing at me.

"Billy!" his attorney shouted.

"Mr. Granger, do you wish to revoke your right to counsel?"

Billy looked at his attorney, who was seething at his client. His eyes then shifted to us.

"Yes."

"Woods, can you stay here while I get the form?"

"Not a problem," I replied.

"Billy you are making a huge mistake," his lawyer said as he took his leave.

I nodded my head at the camera in the corner of the room. My team would make sure the lawyer didn't make any calls. I turned to face Billy as tears began to streak down his face. Illingworth came in a moment later with a form and a pen. Billy signed it without even reading the document. Placing the pen down softly on the table he looked at us.

"I don't know where any of the young are," he stated.

"Where's Chloe Nichols?" I asked.

"What?"

"Chloe Nichols. The female you helped break into my home, where is she?"

"She's staying with Troy," he replied.

"Where?"

"He has a house in the north part of town."

"We need an address?"

"8930 Beverly."

"Do you know where Isobel Daring is?" Illingworth asked.

"No...I swear. Troy never said anything about her."

"What did Troy say?" Illingworth asked.

"He told me the defect was trying to take WPG down. He said we were trying to help witches and the way to do that was to protect our organization. We were there to prevent witches like her from poisoning our bloodline. We had to find a way to make our species whole again."

"What do you know about H&W Clinical Research?" I asked.

"They sponsor us," he cried. "I don't want to die."

Ryan entered the room. We all looked at him.

"Be back in a moment, Billy," Illingworth said.

We followed Ryan out, shutting the door all the way this time.

"I'll finish up with Billy. Here is your warrant for Chloe Nichols. Cain is back with the charm and is working on a warrant for Troy. I want you to get over to that address to see what we can find out from Chloe."

"My team and I will head there now."

"Your team followed the lawyer out, should I be asking why?" Ryan gave me a hard look.

"Nope."

With that I headed out of the station. Meri and Watts were standing by the cars. Meri with a smile on her face. Watts looking a little green.

"Where's the attorney?" I asked.

"At home, packing for a vacation," Meri said.

I smiled knowing what Meri had done. She had used her ability on the male to ensure he didn't call Troy. If Troy found out Billy broke, it could mean terrible consequences for us and Isobel, if she was still alive.

"Whose car are we taking?" Meri asked.

"Mine," I replied.

"What did Billy give you?" Watts asked.

"My mother. He didn't know where Isobel was but he knew where to find Chloe."

"Do we have the warrant for her arrest?" Meri asked.

I waved the paper I had in my hand. I unlocked the Suburban and we all climbed in. Watts in the back seat with Meri and I in the front. I drove away from the station as the excitement of the hunt began to fill me. The hum was different than it was normally. This hum was more angry. Angry at them for taking Isobel. Angry at the fact that no one seemed to care about the other young that were missing. Angry at the fact that my mother was part of all of this. Anger was good, it helped make what was about to happen easier. My mother was going to talk if it was the last thing she did.

Chapter Twenty-Five

We arrived at the address Billy gave us twenty minutes later. The house was located just outside The Gallery. I parked down the street from the house, watching for any movement inside. There was a chance that no one was even there. What if Chloe and her consort had already left town? I would chase them across the globe, if I had to at this point. There would be no stopping me until I found Isobel and I had all of the answers to my questions.

"You ready for this?" Meri asked.

"Yup."

"You know Embers and I can go in and do this, Woods. You could sit this one out," Watts offered.

"That's kind of you Watts, but I'm fine. I can handle whatever is going to happen next."

"She's your mother," he pointed out.

"No, she's not. The word mother would imply she did more than be an incubator. She is a suspect, nothing more. Now are we done with the chit chat or do we need more of this touchy feely bullshit?"

"Nope. We're good," Meri answered.

"Good. I'm going to pick the lock, as soon as I get the door open we move fast. The first to get their hands on her take her down. Do not shoot to kill, we need her talking. Maiming is acceptable," I said, shrugging my shoulders.

They both nodded. I climbed from the car first and did the walk up, Meri and Watts gave me a thirty second head start before they followed. I scanned the neighborhood, seeing nothing suspicious. I had placed my lock picking kit in my back pocket before we left the station. I pulled the small kit from my pocket and grabbed the tools from the pouch. As soon as I got to the door I knelt down and began to work the tumblers inside the lock, it was a basic lock with nothing special. It took me less than a minute to get the door open. I replaced the tools in my pouch before slipping it in my back pocket. I kept my gun in the holster, instead I pulled on a ley line. The feel of the energy as it flooded my body was like a second skin, as we moved through the small house silently. The living room was small, connecting to the kitchen. Watts took the kitchen clearing it with his gun pointed slightly down. Meri and I took the hall that was next to the kitchen. We reached a T in the path. I waved at Meri to take the right while I went left. We moved without saying a word. I heard Meri open the door at the other end of the hallway. I waited until she stepped out and shook her head. I opened the only door that was left finding my mother still in bed. Her red hair was splayed across the pillow, Chloe's head turned away from the door. She was wearing a peach colored silk gown with the sheet that was tucked under her arm. The other arm was up under the pillow she lay on. Some things never changed. My mother was never an early riser. I should have known there was no reason for concern that she would leave town early in the morning. Chloe showing up at my house at eight a.m. a couple days ago should have been the real shocker.

I softly touched her cheek, it was enough to stir her but not enough to wake. She leaned her face into the touch. I waited for her to settle before I placed my right hand around her slim throat. I applied pressure until her eyes flew open.

"Hey, Mom. How's it going?" I said as I pulled her from the bed. Panic set in as she realized the situation she was in. Her hand went to the one wrapped around her throat as her feet tried to find traction, I forced her against a wall. A small oomph escaping her body.

"Watts, we found her," Meri called down the hall.

I could hear his heavy footfalls as he ran from the front of the house.

"I bet you're wondering how I found you? It was easy once I threatened Billy Granger with a death warrant. Self preservation will win out more times than not."

"I told Troy not to trust him," she wheezed.

"You were right. But hey, I'm not here to talk about Billy. I'm here to talk about Isobel Daring. You know where that female is. Tell me!" I demanded.

"I don't know what you're talking about," she smiled. Her eyes never left mine as I held her against the wall. She knew where the female was.

"The fuck you don't. I know that look. You want to use her disappearance, for what? To make money? Or was there something bigger?"

"I assure you, dear, I have no idea what you're talking about," she gave me a feline smile, as if I wasn't willing to kill her. Boy, was she wrong.

"You are going to tell me what I want to know or so help me to whatever God there is, I will burn you alive."

"You wouldn't do that. I'm..." her words cut off as I squeezed her throat tighter.

"Why because you gave birth to me? Believe this, there is nothing I want more than to see you burn." I let the energy flow like my rage. My hand on her throat became a heat source. Her blue eyes grew large. "You have two options, tell me what I want to know or burn slowly to death. I will make sure you feel every flame as it engulfs you. Your screams will do nothing to sway me."

Any arrogance that had once played across her face was gone. Her weak hands were pulling at my hand as the energy poured through me into her flesh. I could see the red that was starting to spread from under my hand down her body. She gave me a short nod. I pulled back the flow of energy and let my hand go slightly slack. She gasped for oxygen as tears started to roll down her face.

"If I tell you, you have to promise me a deal."

"A deal? You think I'm here I negotiate. No! The only deal you'll get is me promising not to kill you once you tell me where Isobel is."

"You think Isobel is the only young that has been taken? I have all the information you need on Travis and H&W. What Travis has been doing for the last fifteen years. You want to know where your precious hybrids are, you will get me a deal."

Son of a bitch! She had a trump card.

"Watts, call Ryan and Illingworth, tell them to get down here now. Let them know Chloe Nichols is willing to make a deal," I gave Chloe a hard look before I went on. "In exchange for what?" I asked her.

"Let's say thirty maybe forty hybrids." The arrogance that had been absent moments ago was back once more.

"Fucking hell," Meri said from behind me.

Watts moved out of the room as he pulled his phone from his pocket. I held Chloe where she was as rage began to replace anger. I was not going to just stand here and wait. I wanted information now.

"Is Isobel Daring still alive?" I asked.

"I told you, dear. I want a deal."

"Well, we're going to be here for a while, so why don't you start talking?"

"That's not how this works."

"You want a deal, you have to give me something before the humans get here. Or I'll tell them you have nothing. So why don't you tell me about Isobel? When the cops and F.B.I. get here you can spill on all of the other little details you have," I said placing my face close to her.

Her eyes were measuring the truth in what I was saying. She must have seen something because she began talking.

"Isobel is still alive. Lucy couldn't get her out of the city and neither could Beau. They've been waiting for the search to be called off."

"Where are they?" I demanded.

"You will have to wait for that piece of information."

"Meri, you got any flex cuffs on you?"

"Yup."

"Good."

I released my hold on Chloe long enough to grab her by the shoulder and spin her around. Her chest hit the wall with a thud. My hand went to the nape of her neck holding her in place as I forced her legs apart.

"Put your hands against the wall," I ordered her.

She did as she was ordered. Meri stepped up and ran her hands down her legs and body. Chloe tried to jerk away from the touch but I held her in place.

"You move again, you will lose a limb," I warned her.

"She's clean," Meri said as she grabbed my mother's arms roughly.

She was cuffed and we moved to the living room. I forced her down into a brown chair and stood over her. Meri stood behind her. Chloe looked at me then at Meri.

"This is what you traded your family for?" she spat.

"Yeah, for a real family. Now why don't you sit there quietly while we wait."

I crossed my arms over my chest as I stood over her. The look she gave me was one of hate and disgust. I returned her look, my feelings of disgust, hate, and distrust showing on my face.

"The worst mistake in my life was having you and letting you live," she spoke leaning forward.

"No, your worst mistake was coming here. And if you talk to my family that way again I'm going to bleed you dry," Meri said as she pulled her back roughly. Chloe looked at Meri, unsure what to say after that. All I could think was how much I loved Meri at that moment.

It took Ryan, Illingworth, and Cain thirty minutes to arrive. Watts stood next to me, looming over all of us. The look on his face was a look of dread with anger mixed in because he knew what would happen next with Chloe.

Ryan took in the scene as he entered with Illingworth on his heels. Cain remained at the door leaning against the door jam.

"Chloe Nichols?" Ryan asked.

"Yes," she answered.

Ryan moved into the house taking my place in front of Chloe. I took a step to the right.

"I understand you have some information for us."

"What kind of deal are you going to give me?" she asked, smugly.

"The bigger question is, what can you offer us? You talk to me first. If your information is good then you get your deal."

She looked between Ryan and myself.

"Tell him what I told you," she demanded. I sighed, not liking the situation.

"She says Isobel is alive and still here in the city," I said.

"Where?" he asked.

"Not until I have a deal in front of me."

"No," Ryan said shortly.

"Excuse me!" she demanded indignantly.

"This is not how it works. You tell me where she is. If she is still alive and we get her back, then you get your deal. Otherwise, I charge you with kidnapping and possibly murder. Agent Illingworth charges you with eight counts of kidnapping and a slew of other charges. You either give us Isobel and whoever was involved or I walk out of here and get a death warrant for you. From the look of your neck, your daughter would be more than willing to execute that warrant," Ryan explained. His voice was calm the entire time he spoke.

Chloe had a moment of indecision as she stared up at Ryan before she spoke. She turned her head to look at the federal agent as he stood with his arms across his chest. He didn't flinch or offer to step in. He just stared at her.

"Fine. She is at a safe house Troy owns."

"Where?" Ryan asked.

"The address is in my phone."

"Where's the phone?" I asked.

"In the kitchen."

"Watts, go get the phone," I said.

"How does your mate fit into this?" I asked.

"He works for The Wellness Group. They get information about the hybrid young from hospitals and doctors, like any other drug company."

"Then what?" Ryan asked.

"They research the families. If the family doesn't want the young, they buy them and take them to H&W Clinical."

"What happens to them there?" Ryan asked.

"What do you think?"

"They test drugs on them," I replied.

"Not exactly," she said with a smile.

Watts came back in with her phone in hand.

"She has a passcode for it."

I leaned down in her face.

"What's the code and if you lie, it will be your death," I whispered menacingly.

"2550," she replied.

I stood up and waited for Watts to enter the code.

"It's in the last message Troy sent me," she said.

"Got it," Watts replied.

I looked at the address. The location was located to the east of my home. Watts sent the address to all of us from his phone.

"Cain, take her to the station and put her in an interview room," Ryan ordered. Cain stood up straight and made a move towards Chloe.

"Can I at least get dressed?" she demanded more than asked.

Ryan looked at me.

"Get up!" I demanded pulling her by the arm. "Meri come with me."

I dragged my mother by the arm down the hall, into the bedroom where I pushed her down on the bed. I didn't have to ask Meri, she knew where I needed her. She stood over Chloe as Chloe righted herself. I threw the closet open and pulled out a suit and tossed it on the bed.

"I'm going to cut the cuff off of you. You try anything and I will not hesitate to do what I need to stop you. Do you understand me?" I growled.

"Yes," she snapped.

She turned so I could get to the cuff. I used my knife to cut the plastic in the middle of the cuff, freeing her enough so she could use her arms. The cuffs themselves were still in place around her wrist but she could move her arms.

"Get dressed," I growled at her.

"Can you shut the door?"

"No, I can't."

She looked at me with pure hatred. Anyone who says a mother can't hate her own child, had no understanding not all mothers were made equally.

Chloe dressed, keeping her eyes on me the entire time. I pulled out a pair of shoes for her tossing them at her feet.

"Meri, you have any other cuffs on you?" I asked.

"No, I only grabbed the one set. Sorry," she apologized.

"Ryan or Cain will have some."

I grabbed Chloe by her upper left arm and pushed her forward. Meri fell into step as soon as we were in the hall, grabbing her other arm as we perp walked her into the living room. Cain was ready with a second set of cuffs. He pushed the first set up her arms and cuffed her hands in front of her. I handed her off and watched as she was walked out of the house. I hadn't seen my mother in almost twenty years and now I was arresting her, wishing I could put her to death. She would roll on her mate and whomever else she needed to in order to be free and clear. It pissed me off that she would get no time for her part in this. Not that she would actually admit to all of her wrongdoing. Sometimes that's how the justice system worked. Guilty parties could go scott free because they had a bigger fish than themselves to give up. I was really hoping Beau didn't leave everything to her. Being sent back to the poor house would at least be some form of justice or karma. She deserved worse.

"The D.A. will take a couple hours to get over to the precinct but we can move on the address she gave us," Ryan said.

"That's where we're heading next," I answered.

"Illingworth and I are coming with you," Ryan informed me.

"What if her consort comes back here?" I asked.

"I'll leave a couple of uni's here."

"Are you sure they can handle a witch?" I inquired.

"They'll have too."

I didn't like the idea of Ryan and Illingworth coming with us. We had no clue what we were walking into. Meri and I could handle whatever they could conjure up, I wasn't sure about the humans. Looking at Ryan I saw the resolve in his eyes. There would be no convincing him to sit this one out.

"Then let's do this," I answered.

Chapter Twenty-Six

We parked our vehicles far enough away from the address Chloe had given us, so no one inside would take notice of us but close enough for us to see what we were possibly dealing with. The house was located on a large plot of land, similar to my own home. The difference was my house was much larger than the one we were looking at. The house was set back on the property away from the street. From the outside, the house looked as if it was less than fourteen hundred square feet. I didn't think more than one or two individuals were inside. Chances were good they had no clue we were coming. There was a chance that the doors could be wired with explosives or charms that could cause injury to us. We wouldn't know until it was too late if there were. My gut said there would be no traps set up. Troy Salazar was confident Billy was willing to go down for him and his cause. His arrogance would be his downfall, overconfidence would make him neglectful. If Billy did roll, the kid had no clue as to this part of the plan. I was confident they believed Chloe would keep their secrets. I was also confident they had no clue what the female knew. Chloe wasn't stupid, she would find out everything she needed to know to ensure she was protected. From the little she had said so far I was right.

The problem in breaching the house was the approach. There was no way to approach the place without being seen. There were no trees or other buildings for cover. If anyone was looking out the window they would see as we pulled in. Things could turn ugly quickly, which would put Isobel in more danger than she already was. Sending in S.W.A.T. could add to the casualties. I continued to study the house saying nothing.

"How do we approach this Woods?" Watts asked.

"Three of us take the front, while the other two take the back."

"Are you sure that's a smart play?" Illingworth asked.

"What do you have in mind?" I asked.

"We get an assault team to breach the place."

"No, too dangerous," I said dismissing the idea quickly.

"Why?" Ryan asked. He wasn't questioning my judgement; he wanted me to explain my thinking. It was a more peaceful way to handle the F.B.I. agent's questions about my judgement.

"We don't know where Isobel is nor do we know how many hellborns are inside. There is also the question of how far is anyone willing to go to save themselves. There are five of us. Meri and I each take point at each of the doors. Any hellborn who tries to run we deal with. One of you grabs the girl, make sure she is removed from the property and quickly. Hopefully, we get the human alive and get her talking," I explained.

"An assault team could be here in the next two hours. We let them go in, handle whatever is in there and we deal with whatever is left," Illingworth suggested.

I shook my head at him. It was a terrible idea. We had no clue what type of magic was inside being used. There was also the chance that one of the individuals inside would use Isobel as a shield or that she could be killed by a stray bullet. Illingworth had no clue what he was doing when it came to hellborns.

Ryan looked at me as if he was sizing me up. I had a feeling he was more than likely sizing up my plan more than me. He knew my skill and how I worked. Illingworth he didn't know. The human we were up against had access to spells, it was smarter to treat her as a hellborn.

"We go with Woods' plan."

"You can't be serious," Illingworth said with disbelief in his voice.

"This is technically a hunt that means you and I are along for the ride nothing more. What do you want to do, Woods?" Ryan turned to me. I looked at the house as my plan began to form.

"Myself, Watts, and Ryan take the front door. Meri and Illingworth you take the back. There is no way to approach the house without being seen. So Meri, you and Illingworth take Ryan's car and approach from the back of the property. Meri is the first to enter," I reminded Illingworth, looking at the agent as I spoke. "We drive to the front, block the driveway and garage with my car and go in. Watts, your job is to find Isobel and get her the fuck out of there," I ordered.

Ryan handed the keys to his sedan to Illingworth.

"You two take the lead on the approach. This needs to be fast and dirty. It's the only chance we have to catch them off guard," I said.

"Let's try to take our suspect alive," Ryan ordered.

We all nodded before we headed to the vehicles. Watts took the backseat while Ryan took the front passenger seat. No one put on seat belts. Illingworth took off first, I gave him a forty-five second lead off before I took off after them. It was enough to give them the time to turn in and begin their progress to the back of the house. I pulled in blocking the garage door. Ryan and Watts both had their guns out. I pulled on a line, I could feel that was running along the house. Ryan took a step back before he kicked in the door next to the doorknob. The door gave way as wood splintered. He stepped to the side allowing me to go in first. The door breaking open startled the woman, she hit her feet as I entered the small room. She had been sitting at a small table in the corner eating, part of an uneaten sandwich sat there. Everything moved at warp speed from there.

In the center of the room sat an ugly brown sofa with a pull out bed. Laying on the bed was Isobel. Tears running down her face as she curled into a ball clenching her stomach. The blond woman, Isobel had known as Bree, made a move as if she had a gun at the small of her back. The energy from the line filled in my left hand as I raised it up. She saw the bright blue flame in my hand and put her hands in the air. There was the sound of running feet and a squeal like a pig before the sound was cut off. A second later, Beau Nichols wide body came out of a room to the right of the sofa-bed just as the back door was kicked in. Beau's hand raised as if he was ready to throw something. Ryan didn't hesitate to fire his gun. Beau Nichols' head jerked back and his body went down.

Watts scooped Isobel up into his arms and carried her out. I could hear him talking as he took her from the scene. I approached the human who had moved away from the table, turning and placed her hands on the wall. She knew she was done. I kicked her feet wide and ran my hands down her body searching her for any weapons. She had a gun at the small of her back with a knife at her ankle. Ryan handed me cuffs that I used before I forced her ass back into the cheap wooden chair. Meri and Illingworth came in from the same direction where Beau had gone down. Meri had Troy Salazar by the throat dragging him into the room. I let Ryan take control of the human while I went to Meri.

"He tried to run until he saw us coming. What happened here?" she asked, as Troy pulled on Meri's wrist.

I bent down and pulled a small bag from Beau's hand. The material of the bag was sheer and stunk. I knew this charm from the smell of it. It was a charm that would have made it difficult to breath until we all collapsed. I looked at Beau, seeing the small entry wound, no bigger than a pencil eraser in the front of his head. Blood was already spreading out onto the brown carpet. There was blood spray and brain matter on the wall where his head had been. I looked away from the dead witch wishing it had been me who had taken the shot.

"He tried to throw this," I said holding the bag up.

Meri's nose scrunched up at the scent of the charm.

"You think Chloe will be upset that he's dead?" Meri asked.

"Doubtful."

Troy began to gag at that point, I looked at the witch who was still being held by Meri. His face was turning red, her grip on him had increased enough where oxygen was being denied to his brain.

"I told you I would be coming for you," I said with a smile.

He tried to talk but all that happened was his lips moved as his skin began to turn blue.

"Meri you have to ease up."

"Do I have to?" she asked.

"Unfortunately, we don't have a death warrant for him, yet. But when we get one you can do the honors."

"Really? You say the sweetest things to me" she replied with a smile.

"What can I say I'm a giver," I shrugged.

Meri's grip loosened enough for oxygen to start flowing through Troy's lungs again. He coughed hard for a good two minutes as Meri kept him against the wall.

"You don't have anything on me," he finally spoke, his voice was raspy from the choking he had experienced.

"I don't. Well let's see, a wanted witch by the name of Chloe Nichols was found this morning in a home belonging to you. There is also the fact that Billy Granger says you asked him to help break into my home with Chloe Nicholes," I answered.

"Chloe knows nothing," he shot back.

"Really? Interesting you think so. She really is a very good con artist. According to Chloe, she says this is your place and you have had Isobel here for two days. And she seems to be able to connect you to a number of other missing hybrids. My guess is once she finishes giving a statement, I'll have you on more than just aiding and abetting and conspiracy to commit a crime," I said with a smile. I went to turn away before I remembered one more thing. "Oh and the F.B.I. is looking into your financial records, which means if I can't get you for kidnapping, they will."

The look on his face said it all. Oh how the mighty fall. I let Meri turn him around as she grabbed him by the back of his neck forcing his face into the wall. She pulled a flex cuff from the small of her back. As she reached for his wrist, Troy began to fight. He bucked his body, throwing his head back with a hard jerk. Meri was prepared for it. She moved her head back just before he made contact with her face. I grabbed a handful of his hair on the back of his head and slammed his face into the wall. There was a loud crunch as he howled in pain. Blood burst from his broken nose, rushing down his face. I continued to hold his hair as Meri grabbed his arm twisting it up as we took him to the ground. Ryan and Illingworth came over to the small hallway as Troy went face first into the bloody carpet. He was still trying to fight when Meri gave a hard twist to his wrist. There was another crunching noise as his wrist broke, all those little bones were going to be useless. He screamed in pain as I slid the busted wrist that was at an odd angle and his other hand into flex cuffs. I pulled them tight preventing him from being able to move.

"What the hell happened?" Ryan asked.

"He tried to fight," Meri answered.

"And his wrist?" Illingworth pointed out.

"You guys saw he was still putting up a fight. We had to subdue him," Meri argued.

"Embers can you get this guy out of here without breaking him more?" Ryan asked.

"For the record I broke his wrist, Savannah is the one who broke his face," she pointed out.

I helped Meri pull Troy up on his feet as she walked him to the front of the house. Troy's legs looked like they were on the verge of giving out on him. If they did, Meri would just drag his ass to the car.

"Illingworth, why don't you move the car around so Embers can place one of our suspects in the back."

"Yeah," he said as he looked at me. Illingworth looked irritated.

I wasn't sure if he was mad at me for breaking Troy Salazar's nose or if it was because my plan worked. Maybe it was a little bit of both. I stepped out of the hall following Ryan to the living room where our kidnapper was still sitting calmly. Her blonde hair was the color of straw, telling me it was a die job. Looking at the dark brown eyebrows and her light brown eyes I would say she was naturally a brunette. She looked at me with a smile. It wasn't one of arrogance, more that she had enjoyed the show. I stood in front of her while Ryan pulled out his phone. He walked to the front door as he talked.

"You have anything to say?" I asked.

"No, other than I wish it had been me who broke the fucker's nose."

"Why is that?"

"I was tired of him hitting on me. For the last three months he has been trying to fuck me."

"You don't seem like a woman who takes that kind of crap," I pointed out.

"Normally I don't, but I couldn't hit him either. It would have screwed my job here."

"How so?"

She smiled as she sat back in the small chair.

"No. I'm not telling you shit until the F.B.I. agent gets me a deal."

Another one who wanted a deal. I just shook my head.

"What can I say is your mother made the right play," she smiled.

"How do you know she did? I could have been bluffing."

She shook her head at me.

"Your mother can read a situation better than any of these males could. They all underestimated her."

"Don't envy her too much."

I stood over the suspect as Ryan came back into the room.

"I have a team coming out to dust the place and collect evidence along with two ambulances. They should be here in ten. Did she say anything?" Ryan asked.

"Nothing worth repeating."

Watts came running in at that moment.

"Woods! There's something wrong with Isobel."

I took off outside. Isobel's brown hair was in tangles as she sat in the back seat of my Suburban. She was clutching her stomach, her small body folded in the middle.

"Hi, Isobel. My name is Savannah. Can you tell me what's wrong?"

She shook her head, closing her eyes tight. I tried to touch her, she moved away from my touch before she winced.

"Isobel, I know you're scared but I'm here to take you back to your mom and dad. But I need to check you out. It looks like you don't feel good. Can I please help you?" I tried again.

She sat there crying. She didn't know who to believe. I didn't blame her in the least. I turned, pulling my jacket off my shoulders.

"Isobel, can you open your eyes. See my mating mark. I am part of the Black Grove Clan. My mate is Santiago De los Rios. I am here to help you. Will you let me?"

The little female looked at my mark then nodded. I turned back to her pulling my jacket back in place.

"Does your stomach hurt?" I asked softly.

She nodded her head again. I touched her head, feeling she was hot to the touch. I wondered how many times they had dosed the young with the tea or a sleep charm. I was confident her little body was rebelling against all of the charms she had engusted. There was also the chance if they gave her more than one kind of charm, it could do more than just make her sick. It could be an overdose of mandrake, which could cause death. It could be another herb that shouldn't be mixed with mandrake. Or it could be something completely different.

"How long have you been feeling like this?" I asked.

"I don't know," she cried.

"Okay. This is my good friend Antoine, he works with me and the human police. Is it okay if he sits with you? I need to go back inside for just a moment."

"Yes," she said.

"An ambulance is on the way. I need you to hold her while we wait. I'll be right back," I said to Watts.

I went back into the small house. Ryan had his arms crossed over his chest.

"What charm did you give her and how much?" I demanded.

"Like I'm going to tell you before I have a deal. Fuck that!"

"Ryan, I think you should step out to see if you can find out when CSU will get here," I suggested.

"Is the kid okay?" he asked.

"I don't know. As of right now it looks like an overdose but I can't be sure until I know what they gave her," I explained.

He looked at the woman and headed toward the door. He gave the two of us one final look before he stepped out. Ryan was a man who played by the rules but he was also a father. I had a feeling the man who walked out of here was the father, not the cop.

"You think I'm scared of you," she said with a smile.

I said nothing as I stood over her. She met my stare head on. She wasn't scared but she should be. I balled up my fist as I brought it across her face hard enough for her to fall back. The chair tipped back with the force of my hit and her body's reaction to it. I didn't wait, I pulled the chair free from her body tossing it across the room. I jumped on top of the woman and hit her again.

"You will tell me what you gave her or I will do more than beat you into the fucking ground."

"I'm human, I have more protection under the law than you do. If you do anything more I will own your ass."

"You think any of the cops care what I do to you. The Lieutenant is the most law abiding individual there is. He walked out. Do you really think anyone will stop me?" I said as I leaned down over her.

"You need me if you want the other hybrids.

I laughed harshly at that.

"You were right, Chloe did ask for a deal. The part you miss judged about her is that she can give us all of that information. She never gets into anything without holding all the cards. So if you want a sweet fucking deal, you will start by telling me what you gave that female," I replied as I pulled my knife from my thigh. I ran the blade down the front of the woman's chest. "I cut hellborns up for a living. Do you think I care about doing the same to you?"

She looked at the blade and then at me. No panic was there, just a calculating look.

"Troy gave her mandrake two hours ago."

"How much?"

"I don't know."

"How much has she had in the last day?" I demanded.

She looked at me. I pressed the tip of the blade into her flesh enough to get her attention to how serious I was.

"He has kept her sedated since we got here," she answered.

"See that wasn't that hard was it."

I stood up pulling the woman to her feet. Her face was starting to swell as we left the house. I handed her to Ryan and headed back to Isobel. Her eyes were closed but she was still whimpering.

"Isobel, can you look at me?" I asked.

She opened her eyes enough that I could see that her pupils were dilated. I needed to do something to help her now. The problem was I had no clue what I could do aside from giving her water. She needed a cleansing solution and fluids. I went to the trunk and found a water bottle. Maybe I could start flushing her system. I wasn't sure if it would work but we still had five minutes until the ambulance arrived.

"Isobel, I need you to drink this water," I spoke softly as I opened the bottle.

"My tummy hurts," she said with a shiver.

"I know it does but this will help. Can you try to drink it?"

She started to cry and the sound broke my heart. Normally, I wasn't a kid person but the sound of her weeping as pain and fever rode her body just broke me. She didn't ask for any of this. I lifted the bottle to her lips and helped her drink. The entire time she cried as I gave her little by little of the water. After every few sips she would beg for me to stop. All I could do was keep encouraging her to drink. Watts looked at me as if I was a cruel beast or maybe it was the situation that was doing it. At the moment I felt like it was me, so why wouldn't he too?

The ambulances finally arrived one after another. Watts carried little Isbol over to the medics with me following behind.

"Seven year old, hybrid who was given an overdose of mandrake root. I've given her water but she is in a lot of pain," I said to one of the medics. Watts set the girl down softly on the gurney. He went to step away when Isobel's tiny hand reached out to him.

"Cannnn... Antoine goooo... with me?" she asked around her sobs.

"Yes, Isobel, he can. I'm going to call your parents right now and they will meet you at the hospital."

She nodded. The medics began an I.V. with a cleansing solution in it. They took her vitals next as they tried to keep the female calm. I pulled out my phone and dialed my first contact in my favorites.

Santiago answered on the second ring.

"Mi Amor, please tell me you have her."

"She is on the way to the hospital now."

"Is she alright?"

"She has been given an overdose of mandrake. The paramedics are working on her now. Other than that she is okay," I explained

"I will go and retrieve the Darings now. I will meet you there?"

"Yeah."

"I love you," he said.

"I love you, too."

I hung up as I watched Meri pull Troy Salazar from the back of Ryan's car. She walked him over to the paramedics who looked at the mess we had made of him. I could see the medics were wanting the cuffs off of him and Meri was refusing. They would need the cuffs off if it meant they were to treat him. It was truly a waste of medical treatment being that he would be put to death soon enough. I walked over and released the cuffs. I forced Troy down onto the gurney while Meri stood over him. Just as I had done with my mother, I did with Troy, keeping the cuffs on his wrists.

"Ride with the medics and I will meet you guys at the hospital," I ordered Meri.

"Are you sure?" she asked.

"Yeah, Watts is riding with Isobel and you can make sure he doesn't try anything."

"Okay, see you there," Meri replied.

Isobel was already loaded into the back of the ambulance and on the way to the hospital while the other medics worked on Troy. I walked away from them, heading back to Ryan who was handing off the human to a uniformed officer.

"You know I shouldn't have let you do that?" he said.

I shrugged my shoulders at him.

"All I could think of this entire case was what if it was my kid," he said.

"I figured that's why you walked out of the room," I replied.

"This one...I feel like I need a few days off."

"If the department asks, tell them I did it. Tell them you have benched my team for a week."

"I can't do that, Woods. You have worked night and day on this. It's not fair to you."

"Yes, you can."

"You're not the only one at fault."

"Look, I was suppose to be off this week. It just means I get next week off," I pointed out.

"It's not right, Woods," Ryan argued.

"Knowing what they gave Isobel, probably saved her life. I don't regret what I did and I'll tell the department that."

"Could she die from what they gave her?" he asked.

"Yeah, she could."

He shook his head.

"Do you think there's others? Or could it all be a lie?" he asked.

"I believe Illingworth had it right. They're all connected and there is more to this than we know. My guess they're in Fairetree."

"Fucking hell."

"Don't question the human until I get to the station. I'm going to the hospital. Isobel's parents are on the way."

"You already called them?" he questioned.

"No, I called Santiago. He's going to pick them up now."

"I'll see you at the station."

I nodded and left the scene. It was already mid afternoon and I was ready for the day to be done. I was glad we had found Isobel alive but from the sound of it there was more than the F.B.I. knew about. The question now became, why were they taking hybrid young? Chloe had said they were experiments on them. How far did that testing go? I had a feeling the answer to that was going to be like nothing we had ever faced before.

Chapter Twenty-Seven

I arrived at the hospital after Santiago and the Darings. The waiting room was large and painted in a pukey yellow with padded chairs. The chairs were lined up in a horseshoe pattern, with a single row of six chairs back to back in the middle of the formation. A television hung from the ceiling with no sound, just subtitles. The Darings were both standing in the middle of the waiting room with fear on their faces. Santiago was the first to spot me, meeting me halfway between the sliding glass doors and the waiting room. He pulled me in close, wrapping his arms around me. I took the moment to fall into his embrace. The feel of him was refreshing as I wrapped my arms around his waist. I lifted my head up so I could look at him. He kissed me gently. The kiss was not nearly long enough but I would take it for now. When all of this was done I planned on taking as much time to be with him as I could.

"Are you alright?" he asked softly.

"I'm okay. I can't stay long but I wanted to see how Isobel was doing and collect Meri and Watts."

"Were they hurt?"

"No. Isobel connected with Watts and wanted him to ride with her here. Meri rode over with Troy Salazar, the head of the WPG of the region."

"Was he involved in the kidnapping?" Santiago questioned.

"Yes. He is also part of some larger plot or ring. I'm not sure what as of yet but according to the human and Chloe there are more hybrids that have been taken. That's why I can't stay long. I want to be there for the interviews."

"What can I do?" he offered.

"Nothing right now but I may need you to contact a few of the clans in Georgia, California, Nevada, Oregon, Washington and I think New York," I replied."

"Why?"

"Those are the young we know about that have been taken or at least where they were taken from. If the number is in the thirties or forties, there may be more clans to contact. I don't know what kind of facility we are dealing with, which means I may need help breaching it."

"You want their permission to take custody of the young and obtain their assistance," he finished my thought.

"Yeah."

"What if I was able to offer you the manpower you need? I can make calls and ask the other clans if they would allow the Black Grove Clan to take custody of the young until all of the details have been sorted out."

"It would mean we could move sooner."

"Yes and you would know your team as well," he pointed out. Trust was a big thing when it came to making a breach, you needed to know who had your back.

"I like your idea," I smiled at him.

"Do you know which territories each of the young are from?" he asked.

"I don't, at least not off the top of my head but I have all the information in my office. It's on our desks."

"I will stay with the Darings long enough to find out how Isobel is fairing. Once we know she is, I will go home and make the calls."

"Thank you," I answered, standing on my toes giving him another kiss.

We both looked over at the Darings as they clung to one another in the waiting room. Emma stood with her arms wrapped around her mate's waist as she looked out seeing nothing in front of her. Brian had an arm around Emma's shoulders with the same distant look in his eyes. I dropped my arms from around my mate and took his hand instead. I needed to approach them but I had no clue what to say to them. At this point, I didn't think they cared what came out of my mouth. They just wanted their daughter in their arms. We approached the Darings slowly, Brian's distant look broke first, his eyes met mine. The pause he took only lasted long enough for his brain to register who was standing in front of him before he launched himself at me wrapping me in his arms in a huge hug. It was the best description I had as he engulfed me. Santiago stepped back allowing the other male to hug me. I gave Brian two pats on the back as the signal that the hug should end, instead he just kept hugging me. I tried again, this time the pat was harder. He took a step back, tears in his eyes. I looked at Emma next, about to speak when she hugged me as well. The life that had been missing in her eyes over the last several days was there as she began to cry.

"Let's sit," I suggested as I stepped out of the embrace.

They both took a seat next to one another. They found each others' hands and looked at each other in shock. I could only imagine the hell they had put one another through for the last three days.

"Isobel is being treated for a Mandrake overdose. Before the medics arrived I had her drinking water in hopes it would help flush her system."

"They wouldn't let us see her. You've already done so much to help us but do you think you can get them to let one of us in with her?" Brian asked.

"Antoine Watts is with Isobel, as we speak. They have made fast friends, the two of them, she insisted he ride with her to the hospital. So at this point, I say let Antoine stay with Isobel while they make sure she's stable," I suggested.

"Do you know...Did you find Bree?" Emma asked.

"Yes, we did find Bree. The police have her in custody now and will be getting a statement from her sometime in the near future. Santiago and I will stay with the two of you until we know Isobel is okay," I explained.

"Thank you, both of you. We are no one's inside of the clan and you have been with us through this entire nightmare. We don't know how we can repay you," Brian said.

"You are not no one, you are the Darings who are part of our family. You do not need to be part of the hierarchy for you to matter to us," Santiago replied. "You owe us nothing. We were happy to be of assistance. I did very little, it was my mate who worked day and night to find your young. So the gratitude goes to her."

I flushed at the complement my mate had given me. He had been more helpful than he realized. If it hadn't been for him, I would have lost it more than once during this entire case. I reminded myself we weren't even done yet. We only seemed to be half way there.

A doctor in dark blue scrubs came out as we sat there.

"Isobel Daring's parents?" he called to the waiting room.

Brian and Emma stood up together and moved towards the doctor. Santiago and I followed behind them. The doctor looked at us. Brian looked from the doctor to us.

"They're welcome to stay. Please what's happening with our daughter?" he pleaded.

"She is doing fine. We were able to give her fluids and a cleansing solution to clear the mandrake from her system. We are moving her up to pediatrics in a few minutes. I am admitting her for the next two days just to ensure she has nothing else in her system."

"Can we see her?" Emma asked.

"Yes. Why don't you follow me and you can ride upstairs with her."

We followed as the Darings headed into the bays in the E.D. She was in a private area with a sliding door. Isobel was awake talking to Watts. She had a smile on her face as Watts laughed at whatever Isobel was saying. It was amazing how fast kids could bounce back. She had endured so much and yet here she was laughing and smiling with one of my partners. The Darings watched for a moment before they went in. The three greeted each other with tears and joy. Santiago and I stood at the door watching as the family unit reunited. Her mother pulled her into a tight embrace as dad hugged both of them. Emma Daring was crying once more as Isobel's thin little arms wrapped around her neck. It was a good moment to experience. Santiago placed an arm around me as we stood there. I leaned into Santiago, resting my head on his chest as the reunion continued. Watts had stood up and moved to the back of the room. Isobel was the first to pull back from her parents.

"Mom, this is my friend Antoine. He saved me," she said with excitement.

"Well I didn't do it all by myself," Watts smiled down at the girl.

"You carried me out."

"I did."

"So you saved me from Bree," she said it so matter of factly it made me smile.

Brian Daring went around the bed pulling the bigger man into an embrace, just as he had done to me. Watts looked around unsure at first before he returned the hug.

"Thank you for everything you've done for my family."

"It was my pleasure," Watts answered.

"We need to get going," I said, breaking up the happiness.

"Can't you stay, Antoine?" Isobel begged.

Watts bent down so he was at eye level with Isobel.

"I can't right now but if it's okay with your parents I would like to come back tomorrow and see you," Watts looked at them both. Emma looked hesitant. I didn't blame her, the last human they trusted kidnapped their young and drugged them.

"Please Mommy. He isn't like Bree, he saved me."

"We would love for you to stop by tomorrow Antoine," Brian said as he rubbed his wife's back.

Isobel leaned forward and hugged Watts. He returned the hug before he stood up moving out of the room.

"I will be taking my leave as well. I plan on sending two guards from the clan to ensure you are protected," Santiago informed them.

"Thank you," Brian said bowing to Santiago.

We took our leave, letting the door slide closed. I pulled out my phone and dialed Meri.

"Hey, where are you?" she asked.

"In the E.D. Where are you?" I asked.

"Same. Waiting for Troy to get patched up. They just took x-rays and now we're waiting for the doctors to tell us what's next. They have him sedated."

I looked around the E.D. seeing Meri at the opposite end standing just outside the curtain.

"Good. Let me make a call and get some guards on him. When they get here, meet us in the parking lot."

"Got it."

I hung up and went to call Ryan when Santiago placed a hand on my arm.

"I am already sending someone to guard Isobel, why don't I send two more to keep an eye on him?" Santiago offered.

"It should be a hunter or law enforcement. Technically, he's in police custody."

"True but he harmed a member of the clan, which gives us claim to him as well. Our vampires can handle him better than humans can."

I thought about what Santiago was saying and felt like he was pulling one of my tricks of stretching a loophole to fit his needs. There was a reason he and I worked so well together. I smiled at him.

"Sure," I said agreeing with Santiago.

He got on the phone as we headed out of the hospital. I let go of him as he spoke into the phone. I looked at Watts seeing a worried look on his face.

"You doing okay, Watts?" I asked.

"I've never worked a missing child's case until now. My head keeps going through the what if we hadn't gotten there in time?"

"I get it. I've been playing that same game over the last few days."

"I'm just glad we found her alive."

"Me too. There is a bright side to all of this," I offered.

He gave me a sideways look.

"You have a forever friend in that little female and her parents."

"The happy ending was pretty nice. You know as a cop we don't get a lot of that. So much of what we do is questioned. I get it. There have been some questionable calls but it makes it difficult to remember why we do the job. It's not often we get that level of gratitude," he stated.

"Hold onto that feeling. The feeling of knowing what you did for that young and her parents. You're going to need it for what's next."

"Why's that?"

"I have a feeling we have only closed part of this case. The other shoe is about to drop," I answered.

"You think Chloe was telling the truth?"

"I do and the human who stole Isobel is going to confirm that."

"Shit!"

I felt the same way as Watts did. Isobel's case had been enough for me. Now we were looking at something even worse than what we had imagined. I wanted to be done. Technically, I could have been. I could step back and let the F.B.I. take over the investigation and enjoy my time with Santiago until our mating ceremony Maybe even have a repeat of the night before. The problem was the F.B.I. didn't seem to know much about hellborns. How many young would die because of their lack of knowledge? I wouldn't be able to live with that. I didn't think Meri or Watts could either. We would face this ugly situation head on and then deal with the psychological aftermath later.

Chapter Twenty-Eight

It took the vampire guards forty-five minutes to arrive at the hospital. The guards for Troy were Kabel and Abel. They were the opposite of one another but they were also the best team for the job. They could almost communicate without speaking to one another. There was no way Troy would get around the two of them. Isobel would be guarded by Tony until she went home. Santiago introduced him to the Darings. I was confident Santiago would place a guard at their home until all the guilty parties were caught and dealt with.

Isobel would have to make a statement to the police eventually but I would try to make sure one of us took it. She was already comfortable with Watts, he would be the best man for the job. I said goodbye to my mate. He had his own job to do for the next part that was to come.

My team and I headed to the station from the hospital. The place was busy as officers milled around wanting a look at the two suspects who were currently in custody. I found Ryan and Cain both in the electronic monitoring room. Chloe was in interview one with a salt and pepper haired man. He was lean with a dark blue suit. He was an ADA for the District Attorney's office. We watched as he walked out of the interview room, my mother sat back in the metal chair with a smile on her face.

"Hunter Woods, I didn't realize you were on this case. Aren't you supposed to be getting mated this week?" Richard Jimenez said as he entered the room.

"ADA Jimenez. How are you?" I said with a polite smile.

"Are you the reason both of my suspects look beat to hell?"

"They resisted. I was just doing my job," I answered.

"No, what you are doing is making my job harder. Lieutenant maybe you should explain to Hunter Woods the way to handle a suspect."

"Woods did what was required to find Isobel Daring," Ryan defended me.

"You people," Jimenez shook his head.

"What's going to happen with Chloe Nichols and Bree Miller?" Ryan asked curtly.

"I'm dropping the charges against Chloe Nichols for the breaking and entering and conspiracy charges. The U.S. attorney will have to decide what they want to do with her. Chances are good she'll get immunity."

"Are you kidding me!" I demanded.

"After what your hunter did to her neck it was the best I could do. The human's real name is still in question as of right now. The name she has given us is Lucy Whitbar. We will be reducing her changes. The F.B.I. will get first crack at her."

I looked at the other monitor seeing Illingworth already questioning the human.

"Ms. Whitbar is demanding Hunter Woods be in with the agent for her questioning. Can you tell me why?" He looked at me.

I had no clue what she wanted with me but I was more than happy to oblige. I shrugged my shoulders at him.

"A U.S. attorney should be here in the morning to take Ms. Whitbar into custody," the ADA said as he left.

I was left shaking my head.

"Woods, get in there with Illingworth," Ryan ordered me.

"Fine but then I want to talk to Chloe Nichols."

"You're to stay away from her," Ryan answered

"What!"

"It was part of the deal Jimenez made with her," Ryan informed me.

"What about me?" Meri said.

"She didn't say anything about you Embers, just Woods."

I looked at Meri who was smiling wide. She wanted a piece of that witch. I left the room and headed down to the second interview room. I knocked on the door as I entered. Illingworth and the human both looked at me. Illingworth nodded his head before he returned his attention to the suspect.

"What have I missed?" I asked.

"Ms. Whitbar was just about to tell us what she knows about these hybrid children."

"Where's my deal?" she asked.

"There is no deal until you talk. That's how this works. Now I have Mrs. Nichols in the next room. I can go over there and see what she says or you can be the first to talk and get the deal."

She looked at both of us and smiled.

"If I talk, how do I know you'll get me a deal?" she asked.

"You don't. You can either spend your life in prison, if you're lucky or you can talk to us and have a chance at not getting life."

She looked less than happy at what she was facing.

"What do you want to know?"

"Where are the hybrid children?" Illingworth asked.

"In Fairetree at a facility," she replied vaguely.

"What type of facility?

"A medical facility."

"I need more than that," Illingworth replied.

She was looking at me with a smile.

"You got something to say?" I asked with my own smirk.

"Your mother is a piece of work, you know that. She asked that bag of money of a husband of hers to kill you."

"Am I supposed to be sad or hurt?" I replied dully.

"No, it shows me what makes you tick. You were good in that room. I actually believed you would cut me up."

"I would have,'" I said leaning forward on the table. "Is that why you wanted me in here? To ask me if I was really going to cut you up?"

"No, I just like a girl who knows how to get answers," she said with a smile.

"Is that what you're looking for? Me to rough you up again?"

"Why don't you ask me the questions Mr. F.B.I. wants me to answer?"

I glanced at Illingworth as he watched our exchange. He gave me a glance and a nod of his head. I turned my stare back on the human.

"What type of facility are the hybrid young being held in?" I asked.

"A research facility."

"Is it H&W Clinical Research?"

She nodded with a smile meant only for me.

"Why do they want hybrid young?" I asked.

"They are trying to turn them into pure witches. Get rid of the vampire DNA," she answered.

"Cleansing the species," it was more of a statement than a question.

"Yup."

"How many do they have?" I questioned.

"The last count I knew of was forty-five but I'm sure at least one or two of them have expired by now."

I was confident I knew what she meant by expired but I still had to ask the question.

"What do you mean?"

"What do you think I mean?" she smiled a cold smile as she leaned back in her chair.

I wanted to vomit right there. What could they actually be doing to those kids that would kill them? They wanted to cleanse the species. Bigotry at its finest. It made me want to burn the place down.

"Do you know what type of experiments they're doing?" I asked.

"No. They don't tell us that. Our job is just to acquire subjects, nothing more," she answered calmly.

"How do you find the hybrid young?" I demanded.

"That's where Beau and his company come in, or did. The Wellness Group goes to hospitals, free clinics, and doctors as reps who are looking for ways to help patients with minor illnesses. They get the patient lists with their species and the cold calling begins. When they find one, they send one of us to get to know the families and children."

"Then what?" I demanded.

"If we see the family is as disgusted as the WPG is with the kid, we buy them from the family. If they're like the Darings then we take them," she explained as if she was talking about buying groceries.

"Is that how you found Isobel?"

"No, actually Troy found her. He had been giving one of his sermons about how purity was so important. When a couple approached him after the meeting, saying their daughter had become a hybrid and their grandchild was one. They wanted more for the poor kid," she laughed.

Now that connected Troy and the Brazens to Isobel's kidnapping. I guess I would be going back to see the Brazens just as I promised I would.

"So Troy knows what's been happening at H&W?" I questioned.

"Yeah, he knows. He's a shareholder with the company."

"Where is the facility exactly?" I asked.

"You know where."

She was right, I did know where it was. It explained why Chloe took the sticky note from my desk. I moved on.

"The Fairetree police department doesn't know what they're doing?"

"It's called money," she answered me like I was stupid.

"H&W buys them off," I said.

"Why do you think they chose to set up there?"

"I don't know," I answered as if I had no idea.

Lucy smiled at me as she eyed me. She didn't believe the dumb act for a second.

"Because it's a small city with no hunters and a small hellborn population. It costs less to pay off the cops and the mayor there than it would a city like L.A."

"Tell us about these kids?" Illingworth showed her the photos of the young he had brought us. She ignored him and continued to stare at me.

"What do you know about these young?" I asked.

"No, I think I'll wait for my deal," she smiled.

"What can you tell us about the facility?" I asked.

"I've given you enough to get my deal. You want anymore out of me, you'll have to get the F.B.I. here to get me my deal. Then I'll answer every question you have Savannah," she said my name as if we were old friends.

"We'll be back," I said. Illingworth and I stood up.

"You could wait with me," she offered.

"No, I think I've had my fill of you."

Illingworth was at the door waiting for me. I moved towards the door when she spoke again.

"You know I was given your name before I took this job. Matthew said you were good but I didn't believe him."

"What did you say?" my heart stopped as she said his name.

"Matthew. He says hello. He misses his little witch."

Only days ago I thought I had seen Matthew on the street. I had felt at the motel as if I was being watched. Turns out I had been right.

"Where is he?" I demanded.

"You know he's a damn good time. Knows just how to make a girl scream his name."

"Where is he?" I growled.

"Sorry not happening."

I moved towards her and leaned down with my hands on the table forcing her to look up at me.

"What do you want for it?" I offered.

"Nothing you can give me. He sent a message in case we crossed paths."

"And?"

"He said he can't wait to taste you again," she was smiling as she said it.

I went for the human, only Illingworth's hand on my arm stopping me. He pulled me from the room. That bitch knew how to find Matthew. Fucking hell! Matthew had been two hours from me for how long? Maybe he had been closer. The thought of the hitman made me come unglued. I had been living in this limbo for a year. Not knowing when my next message from him would come or if he would make his move to take me. Normally, I could keep it all in check. This week had been hell and it didn't seem to be getting any better.

"Let's go, Woods," he said as he pulled me out the door.

"No! I'm not done with her yet."

She smiled as Illingworth pulled me from the room. The door closed as I tried to push Illingworth off of me.

"Let me go!" I growled.

"Like hell I will. You go back in there you'll fuck everything up. We still need her."

"I need to ask her more questions."

"No, you don't," he had forced my back against a wall. His hand still on my arm.

I pushed him off of me, turning to go back in the room finding Meri in my path. I hadn't even noticed her arrival. I looked at her and she stared back.

"I need to know where he's at," I said to Meri.

"I know you do but you can't right now," she said calmly.

"She knows where Matthew is."

"What's more important, getting info on Matthew or the hybrids? She isn't going to give him up without some convincing. And there is no way to do both. Are you willing to give up the hybrids for him? If you are, I'll back your play but you better be sure. What will it be?" Meri asked.

Fuck! She was right. The human was not going to give me Matthew unless I was willing to do what I had threatened to do back at the tiny house. Then what? Murder charges for me? Not what I saw for the rest of my week. I couldn't go after Matthew and save the hybrids from whatever was happening to them. Life is about choices. You didn't always have to like the choices you were given, but you did have to pick which way you were going to go. This was one of those moments. I let my back hit the wall as my head fell back.

"The hybrids," I answered. She rested a hand on my shoulder.

"Okay."

"Who's Matthew?" Ryan asked from my other side.

"A past case," I answered.

"In my office, Woods," Ryan said anger was in his voice.

I followed him to his office. He stepped to the side allowing me to enter in first. He shut the door firmly behind him.

"I know almost every case you've been on. I would remember if a suspect got away by that name. I'll ask again who's Matthew?" he demanded.

"He's a vampire I have been looking for for the past year."

"What case?"

Holy hell! I had been keeping this secret for a year and now it was all going to come out. Did Matthew send her? Or was he just one of the paid kidnappers? Did it matter at this point? No, not really.

"Daniel Adams' case," I answered.

"Daniel Adams ...Daniel.... The wolf who was working with a vampire?"

"Yeah."

"How is this Matthew connected to it?" he asked, his voice taking on an edge.

Now I had to decide how much I was going to tell. The whole truth? Half? Or just enough to get myself out of this?

"He's the vampire who was controlling Daniel Adams."

"Fucking hell! How long have you known his name?" Ryan yelled at me.

"I've known about it for the last year," I admitted.

"How did you find him?"

"He found me."

He was pacing behind his desk as I answered his questions.

"Please tell me you had a good reason for keeping this to yourself?"

"I was worried he would come after you or Cain. Not to mention I'm not sure his name is actually Matthew."

"Why would he come after us?"

Decision time was now.

"Because he wants me and if he thought you were standing in his way, he would not hesitate to kill you or Cain. If he felt you were a liability to me, he would remove you. As it is, I worry he'll go after Santiago."

"You should have told me," he said as his ass found his chair.

"I did it to ensure you guys were safe."

"The head of that wolf you got three months ago?"

"Came from him," I answered.

"What did the wolf do to you?"

"He was the one who attacked Vanessa Sanders. I've been looking for a mole inside the Falls Wolf Pack for the last year. I believe he was just finishing cleaning up any one who could tie him to the murders," I lied. I dropped my head afraid Ryan would see the lie in my face.

If I told him about my attack he would know I had help from somewhere. If he started digging he would know Cain had helped me and I wasn't willing to let Cain take any of this fall.

"Can I trust you to do your job?"

I looked at him.

"You can. I have never lied to you before Ryan. I kept this from you for your protection."

"I want to know everything you know about this vampire. And I mean everything," he replied.

"Fine. I don't know much because I don't know his actual name. I only know him as Matthew and the alias he used during the murders a year ago."

"When this is done, you and I are going to have a sit down about all of this."

He was silent for a long moment.

"Does that mean I'm still on this case?" I asked.

"For now," he warned.

"Thanks Ryan."

"Don't thank me, not yet. If you ever do this again I will have your hunter's license up for review. Even if they don't take your license I will end your contract with the PD. Do you understand me?" he asked.

"Got it."

"And you are off for the next week, your entire team is," Ryan said stabbing his finger hard on his desk with each word.

"Fair enough," I replied, raising my hands in surrender.

"Cain and Embers will do the interview with your mother. Let's go."

I walked out of Ryan's office with him following behind me. I needed to figure out how much more I could tell Ryan. I knew Matthew was related to Dante and the Moore family clan. If we started making calls to the Moore family, how much would they tell us? Would Matthew find out? What would he do? There were too many what if's for this situation. Right now, I need to focus on the hybrid young. They needed to be my main focus. Matthew had waited this long, he could wait a little longer.

We walked into the electronic monitor room. All heads turned to us as we entered.

"Embers and Cain go talk to Chloe Nichols, see what you can get her to say about the facility. The more we know the more prepared we'll be," Ryan ordered.

The two left the room and I took Meri's place next to Illingworth.

"I'm sorry for my outburst," I said as I watched the screen. Cain and Meri were just entering the room, taking seats across from Chloe. She wiggled slightly as she sat herself into a more upright position.

"Are you okay now?" he asked.

"As much as I can be."

He looked me up and down before he returned his stare to the monitor.

"What can you tell us about H&W Clinical Research?" Cain asked.

"They're a medical facility who are trying to cleanse hybrids."

"And how are they doing that?" he asked.

"They're testing theories, currently nothing has worked," she smiled at the idea.

"What kind of theories? We need specifics," Cain said waving his hand in a circle, encouraging her to say more.

Chloe said nothing as she looked at the two of them.

"You were given immunity on all charges. You can either tell us everything or we file charges," Cain reminded her.

"Is my daughter watching?"

"Why is that important?" Meri asked.

"I know how much she adores the defects, being that she's one. I figured she wouldn't want to miss this part. If only we can choose our young. How much easier it would be? No worrying about them becoming the thing you hate the most."

Meri growled deeply at her.

"What kind of theories?" Cain said again loudly.

"You want to know what they are doing to those...abominations," she put some effort in the annunciation of the word abomination. "They're testing ways to kill the vampire DNA. They've injected human and witch DNA into some of them. The results have been less than pleasant. They are currently trying stem cells from witches that were donated to the company. They're also working on a drug regimen."

"What kind of drugs have they been using?" Cain's voice was harsh as he asked.

"I don't know what drugs. I just heard Beau on the phone discussing it about it a week ago."

"You said something about the results having less than pleasant affects, what did you mean?" Meri asked.

The smirk she gave was nasty in nature as she began to pick at her fake nails.

"Some have died while others have become ill. From what I understand when they tried to use wolf DNA some of the children had partial transformations. It was quite painful for them."

Meri growled at her once more.

"You're thinking about that female you call family right now. Will you still love her when she's defective?" Chloe asked, looking at Meri.

"Now I see why you said you wouldn't have a problem arresting her," Illingworth said. I glanced at Illingworth.

"There is no love loss between the two of us," I replied before I returned my attention back to the interview.

"H&W has killed some of the children they're holding?" Cain asked. His voice was filled with disgust.

"Kill would imply it was intentional, they just weren't strong enough to handle the treatments they were given."

There was a pause in the questioning as we all took in what she was saying.

"What else can you tell us?" Cain moved on.

There were at least forty young being tortured as we stood listening to Chloe brag about what was happening. I wanted to drive down there now and pull as many young as I could from the building. It wasn't a smart move. The only people who knew what fail safe plans they had in place would be employees or the owners of the company.

"The last I knew they had forty-two young. Your sweet Isobel would have been forty-three."

"How do they keep the young from leaving?" Meri asked coldly.

"They're kept on the third floor under lock and key. The doors of their rooms are reinforced with steel so they can't touch the doors without burning themselves."

"Is there anything else you would like to add at this time?" Cain asked.

"No. Now where is my consort?" she asked.

"Dead. He was killed in the rescue of Isobel Daring," Cain answered coldly.

"I guess it's a good thing I made sure he added my name to everything. Am I free to go?" she replied.

"Unfortunately, yes," Cain and Meri both stood up.

Chloe came around the small table and headed for the door.

"Make sure you tell my daughter the next time I see her will be at her funeral. Hopefully, sooner rather than later."

Meri took a step towards her as Cain stepped in her path.

"Get the fuck out of here," he ordered Chloe.

Chloe gave Meri and Cain one more smirk before she left. I took a step towards the door when Watts stopped me.

"She isn't worth it, Woods."

He was right she wasn't worth my time but it didn't mean I didn't have a few things to say to my incubator. I walked around him and headed down the hall.

"Hey!" I yelled.

She kept walking as if I hadn't said anything. I picked up my pace and grabbed her arm, spinning her around.

"You think you were clever in there? Like you won something. The only thing you won is now you're on police radar. You breathe wrong and they will come for you. I pray I'm the hunter they call to put you down. You are nothing but a worthless bag of skin."

"You know when I found out I was pregnant, your father was so happy. He thought you would be a boy. It's why he left you behind. He had no use for a daughter. For me, I knew as soon as I saw you what a mistake you were. Life always weeds out the weak dear, eventually it will come for you."

I let her walk away. Watts had been right she wasn't worth it. It wouldn't be long until she went back to being Chloe Woods. The thought was enough for me to realize it was time to let go of my past and that meant my last name as well. I would have to change my company name but it would be worth it. It would kill any connection I had to the female. I was ready more than ever to be rid of the black spot in my life.

"Woods, are you okay?" Ryan asked.

"I'm fine. Do me a favor?" I said.

"What's that?"

"Don't call me Woods anymore. I'm taking Santiago's last name."

"What about your company?"

"Well you gave me a week off so I'll start filing all the paperwork for a name change. Maybe I'll dissolve the thing and create a new one for Meri and I. Either way I'm done with the name of Woods."

Chapter Twenty-Nine

By the time I arrived home, I was thankful to be free of the baggage of my past. The decision to change my name had been a decision made in the moment. As I climbed out of my car, I knew I had made the right decision. It would take some time getting used to saying De los Rios but everyone, including me would get used to it. Changing my name was part of letting go of everything from my past. My future was with Santiago and our clan. The fact I was seeing the clan as my family said how much I was moving forward in my life.

From what we had learned so far, H&W Clinical Research had been abducting or paying for hybrid children in order to try to separate the two parts of the DNA that made them. Young had died during this testing and no one even noticed. How could they get away with this and no one care? The answer wasn't complicated, it was rather simple, actually, hybrids were the one species no one cared about. They weren't one or the other, they were not really accepted by witches or vampires as a whole. My clan was different. The Black Grove Clan cared about hybrids because Hugo and Santiago were different about their views in regards to hybrids. Few clans were like ours.

We still had a long way to go. There would be a second interview with Lucy Whitbar the next day and we still had to figure out how we would get the young out of the facility. I needed to see floor plans for the facility and do some surveillance. I was confident the company would know they had a few employees that were missing, it meant we would have to move fast. Meri and Watts would not be enough to breach the place. We needed more hellborns for this job. Santiago was more than willing to provide vampires to assist in getting the young out but I would need fighters too.

I walked into the house as Santiago was descending the stairs from the second floor.

"I am glad you have made it home, Mi Amor," he said in greeting as he gave me a quick kiss.

Prior to Santiago, I had been fine living on my own. I had few ties to hellborns or humans. Coming home to a greeting as simple as a kiss and a hello, had made the worst of my bad days into good days. I loved coming home to him.

"Yes, I finally made it."

"Dinner should be arriving shortly. Why don't you go take a shower and relax before it arrives?"

"Sounds like a great idea but I would much rather you join me," I said kissing him again, trying to tempt him into joining me.

"That is a very good idea but who will answer the door when our food arrives."

"Too true. How about I sit and wait with you? We can always head upstairs after dinner together."

We kissed again, this one long and passionate.

"Agreed," he said as he turned us towards the living room.

I took off my knife, then stripped my holster and gun from my side. I sat down next to Santiago and slid out of my boots before I curled into his body. He draped his arm around me pulling me closer to him. It felt so good being there with him, my head resting on his chest.

"How was the rest of your day?" he asked.

"Well, it looks like H&W Clinical is more than they claim to be to the government. They've been testing on hybrid young in order to make them all witches. They're trying to "cleanse the witch species". Chloe's words not mine," I answered.

"How many young have they taken?"

"I don't know. All we know is they have somewhere around forty young."

We were silent as we sat with one another.

"I made calls to the vampire clans, most of them knew little about the hybrids who were kidnapped but have given us permission to act on their behalf," Santiago informed me.

"I guess that's a plus. I can cross that one of my lists."

"What can I do to help?" he asked.

"I don't know. Having a guard with Isobel has been a big help. And thank you for the assistance with Troy. He has to have surgery on the wrist Meri broke tomorrow morning."

"It is my pleasure to help where I can."

"We have a second interview with the human who took Isobel tomorrow. I need to get plans for the building where the hybrids are being kept and have to set up surveillance for the place," I replied.

"The plans should be easy to obtain."

"Normally, I would say yes, but from what I understand local law enforcement is helping cover this up. We can't just get the plans without tipping them off."

"Why not send Meri to obtain them?" Santiago suggested. I sat up a little looking at him.

I almost pointed out again about the local authorities being paid off when it dawned on me what Santiago was saying. Meri had a way around the problem. I had been completely up in my head with the bullshit with my mother and the human knowing Matthew, I hadn't thought about Meri or her abilities.

"I didn't even think about that. Hold on," I said sitting all the way up.

I hit her contact in my phone and waited. It took her awhile to answer but she finally did.

"What?" she growled.

"Hey how do you feel about driving down to Fairetree tomorrow and getting the building plans yourself? You could take Duncan with you." I offered.

"Can I call you back later?" she said a little breathy.

I wasn't the only one who had been using her mate to disconnect from this case. I could feel my face turning red from embarrassment for the interruption.

"Just give me a yes or a no?"

"Fine, I will do it," she growled again.

"Great call me in the morning before you get there."

"Yeah, sure. I gotta go," she said, hanging up on me.

I leaned back, falling into Santiago once more.

"That's another thing off my list," I said.

"When do you plan to rescue the young?"

"Soon, not tomorrow obviously but within the next day or two."

"Will it be before the ceremony or should we begin postponing the event?" he asked. His voice was careful and controlled. We were mated, technically, but the ceremony would be in front of all of the movers and shakers of the city, plus a few of my friends. Postponing would mean calls would have to be made, more money spent, and for Santiago a delay in us moving forward. Our ceremony was more than a party. It was showing the second in command in the Black Grove Clan was mated. It was a change in power in some ways for Santiago. The thing was that he didn't care about that part, this was a step for us to move forward. Hugo had demanded the ceremony but Santiago wanted and needed it too. I had been the one who didn't care much for it even though it would be a witch's ceremony. I had to close this case before our ceremony. Delaying was not in the cards for me.

"No, we won't. These people who are running this place are meticulous. I imagine they'll notice their people are missing. So I think I can plan on going in within the next day."

"Are you sure? I do not wish to delay but I also want to know you will be at the ceremony in one piece."

I looked up at him and could see the worry on his face. I placed a hand on his check.

"I promise I will be there in one piece. I will be as safe as I possibly can be." I kissed him hoping the feeling of my body would erase the worry.

"Who will go in with you?"

"I don't know. Meri and Watts, of course, but all I have are humans. I don't want Cain or Ryan to get hurt. I'm sure the F.B.I. will want in on it. They can't handle what could possibly be inside without serious injury or death."

"I have already offered vampires to you," he pointed out.

"It would be great but the law says hunters only are allowed to execute the warrant. The vampires are only there for retrieval."

"They will fight back if engaged," he replied.

"I know."

"Let me help you with this. I do not often ask to be part of your work, but this is different."

I said nothing as I sat there looking into his dark eyes. Could I fight beside my mate? I wasn't sure I could. It wasn't that I didn't think he could handle himself. It was more that I didn't know if I could handle someone coming at him. The mate inside of me wanted to growl at anyone who would think of causing him harm. I knew he felt the same as I did and yet he found the strength to watch as I went out day after day doing just that. Could I say no with that thought in mind? I didn't think I could. If I said yes, it would mean one more problem off my list. Maybe he could even get a team out there tonight to do surveillance. It would solve so many problems for me. Yet, I was hesitant to say yes. If he could stand back and watch as I went out, putting myself in danger all the time, then I needed to be able to do the same. What if Matthew showed up? He would go after Santiago. Could Santiago win that battle? It scared me to think about it. Would Matthew let him put up a fight? Or would he take him when he wasn't looking? I wasn't sure.

"I would rather be at your side and know you are okay than sit on the sidelines fearing I have lost you. On any given day I am able to handle the uncertainty of your work. This one is different, it is not you going against one hellborn but multiple."

"Matthew may be there?" I cautioned him.

"What?"

"The human knows Matthew. He warned her about me. From what I understand they're lovers, which means he could be there. I'm worried if you're there he'll target you. I don't think I can handle that?" I explained.

"If he is there, I will deal with him. I am more than capable of handling myself in battle."

"I worry he will wait until you have your back turned. You won't see him coming."

"And I worry he will find a window of opportunity in the chaos that will ensue and will take you from me. Do you think I do not worry about him taking you anytime you are alone? You will fight him, I know you will but what happens if he takes your vein again. He could fill you with Euphoria and take you. The only time I am at peace is when you are with me," he argued.

Wow!!! Santiago had been under the same black cloud I had been. I never even saw it. This was unfair for both of us to live this way. God, I needed to kill Matthew in order to remove the black cloud. Would we ever find total peace? I didn't think we would until he was dead.

"Okay," I said, placing a hand on Santiago's face. "We need a team of at least..." I thought about what we were doing. I didn't know anything about the building, other than the children were kept on the third floor. "Ten vampires. We want individuals who not only can fight but won't lose their head when things become chaotic." Santiago smiled at me.

This was going to be a battle. It wasn't just serving a warrant, it was going to be a bloody mess. Chaos would ensue no matter how much planning we did. The best we could do was to control the havoc for as long as possible. We needed to get in quickly and take control as fast as possible.

"Can you send two of your fighters out there to start surveillance? We need to know roughly what we are dealing with and how many hellborns are there at all times," I pointed out.

"Let me make a call to Hugo. He will want to be a part of this, from a distance," he pulled his phone from his pants pocket, unlocking it with one hand, and going to his contacts.

As soon as he got Hugo on the phone, Santiago started telling him about the hybrid young who had been taken. There was some back and forth. I was imagining Hugo wanted some credit for offering soldiers for the breach. I would give him what he wanted, if it meant he agreed to give us the soldiers we would need. Santiago said Dante's name followed by a hard no. There was some more back and forth that switched from english to spanish. I sat silently as they spoke to one another. After fifteen minutes of discussion the call ended.

"Hugo has agreed to help..."

"As long as the press knows the clan helped with the rescue," I finished.

"Yes."

"Not a problem."

"He is sending Malcolm and Devon out tonight. All I need from you is an address," Santiago handed me his phone, the contact already pulled up with a message. I typed in the address and hit send.

"Are these two good? I mean they have to be as inconspicuous as they can be," I asked.

"Malcolm and Devon were thieves at one point in their lives. They worked in different areas of thievery but they do know how to move without being seen."

"What kind of thievery did they take part in?"

"Malcolm was a master at B and E. He knows how to get in and out of places without being seen and he knows about security. Devon has a pretty face, he grifted more than he did anything else," Santiago explained.

On a normal day, I would have been bothered by the thought of using ex-thieves but they sounded perfect for what we needed. I would have preferred doing it myself but I needed to be here for the second interview with Lucy. As much as I had grown into having a team, I still wanted to do everything myself. The problem was I couldn't do it all. If I had still been working by myself, I would not have been able to cover as much ground as we had with this case. There was a chance Isobel would have died or never been seen again. It was a terrifying thought but it was the truth. It made me grateful to have Meri and Watts. Soon enough Meri and I would be back to just the two of us. Watts was going to return to his role as a detective. The thought made me sad. He was a good cop but he would have made a damn good hunter. He was always willing to learn. You didn't find a lot of that in law enforcement, the longer someone stayed with the department, the less they were willing to learn. They got stuck in their ways of thinking and working. Watts seemed to want to know everything he could about hellborns. He was good with hellborns. He had forged a bond with not just Isobel but Brian Daring as well. He also could handle himself, which he was proving more and more. I was beginning to wonder if there was a way to convince him to join our team on a more permanent basis. Ryan would hate the idea but he'd get over it.

The doorbell rang bringing me back to reality. I sat up allowing Santiago to stand up. He went to the door. I watched as he signed the receipt and took the square box from the delivery guy.

Very rarely did Santiago order pizza. I was the junk food queen in the relationship where he preferred having an actual meal. Pizza in Santiago's mind was a waste of a meal, it was more of a half meal that provided nothing to the body. He was right but sometimes you just wanted to waste the calories and eat. He sat the pizza down on the table.

"It has been a long day for the both of us. I thought this was the easiest option for tonight," he said.

He went to the kitchen to retrieve plates, while I pulled the box open. The smell of pepperoni, tomato sauce, and bell pepper greeted me warmly as I moaned aloud. Santiago returned a moment later with plates, glasses and a bottle of wine. I took both putting a couple slices on each plate and sat back licking my fingers.

"Thank you for this," I said before I took a bite.

"I am the one who must make sure you eat. This week has been long and I know the only food you have been eating is the food I have been preparing you."

"It's true," I said around a bit. "I have been skipping more and more meals this week. This case has just been...difficult. Everything about it has been rough and I don't think about food until I get home and you say something. Thank you for the pizza. I know you don't enjoy it much but it's exactly what I needed tonight."

"It is my pleasure," he replied as we ate. "What time should we arrive at the station?"

"What?"

"You will be planning the assault on H&W tomorrow, correct?" He asked.

"Yeah."

"Then our vampires should be there for the planning. We need to know what we are dealing with as well."

He had a point. I had planned on waiting until the day we went into the facility to bring the vampires in because I didn't know how I was going to explain it to Ryan or the F.B.I. I guess I would be doing that tomorrow. I chewed slowly waiting to answer him.

"I don't know when Meri will be back with the plans or when the F.B.I. will be there," I answered before I took another bite.

"You are stalling, Mi Amor," he said eyeing me.

"No, I'm not," I answered, eyeing my pizza.

"Yes, you are. What is the matter?"

I gave him a sideways glance before I returned my focus on my pizza. I took another bite. His gaze never leaving my face. Eating was not going to make him give up.

"I have no idea how I am going to explain I'm taking vampires in instead of law enforcement."

"We have permission to retrieve the young, they do not," Santiago said simply enough.

"They aren't going to see it that way. These young are part of a federal investigation, meaning the F.B.I. are supposed to do the rescuing. My team is there for clean up, nothing more."

"Can you list us under your license?" he asked.

I thought about what he was asking before I answered.

"Maybe or make each one a temporary employee. It could work but I don't know with the numbers we're talking about."

I could make them employees for a day, maybe two but was the loophole in the law big enough to cover all of them. I liked to stretch things but this may have been taking it too far. I guess the only way to know was to try. Sometimes it was better to ask for forgiveness than permission. I think this was one of those times. Would I have to pay them? What would it do to my taxes?

"Let's try the employee route. We may be reaching too far."

"I will ask again, what time do you wish for us to be there?" he said with a smile.

I didn't know how long it would take for Meri to get the plans back here. I would imagine it would take only a few hours but what if it took longer. What happens if they got caught? Maybe it would be better if I went? Okay, the last question was more about me wanting to do everything than anything else. If Meri was caught she would deal with it and get herself out. She could handle herself and she would have Duncan with her. No way he was about to let anything happen to her.

"Let's say one o'clock. I have to get all the paperwork ready tonight. You will have to bring it with you when you come to the station," I said.

"I will take care of it."

I ate more of my pizza, when I realized I hadn't told Santiago everything about my day.

"One more thing I need your help with."

"What can I help you with?"

"I need to change the name of my business and add Meri to the ownership. You handle all of the business stuff for Obsidian and the other businesses. Can you help me do that?"

"Why are you changing the name of your company?" he questioned.

I set my plate on the coffee table and turned to face him.

"I'm dropping my last name and taking yours, like humans do."

"Are you sure you want to do this?" he asked.

"Yes. Today my mother got off scot free and there were things said between her and I. I want no part of me associated with her. The best way to ensure that is to change my name."

"Mi Amor," he pulled me into him. I wrapped my arms around him.

"I'm okay. I swear. I just need to do this. So can you help me with the paperwork?" I asked as I pulled back.

"I would be happy to help you. You know you will have to inform the board of this as well."

"I can take care of that next week."

"What about work?" he asked.

"I will have all of next week off. I kind of got rough with the human who kidnapped Isobel. Ryan knew I would but I'm taking the hit on this one. So I'm benched for a week."

"We will take care of the paperwork while you are off," he said.

We went back to eating, turning the conversation to a lighter subject. We spent the night talking about what my new company name would be. I had no clue what I would call it but I would figure it out. Adding Meri as an owner was a big step on my part but one I was happy to do. She had earned the right for all the years she had worked as my back up, she had been there at my side through the attack three months ago and now as she worked to get her license. Putting her name on the business, also meant if something happened to me, she would continue as a hunter. She didn't need to work but I saw she enjoyed it. Duncan had his own businesses and now so would Meri or at least one she shared with me. It was a way I could not only thank her but ensure she would be okay if I died. I didn't like thinking about my death. Before Santiago, death was just a part of life I dealt with on a regular basis. I hadn't worried about it. I had lived my life with the thought, if it happened so be it. Santiago had changed that way of thinking. Now the thought of one of us dying was terrible. I lived a dangerous life, my mate was the number two in a large clan, it made both of us a target. I needed to make sure things were in order in case death did happen.

Chapter Thirty
Three Days Before the Ceremony

I woke up early the next morning, lying next to my mate thinking what the day would hold for us. I had printed out fifteen forms for new employees the night before, filling out my portion of the information. I only needed ten but I wanted to make sure there were extra forms if needed. My business was going from three employees to almost fifteen for two days, just to go back to three individuals for four months. I was pretty sure there would be some questions at some point, for now I would not worry about it.

I was hoping Meri was already on the road to Fairetree. The sooner she got the building plans the better. I wanted her in and out of Fairetree before anyone took notice of her. I thought about calling her and dismissed the idea as fast as I had the thought. She could do this without me checking on her. The city wasn't a small town but it was smaller than our city was. I didn't want anyone to take notice of a vampire asking questions about H&W. I had to trust Meri could get in and out with the plans and none the wiser.

My brain moved to the interview today with Lucy Whitbar. I had to stay on the hybrid young and not deviate to Matthew. The fact that he was only two hours away wasn't a shocker, Matthew had been wanting me for himself. It was more than likely how he kept tabs on me. Two months ago, he sent Robert's head to me, making it clear he had been watching as my life continued to move forward. Santiago and I mating had been out of his control. The mating ceremony that would be happening in three days would be salt in the wound for him. Knowing Matthew was involved in the kidnapping of hybrids made me despise him more. I hated the idea of Santiago going with me, I felt like I was putting a target on his back for Matthew. Santiago felt the same way about me. If there was a way to get Matthew and the young, I would. This was not one of those situations. It was one or the other. I was beginning to wish I could multiply myself.

My phone went off, stopping my thoughts. I rolled over pulling my phone from the side table. It was a message from Ryan. The U.S. attorney would be at the station in an hour. I needed to be there because the second interview would start as soon as Lucy Whitbar signed her deal with the federal prosecutor. I sent a quick message back saying I would be there.

I rolled on my back, looking at my mate then rolled my body to face him. I touched his cheek softly. That one touch brought his hand up to cover mine. He turned his head slightly and laid a kiss on my palm.

"You have been lying there worrying for some time now, Mi Amor. Do wish to talk about what is bothering you?" he said as his dark eyes focused on my blue ones.

"Have you been awake this entire time?"

"No, only part of the time. What is bothering you?"

"I don't know... everything. I mean... I want to be the one who is surveillancing the facility but I can't. I wish I was with Meri right now, just so I know it all goes smoothly. Then there's the interview today, I want to know where Matthew is but I can't ask. She's not going to give him up unless I beat it out of her but then we won't get all of the information on the hybrids."

He wrapped one hand around my waist, pulling me closer to him.

"You cannot do everything. Devon and Malcolm are very good. They will get everything you will need about the facility. Meri has Duncan with her, correct?"

I nodded my head.

"She will be able to get the building plans without anyone being the wiser. As for Matthew, we will handle him when the time is right. There is nothing we can do about him right now. I know you fear he will be there when we go in. I have lived for four hundred years. Do you not believe I can take care of myself?"

"I feel like I'm putting a target on your back. I know you can handle yourself. I still worry," I answered.

He brushed my hair away from my face.

"I swear I will not take any more chances than I must as long as you can promise me the same."

"I have to go in there Santiago..." he shook his head as I began to speak.

"I understand what you must do but there are risks we must take and there are unnecessary risks. I need you to swear you will not take any unnecessary risks. Can you vow to me you will not take any unnecessary risks?"

I understood what he was saying. If I have to choose between my life and another's life, I was to make sure I got myself out.

"It will break me if I lose you," he said.

"I feel the same way about you."

He leaned in kissing me. The feel of his lips, as his tongue slid into my mouth was enough for me to forget my worries. I wanted to stay in bed with him for the rest of the day. Unfortunately, my phone went off once more reminding me I had to get out of bed.

I rolled away from Santiago seeing it was a message from Meri. She had the plans, which made no sense, being it was before eight in the morning. Most county offices didn't open until nine at the earliest. I had a feeling I wasn't going to like how she got the plans. I looked at the time before I rolled back to face my mate.

"I have to go," I said kissing him again.

"I know." Santiago rolled onto his back taking me with him. The feel of his bare skin against mine made my body respond. I kissed him one more time before I climbed from the bed and headed for the closet. I didn't want to leave but my obligations said I had to. All I had to do was make it through the next two days and I would have a week to spend with my mate. I kept that thought in mind as I pulled clothes on.

"I forgot to forewarn you, Hugo is throwing us a party the night before the ceremony," Santiago said from bed.

I stepped out of the closet in a black bra and my skin tight hunting pants.

"What?"

"He wishes to have a party for the clan. Not all of the members were invited to the ceremony and he wishes to allow them to celebrate with us."

I hated clan events for the simple fact that the general population bowed to me. It was awkward for me. I wasn't sure I would ever get used to the fact that I received the same level of treatment as Santiago. He had been the second to Hugo for years. He had earned their respect. I felt I still had a ways to go to earn their respect.

There was also the fact that any event Hugo was hosting became about Hugo. His wanting to throw a party for us, meant he wanted an ego boost. A night of Hugo and Dante was not how I thought I would spend the night before my mating ceremony. Maybe the paperwork for my case would take longer than I could anticipate. As I thought about it I kicked my own self for the thought. This was part of the responsibility of being mated to Santiago. I needed to get over my hang ups.

"Fine," I said, feeling defeated.

Santiago sat up and pulled me into the bed, a smile on his face.

"I know you hate these events. Thank you."

He kissed me as his hand slid down my neck to my breast. Santiago's hand brushed the top of my breast making me catch my breath. I pulled back from his kiss looking into those almost black eyes.

"I don't hate them. I just feel uncomfortable at these events. Besides it means you get to bring me back here and make it up to me," I said with a smile.

He smiled at the idea and kissed my neck. Santiago brushed my neck with a fang as my hands found his hair pulling him in closer. His mouth began to travel down my body. He reached the top of my breast and stopped. I looked down at him seeing his eyes heavy with sex. Santiago gave me a sly smile.

"You have to finish getting ready for work. We will finish this tonight," he promised as he laid back, placing one arm behind his head. Seeing his built body stretched out like that was evil in so many ways.

"I could be a little late. It's not like the human will talk to anyone but me."

I moved, repositioning myself so I was straddling him. I leaned down kissing his bare chest. A low growl came from him as I moved down his body. I pulled the blankets back finding him hard. I slowly moved down his body until I reached his pelvis. I licked the head of his erection as he let out a hiss. I raised my eyes up the length of his body, seeing him watching me. I took him in my mouth, sucking hard as I took all of him.

"Mi Amor," he breathed.

I continued to suck on him, my eyes never leaving his face as his eyes lost focus. I pulled his erection free of my mouth and smiled slyly.

"Maybe you're right I should finish getting ready for work," I said. I licked the head again slowly.

He grabbed my arm and pulled me up against his body kissing me hard. He flipped us over, putting me on my back as his teeth found the front of my bra. The lace didn't stand a chance as he tore it from my body. He sat up long enough to pull my pants off. I was grateful the pants survived, unlike the pair from the other night. He didn't waste anytime as he came down on top of me. His erection powered into me as I latched onto his back with my nails. Santiago moved hard and fast in and out of me until I was withering with his name on my lips. I pulled his head down as I turned my head. His strike was just as rough as the sex was. He drank at my neck as he plowed into my body repeatedly, never slowing down. I felt as his pace changed. I cried out as I orgasmed, a second later he came while I organsm. He pulled his fangs free from my neck, he licked the bite lovingly.

"You are magnificent and very late for work," he whispered against my skin as he kissed my neck where he had struck.

"It was totally worth being late for," I panted.

We laughed together as we lay there a little longer enjoying the peace.

I ENDED UP BEING THIRTY minutes late. By the time I arrived, Ryan was blowing up my phone as if the sky was falling. He met me at the front of the station house hands on his hips.

"Where have you been?" Ryan asked.

"I didn't know I was punching the clock with you now."

"I texted you when the U.S. Attorney would be here. I expect you to be here on time," he snapped as we walked deeper into the station.

"Did I miss anything important?" I snipped back.

"She won't sign the deal until you're in the room with her."

"Oh, for fuck sake! I am sick of this woman."

"The U.S. Attorney is waiting for you in interview one."

I walked into the squad room as cops continued to work on other cases. Ryan was a step behind me, as if he was escorting me to the room. I ignored his presence and kept moving to the rear of the squad room. As I hit the hallway Ryan stopped me.

"Are you okay to do this?" he asked.

I met his stare evenly.

"Yeah."

"You can't ask her any questions about the vampire."

"Look, I made a choice yesterday. I chose to go after the hybrid young. I know the line. I'll be fine."

"If I think you can't handle this, I'm pulling you from the interview."

"I figured you would," I replied sarcastically.

"Where's your team?"

"I sent Meri on an errand. She should be here within the next half hour or so. Watts is on the way now. I didn't call him until I was on the way myself."

Ryan nodded. I took that to mean that I was safe to proceed. I headed into the interview room. The U.S. Attorney was a woman in her forties. Her strawberry blond hair was long, hanging loosely down her back. She wore a navy blue suit. Her bright green eyes met mine as I entered the room. She stood as I moved towards her.

"I'm Hunter Savannah De los Ríos," I said, sticking out my hand.

"Ms. De los Ríos, I'm Victoria Hudson," she introduced herself. Her eyes slid over the mark on my neck.

She shook my hand with confidence, grasping my hand instead of barely touching me.

"Sorry, I'm late."

"We were beginning to worry about you," she stated.

I took a seat on the other side of the attorney. Lucy watched me as I moved. I didn't look at her until I was seated. I sat back in the chair folding my hands in my lap.

"What were you doing Savannah?" Lucy asked, seeing the bite on my neck.

"None of your concern," I answered. "Now can we get this done. I have better things to do today than waste my day with you."

The attorney cleared her throat as she set a thick set of documents in front of the suspect.

"This deal is with the federal government. You will serve ten years in a minimum security prison. In return you will give the government information on H&W Clinical Research and The Wellness Group. Do you agree to these terms?"

Lucy was looking at me waiting for a response from me. I gave her a deadpan look.

"Sure."

"Sign here."

The U.S. Attorney showed her where to sign. Flipped the page to another spot for a signature. Lucy signed the document with no pause. She set the pen down on the table, her stare returning to me.

"Ms. Whitbar, what can you tell us about H&W Clinical Research."

"I know lots of things. You need to be more specific. Oh and I want her to ask the

questions."

The attorney looked at me and I continued to stare at Lucy.

"What are they using the hybrid young for?" I asked.

"They're trying to separate their DNA. WPG as you know feels hybrids

weaken the witch species."

"How are they doing this?"

"They have added DNA from witches, humans, even wolves to see if they could flush out the vampire part. The wolf DNA I think was just to see what would happen. The scientists get bored," she said with no infliction in her voice.

"What else have they done?"

"They have tried draining them and replacing their blood with pure witch blood. They tried washing a couple with bleach, I believe. Again, probably more for fun than anything productive," she smiled.

I wanted to beat the crap out of her, instead I kept asking questions.

"Have they done anything else?"

"They tried injecting them with synthetic blood, right into the heart. Most of those kids died."

I was getting a clear enough picture as to what had been done to them. I moved on.

"Why did you not take Isobel there as soon as you had her?" I asked.

"That's not protocol. When you take a hybrid most law enforcement don't care. They spend a couple days looking for the kid and then move on. So once you have the kid you wait a few days in some cheap motel for the dust to settle. Once the cops stop, you drive out of town and meet with your handler. You hand the kid off, he gives you a payment and you move on."

"Was Beau Nichols your handler?" I asked.

"Yes."

I moved on. There was nothing to gain from that area of questioning.

"What can you tell us about the building?"

"Not much just what Matthew has told me," she smiled.

I took a deep breath before I moved forward.

"What did he tell you?"

"It's three stories, a square building. The kids are kept on the third floor. Each door is locked and can only be unlocked with a key card. They automatically unlock on the inside when you approach them or they do for staff. The doors have steel on the inside to keep the little tykes away from them. What I understand, it burns like hell when they touch the doors," She smiled at the last part of her statement.

"Any windows?"

"They have small slits for windows up high. To ensure none of the kids can get out."

"How many employees do they have?"

"I don't know."

"What else do you know?" I demanded.

"That's everything."

"What about The Wellness Group?" I asked.

"There are only a handful of employees," she shrugged.

"How many is a handful?"

"Ten, maybe fifteen," she answered.

"Are they hellborns or human?"

"Hellborn or at least most of them are. Beau kept it small so there was less chance of getting caught," she answered.

"Do you know any of the other kidnappers?" I asked.

She smiled at me.

"Do you think we had office Christmas parties or something? Beau kept us from knowing one another. I only met Matthew when I was meeting with Beau after I bought a kid off a family. He helps secure the new patients when they arrive."

There was a chance he would be there when we went in. I wanted to ask her more questions but all of them were dealing with Matthew. If I did that I would be pulled out of the room and her deal would get sweeter. I moved on.

"We need you to look through photos of eight hybrid young. You will identify the young you took," I ordered.

Ms. Hudson placed each of the photos across the table. Lucy looked down at the photos taking each of the images in one by one. There was no emotion as she pointed to three of the pictures. Andrew Corker, Jay Guzmen, Faith Holder, and Meg Travers. She sat back and looked at me. I was tired of this bitch. I was tired of talking to her. I was tired of her smile. I wanted nothing more than to put her down. Unfortunately, the law didn't allow me to kill human pieces of crap like Lucy Whitbar. No the State did that with drugs, making it as painless as possible or they served time in prison. More times than not they got prison and served only half of their sentence.

Ms. Hudson took the photos and placed the others in a separate stack. She turned to the camera in the corner of the room behind us and waved. Ten seconds later two large men walked in with chain cuffs.

"These are U.S. Marshals, they will be escorting you to the Federal prison before your hearing in a few days. From there you will be transferred to the minimum security prison you will be spending the next ten years in," Ms. Hudson said as she headed for the door.

I watched as they shackled their prisoner's feet first, then her hands.

"You know I'll only serve five maybe seven years at the most."

"No, you will serve all ten years. I will ensure you will," Ms. Hudson said before she left. I smiled my own cruel smile as Lucy started her shuffle to the door.

"Do you really think Matthew will leave me in there? He'll get me out."

I laughed coldly at her.

"You know I thought you were smart but that statement just proved me wrong. He will leave you there because you were nothing more than a messenger for him. Chances are good while he was fucking you, he was thinking of me."

I hated the fact Matthew wanted me but it felt good to burst her bubble. Hell, it felt better than good, it felt fucking great.

"I know things about him," she shot back.

"Bad luck for you then because it means you'll be dead soon enough."

I walked out ahead of her, all humor was gone from Lucy's face. I walked away with the satisfaction knowing it was the last time I would ever see Lucy Whitbar. Matthew would never leave anyone alive when he was done with them. For once I was grateful.

Chapter Thirty-One

I met the others in the electronic monitoring room. Cain was sitting in front of the monitor for the interview room I had been in with Lucy Whitbar. Ryan was standing next to him, while Illingworth was leaning against the wall behind the other two. He had his arms casually crossed over his chest.

"You did good in there," Ryan said.

"Thanks."

"What's our next move?" Cain asked.

"Meri should be here soon with the building plans for H&W. We can look them over and make a plan on how to enter the building. Chances are good that I'll need to bring in my IT guy to help with the security system," I said.

"We need to get a team out there to do surveillance on the place," Illingworth added.

"I already arranged that last night. I'll call them in a little while to see what they can tell us, so far."

Illingworth looked at me, a smile playing on his lips.

"This is now F.B.I. jurisdiction. We will be taking over all operations from here on out."

"No, you won't actually. This is hunter jurisdiction. These are hellborns who took other hellborn young. It means I have the right to go in and serve warrants on the facility," I pointed out. "Not to mention I am licensed to hunt in Fairetree."

"These kids were taken across state lines giving..."

"And I have permission as the second in command's mate of the Black Grove Clan to go in and retrieve them for multiple clans. The way I see it between the vampire clans and my standing as a hunter,

I run the show. You're just a visitor in my world, Illingworth," I shot back.

Illingworth straightened from the wall and took a step towards me. He was trying to use his height to intimidate me. It didn't work, I stared right back at him with my hands on my hips.

"Alright, enough," Ryan said, moving Illingworth away from me. "There has to be a way to do this so everyone gets their piece of the pie."

I looked at Ryan and nodded.

"I have a team coming in at one. I will take my team in to clear the path for the F.B.I., they can enter to get the young out. We will take the lead and he can head the rescue team. Fair enough?" I offered.

"You do realize I can get an assault team in place and take control of the place now. The F.B.I. is the best at this," Illingworth said.

I chuckled at his arrogance.

"My team is a team of vampires and one human. You really think your humans are

Better equipped than my team," I pointed at myself.

"You're taking vampires in?" Cain asked in disbelief.

"As Santiago's mate, I have the ability to call on others to assist me," I responded.

"Woods.... I mean De los Rios," Ryan corrected himself with irritation. "They are not licensed hunters; they cannot go in there to serve a warrant."

"They can as my employees," I pointed out.

"That clause is for one maybe two individuals, not how many ever you're using for this," he almost yelled.

"Technically, the law doesn't say how many employees I can have under my license. The paperwork was filed with the state last night. I will have all employee records for you by one p.m. today," I answered.

"You know damn well the purpose of the statue is meant for one," he was yelling now.

In Ryan's eyes I was stretching the law too far.

"The law is unclear what it means and the last time I checked you aren't a judge, Ryan."

"Woods," he warned.

"If we go in with humans, the death rate will be greater than if we do this my way. Do you want to explain to the families of those that die or to the media why you didn't go in better prepared? By the way, it's De los Rios now."

He was quiet, everyone was quiet. Ryan had his hands on his hips as he looked at me. He knew I was right. We lived in an age of twenty-four hour news cycles. Add to it that, someone would talk to the media. In a matter of hours it would go from a failed assault on a medical building, to several dead police officers who ignored the advice from a local hunter. The storm that would rain down on Ryan and the department would be a mess. I was confident Hugo would take the opportunity to point out the clan had offered their assistance. The hellborn community would be up in arms for their ignorance. The F.B.I. would also get their share of the responsibility and every fuck up they ever had would be revisited.

"Fine... we will offer support for the assault. I will run the recovery," Illingworth agreed.

"Then Cain and I are coming with you," Ryan said to me.

"You can go with Illingworth, you're not entering in with us," I answered.

"No. We're coming in with you," he said with force.

Ryan's look of this was non-negotiable.

"Fine but you will wear a vest and follow all of my orders," I shot back.

"This is going to be fun," Cain said.

"Shut up Cain," Ryan and I said as one.

IT TOOK MERI ANOTHER hour to arrive at the station. By the time she arrived we were all ready for the next step. Illingworth had begun to get the federal warrants we needed with the U.S. Attorney. Ryan, Cain, and I sat around with nothing to do but wait. Ryan and Cain were both in chairs while I rested my ass on one of the tables. My feet resting in a chair. My eyes kept going over the board looking at the faces of the young. Waiting was the worst part of the job, whether you were a cop or a hunter, it didn't matter. It was terrible. All you wanted to do was act, do something productive, or at least feel like you were being productive. Sitting and waiting made you feel like you were doing nothing. The truth was sometimes you had to wait, there was no other option.

Meri and Watts walked in with the building plans in hand. The plans were a thick cylinder of paper that was three feet long in length. She grinned at me as she walked in.

"What did we miss?"

"Not much. How did you get the plans so early? And why is Watts with you?" I asked.

"I took him with me instead of Duncan. And I have my ways," she replied.

Watts walked into the conference room we were using. As he walked past me he whispered.

"Don't ask."

I had already had enough fights this morning I didn't need another one. I let it go. I stood up as Meri came over to the table. I looked at the black and white drawing of the building, it was nothing special, just a square building as Lucy had told us. I looked at the first floor seeing it was a simple layout. There were two entries.

The first was the front doors. A reception desk and two doors that led to a bank of elevators, and smaller rooms. To the right of the reception desk were the emergency exit stairs. My guess was that was where they examined the witches that were part of the medical trial, the NIH knew about. The second entry were two large doors that looked like a loading dock. I could also see a set of stairs to the left with a much smaller door.

I turned the page seeing the second floor. Three rather large rooms were along one side of the building. There were two rooms, at both ends of the hall. Those rooms were the biggest on the floor, measuring four hundred square feet each. I had no clue what the rooms were used for. The room in the middle was smaller than the other two. I could also see a long, wide room across the hall that had small dividing walls and doors. The plans showed multiple built in counters. My guess was that it was a lab of some kind. A facility like this would need to have a lab on site.

The top floor was divided into much smaller rooms on one side of the building. The elevators opened up to a foyer like space with three load bearing walls. The smaller rooms would be where they kept the young or at least that was my best guess.

The last page was the basement. There was nothing special to the room. There appeared to be a boiler in the building but that was it. It could only be accessed by an elevator from what I could tell.

I flipped back to the first page looking over the ground level again. There was a set of stairs at one end of the building that went all the way up to the top floor. I wanted to start planning now but I wanted everyone here before I did that. The only other piece I was missing from the plans was the location of the security system.

"Can you call Duncan? I think we need him for the security system," I asked Meri.

"Shouldn't be a problem."

"I need him here in the next thirty minutes."

"Be right back."

"Savannah, do you have a plan?" Watts asked.

The fact he used my first name made me stop and look at him.

"You called me by my first name. What's up, Watts?" I said as I stood up.

"I thought it would be easier with the name change and all. I have to admit it was odd I've always called you Woods. Saying your first name just didn't feel right."

I smiled at him. Watts looked tired as he sat back in the chair. The more I looked at him, the more I was glad we would be off for a week. When Watts joined our team, the plan had been for him to shadow me. I had turned it into a job for him. He was learning about hellborns along with the role I played in every case. I even made sure I paid him for his work. This was the first time I had seen Watts worn down. We all were feeling the affects of this case. I was worried Watts would not be able to handle the breach, maybe rescue would be a better fit for him. He had done a great job with Isobel. I sat down in the chair next to him. I looked at him and leaned towards him.

"Would you rather be on the assault team or the recovery team?" I asked quietly.

"What?" He leaned forward with his elbows on his knees.

"This case has kicked all of our asses. I see the weariness in your face. So if you're more comfortable on the recovery team, it's fine. I have a team of vamps who are coming in. But I need you to be honest where you feel you need to be."

"I want on the assault team," he answered with all seriousness. "After being with Isobel, I was worried about breaching the place but you had already made up your mind where I was going to be. I was willing to because I follow your lead. Then I heard what that human and your mother said. The assault team is where I need to be."

"Are you sure?"

"Yeah."

I studied him seeing the resolve in his dark eyes.

"Okay. Then you need to be prepared. There is no shooting to wound tomorrow, it's all shoot to kill," I informed him.

"It won't be a problem."

I nodded at him as Meri came back in the room.

"Duncan is on the way."

"I should call Santiago to see if he and the others can get here sooner." I hit his contact as I stood up and walked to the door. He answered on the second ring.

"Hello, Mi Amor."

"Hi," I smiled at his greeting. "I know I said one but I was wondering if you and the others could be here sooner?" I asked.

"We can arrive within the hour. I will call Kabel and Abel to have them meet us at the police station."

"I'll see if Ryan can send officers over to guard Troy and relieve them," I replied.

"I will see you soon."

"See you soon."

I hung up and smiled for a moment at my phone. Ryan was looking over the plans, flipping between the pages.

"Ryan can you send a couple uniforms over to the hospital to relieve my guys."

"Yeah, not a problem," he replied. "Cain get Smythe and Royce over to the hospital now. And see if they're done with Troy Salazar's surgery. If they are let's set up transport."

"Got it, Lieutenant."

Cain headed out of the room. I came around the table with my arms crossed over my chest looking at the drawing once more.

"You know this is going to turn into a cluster fuck?" he said to me.

"Yeah, I know."

"Look at this area on the third floor," he pointed to

"I'm confident those are rooms where they are keeping the young."

"How are we going to get to all of them carefully and systematically?" he asked.

"Carefully. We need to clear a path on all three floors for Illingworth's team. That's what you and I need to focus on. Let Illingworth focus on the retrieval."

"What if we can't get to those rooms? We don't even know what type of security they have or how many witches are in there?"

"I'm working on all of that," I replied.

"When are the blood suckers getting here?"

"Soon and don't call them that."

"Are you sure using them is a good idea?" he asked.

"Can your cops handle spells being thrown at them?" I waited half a second before continuing. "The vampires can be taken down with a spell but they're stronger and have better reflexes. They're motivated to help."

"Why is that?"

"Because of the Darings. The clan is a family," I answered. Ryan opened his mouth to argue with me when I stopped him. "I didn't realize how much they are until I became part of them. Most of the clan members are family. Not all I'll admit but most are. So you fuck with one, you deal with all of them. Hugo is very much about no one harming his family. Santiago and I are as well. They want to stop these assholes probably more than you do. It makes them perfect for the job."

"Doesn't mean I have to like it."

"You don't need to like it because you have to follow my orders for a change."

He shook his head, scowling at me.

"This should be a law enforcement matter. It has nothing to do with you being in charge," he explained.

"So it's for humans to handle?" I questioned.

"That's not what I mean."

"Look, I respect you for always being willing to do right by any hellborn who falls victim to whoever. I respect you for being a cop but this is a hellborn matter. Humans are not equipped to handle this. There is also the fact that not all cops are as honorable as you are Ryan. Can you ensure there would be no cops with any bigotry against those young?"

"No, but neither can Illingworth," he pointed out.

"I know that, that's why they go in after us. I have to take him with me on this because I have no choice. If I had the option they would stay behind. If one of those guys hates hellborns or hybrids they will do the least amount they can. If things get ugly they will not sacrifice for those young. We are the best for this job because we will."

"Okay, De los Rios," he said, putting an emphasis on my new last name.

I smiled at the emphasis. I understood how Ryan was feeling. I had been feeling the same way since the night before. I wanted to be everywhere, doing everything. The problem with that was you couldn't and some jobs are better dealt with by others. He didn't have to like it anymore than I did but we both had to accept it.

Chapter Thirty-Two

Duncan was the first to arrive. None of the officers in the squad room took much notice of him as he walked through. In terms of vampires, Duncan had a very understated look about him. It wasn't that he couldn't be fierce or terrifying. If anyone tried to harm his mate, you would see how furious and ferocious he could become. Outside of life and death and Meri, Duncan had other talents. He could take your life and ruin it in less than ten minutes. His thin narrow build and quiet demeanor made others take little notice of him. For this job, he wouldn't be entering the facility he would be outside ensuring our presence was not detected until we entered. He was the best male for the job and I was glad he would have my back.

The next to arrive was Abel and Kabel. Ryan was called by the receptionist at the front desk, the poor human didn't know what to do with the two vampires. I went with Ryan who seemed just as overwhelmed with the two as the receptionist. Abel and Kabel were a lot to take in with their contrasting personalities and physical characteristics. Abel with his dark skin, thin build and scar across his neck was standing next to Kabel in all his brightness. Kabel stood six feet six with blond hair that he wore long. His bright green eyes were always filled with humor as Abel's were always serious.

Abel kept a straight face while Kabel smiled and greeted the Lieutenant as if they were old friends. I tried to hide a smile as Ryan looked at me with a mixture of, is he serious and what have I got myself in. As soon as the two stepped clear of the front desk. Abel stepped forward; he bowed his head to me and then offered me his scarred hand. It was always the same with the vampire. I shook his hand quickly. He stepped to the side allowing Kabel to greet me. Kabel only gave me the proper bow when we were in a clan setting. This was not that so instead he bent down and scooped me up giving me a bear hug. In some ways I hated it. Outside of Santiago, I didn't let anyone, hellborn or human, pick me up. It made me feel like a child. With Kabel it was just the way he was. I gave him a hug back giving him two solid taps on the shoulder. He leaned his head back with a smile.

"Now you can do better than that female," he said with a smile.

"No, I can't. Now put me down Kabel."

He placed me on my feet and smiled down at me. I smiled despite my desire not to and shook my head.

"Why don't you follow me," Ryan said with a serious tone.

We walked through the squad room. Officers looked at both vampires. Kabel took the attention in stride, waving at a few of the women officers. Many of the gazes were on Abel as we moved. Between the scars he carried and the look he wore, he had a tendency to make humans nervous.

"So I hear we get to help kill the fuckers who took Isobel?" Kabel said with excitement.

"Yeah, you do," I answered.

"I can't wait. Abel and I were stuck with that asshole all night. Let me tell you what a whiny bitch he was all night long. "Oh the pain! My wrist hurts!" Kabel imitated Troy. I laughed because what else could I do but enjoy the show. "I can't wait for you to become one of us," he said, giving me a side hug.

"What did he say?" Ryan asked as we entered the room.

Crap! I hadn't told Ryan or Cain what I had planned or really what Hugo had planned for me. Kabel looked from me to Ryan. He gave me a look of contrite, before mouthing sorry to me.

"Sometime in the near future, I am to become a hybrid," I answered.

Ryan had stopped moving just outside the conference room. His face was tight and his eyes had a fire in them, like I had not seen before. If I didn't know any better I would think he was a hellborn.

"We'll talk about this later," he almost growled.

There was nothing to talk about. Whether Ryan liked it or not I was going to become a hybrid. He could bitch and complain all he wanted, it wouldn't change the outcome.

As soon as we walked in Kabel grabbed a hold of Meri giving her a big hug as well. She wrapped her arms around his neck, smiling. He whispered something in her ear, which made both of them laugh. As he put her down he looked at me with his big smile.

"See that's how you hug."

"No, that's how you two hug," I corrected.

Illingworth and Ms. Hudson both stood from their corner they had been working in.

"Kabel, Abel this is SSA Illingworth and the AUSA Victoria Hudson," I introduce the two feds.

Abel shook their hands quickly and stepped back away. He moved to the far wall placing his back against it so he could see the entire room. Kabel went over shaking hands, smiling at the two. Illingworth looked at the vampire, not sure what to make of him. Victoria Hudson on the other hand smiled at the male. She had put on an award winning smile as she straightened her suit and smoothed her hair. Kabel gave her a smile before I turned him away from the human.

"This is Sergeant Marcus Cain," I said.

Cain stepped forward shaking Kabel's hand. Abel just nodded at him from his wall.

"Hey, are you the one who helped out our female a while back?" Kabel asked.

"Yeah, that was me," Cain said unsure of what was coming.

"You're the best. Thanks for looking out for her."

Ryan was looking at all of us trying to figure out what he was missing. I ignored his stare and hoped Kabel would stop talking.

"I....uh..." Cain saw the look on Ryan's face. "It was nothing."

The phone rang once more stopping Ryan from asking any questions. I was betting it was the other vampires. I was grateful Santiago had shown up. There were days he had impeccable timing.

"Yeah," Ryan answered. "Send them back," he said shortly.

He walked past Kabel and Cain, stopping next to me. "I have a feeling I'm missing a big piece of some puzzle I had no clue I was missing. We will talk about all of this later."

"Yeah, I figured," I answered. What the hell was I going to say? At least I had time to figure it all out.

He walked to the door and opened the way for Santiago and the others as they crossed the squad room. There were eight vampires in total. Santiago and Cristian led the way, with Francisca and her mate Michael right behind them. They were both tall. Francisca was curvy like I was but had killer legs and caramel skin to make her even more breathtaking. Her dark hair fell in waves around her face. And her eyes were as dark as my mates. Her mate Michael was six foot seven making the others look small and built thick. His dark hair was almost as dark as Francisca's but not quite. The auburn highlights in his hair were subtle. He had dark grey eyes and soft tan skin. The pair made the rest of us look dull.

Ainsley was next to them dwarfed by the bigger vampires around her. She was my height making her the smallest of the group but she also had a bad ass ability. She could read thoughts. I had never seen her in a fight but she was almost a hundred and fifty years old, meaning she was probably lethal as hell. Females our size survived by knowing how to protect ourselves. Her delicate features made her look soft. Her blond hair was streaked with a soft brown color. Her eyes were almost a teal color with knowledge behind them. She was not nearly as curvy as myself, she was built more petite than curvy.

Behind her was Elizabeth, with her tall lean body. She wasn't as tall as Francisca who was almost six feet tall but she was close, only a few inches shorter. Her pale skin was flawless as she carried herself with elegance. Elizabeth had soft brown hair almost toffee color. She had an angular face but not in a harsh way. She would have been great on a fashion runway in New York or Paris with her build and looks.

Liam, my favorite Irishmen walked next to her. He was lean with muscular arms. Liam had a dry sense of humor and knew a thing or two about bombs and many assorted other things. He also only shared that sense of humor with those he knew well. Anyone who didn't know him or he didn't like only saw the cold exterior. Liam was smart and could read a situation as well, maybe better than I could. His intelligence light green eyes always watching what was happening around him. When I was attacked three months ago, Liam had been one of the vampires who had guarded me. He had made it his personal mission to keep me safe, until Robert's head showed up on my doorstep. I liked Liam better than most.

Bringing up the rear was Tony. He was tall and as thick as a wall, with muscles that were as large as the rest of him. Tony also had a heart of gold, he had taken my safety personally, just as Liam had. Tony and I became friends a year ago when I had threatened to set his family jewels on fire. For some reason it had made the large male like me.

I gave Santiago a quick hug stepping to the side allowing each of them to step into the room. They each bowed their heads to me as they entered. I gave Tony a pat on the back, which made him flash his bright pearly whites at me.

"Here are all the employment records for each of us?" Santiago said, handing Ryan a file.

"Thanks," Ryan took the file and saw the top page. "What? You are joining your wife on this?" Ryan asked.

"My mate and yes, I am. As the second in command of the Black Grove Clan it is my duty to take part in this operation," Santiago answered.

Ryan shook his head.

"I don't think this is a good idea for the two of you to do this together. You could become distracted and end up getting someone else hurt," Ryan pointed out.

"That's why we will be in two different groups. It will be fine, Ryan," I replied. "Now let me introduce everyone."

Introductions took some time. There was a lot of hand shaking as the vampires met the humans. It took several minutes for the room to quiet down and everyone to find their place. I cleared the whiteboard as they all took seats. Kabel seemed to be making fast friends with Cain. They sat next to each other laughing at one another's jokes. The only one left standing was Abel. He was still standing close to the door against the wall. I drew out a rough sketch of the bottom floor on the first whiteboard. I moved to the second board and drew the second floor.

"Okay. Here is a diagram of the ground floor of H&W Clinical. There are two entry points. We will be splitting into two groups. We don't know what kind of security they have as of yet but let's assume they have cameras on each entry point," I said as I marked the map. "Duncan, your job will be to get into their security system and make sure we have free movement throughout the building. I don't want them to see us until we enter the building," I ordered.

"It shouldn't be a problem. I'll see if I can find out what system they have. It will make it easier to bypass it."

"I have Devon and Malcolm outside the facility observing," Santiago said.

"If anyone can find out what they have it's Malcolm," Duncan replied.

"I will take a team from the front. While Santiago breaches from the back side. Team A is my team. Santiago, you are Team B. Meri, Watts, Liam, Tony, Cain, Ryan, and Kabel will be with me. The rest will be with Santiago."

"May I make a suggestion?" Santiago spoke up.

"Okay," I said with a tight smile. Santiago was used to being in charge as much as I was. Us working together on this was going to be a challenge.

"Tony should be on my team and you should take Ainsley."

"Why?" I asked.

"Because of her ability," Santiago pointed out.

"Her ability?" Illingworth questioned with narrowed eyes.

"I can read minds," she answered with a smile. "Francisca would be a better choice for Savannah's team than I would be."

Illingworth looked nervous. I smiled at Ainsley and then thought about what she was saying. Francisca had an interesting ability, it was like Meri's but was different, better in some ways. I hadn't asked her about it but I knew she could manipulate an individual's mind. Meri could get others to do what she wanted. Francisca could manipulate their thought process entirely. Ainsley was right with her assessment.

"I agree with Ainsley on this one. Francisca, you're with me. Tony you're with Santiago. Francisca depending on what the other two can tell us, I want you going in as one of the first to stop anyone from sounding an alarm."

"I can do that," she responded with a grin.

"Good. We don't know how many employees will be there but everyone should be prepared that they will be using charms on all of us. We have no clue how lethal the charms are but let's assume they will have deadly charms," I explained.

"How do we get into the loading docks?" Cristian asked.

"That is a question. I don't have an answer yet," I said. "Santiago, let's call Devon and Malcolm to see what they can tell us."

"As you wish."

He pulled his phone from his pocket and hit the contact for one of the vampires, placing the call on speaker. Devon answered after a few rings.

"Hey, Santiago."

"Devon, I am here with Savannah and the police. We were wondering what you and Malcolm have discovered about H&W?" Santiago asked.

"The place opens up at six in the morning. Most of the staff arrive around then. They enter through the front of the building. No key card or keys needed. There is a loading dock but we haven't seen any deliveries come through all day. From what we can tell there are three guards on duty at night. It looks like they are either human or witch. Most of them look like they won't be much of a challenge," Devon explained.

"What about cameras?" I asked.

"They have plenty of those. One on each corner with two on the front door. There is also a six on the back side. One on each corner, two covering both doors."

I marked the map as he spoke.

"It's Duncan. Do you know what system they're running?" Duncan jumped in the conversation.

"Yeah, I got in there this morning asking for directions. The receptionist was extremely helpful. They have SafePlace Security." Duncan made a note in his phone. "There are two doors behind the front desk. It looks like she has to buzz in anyone who wants to go through the doors but I'll see what I can find out tonight."

"What do you mean tonight?" I asked.

"I have a date with the receptionist tonight."

I rolled my eyes. Devon was a grifter and easy on the eyes. If she had any secrets Devon was about to get all of them out of her. He was damn good at being a thief. Rumor was he had grifted a De Vinci painting from another thief that had stolen it from an art gallery. He then turned around and sold the painting with a con-cocked story about it being handed down by his father. He made millions from it. I had no clue if it was true but if it was it was a testament to how good he really was.

"There are witches coming and going out of the place as we speak. I don't think they're employees though."

I nodded. Chances were they were the clinical trial patients.

"What time did that start?" I asked.

"Nine."

Patients? Once this was all done we would have to track all of the patients down to find out what they knew.

"Are there any buildings near the facility?" Ryan asked.

"Who's that?"

"Lieutenant Jamison Ryan of Sweetclover P.D.," Ryan said sternly.

"Damn... uhm... I mean not really. The area is an undeveloped area. There is a building half a mile from the place."

"What's the name of the business?" I asked.

"The Wellness Group."

Well we knew where they were located at least.

"Illingworth are you going to have a team on that building?" I asked.

"After the raid the other team will move in to collect documents from The Wellness Group," he explained.

I nodded my head.

"Let me ask you where is a good place to meet up?" I asked Devon.

"We parked a few miles out and walked in. The area around the place has grass that hasn't been cut in a while. Malcolm found a spot to hide out for the night," he explained.

"Malcolm, what is your take on the place?" Duncan asked.

There was a moment of pause in conversation when a deep voice came on.

"It's a secure facility. If you can get control of the cameras and the alarm system you can get in. The loading dock, I would guess is operated electronically so either you need to get in the system or you blow the fucking thing."

"What are the doors made of?" Liam asked.

"Steel," Malcolm answered.

Liam nodded, taking in the information. I could see the wheels inside his head turning.

"I'm coming out tonight. I'll be there by eight can you take me out to your hide?" Duncan asked.

"Can do," Malcolm replied in the affirmative.

"Savannah, when do you want to go in?" Duncan inquired.

I looked at the diagram of the building. We knew what time the staff arrived but not when they left.

"What time does your date get off work?" I questioned.

"Five," Devon replied quietly.

If most of the staff left between five and seven, the best time to hit the facility would be three or four a.m. Whatever security personnel were there, would be small. It would be late into the shift, so they would be bored and less focused. We could go in fast and hard eliminating all of the staff quickly. Less chaos than I had planned for.

"Three a.m.," I answered.

There were a few groans in the room, mostly from Cain.

"I'll send you a location where to meet us and we can drive you in," Malcolm said to me.

"Thanks Malcolm and Devon," I said.

Santiago ended the call and I looked once more at the diagram before turning to the waiting vampires and humans.

"Duncan, if you can't get the doors open I'll need to know ahead of time," I said, turning my attention to Duncan.

"You'll know by two," he replied.

"If you can't. I can take care of the back door," Liam offered.

"I figured you could," I smiled.

"What? How?" Illingworth asked.

"Liam has a colorful background and he is very good with explosives," I explained.

"Aye. Don't worry your pretty little F.B.I. head," Liam grinned at Illingworth.

"If Duncan can get the doors open, we stick to our teams and move in. We are taking only young alive out of the facility. If any witches get in the way, we have death warrants. Our job is to clear a path for Agent Illingworth and his team," I said to the room.

Everyone nodded their heads in understanding.

"If you see any young and you have the opportunity to get them out. Do it," Ryan chimed in.

"Illingworth, how many men are you bringing with you?" I asked.

"Fifteen."

"Okay. Once we're in you wait three minutes before you enter. We should have the bottom floor cleared and moving to the next floor, maybe even to the top floor," I said.

"Are you sure three minutes is enough?" he asked.

"Yeah, I am."

Ryan jumped in before Illingworth could argue.

"Everyone needs to be here by twelve thirty and we caravan from here," Ryan added.

"Meri and I can drive both of our vehicles."

"I will provide two of the vans the clan owns, as well," Santiago added.

"Do we need that many vehicles?" Cain asked.

"I want as many vehicles there as we can to move the young out of the facility to here," I answered.

"What about ambulances?" Cristian asked.

"No, it would tip them off. These hellborns have deep pockets." Ryan answered.

"We only call for an ambulance if one of the young is seriously hurt or one of us. Minor injuries we transport them back here. I don't trust anyone outside of the individuals in this room," I ordered.

"Any questions?" Ryan asked. There were a few head shakes. "Okay, see all of you tonight."

Chatter broke out once more as vampires and humans stood up.

"You mind if I head home with Duncan?" Meri approached me.

"No, go. I'll see you tonight."

I watched as she and Duncan headed for the door together. Her arm hooked in his as they left. Watts was next to follow saying goodbye to everyone. He fell right in with the vampires as if he was talking to a human. Most humans were either star struck by them or scared shitless. Watts didn't do any of that. He shook hands and spoke with everyone. I noticed Ainsley taking an interest in the human as they walked out together.

"Savannah..." came a soft deep voice from behind me.

I turned to find Abel, his face as serious as ever.

"I need to ask a favor?" he spoke softly

"Okay. What's up?"

"You need vehicles tomorrow. I was wondering if I may drive myself. I do not enjoy riding in those vans, they make me feel like... I...like I am being locked away."

I looked at the vampire who struck fear in most individuals. Right now, he looked nervous. If I was right about Abel's past it made sense why he would not want to ride in the vans.

"Yeah, that's not a problem."

I could see him relax enough for the hard look he always wore to return to his face.

"Thank you," he said bowing his head. He and Kabel left shortly after. One by one, everyone was gone leaving only Santiago, myself, and the three law enforcement officers.

"Are you coming home?" Santiago asked.

"I am. I want to sleep next to you before we do this tonight," I answered, taking his hand. "I just need to erase this first. Can you grab those plans on the table?"

"Of course," he said, pulling my hand to his lips. He kissed my knuckles causing me to catch my breath. I wasn't sure how much sleep was going to happen when we got home.

I erased the whiteboard. I didn't need anyone walking in here seeing what we were planning. Illingworth came over as I finished up.

"Is that really necessary?" he questioned.

"Yeah it is. I want to make sure there are no leaks."

"The U.S. Attorney is getting the warrants around four today. She knows a friendly judge who leans more towards hellborn rights."

"Good. I'm going to head home with my mate and get some sleep. If anything changes let me know."

"Listen Woods or De los Rios... I'm sorry for questioning your dedication to this."

"I understand why you did but thanks for saying it."

"Is the vampire really your mate?" he asked eyeing Santiago as he spoke with Ryan and Cain.

"Yes, he is. Why?"

"You two just seem different from each other."

I laughed at him.

"Trust me when I say there is more to my mate than meets the eye. Don't let his nice suits fool you."

"If you say so," he replied, eyeing Santiago.

"Trust me Illingworth my mate will be fine."

I walked away from him knowing he was watching as I headed over to my mate.

"We're going to head home," I said to the other two.

"That's a good idea. Cain and I are doing the same," Ryan said. "That vamp Liam, was he serious about using explosives?"

"Yes, Lieutenant, he was," Santiago answered.

"I hope Ember's mate can get those doors open," Ryan said.

"So do I," I replied.

"We will see you both tonight," Santiago said. We turned and headed for the door when Santiago stopped once more. "Agent Illingworth will you be here tonight as well?" Santiago asked.

"Yeah. I'll be here."

"Good, I look forward to working with you. Maybe we could share a vehicle tonight," Santiago offered with a smile.

I looked at my mate as we walked out of the room. I had no clue why Santiago would offer to ride with the F.B.I. agent. I waited until we were outside the station before I spoke up.

"What was that about?"

"He has taken an interest in you," Santiago said.

"And?"

"And I want him to understand whose mate you are."

"I already did that," I said.

"I am well aware you have but I am not sure he received the message."

I stopped Santiago in the parking lot, turning to face him.

"You know I have no interest in the human, right?"

"Yes but I do not like the way he looks at you. I have a right as your mate to put another male or man as it may be, in his place." I shook my head as I smiled at him. "You should also be aware if Matthew shows his face tonight I will eliminate him with no hesitation. The man in there I can handle with words. Matthew I will not," he placed a hand on my cheek. I leaned into his hand.

The thought of Matthew showing up added another element I didn't want. It made me want to switch the teams up and put Santiago on my team. The problem was I didn't want either of us to become distracted by the other.

"I know you will." He pulled my face to his and kissed me quickly. "Let's go home," I said as I stepped back. I looked around for his car.

"I rode with Cristian. We had business to discuss on the way here," Santiago explained. I unlocked my car. Santiago walked me to the driver's side, he opened the door for me. I

climbed in and started the car as he shut my door. He climbed into the passenger seat and we were off heading for peace and quiet that was all ours. I was looking forward to the next six hours we would have together.

Chapter Thirty-Three

Santiago and I arrived home and only slept for a few hours. When we left the station, I could feel my nerves starting to set in. We were going to a large facility to rescue at least forty hybrid young. There were going to be nerves because there were too many possibilities for things going wrong. What if the young were killed? What if one of our vampires were killed? What if Meri or Santiago were? The injury count could be small or it could be big. I hated this. Too many ifs and questions and not enough answers.

The alternative was we sat on the sidelines and human law enforcement was killed. If that happened, I couldn't live with myself knowing I could have done more. If you have the means at hand to act, then you should. I had the means to act and my involvement could mean less casualties over all. It was all that mattered. If I could stop Santiago from going in I would. I had a moment as I lay in bed next to him where I thought about just knocking him out. But then how long would he be down? When he came to, it would cause more problems than we needed. He would be rightfully angry at me. Not to mention, this was the way Santiago lived his life everyday with me. He always seemed calm and okay with it and yet every time I went to work, he had to deal with the worry that I wouldn't return. I was getting a taste of what Santiago went through and I was realizing how lucky I really was. Still I hated the idea of him being in danger.

I tossed and turned for a while, running the plan through my head repeatedly going over the steps to see if I had missed anything. Maybe I needed to force Illingworth to wait longer before he entered? Three minutes was going to be pushing it for him as it was. Five minutes would be too long because he would not be able to stand waiting that long. Maybe I should partner everyone up? No, that wouldn't last when things went crazy. I hated Ryan and Cain coming in with us. In truth I hated Watts going in as well. This was no place for a human. I was afraid they couldn't handle seeing twelve hellborns let loose on other hellborns. Saying it was going to get messy was an understatement. Maybe I should place a few people at the doors? To get anyone who we missed. That didn't seem like a bad idea but then who do I choose for that job?

I couldn't take laying in bed any longer, I checked the clock seeing I still had a couple of hours until we left. I needed to do something. I could feel the start of adrenaline as I headed for the closet. I could pack my bag, it wasn't much of an activity but it was better than fidgeting. I pulled a bag from a rack over my head. My normal hunter bag was already in the car, this one needed to be different. It needed weapons, blankets, water, extra clothes for Santiago, maybe extra supplies for my first aid kit. You could never have too many of those. I started with the blankets. I walked out of our bedroom and headed to the spare room two doors down from our room. The closet held spare bedding. I slid the doors open and started pulling blankets down. I had to pull the winter blankets out of my way. I dropped them on the floor as I went for the old ones I had before Santiago. The ones I had used when I curled up on my couch by myself in my townhouse. The ones I used during summertime. They were perfect for this. We had no clue what condition we would find the young in. We could only guess they would be in bad shape. I grabbed the blankets and threw them on the bed. I was just picking up the bedding from the floor when Santiago came in. He leaned against the door jamb in his pajama pants, bare chested watching me.

"What are you doing?" he asked.

"I'm getting a bag ready for tonight."

"What are the blankets for?"

"In case we need them for the young. Fairetree is two hours away to the south, it'll be colder down there than it is here. I want to make sure the young are warm."

"The F.B.I. is doing the rescue part of this or have you forgotten your own plan."

I stood on my tiptoes trying to shove the blankets back on the shelf finding it more difficult than it was to get them down. Santiago came over taking the bedding from me and placing them neatly back up on the shelf.

"I know they are, but we don't know the exact number of young that are in there and what if they don't have enough or we need them for the back of the cars. It can't hurt to have them," I answered staring at my mate. He placed his hands on his hips looking down at me.

"I know you are nervous about tonight but is this all necessary?"

"I don't know ...probably not but I have to do something."

Santiago nodded his head at me as he looked at the blankets on the bed.

"What else do you wish to pack?" he asked.

"Clothes for you and extra weapons. We should leave early to get water, just in case."

"Why would I need additional clothes?" he questioned.

"If your clothes are damaged during the breach then you have something to change into," I explained.

"I will be fine."

"You say that now until you end up in a tattered shirt and no replacement."

"Mi Amor, if I end up in ruined clothes I will be fine until we arrive home," he reassured me.

"I'm bringing extra clothes."

There was a pause as Santiago stared at me.

"There is no talking you out of this?" he questioned.

"No."

He kissed me on the forehead.

"I will take care of pulling out extra clothes while you pack the blankets and your weapons. I will call Cristian and have him bring two cases of water from the club," he offered.

I smiled at him as he headed for our room. I watched as he walked away enjoying the view. I closed the closet and picked up the blankets I had picked out, heading back to our room. I could hear Santiago in the closet talking on the phone. He was digging in a wood trunk in the corner of the closet, pulling out clothes.

"Yes, three cases. Add the replacements to the next order for Friday morning. Good. Thank you Cristian," he ended the call as I went to the safe.

"Three cases?" I asked.

"If we are going to plan for worst case scenarios, I thought three would be appropriate."

"Planning for worst case scenarios has always worked in my favor," I pointed out.

I headed for the bathroom finding my extra supplies in a basket under the sink. I added a few rolls of gauze, a box of gloves, and an unopened bottle of witch hazel, an extra box of bandages and surgical tape. I tossed them all in the bag. I looked at the supplies, I was packing and was beginning to worry Santiago was right, I was going overboard. I shrugged my shoulders and moved on.

I pulled out my nine millimeter and then the .22. I also grabbed two additional, loaded clips for both guns. I would carry my knife on my thigh along with a new purchase I had made only weeks ago. It was a long thin blade I could wear down my back. It came with a nylon shoulder harness that fit smoothly under my clothes. I would wear my hip holster for the nine and the twenty-two. Next I pulled out my own clothes. I pulled out a pair of my black pants along with a black tank top and a long sleeve black cotton shirt. The long sleeve would help with the chill in the night air and also help hide the knife. I slid the new blade into the bag. I would go with the guns on my hips along with the knife strapped to my thigh. The knife strapped to my back would wait until we got to Fairetree. It would be uncomfortable if I did it now. I zipped up the bag and threw my clothes on top of the bag. I grabbed my boots next and carried everything to the bedroom.

I dressed and began to strap on my holsters one at a time as I went. The first was the shoulder sheath over the tank top. The nylon was soft but I knew hours of wearing the thing would start to irritate my skin. I wanted none of that. The tank top would help prevent skin irritation. The long sleeve went on next. I hooked my belt on my pants and clipped on the nine millimeter. Next was the knife on my thigh. I pulled the velcro tight around my thigh and then checked my blade. I had no clue why I was checking the blade. I kept my weapons well taken care of. A man is only as good as his tools and all that jazz.

"Here are my extra clothes, as requested," Santiago said pressing his body against me as he brought laid clothes on top of the bag. I turned to see he was dressed. He wore a black T-Shirt that was tight over his shoulders, chest and arms. The shirt laid flat against his flat stomach. No one could ever really tell how well built he was unless you saw him in his more casual clothes. I had never known until the first night we had kissed how well he was built. I still remembered the surprise at the feel of him in the suit.

The shirt was tucked into black military style pants with combat boots. Santiago looked damn good dressed for a fight. I ran my hands up his hard chest enjoying the feel of him.

"Damn you look good." I said smiling.

"As do you."

"Maybe I need to take you on more hunts with me," I said.

He smiled showing his fangs. I hooked a finger in the neck of his shirt and pulled him down towards me. We kissed one another, feeding off each other's need. If we weren't careful, we would have to get dressed again. He pulled my body into his. I could feel his body responding as his hard erection pressed into my stomach. His hands slid from my waist down to my ass. My own body grew tight. Santiago growled as my scent changed. My hand was sliding down his body when my phone went off. I cursed as I broke the kiss, seeing a message from Duncan. He was working on the security system now and had already gained access to the cameras. I shot back a text releasing my hold on Santiago. As soon as soon my body lost physical contact with him every bit of nervous energy was back.

"We'll finish this later," I said, rising up on my toes and kissing him. A growl rolled up his throat in anticipation. The sound making me want to finish it now. Unfortunately, we had a job to do. I turned away from him placing his clothes in the bag and zipping it up.

"We most certainly will, Mi Amor," he whispered against my neck as he brushed my neck with his fangs making me want him even more. He took the bag from my hand and walked away from me. I was left standing there, wishing I was doing something completely different at the moment. I leaned against the bed, so I could step into my boots. It took only a minute to zip up my boots. I leaned back on our bed as I took a few deep breaths before I moved. I left the room trying to ignore my own needs, as I followed after my mate.

He was waiting at the door with keys in hand.

"Are you ready?" he asked

"Yes."

"Do you mind if I drive?"

"You hate driving my car," I pointed out.

"Tonight I wish to drive."

"Uh-huh, sure you do," I said with suspicion.

He was smiling at me as he ushered me out the door. His desire to drive had to do with Illingworth I suspected. I shook my head trying not to smile as we climbed into the car.

WE WERE THIRTY MINUTES early for the meet up but Illingworth and Ryan were already there. The teams would be arriving soon enough. The two were leaning against Ryan's unmarked sudan. I waited to exit the Suburban until Santiago opened my door for me. I placed my hand in his as we approached the two LEO's. Illingworth looked at both of us before dropping his gaze to the ground. Ryan was in tactical gear similar to Santiago's. It was weird seeing both of them out of suits.

"I should have known you were going to be here early," I said.

"I couldn't sleep," Ryan replied. "It's been a long time since I was involved in a raid."

"Don't worry, it's like riding a bike, you never actually forget," I remarked with a smirk.

Ryan shook his head at me.

"We got the warrants we need," Illingworth said.

"Good. We haven't gotten any calls from our guys. So it looks like H&W is none the wiser," I added.

"The tactical team should be here soon. None of them know what we're hitting," Illingworth added.

"It sounds like you don't trust them," I pointed out.

"I trust them to do their job but you made a good point about not knowing what they do outside of their job."

As we stood there talking, another vehicle pulled in followed closely by three other vehicles. The first vehicle was Meri's Range Rover. Next was the two vans the clan owned, followed closely by a Dodge Ram. I was confident that it was Abel's vehicle. I watched as all of the vampires exited the vehicles. The shocker was seeing Cain climb from one of the vans as he laughed it up with Kabel.

"I take it none of you could sleep either?" I asked as they approached.

"We can sleep after," Kabel replied, hugging me. He bowed his head at my mate.

We all stood talking to one another while we waited for the humans to arrive. It wasn't a long wait, five large Suburbans pulled in fifteen minutes later. I moved in beside Ryan and Illingworth as the humans climbed from their vehicles. I let Illingworth take the reins as the humans looked at all of us, knowing we were hellborns. There were some stunned faces, some who were not sure what to make of us, and only a few who didn't like we were even there.

"Alright let's get the show on the road," Illingworth called as he led everyone inside. The conference room was packed as everyone filed in. A map of the third floor of H&W was drawn on one side of the board with a drawing of the first floor on the other. Illingworth must have taken a photo of the plans earlier in the day. I stood next to Ryan off to the side of the board as Illingworth took center stage. My people knew the plan. I would speak when I was needed.

"I need everyone to turn off all cell phones now." Illingworth instructed the room. Everyone including my team followed the order. As soon as Illingworth was sure the phones were off he went on.

"We will be breaching a facility called H&W Clinical Research. We are entering a facility with a minimum of forty hybrid children. Our job will be to get the kids out while Hunter De los Rios and her team take care of the hostiles. They will enter through two points: the front door and the loading dock. We will wait three minutes before we enter. The kids are located up on the third floor in a maze of rooms. This is where it will get messy, so I need everyone communicating as we clear the rooms. We will be using channel three on the radio." Illingworth pointed to the map on the board.

"Why are they doing the entry?" one man piped up.

"Because serving a death warrant is a hunter's job, not ours. Our job is to retrieve the kids." Illingworth answered. "Any more questions?"

"So we're letting the monsters go in while we sit back? This is bullshit," the same man said.

That got a response from my people and a few on the rescue team as well. I watched as Liam began to stand up from a chair. Ainsley pulled on his arm giving him a shake of her head.

"Johnston..." Illingworth started as I stepped forward next to him.

"The facility we are going into is full of witches, who have been using these kids as test subjects. So yes, we monsters are going in first. They will have charms and possibly weapons. As a hellborn we can handle both better than the human body can. If you can't handle that there's the door," I replied, pointing at the door. The human stared at me and I stared right back.

"You have your orders. Johnston, if you can't handle your job, I can reassign you. Does anyone else have a problem?" Illingworth raised his voice as he spoke. "If there are any hostiles you come across you have the green light to shoot. No one is to move in until I say so. Now any more questions about the mission?"

No one said anything else.

"We will be meeting up with a few of my team members about two miles outside the facility. We will get final details there and gear up," I instructed.

"We follow De los Rios' team out. It's a two hour drive so get comfortable. Let's go," Illingworth added.

With that there was shuffling and loud scraps as humans and hellborns made their way out of the conference room. I walked beside Ryan behind the crowd. Illingworth was angling himself towards the man who had questioned the plan. I let him handle his people. I had enough to worry about than some asshat human who couldn't seem to follow easy enough orders, without spewing his hate. My team began to load up. Meri and Watts in her car. Cain climbed into one of the vampire vans while Ryan rode with Santiago and me. Santiago offered Illingworth a ride once more. He declined as he moved up beside Johnston. Illingworth was on that guy's ass climbing into the same SUV. It was going to be a long two hour drive in that car. We pulled out first with a train of vehicles to follow. If I thought the nerves at home were bad, now they were ten times worse. I could feel as my stomach tightening up as we hit the highway. I said a silent prayer that everyone one would come out of this alive including the young.

Chapter Thirty-Four
Two Days Before the Ceremony

By the time we met up with the others, Duncan was inside their network taking complete control of the security system. He tried to explain what he was doing but I couldn't follow all of his steps. My attention was on what was about to happen, not what Duncan was doing. All I cared about was that he could get us in without anyone seeing us until we were inside.

Devon's date had gone well. The witch didn't know much about what was happening but had given him information about the elevators and how many employees they had. There were a total of one hundred employees but at night only thirty were in the building, half of them were security. All she knew was that they were working on improving life for witches. She was not allowed on any of the upper floors. All I could think was how stupid she was. Who would work for a company that didn' allow you past the first floor? Wouldn't you want to know what was going on? Or maybe that was just me.

Devon would be staying outside of the fight, watching Duncan's back. It made me more comfortable knowing someone would be outside with Duncan. Malcolm would be going in with us. He had seen enough to know he wanted in. I set him on my team. He was thin and only a few inches taller than myself but he knew how to move quickly. He wore his black hair short, a buzz cut style and tonight he was wearing a skull cap hiding the top of his head. His black eyes against his fair skin were a stark contrast. His all black clothes reminded me that he was indeed a thief at some point in his long life but tonight he was a fighter.

We all geared up, the humans and I. I added the long blade to my body. I pulled my hair back in a tight ponytail. I double checked my clips before I strapped them to my belt. I watched as Ryan, Cain, and Watts strapped on additional tactical gear. I was glad they had some form of protection. I didn't know if it would do a lot for them but it couldn't hurt.

"I'll keep an eye on Marcus," Kabel said as I finished getting ready.

"Excuse me?"

"I know three of those humans are your friends."

"They are. Is that way you've been nice to him?" I asked.

"Nah. I actually like the guy, he's funny as hell. And has some of the best stories about you."

I rolled my eyes and made a note to smack Cain when this was all done.

"Don't worry. We got this," Kabel said patting me on the shoulder.

"Listen Kabel, I appreciate you watching his back but make sure you're keeping yourself alive as well," I ordered.

"I got this," he said, giving me a quick hug. I couldn't help but smile at him. He walked away joining the others. I checked the time it was almost time to move. I watched as he joined Cain. The two started up with their jokes once more.

"Here," Illingworth said, coming up behind me. He handed me a clear radio that hooked around my ear.

"What's this?" I asked.

"So we can communicate with your team."

The earpiece connected to a small radio that was no bigger than a key fob.

"Thanks." I hooked it on and could hear the chatter as individuals checked their radios.

"I brought enough to equip all of the teams," he added.

"I really appreciate it."

He nodded at me as Santiago came over.

"Are we ready?" Santiago asked me.

"I think so."

"May I have a moment with my mate, Agent Illingworth?" he asked.

"Not a problem. I'll get the troops organized," Illingworth walked away while I turned to face my mate. The thought of knocking him out and throwing him in the back of the Suburban was still an option in my head.

"Please be safe," Santiago said, placing his hands on the side of my face.

"You too. We have our ceremony in two days. I don't want to be left without a mate for that," I tried to joke with him.

We kissed tenderly for only a moment.

"I will see you inside, Mi Amor."

"Okay," I said. Santiago went to join his team while I closed the back of my car up. I handed my keys to Devon before I joined everyone. I took a steadying breath as I watched my mate walk away. Why did he have to be here? I would have been nervous without Santiago here. His presence made the pressure and anxiety worse. I scanned the area once more seeing nothing and no one around.

We headed out in two groups towards the building. I held my gun low at my side as we moved. There was a black fence around the property, Malcolm had already picked the lock on. We slipped inside and moved across the open field quickly. I took my group to the left of the front doors as Santiago took his group around the back. The front doors were two glass panel doors. I looked at the doors and knew as soon as we approached it would begin. I could see three guards at the front desk as we stood to the side. Francisca stood beside me. I waited for a voice to say in my ear team B was in position. One more breath and the count of three in my head before I shouted into the radio.

"Go!"

I moved on the doors as I pulled on a line that ran under the building and hit the glass double doors with an energy ball. The glass exploded with shards flying inside. I moved quickly as the glass hit the ground. I didn't look at my team as I moved. Instead I took the first guard out, who popped up from behind the long reception desk. Two shots to the chest had the guard's body jerking back before it fell to the ground. Another came around the desk, Francisca moved on him quickly, grabbing the witch around the throat and forcing him to look at her. He was a ley line witch. I watched as a ball of red fire formed in his hand. I was about to call a warning when he took the energy and shoved it at the desk he had been sitting at. Screams filled the air as the desk went up. Someone had been hiding behind the desk. I watched as a male took off running towards a door to the right, his body engulfed in flames. The witch Francisca had by the throat, was thrown on the flames engulfing the desk. No sound came from him as his body caught fire.

My team was already heading to the doors that lead to the elevators and the stairs. I moved with them. As soon as we were on the other side I waved Ryan, Cain, and Kabel to do a search of the rest of the floor. I could hear fighting in the back of the building as we went through the doors. Two of Santiago's team came through the door. The mate in me wanted to go back there but instead I moved to the end of the hall where the stairs were located. We ran up the stairs. Watts, Liam, and myself took the second floor while I sent the others up the third floor. Watts pulled the door open, holding it while Liam and I went through. As soon as we entered the floor, witches started coming out of rooms. Charms were launched at us. Watts began to fire, while Liam moved down the hall as if nothing could touch him. The growl that flowed out of the male was a sound of fury. He grabbed a witch, who had a charm in his hand. The witch tried to bring the spell down on Liam's head. He was too slow as Liam grabbed the witch's arm, breaking the limb. There was a scream as the bones shattered. Liam wasted no time breaking the male's neck before discarding the body. Witches and humans poured out of the room to the right of us. Chaos had begun. Charms and magic began to fly. Liam moved quickly as he grabbed another witch, I watched as he sank his teeth into his next victim's throat and pulled back. He dropped the male with blood pouring down his front and continued to move as if nothing had happened.

I moved down the hall firing my gun until it clicked empty. I dropped the clip and added another in one fluid motion. I saw as a large charm, the size of my fist as it began its descent on me. I threw a shield up as the spell hit. The spell had been powerful enough for me to feel the impact on the shield. I holstered my gun as I staggered slightly under the impact. Liam was moving too fast for me to track and I was worried I would hit him. I dropped the shield as I pulled more energy from the line. I threw an electric blue ball, hitting two witches at the same time. Both went down twitching as the magic ate away at their bodies. I pulled the knife on my back as a human approached. He had two charms in his hand. I gave him no chance to act as I ran at him swinging my large knife. I took him in the side cutting deep into his body. I pulled the knife free and moved on as the man died slowly on the floor. Screams and growls were everywhere punctuated with gunshots.

I entered the first room on the left side of the hall. The room was large with an operating table in the middle of the room. A large light sat overhead. There was a team of humans and witches with masks and gloves standing over a young's body. The young was female, no older than four. She was asleep, strapped down to the table with steel bands at her legs and around each wrist. The surgeon had a scalpel in hand. I switched the blade to my other hand and pulled my gun.

"This is a sterile environment. You can't..." I raised my gun at his head as I moved in on all of them.

"Drop the scalpel," I ordered.

"This is..." the doc got no further when I put a bullet in the female witch standing next to him. The blood from her head splattered across the doctor's scrubs.

"The next hellborn or human who moves without my permission gets the same treatment. Now, please put down the scalpel and wake that young up. Get her ready to move out of this room."

He set the scalpel down slowly. He nodded to a human who was at the young's head. I watched as he injected meds into an I.V. One of the nurses began to pull the tube from the female's throat. I saw the movement to the left of me. A female began to move towards me. My bullet took her in the chest. She jerked and collapsed. I moved deeper into the room. I swung the large blade up and out sliding it back into its sheath.

"Anyone else?" No one made a noise. I pressed the small button on the radio. "I have a young on the second floor."

"On the way," I heard a voice in my ear.

"What were you doing to her?" I demanded.

"We were doing exploratory surgery. The female has developed a lesion on her liver."

"What's her name?"

"Number 56971," the surgeon answered.

"That's not her name. What is her name?" I growled.

"When the specimen enters the facility they're only referred to by their case number," the doctor explained.

Specimen? These were young and they were referred to as specimens. No names, just numbers. The door opened and Ryan came in.

"What do we have, De los Rios?"

"Female young, who needs to be moved out."

Ryan approached the table. "Release the bands now," Ryan demanded.

A nurse reached under the table. I turned my gun on her.

"The release is here," she said with panic in her voice.

I gave her a nod. I heard metal moving against metal and the steel straps pulled away from the girl's extremities. I could see burn marks from the straps on her legs and around her wrists. Her poor little wrists were bleeding. Ryan picked the girl up gently and removed her from the room. I could hear her moan slightly. Ryan made a soothing noise. I waited for the door to close behind him before I did anything else. I shot the other two witches in the room. I dropped the empty clip from the gun and added the new clip. I released the slide, chambering a round, before I pointed it at the human surgeon once more. There were three humans left for me to deal with. I wanted to kill them as I had done with the witches but the warrant didn't cover them, unfortunately.

"Was that necessary?" he asked.

"Yeah it was. I have a death warrant for the hellborns who work in this facility. Would you like to join them?"

He looked at me as if he was unsure if I was serious or not. I let the feeling of death fill my eyes.

"You wouldn't," his voice shook a little.

Liam popped his head inside the room. He took in the sight of the dead bodies on the floor.

"The floor is clear but your human is down," Liam said.

"Which one?"

"Watts."

"Is he breathing?" I asked. I could feel the panic inside of me.

"Aye."

"Get him down to the vehicles,"

"You want me to take care of these?" he nodded his head towards the three humans."

"No." Liam said nothing else just left me to it. "Line up against the wall. Hands up."

Instead of killing them, I patted each of them down finding nothing on them.

"Walk," I said, forcing my gun against the surgeon's head. They fell in line one at a time. As soon as we were out in the hall. They each took in the sight. There were bodies scattered with blood painting the white tile floor. Blood splattered the walls as well. The human nurse started to cry.

"Move towards the stairs," I ordered.

They continued to follow orders. We reached the stairs with the woman sobbing as we moved. I was beginning to wish I had shot them. They entered the stairwell and moved just as two agents were coming up.

"You two take them down and cuff them," I ordered.

"We have more kids up there."

"I'll go up, you take them,"

They did as they were told. I watched as the humans walked down the stairs before I moved on.

The top floor looked a lot like the second floor did. Blood and broken bodies lay on the ground. I holstered my gun. It appeared the fighting was over. The main door to the third floor was propped open. I watched as young after young were walked out or carried through the door. I slid past two agents who were helping three young to the elevator. The young were sickly thin and scared as they were ushered out.

I entered the space where the young had been held prisoner. I looked at the young as they were slowly moving towards the door. One of them was my height but he was thin, almost skin and bones. His fair skin was pasty white and he had dark circles under his eyes.

Another of the young had brown eyes that had a dazed look as if she were a walking zombie. The zombie was maybe nine years old. They were all so thin and frail looking. I could see burn marks on their arms and legs. They all wore hospital gowns as they moved. Another male was covered in what looked like small round burn marks. There was a female being carried out by one of the F.B.I. agents. She had dried blood down her leg. I could fill in the blanks as to what she had endured.

I found Meri in the maze of rooms. Hands on her hips looking like a mess. I could see she had a bruise under her right eye. Dry blood coated her arms and hands. A burn on her side, her blackened flesh showed through a hole in her shirt. Any pain she may have felt held no weight as what we were witnessing. She watched as each young was carried out. The horrors we were seeing were like no other.

"There you are?" she said as I approached.

"How's it going?"

I looked at the room for the first time. It was a six by six room with a bed, a tankless toilet and nothing else. I moved to the small bed finding a crank of the same kind that was on the gurney in the O.R.

"You turn it and steel straps come up to lock them to the bed," I said.

"For fuck's sake," she spat. Meri had a look of disgust. "We found one young who has fur coming out of her body. Another is blind."

"This is so much worse than I thought it would be," I said quietly.

"Most of the young are out," she informed me. Meri's voice was hollow as she spoke.

"Let's start searching rooms together to make sure we don't miss anyone."

She nodded and we moved as one through the place. Every room was a carbon copy of the next. There were no pictures or anything other than a toilet and bed with those terrible straps. We were in the fourth room when a call from Duncan came through the ear piece.

"We have a straggler in the loading dock!" Duncan yelled.

There was some chatter as one talked over the other. Meri and I kept moving looking under each of the beds as we searched. We had only gone into three more rooms when Duncan came back on.

"SHIT! Someone get down there and stop that male now!" Duncan yelled.

Less than a minute later.

"He threw a lever before we could stop him," Kabel was speaking now.

I looked at Meri as the radio went silent. Meri and I stood still as we waited for someone to say something.

"What's going on down there?" I questioned.

There was a moment of silence before anyone spoke.

"Everyone out of the building now!" Duncan demanded.

"Smoke," came another voice.

"The stairwell is filled with smoke," came another.

"The building is on fire," Duncan broke in.

I looked at Meri.

"I'll finish searching you go," I ordered.

"Like hell I will! I go when you go," she shot back.

"Meri, don't be stupid. Go!"

The chatter continued, I ignored it as I looked at Meri. I needed to make sure all the young were gone. I couldn't just run out and leave any to die.

"Fuck that!" she spat at me. "I leave when you leave."

"Savannah, where are you," came Santiago's voice in my ear.

"Meri and I are on the third floor."

There was more chatter about smoke filling the corridors below. I heard someone say the fire department was on the way.

"I'm coming in for you," I heard Santiago break through.

"NO! Meri and I are on our way out. Do not come in here! Do you hear me Santiago?" I yelled at him.

There was some more chatter.

"Savannah, I am coming...."

"Don't you dare," I growled over him.

There was some chatter and I turned my radio off and looked at her.

"Let's make this search quick," she said.

We started once more searching each room. It didn't take long for the smoke to reach our floor. It started small with the smell of burning concrete filling our sinuses. We kept going through the rooms one at a time as fast as we dared. We made it to the final room.

"Let's get out of here," Meri said as she scanned the room.

The smoke was almost black and hard to see through. We were leaving the room when we heard a cough. Both of us paused.

"Hello? This... is the police ...Is anyone... in here?" I called out around my coughs.

More coughing came. Meri moved into the room and I followed. Under the bed was a small young, her brown hair was a mess. Her eyes were bright blue as fear set in.

"We're here... to get... you out," Meri told her as she pulled the girl out. Fear filled her eyes as she tried to claw at Meri. She looked the young in the eye and the young female stopped fighting.

Meri didn't wait for any other response just wrapped her arm around the female. I grabbed Meri's hand and began to guide us through the rooms. The entire third floor was filled with smoke now. The flames would be reaching us soon enough. I found the hall that led from the rooms to the stairs. I could feel as my lungs were filling with smoke and soot. My chest felt as if the flames were inside of me. It took us several minutes to reach the stairs. I opened the door feeling the heat of the fire down below. I looked at Meri.

"What do we do?" she asked.

We had to get down. The elevator wasn't safe and flames were definitely in the stairwell. We could stop and hope the fire department reached us before we died or I could try something I had never done before. I heard of ley line witches who could hold a shield as they moved. I had only done it a few times and never more than a handful of steps. I would have to hold it through the fire and down three flights of stairs. The smoke was already too thick to breath around. Smoke inhalation would kill the female and me. The fire would be what would get Meri. I couldn't let either of them die so I was going to go for option number two. If I failed we were all going to die together. If I didn't try it we were all going to die. Boy were those great odds. Both of our mates were outside watching as the building was going up in flames. I didn't know how long either would stay out of the building before they came in for us. I couldn't have that either.

"Is your radio still on?" I asked.

"Yeah."

"Good." I pulled on the line one more time and forced as much energy as I could into my body. My body began to vibrate with the energy as I formed the shield around us. The shield was like a bubble that engulfed us. As soon as it was in place the smell of smoke died away and was replaced with the smell of ozone.

"Should I let them know?" she asked.

I nodded my head too afraid to speak.

"We're good. Savannah and I have a young and we're heading out now."

I took her hand in mine again and we went down the stairs together. I felt the shield shift as we moved with each step. I focused on our protection keeping it in place as my feet moved slowly. I kept my metaphysical hand on the line and prayed I could keep it up. I continued to pull energy from the line pushing out around us.

The little female had started to cry. The trance Meri had put her in was gone. She curled into Meri as we moved. I could hear Meri trying to sooth her but my focus was on the shield, I had no clue what she was saying. We reached the second floor to see nothing but flames and smoke. I pulled tighter on the line and more energy flowed around us. My body felt as if it was coming apart at the seams. My muscles were straining as the magic continued to flow out of me into the shield. I could feel as a small trimmer was beginning in my legs. I ground my teeth and kept moving, pulling Meri and the female even closer to me. I could feel the heat of the flames as we moved. The progress was slow but we made it to the ground floor. I tried to pull the door open finding it took too much of my focus. The shield was fraying on the edges. Small amounts of smoke were seeping into our bubble. I could see small holes as the fire ate away at the shield. Meri released my hand and grabbed the door throwing it against the wall. She grabbed my hand as we moved with her guiding us this time, I tried to keep going. I pulled on the line trying to patch the shield. I could feel my legs become more shaky as we made our way through the first floor. The trimmers were moving up my body now. I could feel it in my arms and chest. Pain was searing through my gut now as if there were hands ripping me apart.

There was a loud crash to the left that shook the floor. Meri pulled me in tighter to her body as we walked. We were almost to the door when a piece of the upper floor came crashing down in front of us. The shield clasped. The heat of the flames was so great I was sure we were about to cook to death. I still had energy flowing through me but I was unsure I could do it again. Another piece of the ceiling came down around us, pieces of concrete flying at us.

I closed my eyes and focused what little energy I had left in me. I clung to Meri as she hugged the small female to her. I was able to get another shield up. We moved around the falling debris reaching the doors, finally. My legs were having a hard time functioning now. I could feel my feet beginning to drag. I almost tripped as we stepped out of the building. I made it a few more feet from the front door before I collapsed, hitting the hard ground. I felt as my face make contact with the concrete walkway. I heard voices and felt a great rumble around me as darkness claimed.

Chapter Thirty-Five

I came to in the back of a car as coughing ensued. My lungs felt like they were on fire and my throat was melting away. An oxygen mask was placed over my face. I tried to open my eyes but didn't have the energy for it. I felt a hand on my face and knew the touch all too well.

"I am here," he whispered in my ear.

I tried to speak and failed. Darkness came for me once more. I tried to fight it but it was no use. I remembered pleading with the gods above that this was not death coming for me.

I woke up a second time. This time the pain I had felt in the vehicle was not as bad. I found I could open my eyes, which was an improvement. I was in a hospital bed with an oxygen mask that was cranked up on high. I could feel as the air pushed harshly into my mouth and nose. I pulled the mask away from my mouth. I looked around the green room seeing no one in the room. Where was Santiago? He was okay, wasn't he? He was in the car with me? Had the first consciousness been a dream? If so, where was Santiago? A panic entered me as I tried to sit up. My body was so weak it couldn't seem to follow my commands. I tried again as a machine began to scream. I was able to get myself upright only a few inches. I heard the door to my right open and a rush of bodies came in.

"Mrs. De los Rios you need to stay calm. You are at Sweetclover Medical Center," said a female voice.

"San..Santiago ...Where is..." I gasped.

"You need to relax, you are okay. I need you to breathe deeply for me," a woman in purple scrubs came into view. She pushed the mask back on my face. I could hear as more than one person moved around the room. It was all a blur as I tried to communicate with someone. Someone had to tell me where my mate was.

"Where...wh...is...my...ma...te.." I tried again.

"Ma'am, you need to calm down," she pushed me back down and I could feel as a hand found my arm. I tried to push it away and failed. Where was he?

I was panting as I tried to communicate with the woman above me. The panting was becoming worse as I tried to ask again where Santiago was. I felt as my arms began to fight the other hands. I couldn't breath even with the oxygen mask on. Dizziness was setting in and my vision was becoming fuzzy. Oh God! Did he go back in? Had Santiago died trying to get to me? Oh no! No this could not be happening! I continued to fight with the hospital staff as a new panic was setting in the center of my chest.

There was chatter around me as I tried to get up again. The next thing I knew a calmness swept over me, followed by a large hand in mine. I turned my head to the left seeing his almost black eyes. There was worry in his eyes as he looked at me. The calmness was like a blanket as it spread over my body. Oxygen was slowly sliding into me now. I could feel tears rolling down my face.

"I am here, Mi Amor. I am here," he pushed past someone and began to stroke my head. The beeping and yelling stopped as my mate took control of the situation. I was trying to breathe normally but my crying was becoming worse as I realized he was alive. The fear he was dead was now gone, replaced with deep gratitude to the fates.

"We need to sedate her before she goes into another panic attack," a female voice said.

"No, she will be fine," Santiago stated finality.

"Sir, your wife has already had one panic attack. If she has another one it could..."

"She is fine now! You will not sedate her, do you understand me," he said shortly.

"Sir..."

"If she has another one then you can sedate her. As of right now she is not. You need to leave this room," he growled as he stood up right.

There was some more talk but I couldn't take my eyes off of him to care what was being said. He looked back at me as he started to rub my head again. The room became quiet as he sat down on the side of my bed. I pulled back the oxygen mask from my face enough so I could talk.

"I woke up... and...you weren't here," I rasped.

"I was checking on a few of our vampires and Antoine Watts."

"I was scared you were dead," I said as I started to cough, the tears were still going. "I thought... I had dreamed... you were in the car with me."

"I am very much alive."

"I am so happy you are," I tried to take a breath to stop the tears and found it hurt to do so. "I thought you went back in for me..."

He brushed the tears away, as I tried to calm down. A new wave of calmness came over me.

"I tried to but it Kabel, Cristian, and Tony held me back. One of the reasons I had to go check on our vampires."

"Wait? What?"

"I broke Kabel's arm in three places and Cristian needed stitches. Duncan did his own damage to Devon and Abel."

"From you?"

"Yes. They should have not tried to stop me. By the time I broke away from them you were out of the building," Santiago explained.

"I'm so happy they stopped you," I reached up to touch his cheek. He took my hand and kissed it as he looked at me. "What if you had gotten trapped?"

"I am grateful to them as well. Just as I am grateful you are alive. I am quite upset with you. You broke a promise to me," he said. I could see the anger in his eyes. As grateful as he was, I was alive, he was down right pissed off at me. He was right, I had broken a promise to him. He had every right to be angry.

"I had to get that female out."

"From what I understand you and Meri did not find her until after the fire had started. You ignored our calls to leave."

I was going to kill Meri for telling him the truth.

"Do not be mad at Meri. I forced her to tell me. I am one of her leaders. She had no choice but to tell me."

He looked at me. I guess I couldn't be too mad at her, he had pulled rank on her. It was exactly what I would have done if the roles were reversed.

"I'm sorry I took a chance but if I didn't that young would have died in the fire. I couldn't live with myself without making sure there were no young left behind," I explained.

"And I could not have lived if you had died."

"I know. I'm sorry."

"I accept your apology Mi Amor, for now," he said.

"Is Devon and Abel okay?"

"They are fine. Nothing a feeding will not fix."

"Did we lose anyone?" I asked.

"Three agents were killed in the fire. None of our people died but we did have some injuries. Antoine was hit with a sleep charm. He is awake now and will be released tomorrow. Meri is healing as we speak. She is in the next room receiving treatment for smoke inhalation and for the burn on her side. She will be released tonight after she feeds. Michael was also injured by a charm, a draught..."

"Draught of the dead. Is he okay?" I finished for him.

"They thought he was dead but he is on the mend. He will go home tomorrow. If he had been one of the humans it would have killed him," Santiago explained.

"When do I get out of here?"

"Tomorrow. If you are lucky," Santiago overrode me before I could argue. "Which brings me to my next topic. I am going to have Hugo cancel the party tomorrow."

"No," I replied.

"You are in no condition for a party."

"I believe that is up to me. I say yes I am. Or I will be," I said defiantly.

"Be reasonable," he begged.

"I thought you were dead just minutes ago. That was enough for me. No, Hugo is having the party and we're having our ceremony in two days. I will not delay any of it, only for something else to get in our way."

"What is one more week?" he countered.

"A week too long. Besides I want the next week to be about us. Not anything else."

He looked at me with frustration.

"If you are sure then we will stick to our plans."

"I am. Now I need to go see our people," I said as I tried to get up.

"Mi Amor, you need to rest."

"I need to go see them."

I was able to push myself up a little when Santiago's hands pushed me back into the bed.

"Savannah, I will take you in an hour," he offered, frustration in his voice. He used my name, which meant I may have been pushing him to his breaking point.

"Why in an hour? No, I need to go see them now."

"I would like to spend this time with you. You are not the only one who thought their mate was dead only hours ago. I thought you were dead. I want to have a little time with you," he said.

How could I say no to that? I couldn't and Santiago knew it.

"Fine in an hour," I said lying back. He pushed the oxygen mask back up on my face as he sat on the edge of my bed.

Chapter Thirty-Six

An hour passed quickly and as promised, I made the rounds to all who had been injured. Meri was my first stop. She was doing well and would be getting out of the hospital in the next few hours. She gave me the details about what had happened to me and the building. According to Meri, I got us more than a few feet from the building. It was more like five or six feet away. As I collapsed, so had the building as if it had stayed upright long enough for us to get out. The F.B.I. was already making announcements that they had taken down a company who were working under false pretenses and kidnapping hellborn young. They even threw a nod our way saying we assisted them. Of course Illingworth had gotten the credit. The owner of H&W Clinical Research was a female named Charlene Montgomery, she was a witch who was from North Carolina. The government now had a federal warrant out for her. Every hunter in the country would be looking for her. Meri and I had a moment, thinking that we should go after her ourselves. Our mates promptly shut the thought down.

The F.B.I. moved in on The Wellness Group. Documents were recovered and employees from both companies were being rounded up. My guess, a number of them were on the run as soon as the news broke.

In total, we had found forty-four young and all of them suffered from malnutrition and a number of them had illnesses that were uncommon for hellborns. Duncan had obtained all the records from the facility dating back to the nineties. Hundreds of young had perished in that place. The worst part was no one had ever noticed or cared until now.

The more Meri told me, the more I was glad I had been unconscious. Duncan was as mad as Santiago at the two of us for our little stunt. I apologized and pointed out I had ordered her to leave. My statement made my mate angry at me once more and Duncan even more at Meri. The two males would have to get over it eventually.

My next stop was Cristian. He was preparing to leave the hospital as Santiago rolled me into the room.

"Cristian, how are you?" I asked.

He bowed to the two of us before he answered.

"I will heal once, I have fed. It may take a few feedings but I will heal fine," he said stiffly.

The vampire had a bandage down his side, along with one across his cheek. He had a black eye on the left side of his face. I wasn't sure which injuries were from the breach and which were from my mate. As I looked at Cristian, I felt guilty for my mate's actions. Santiago, acting upon instinct had harmed three of our people to get to me. His actions were the response to my decision to stay and search the building. The wounds that Cristian had suffered were my fault and not Santiago's.

"Cristian, thank you for keeping Santiago out of the building."

"It is my duty to ensure he was safe."

"Still thank you. If it hadn't been for you, Tony, and Kabel he could have died."

The vampire took a breath and sat down on the bed.

"Santiago, do you mind if I have a moment with your mate?" he asked.

Santiago looked at Cristian for a moment. I looked up at my mate and nodded my head.

"I will wait outside," he answered, squeezing my shoulder.

Cristian waited for Santiago to pull the door shut before he spoke.

"I know you outrank me and I respect everything you did today. You are a smart female and you are good at your job."

"But?" I said feeling the word was right there on the tip of his tongue.

"What you did was reckless and not only did it almost kill you but him. You are more than just a hunter now. You are Santiago's mate and part of our clan. Taking a risk like you did would have had greater consequences than just you."

"I had to make sure we had all the young, Cristian. I wasn't trying to be reckless, I was trying to do my job," I defended my actions.

"The problem is you have more than one job now. What if we hadn't stopped Santiago from going after you? You both could have died. Where does that leave the Clan? Don't you think Dante would have tried to move into his place? What if you had died? Do you know what it would have done to Santiago? Vampires have died from the loss of their mate's."

Cristian was right if Santiago had died Dante would have been free to make a move for his seat and then Hugo's. The thought of Santiago dying hurt deep inside my chest. I rubbed the center of my chest trying to ease the pain that had suddenly flared to life.

"What are you saying I should do? Quit my job? Walk away from Santiago?" I questioned.

"No... I'm just saying you need to think before you act. You need to remember there is more than one hellborn relying on you. There is a clan of vampires that need the two of you. You and he are good for one another. I believe you are good for the clan. I am asking for all of us, for you to stop being reckless and start thinking about the rest of us."

What Cristian was saying was somewhat true. I didn't regret staying because I saved the little female but the fact that Santiago could have died because of me scared me. What was I going to do? I wasn't willing to give up my job but maybe I needed to think about what could happen if I didn't. There had to be a balance, right? I looked at the vampire in front of me. The worry he was feeling was clear.

"I will do better in the future, for all of you. I'm still learning my role here, Cristian. All I can say for now is that I'm sorry for putting you in the position I did."

Cristian nodded his head before he spoke.

"Thank you," he stood up and pushed my chair towards the door. I pushed the sliding door open for him as he wheeled me out of the room. Santiago was standing beside the door. Cristian pushed my chair into Santiago's capable hands.

"I am heading to the club now, Santiago," he said with a bow.

"No. You need to go home. Hugo has closed the club in preparation for the party tomorrow."

"We do not need a full twenty-four hours to set up," Cristian argued.

"No, you do not. I believe he and Dante are taking time together as well."

"The closer the two of them get the more I dislike it."

"As do we my friend," Santiago put a hand on the male's shoulder. "Now go home and rest," Santiago ordered.

Cristian bowed his head to both of us once more before he turned to leave. Santiago and I watched as Cristian made his way to the exit.

"Is everything alright between the two of you?" Santiago asked.

"Everything is fine."

I could feel the hesitation in Santiago as he wheeled me down the hall. Santiago wanted to know what had transpired between Cristian and I but he would not ask for fear of upsetting me.

"Who would you like to see next?

"Kabel, please. I owe him an apology."

"For what?" Santiago questioned.

"For being a little on the reckless side," I answered.

"Is that what you and Cristian were speaking about?"

"Yes. He made some valid points."

Santiago pushed the wheelchair to the side of the hallway, in front of a bench. He took a seat in front of me and grabbed my hands into his.

"What did he say?"

"That is between Cristian and I," I answered.

"Savannah?"

I looked at him and leaned forward. I kissed him quickly before I sat back.

"I am more than a hunter now. I am your mate and part of the clan. When I made the decision to stay and search the facility, I did it because I was thinking about one of the young dying in a fire. I wasn't thinking about you or the clan. I ordered Meri to leave because I was willing to put my life on the line but not anyone else's," I explained.

His head dropped looking at our clasped hands.

"I need you to start thinking about what it would mean if you died," he said his voice tight.

"I know."

"If you had not made it out... If you had died in there it would have destroyed me." Santiago's voice was rough.

"I am sorry. I am so sorry for what my actions did to you and the others," I leaned forward taking one of my hands from his. I placed it on his check pulling his face up to meet my gaze. "I will do better. I swear to you, I will. I won't stop doing my job but I will stop being so reckless with my life. But you have to promise me something as well?"

"What?"

"If I die you have to swear you will not give up. You have to swear you will carry on and never ever try to come after me again," I said.

"I cannot give you that. I will always come for you. Always."

"I love you for that but the clan needs you. They have to come first," I argued.

There was a long pause before Santiago dropped his head.

"If you die I will carry on without you, I can give you this promise. But I will not swear to the other. I cannot. You are my mate and I will always come for you."

I kissed him and winced as I leaned closer to him. My body hurt. I wasn't sure if the pain was from the shield I had held up, the ley line energy I had pulled through me, or the fire. Santiago pulled back stroking my hair from my face.

"Let's go see Kabel," I said. He nodded and stood up.

Kabel's arm was in a cast up to his shoulder. He was awake and laughing as Cain sat in a chair next to the bed talking. We enter the room with Kabel's boom of a laugh filling the space.

"There she is?" Kabel said.

"Good to see you, Woods. I mean De los Rios," Cain eyed me with a grin. "You know I think I may have to switch to your first name. De los Rios is a mouthful," Cain said.

His clothes were dirty and he had some bruises on his cheek and neck.

"You doing okay, Cain?" I asked.

"Yeah, just a little banged up. How about you?"

"I'll be fine. I get out tomorrow."

"So I guess the big day is still on?" Kabel asked.

"Yes it is," switching my attention to Kabel. "How are you doing?" I asked, reaching for his hand.

"I'm good. I got one of my women coming by to feed me and will be fine by your big day," he said with a smile.

"Good," I said, returning the smile. "Thank you for stopping Santiago from going back in for me. I really appreciate what you did."

"It's all good. Let me tell you, no one had any clue what he was capable of until he did this," Kabel pointed to his arm.

"I saw him inside. Your husband is a badass," Cain added.

I smiled at the two of them.

"Yes he is," I replied. "I also owe you an apology."

"For what?"

"For my recklessness. If I had thought through what I was doing you wouldn't have gotten hurt."

"Look the way I see it, you saved that young, actually all of those young. You were doing your job. And Santiago was just doing what a mate does," Kabel shot back.

"Thanks for that but I still need to say I'm sorry."

"Fine. Go ahead," he said with impatience in his voice.

I smiled at him.

"I'm sorry for putting you in the position where you had to act against Santiago."

"Wow! I have never heard her apologize. I've worked with this female for ten years and never once have I heard her say those words," Cain said.

"Oh for the love. I can apologize for being wrong, Cain. The problem is I'm usually right and you're usually wrong."

All the males in the room laughed at that, including Cain.

"Hey, I have to ask, did you really have to give a statement half naked after you killed a vampire?" Kabel asked. I felt as my face grew hot.

"Really, Cain you told him that story?" I demanded.

"She did, you should have seen her, her pants were torn everywhere. I believe we got a flash of an ass cheek that day," Cain said with a smile.

"Just remember Cain. I have stories too."

"Like what?"

"How about the time that witch hit you with a charm in your coffee. I believe we found you in an interview room barking like a dog."

Kabel laughed loudly.

"Oh please say you have video of that," Kabel asked.

"Maybe," I answered with a smile.

"I like being friends with you two," Kabel replied.

"I have not heard this story about my mate. Sergeant Cain maybe..."

"No!" I shouted. "We have to go see, Watts."

"It's okay, I can fill you later Santiago," Cain added as Santiago wheeled me from the room.

"I swear Cain paybacks a bitch and so am I. You better remember that before you tell anymore stories."

We left the room with the two of them laughing together.

"So how much have the humans seen of your body?" my mate asked.

"More than needed but not nearly as much as you have."

"Good because I would hate to have to kill any of them. I quite like them," he answered with a smile.

Santiago wheeled me down the hall to Watts' room. Watts was asleep but not alone. Ainsley was sitting beside his bed. She jumped to her feet and bowed her head at the two of us as we entered. From the look of it Ainsley had come out of the fighting unscathed. Her clothes held some dirt and blood but nothing more.

"How's he doing?" I asked.

"He is doing well. They had to give him two doses of cleansing solution. He was awake a while ago but the magic is still in his system so they expect to have to give him another dose in an hour," she said.

"Good, I'm glad he's okay."

"I should go," she said.

"No, stay. I just wanted to make sure he was okay. How are you doing, Ainsley?" I asked.

"I'm okay. I wasn't hurt."

"Good, I'm glad to hear that. Will you be at the party tomorrow?" I asked.

"Yes I will."

She glanced at Watts before she refocused on us. I watched her hand as it inched towards his.

"Why don't you bring Watts as your date tomorrow?"

"Hugo has deemed it is for clan members only."

"Oh."

"You are coming to the ceremony, are you not?" Santiago asked.

"I will be, yes."

"So will Antoine, maybe you two could come together. He doesn't have a date," I pointed out.

"Maybe," she responded.

Ainsley looked at Watts for a long moment.

"We should go. Let him know we stopped by. Have a good night, Ainsley," I said.

Santiago backed us out of the room and headed down the hall.

"I believe our Ainsley has an attraction to Antoine," Santiago said.

"I picked up on that, too."

Santiago began to turn me around.

"Now you have seen everyone..."

"No, I want to go see Michael," I said.

"I do not think he is awake yet?"

"I don't care. Francisca is there. She needs to know she's not alone."

Santiago sighed at my stubbornness.

"As you wish," he said relenting.

Michael's room was closer to my room. As I had expected Francisca was beside his bed, holding his hand as he slept. He had some bruises that were already fading from his face. His breathing was slow and soft. Francisca's head popped up from the side of the bed. Tears stained her face, she tried to wipe them away as she stood and bowed her head to us. She, like Ainsley, was dirty and there was dried blood on her but nothing more.

"Please sit. How's he doing?" I asked, waving her back into her chair.

"Everyone thought he was dead. That tall cop was the one who knew what was wrong with him."

I was confident she was talking about Ryan.

"Is he going to be okay?" I asked.

"Yes. They have given him two doses of cleansing solution and also bathed him in solution," she said as she looked at her mate. "The charm had been meant for me, he jumped in front of me. It hit Michael in the face. I was so scared when he went down," I could hear the sadness and guilt in her voice.

"I can imagine you were. Do you need anything?"

"No, thank you."

"Thank you for all your help today. We wouldn't have been able to get all of the young out without you two," I replied.

"We were happy to be of service."

"As soon as he wakes, try to get him to feed. It may help," I offered.

"I will."

She couldn't take her eyes off of her mate.

"We will leave you now. If you need anything from us please call," Santiago said.

We left the two alone. I hoped Michael would wake up soon. Francisca was blaming herself for Michael taking the hit for her. I didn't blame her for feeling that way. I was feeling a similar guilt myself.

We reached my room. Santiago helped me back into bed. I groaned as I stood from the wheelchair and moved slowly to the bed. I was hoping the pain would fade away soon. I was grateful we had not lost any of our people. I felt for Illingworth and the loss of his men. On the upside, we had saved all of the young. I was hoping the eight we had names for were still alive. Within the next several days Ryan and Cain with the hospital staff would start combing through the files to figure out who was alive. I was grateful I wasn't going to have to do any of that work. The survivors of H&W would never be the same but at least they would have a chance to live and heal the physical wounds they were left with.

Chapter Thirty-Seven
One Day till the Ceremony

Meri was released five hours later and made a stop in my room to say goodbye. Duncan was still pissed at the two of us for the risk we had taken. I was done with my apology tour. Duncan would just have to suck it up and get over it. Santiago had, so could Duncan.

Santiago stayed with me through the night. I was released the next morning. I had wanted to go see the young we had saved but many of them were having a hard time coping. They had gone from a facility that had mistreated them and had not fed any of them properly to another facility run by humans. From what I gathered a few had to be sedated and the hospital was trying to ensure they did not overeat or drink. Both could kill them. I would try again in a few days to see how they were doing.

I was glad to be home. I looked at the stairs as we entered the house and then the living room. I could just collapse on the couch was my first thought, when Santiago picked me up. He carried me up the stairs and set me gently in bed.

"Now you are to rest until tonight. Do you understand me? There is no work to be done. Ryan has given you and your team the rest of the week plus next week off," Santiago instructed me as he unzipped my boots.

"I do have paperwork I have to do," I pointed out.

"No, you do not. I spoke with Lieutenant Ryan yesterday and he says it can wait until after our ceremony. Now I will be back," he said, sitting my boots on the floor.

"What? Where are you going?"

"I have to go pick up a gift for tomorrow."

"A gift?" I asked.

"I believe you needed jewelry for tomorrow. I had it ordered and it is ready. Now you do not leave this bed until I say so. Do you understand me?" he said bending down with his face only inches from mine.

"And what if I get hungry?"

"I will be gone at the most an hour. Now lay back and sleep," he commanded me.

He kissed my forehead and left. I stripped out of my clothes and lay naked in our bed. The aches I had felt the day before had dissipated. There was still some pain in my limbs but not as bad as it had been. I had slept only a little at the hospital during the night. Now that I was in my bed, sleep was easy to find.

I slept for hours until I felt Santiago pressed against me. His hand running down my arm. I curled into his embrace. His lips began to kiss a slow trail along my shoulder until he reached my neck. He brushed my hair aside as I angled my head up, he nipped at my neck. I wiggled my butt against him finding him, hard and naked.

"I believe we have something to finish," I said.

"Yes we do," he growled.

His hands were gentle as they caressed my body at first. He cupped one of my breasts rubbing his thumb over the nipple as he kissed my skin. I gasped at his touch. I arched my back slightly turning my head so his lips could capture mine. I rolled slightly forward. It was all the invitation he needed to slide himself inside of me. I felt as he slid in me slowly. He pulled me against him as he moved his hips back and forth. The feel of his hard sex going deep inside of me made me moan.

"I need you now," he said aggressively against my neck. I angle my head to the side. Santiago fangs punctured my neck sharply as he took my vein. He crushed me to his chest, one arm holding me in place against him as he drank, never losing his rhythm as he moved in and out of my body. I could feel as he took great pulls from my neck. Santiago's hips, moving against mine. I rolled my hips forward slightly so he could go deeper inside of me. He knew what I wanted and gave it to me. He pushed deeper and deeper until I was crying out. The feel of him inside of me was glorious as he moved faster. I could feel my own need growing as he rode me. As his hips moved faster so did his mouth as he took from me. I reached behind me holding his head in place as he kept up the quick pace. The sensations became too much as I came around him, milking his erection as he came as well. He released my vein slowly and licked the marks he had left, closed.

I could still feel him inside me and knew he was not close to being done with me. Santiago pulled himself free of my body and rolled me on my back. I spread my legs for him as he climbed on top of me. Santiago was rough as he entered me again and began to pound my core with the pace he had only set moments ago. He put a hand on the back of my neck pulling my head up as he came down on top of me. He growled as he kissed me. His tongue was rough as he licked into my mouth. The kiss was aggressive just as his thrusts were. He released my mouth.

"You are mine and only mine," he growled.

"Yes," I said breathlessly as he rode my body. There was a fire in those dark eyes that hadn't been there earlier. This was not just about a need, this was so much more. I gave him what he wanted as he claimed my nipple with his mouth. I could feel as one of his fangs scored my nipple and he sucked it. He pulled back and looked at me as his tongue began to lick the wound he had created. I watched as he licked it slowly. I lost focus as he captured my other breast with his mouth once more orgasming as he continued to suck on me. He released my nipple and sat up enough to look me in the face.

"Say it?" he growled.

"I am yours, Santiago," I breathed.

It was all he needed to hear. His hips took it up a notch until I was calling his name. He bent over me, pulling my mouth to his as he continued to pump in and out of me. My hands weaved into his hair. I tried to pull my mouth from his but he was having none of it. He kissed me harder. I was on the verge once more when he released my lips.

"Say it again!" he demanded.

"I'm yours."

His eyes held an intensity I had never seen before. I pulled him down giving him my neck once more. He struck on the other side, drinking hard as he rode me. I came over and over again with his name on my lips with each orgasm until he finally came inside of me. He collapsed on top of me. His breath was ragged as we lay there. I was having my own issues breathing normally myself. He looked at me running his thumb over my lips. There was worry in his eyes as we lay there. As great as the sex had been there was something wrong with my mate.

"What's wrong?"

He kissed me again, this time it was gentler than it had been. I broke the kiss brushing a hand through his hair.

"What's wrong Santiago," I asked again.

"He left roses for you. He was at our front door."

I knew the "he" he was referring to. Matthew had come to see me while my mate was gone. I closed my eyes at the dread of it all.

"How do you know it wasn't a delivery guy?" I said stupidly.

He looked at me as if to ask me if I was being serious. Santiago would know because of the scent. It had also been why he bit me on both sides of my neck and had been aggressive with me. It wasn't that I didn't enjoy it, I had, but it had been the predator side coming out in him.

"Was there a card?" I asked.

"Yes."

I closed my eyes once more before I spoke.

"What did it say?"

"You will be mine," he whispered.

I understood more of what had just happened between us.

"I am sorry. I checked the security system, he never entered the house. I tried to stay away from the room until I was calmer. I..."

"No, you have nothing to apologize for. I am yours just as you are mine," I said. I kissed him. He pulled back looking at me.

"I have never felt the need to mark you, as I did just now. The thought of him trying to claim you..." he stated the pain and anger in his voice was thick, I could almost taste it.

"Listen to me. I am not angry with you," I said. I pulled his face down to me and kissed him. I could feel the tension he was carrying. I moved my hips slowly, which brought a moan from him. He pulled back and stared down at me. "I am yours and no one elses," I said to him.

I continued to move my core up and down him until he took over. This time he was gentler. I kissed his neck and chest as we made love. His lips claiming mine over and over again. In between the kisses, I whispered again and again I was his. By the time we were both spent my body had a new ache but it was one I loved the feeling of. Santiago pulled his body free of mine so he could lay beside me. I lay across his chest, listening to his heart beat with my blood pumping inside of him. He ran a hand down my spine.

"We will need to get ready soon," he said.

"I know. I just want to stay here for a little longer."

"As do I," he kissed the top of my head.

WE STAYED IN BED FOR another thirty minutes until we were forced to get up and move. The soreness from the day before was still there along with a completely different tenderness. I showered and dried my hair for the evening before I went to find a dress in the closet. Santiago was already dressed in an impeccable suit and tie. I was staring at my clothes thinking how I had no desire to go to this thing, when an image from the fight at H&W popped into my head of Francisca, followed closely to the image of my fight with Matthew. She had forced the male witch to set the desk on fire without a word. How? I had never really thought about it until now. I had thought Matthew had whispered in my ear when I had fought him over a year before now I wasn't so sure. What if he had the same ability as Francisca? It would explain why I had a difficult time breaking his hold over me.

"Are you alright?" Santiago asked.

"Yeah. Have you heard from Francisca?"

"Yes. Michael is awake and will be going home later tonight or tomorrow."

"So she won't be there tonight. Damn!" I cursed.

"No, she is coming to represent the two of them. Why?"

"I just thought of something I wanted to talk to her about," I answered, turning back to my clothes.

"Perhaps I can answer your questions," he offered.

"It's about her ability."

"She can manipulate an individual's mind," he stated simply.

"I want to know how it works and how many others would have the same ability?"

"The workings of it only she can answer. The second part I can."

I turned and looked at him.

"Only those born as vampires can do what she does."

"What?"

"As you know some vampires can still reproduce after they go through the transition. Not many have the capability to do so. When it happens, it's rare. Those born as vampires grow and develop until they turn twenty one when they stop aging. At that time they also develop their abilities. It is almost as if they go through a transition different from ours. They are quite strong and have the ability to manipulate their prey's mind. Some have other abilities as well, not just manipulation," he explained.

"So all vampire children develop this skill?"

"Yes."

"That's what he is," I said.

"What do you mean?"

"Matthew. The night I fought him, he was able to bite me because I wasn't able to fight him. I couldn't stop it. I tried to fight but at some point my brain said no. I didn't understand why. I mean I had felt Meri's ability in the past but it was like he controlled my brain. I was able to break his hold because I cut my hand on a tree. It was like he couldn't get a hold of all of me."

Santiago had started to growl as I spoke. His head had dropped slightly, his eyes were low. The thought of another male at my vein was more than my mate could handle right now. I approached him placing my hands on his chest.

"Look at me," I whispered. It took a moment for him to focus on me. "He will not get that chance again. Remember what I said to you."

"You speaking about him being against you, at your vein, makes me want to take you right here again, as I did this afternoon."

I looked at the closet floor.

"Well that could be fun but then there may be some questions about rug burn. If I wear a dress it will be pretty obvious," I said with a smile.

That was enough to bring him back to reality. He looked at me.

"Why is this information important?" Santiago asked softly.

"It gets us one step closer to being able to find him. The more we know, the better chance we have at killing him."

Santiago looked at me. I could see he still wanted to mark me again.

"Do you want me to wear a dress tonight?" I asked.

"Yes."

"Then you will have to wait to mark me again with those fangs of yours. As it is I'm going to look like a pin cushion."

He smiled at me. He placed a hand on my neck and pulled me against him. Dropping his head he kissed the marks he had already left on me.

"Wear the black one," he whispered.

A shiver ran down my body making me tight and wet. He released me and left me standing by myself. I pulled the black dress from the closet. It had thin straps that criss-crossed on the back. The straps showed off my marks well. Between the bites on my neck and the clan mark on my shoulder, there was no question whose mate I was. The dress fit snug on the top and flowed out slightly at the skirt and hitting me mid thigh. I slid into the dress and pulled out a pair of black fuck me pumps from the closet. They were four inch stilettos that went well with the dress. I did my makeup quickly and gave myself a once over. I turned, finding my mate standing in the door watching me. His eyes heavy with sex.

"You look beautiful," he whispered.

"Thank you." I walked over to him, placing a hand on his waist.

"When we get home I plan to get you out of that dress and on your back," he whispered.

The image that filled my mind made me catch my breath.

"Let's get this night started then."

Chapter Thirty-Eight

Obsidian was already full of vampires when we walked in. Our arrival was announced as we entered, bringing applause. The overhead lights were on but were low. Large white lights were rigged on the stage, bar, and over the dance floor. Round tables had been set up on both sides of the bar. All of them covered in black tablecloths, with black napkins and tall centerpieces. The centerpieces were in tall, thin crystal stems vases with miniature red roses that were designed into large circular arrangements. Crystal beads hung from the base of the flowers with scattered rose petals around the base of each arrangement. Two small white votive candles were lit inside crystal holders that matched the vases. It was beautiful. Hugo had outdone himself or his staff had. I was sure the decorations had been all his ideas. There were hands to be shaken, bows were given, as individuals approached us with congratulations. The entire time Santiago kept a hand on my lower back, ensuring no one stepped between us. Eventually the vampires went back to their conversations with one another. Soft music played in the background as we moved through the room.

I found Francisca talking with Cristian and another vampire I didn't remember the name of, near the bar. Santiago and I turned in their direction. As soon as Cristian saw our approach, he turned his attention to us, which made the others aware of our presence.

"Santiago, Savannah you both look wonderful tonight," Cristian said with a bow of his head at both of us.

"Thank you," I said before turning to the female vampire. "Francisca, can I have a moment of your time?" I asked.

"Yes, of course," she answered.

"Excuse us for just a moment," I gave Santiago's arm a quick squeeze and moved us away from the earshot of others. There was a small round booth at the back of the room. It was perfect for the conversation I wanted to have with Francisca. I could see the entire room and no one could approach us or eavesdrop easily.

"First, I want to ask you how Michael is doing?" I started the conversation as I took a seat.

"He woke up this afternoon. I was happy to see him awake. He is a little groggy but the feeding has helped. I am only staying long enough tonight to make an appearance and then I am heading back to be with him. He's going home tonight after he feeds one more time."

"Good. I'm glad he is doing well," I said. "Uhm ...I was wondering if I could ask you about your ability?"

She said nothing eyeing me.

"What is this about Savannah?"

I had no clue how much to tell her. I liked Francisca but what if it got out I was asking questions about her ability and others like her. It could reach Dante and Matthew. But she had a right to know why I was asking. Santiago would not have brought her to the raid the day before if he didn't trust her. I took a breath before I spoke.

"A year ago I had a run in with a vampire who has an ability that I had never dealt with before. It was like he was in my head. It was terrifying. I'm still hunting him or at this point it feels more like it's the other way around. I'm trying to learn about him so the next time I'm better prepared. I need to know if he has the same ability as you," I explained.

"May I ask you what he wanted with you?"

"He wanted me for himself."

"How did you get away?" she asked.

"I fought or my brain did. I guess survival instinct. The only way I was able to break his hold completely was I scratched my hand on a tree. The pain brought me out of the trance I had slipped into."

"He either isn't very strong or you are stronger than he realized," she speculated as she gave me a hard look.

"What do you mean?"

"If this vampire is like me, he was born a vampire. Some are stronger than others. I do not know why but we are. Some have more than the ability to manipulate."

"Well ...how does it work? I know with Meri her prey has to make eye contact with her. Do you need the same?"

"No. We just have to touch our prey, usually a hand on the throat or the face does it."

"When he did it he was standing behind me. I was pinned between a tree and him, he didn't touch my head until he moved it for him to bite me."

"Then he knows how to use his ability well."

"Can he hear thoughts while he is in there?" I asked.

"No. He can sense if his prey is under his control or not."

"Francisca is there anyway I can fight it?"

"No more than you did. Now that he has had a taste of you, it may be easier for him to get inside your head," she explained.

"What about after I become a hybrid?" I asked.

"I do not know."

Well that was a peachy bit of information.

"Thank you for the information," I stood up to walk away. She placed a hand on my arm to stop me.

"May I make a suggestion," she offered.

"Yes."

"The first is you need to tell the entire clan about this. We can help protect you. As Santiago's mate it is part of our duty to protect you. The second is you need to go through the transition soon.

It will only make you stronger as a hellborn. If this vampire is after you, you need all the defenses you can gather."

"I can't tell the clan or at least not all of the clan," I answered.

"Why?"

Just as she asked Hugo walked in with Dante beside him.

"There is someone within the clan who brought this vampire here. And I believe they are still in contact. Do you understand what I am saying?"

"Yes," her gaze fell on the skeletal looking vampire.

"Let me help you," she offered.

"I can't ask you to do that especially after what happened to your mate. But thank you for the offer," I replied. My phone started ringing. I looked at the number and knew who was on the other end. I left Francisa sitting in the booth and found a corner to take the call.

"Hello," I answered.

"Hello, Savannah," came Matthew's voice.

"What do you want?" I demanded.

"I had to call you to say congratulations on the big day. Did you like the flowers?"

"No."

"That makes me sad to hear. I know how much your mate hated them. He threw them in the trash. Was he feeling a bit territorial?" he asked with a condescending tone.

"What do you think?"

"I saw when he fucked you. He marked you not once but three times. Was it good Savannah? From what I could tell you seem to really enjoy it. Is that the way you like it? Rough. I am quite good at rough. I'm sure you know that from Lucy. She was so jealous of you the entire time we were together," he all but purred.

"Actually, from what I could tell from my conversations with her you weren't that good."

"I guess you will have to wait to find out, won't you. I have missed these little chats of ours. How is my little bad witch?"

"Be better if you were dead," I shot back.

"You look good tonight, Savannah. I bet you smell delicious. I've been dreaming about you a lot lately. The feel of your body against mine. The way you taste on my tongue. I could come right now as we speak." I wanted to vomit. "I watched you yesterday at H&W, you were good. It looked like you learned some new tricks as well, Savannah," he said my name like he was eating up every syllable.

The sound sent a shiver down me. He had been there, too close to my mate. The disgust I was feeling turned into anger.

"Is that why you called? To brag?"

"I was also impressed with your mate. He may actually give me a challenge," Matthew ignored my questions.

"You will not come near him! Do you understand me? You touch him, and I will tear your heart from your chest and set you on fire."

"It's cute how protective you get over him. We both know you won't kill me. You aren't strong enough and neither is your mate. I will kill him and you will watch as I do it. Once he is dead I will fuck you where you stand until you call my name," he said with confidence.

"Not a chance in Hell that is happening," I growled.

"We'll see. Until then Savannah enjoy your time with your mate while you can."

The call went dead. I looked across the room seeing Santiago as he held a conversation with three others. I needed to do something to stop Matthew. He was right. I hadn't been strong enough last time to kill him but I would be next time. I had one option and that was to become a hybrid. I had in many ways been delaying doing it. I was afraid of not surviving the transition. The fear of Santiago dying was worse.

I headed across the floor to my mate. He had his back to me as I placed a hand on his arm and came around to his side. He took my hand into his and kissed the back of it.

Hugo climbed on stage with Dante next to him. Hugo was wearing a black suit with a red shirt and tie, it was the color of fresh blood. Dante was in his usual black clothes. He couldn't even dress for the occasion. He was smiling, which made his face look more like a dead man walking around.

"I would like to thank all of you for attending this celebration. Our wonderful Santiago and his beautiful mate, Savannah will be taking their vows tomorrow. We are very happy you have joined our family, Savannah," There were applause at Hugo's words. He waited for it to die down before he spoke again. "To add to this happy occasion, I would like to make my own announcement. I have decided to take a mate," he looked at Dante and smiled. "Dante has agreed to be at my side for the rest of our lives." There were applause around the room. Some of the vampires in the room were looking more excited than others. I looked at Santiago and he had the same look of worry on his face as I did. "I hope all of you enjoy the night we have planned. Victor, would you be so kind as to start the music."

The vampire to the left of the stage nodded and flipped a couple of switches. Music filled the space.

"He is making his move," I said to Santiago.

"It appears that he is. We could not expect him to stay still forever."

"No, we couldn't."

Santiago brought his free hand up to my face.

"Hugo is making his way to us, we need to put on a smile for him.

The plus about Hugo was he couldn't smell emotions as my mate could. It made it easier to lie to him.

"My two favorite hellborns," Hugo said with wide open arms. He embraced Santiago first and then me. Dante stood just behind his future mate, his eyes cold as he stared at us.

"Congratulations, Hugo," Santiago said with his business smile. It was the smile he used when he was being polite. It never truly reached his eyes but most wouldn't notice.

"Thank you old friend."

"When's the big day?" I asked as lightly as I could.

"I know you have planned your ceremony in three months but I require more time than that. I am thinking next year. We have not set a date yet."

"We look forward to whenever it is," I replied.

Francisca came to join our little group. She had a smile on her face as she bowed to Hugo.

"I am happy for you, Hugo."

"Thank you, Francisca."

"I just wanted to offer my best wishes before I left for the evening."

"You cannot stay?" Hugo pouted.

"No. Michael is coming home from the hospital tonight, so I must go."

"Give him our thanks for his services yesterday. Which reminds me, Savannah I would love to hear all of the details of your heroics," Hugo said.

"Hugo, perhaps she could at a later date," Santiago offered.

"Of course."

"If you do not mind Hugo, I would like to borrow the happy couple for a moment?" Francisca asked.

"Not at all." Hugo took Dante's hand and walked away.

"Come with me," she spoke softly.

We followed her out of the club. Santiago kept his arm around me as we moved. Franisica turned abruptly to face us, pinning me with a hard stare.

"You are not asking for my help Savannah, I am offering it to you. And you need to say yes," she said seriously. Any smile she had inside was now gone.

"No. I am not putting anyone else in danger."

"What are you two talking about?" Santiago asked, looking at both of us.

"Matthew," I answered.

"That male is going to be the death of our clan," she pointed at Obsidian. "If he is involved with this male you need us just as we need you. You and Santiago will be who leads us next. I have seen it."

"What do you mean you've seen it?" I demanded.

"Remember what I told you inside about the vampires who are like me?" she asked.

"Yes."

"I am one of the stronger ones. You two are meant to rule," she said looking at me.

I said nothing as I let that sink in. She could see into the future? It gave me an entire laundry list of new questions for her. The first was why she didn't see Michael getting hurt? Maybe it was only big events she saw. I would have to save my questions for another time, we had too many other problems to deal with.

"Francisca, I do not wish to rule," Santiago added.

"Would you leave us to him? If you turn from the crown, we will be left at his mercy," She answered. We all knew who he was in this, Dante.

"No. I would not do that to any of you," Santiago answered.

"Good. The wheels are already in motion, there is no stopping what is to come. After your ceremony we will meet at your home.

Until then stay safe, both of you," she stated. She bowed to us and left.

We watched as she walked down the street. I leaned against Santiago as he placed his arm around me. I wanted us to have more time to be blissful but it seemed fate had other plans for us. We were now looking at a war with Dante, ruling the vampire clan, and dealing with Matthew. Would we ever find peace? Or were we doomed to always live in chaos.?

"Let us go back inside," Santiago said. I nodded my head, unsure I could trust my voice.

I took his hand as we moved together. The music had changed while we were outside meaning vampires had taken to the dance floor. Food had been served to many of the tables with half of the guests seated and enjoying what was being offered.

"Dance with me, Mi Amor?" Santiago asked me.

I let him lead me to the dance floor. He held me close as we danced. The feel of him was a feeling I never wanted to forget. My resolve was growing as we moved back and forth with the music. I turned my face up to him.

"Two days after the ceremony, we're going to begin my transition," I said over the music.

He pulled back looking at me seeing my resolve. He leaned back down placing his mouth near my ear.

"It can wait a while longer," he said in my ear.

"No, it can't. Between Dante mating Hugo and Matthew. I can't wait any longer."

"What does Matthew have to do with this?" he demanded.

"He called me right before Hugo's announcement. It's only a matter of time... He will come for me and I want to be ready when he does."

"I will not let him have you," Santiago said.

"As much as you can't lose me, I can't lose you either. He plans to kill you to get to me."

"I expect nothing less from a male of his caliber."

"With me as a hybrid, we will be a stronger team, you and I." Santiago closed his eyes as his head dropped slightly forward. "I love you and I know this is the right decision. We can do it at home and have Meri and Duncan with us. They can make sure no one tries anything," I pointed out. There was a long pause as Santiago lifted his head looking at me.

"Come with me," he pulled me through the room to the invisible door on the far side. He punched in the code and pulled the door open when the release popped.

We said nothing as we headed down the stairs. I walked into the office as he slammed the door shut. He said nothing at first, just paced. I stood there and waited until I thought I was going to explode.

"I do not want you to be forced to do this," he finally spoke.

"I was already forced by Hugo. I have accepted this is part of the deal of him saying yes to us. I..."

"It can wait!" he almost yelled.

"For how long? Hugo will come calling for us to finish it sooner or later. We do it now and we don't have to worry about it."

"No, I do not agree to this," he was shaking his head.

"Santiago, I need you to. I need your vein to do it. If we don't do this our way we will be forced to do it with an audience. And what happens if Matthew shows up in a week? You can't be with me twenty-four hours a day. Please, Santiago," I reasoned. I approached him, placing a hand on his face. Santiago looked at me.

"What if you die?" he spoke softly.

Months ago Santiago had been ready for me to do this. He had offered to do it after I had almost been blown up. I had said no out of fear. Now he was the one afraid of what could happen. I was to but I was more afraid of what could happen if we didn't.

"You will make sure I won't and so will Meri and Duncan."

He dropped his head as his shoulders sagged slightly.

"If we do this it should be here," he spoke without looking at me.

"What?"

"The transition is painful and our home is near humans. If you start to scream, I do not wish the police to show up. If we do the transition here, no one will hear you between the concrete and the noise upstairs," he explained.

I thought about what he was saying. It made sense.

"Okay."

"I want more time than two days," he said sadly, finally meeting my eyes.

"We will have the time after the transition. It gives me time to recuperate and figure out how to handle the new me," I replied.

He nodded his head. I pulled myself against him and he wrapped his arms around me. Neither of us said anything as we clung to one another.

Chapter Thirty-Nine
The Mating Ceremony

Santiago and I didn't stay long at the party after our discussion. Meri and Duncan finally arrived and I broke the news to her. She took it as well as Santiago had. Duncan on the other hand, had been the one who didn't try to argue or debate the decision he just nodded his head and said he would help. It made me love that male a little more.

We had planned for our night to end differently than it had. There had been too many surprises for either of us to want to do more than hold one another. In some ways that was better than the sex we would have had if things had been different.

Santiago woke early the next morning kissing me before he left. He would be heading to the mating venue to make sure everything was set up for the ceremony. Vampire tradition said you didn't see your mate until the ceremony. Mind you, the tradition was written when the two didn't meet until they were giving their vows. I thought it was dumb. I stayed in bed a little longer than I should have. My brain was still working overtime on the events from the night before. Part of me worried Matthew would show up today. It felt like the thing he would do just to teach me a lesson. Meri would be with me throughout the day today and the thought of Matthew showing up meant she was in danger. I had a fleeting thought that perhaps I should just give myself to him to save everyone around me. The thought brought on a horrible image of what was in store for me if I did that. No, I wouldn't do that. I would do what I did best, fight. I would fight until one or both of us were dead.

A greater part of me knew that had been Matthew's goal for the call. He wanted me on edge in order to have power over me. I wasn't willing to allow him to have the power. Not in the slightest. I would go on living my life until the day he did come for me. When he did, I would be ready for him.

I finally got out of bed fifteen minutes before Meri was to arrive. She had planned a day of girly activities for us. Between my hair, nails, and makeup there would be little time for anything else. I didn't feel the need to do any of it but she did. I pulled on a pair of yoga pants, and a ratty shirt I used for lazy days. I would leave my gun at home today but would carry my knife on my thigh. I would have to pack it away for the ceremony but for now I would wear it.

Matthew's call had shaken me up. How much longer would I have my mate before our world split in two? Would I survive the transition? If I didn't, what did that mean for Santiago and Meri? When would Dante make his move? This was supposed to be a happy day instead all I felt was worry, for all of us. If Francisca was right, and I was confident she was, my life was about to become something altogether different. I had no clue what that would mean for my career or how to rule vampires. There was also the issue of Dante. He wouldn't give up the throne willingly. A war would break out within the vampires. The wolves and witches would be forced to choose sides. Francisca was right, the wheels of change were already turning. Dante would take the throne from Hugo, with brutality. We needed to put our own wheels in motion.

My doorbell rang as my head began to swim with every fear I was feeling. I pulled myself up and headed for the door. Meri was standing there looking happy and excited. I tried to push through all of my worries, plastering a fake smile on my face for her but it was no use, her face fell.

"What's wrong?" she asked.

"We'll talk in the car. Let's go," I set the alarm and locked up. As soon as we were in the car Meri started in.

"Are you worried you won't make it through the transition? If you are, maybe it means you should wait."

"The transition is a small worry. Some time after the ceremony, we'll be meeting with a few others. I need you and Duncan there."

"What kind of meeting?"

"One that is behind Hugo and Dante's back," I replied.

"You think Dante is going to take control once they're mated."

"I think he is putting plans in motion to do that. When will he actually seize Hugo's seat, I have no clue. I just know he will. We need to start planning for the war that will come."

"Is that everything?" Meri asked.

"Matthew came to our home yesterday and left me roses."

"Well, that explains the two marks on your neck. I take it Santiago was feeling territorial?"

"You can say that. Then Matthew called me last night at the party. I haven't told Santiago yet."

"Why?"

"Because he was already upset. As good as the sex was, I didn't know if my neck could take any more marks."

"What did Matthew say?"

"The usual stuff about wanting me. He plans on making me watch as he kills Santiago. Oh and he watched us have sex."

"Is that why you decide to go through with the transition?" Meri asked.

"It's part of it. Dante mating Hugo sealed it for me. I need to be one of you or well, as close as I can to being one of you. Also, Hugo will start asking when I am going to do it."

Meri nodded as we drove. We were silent for a while. She pulled into a salon that looked right out of a movie.

"Listen, today is supposed to be a good day. We're going to go in there to have some fun and get you ready for the evening. We need to ignore the other stuff for today," she ordered.

"I would like to but I don't know how to."

"Good news for you, I do," she smiled at me. It was the smile she wore when she wanted to cause some trouble. "So back to the sex," she said.

"We are not talking about that. The only detail you get, was why and that I enjoyed it."

"I share with you. Come on. You know I always thought he would be one of those all about the love making kind of lovers but seeing those marks," Meri said as she raised her eyebrows. "Maybe I'm wrong. Maybe Santiago does like it a little more rough."

"We are so not having this conversation," I climbed out of the Range Rover and headed for the door. Meri followed, keeping the conversation going.

MY NAILS WERE DONE, along with my toes. It took three hours alone for just my hair. Even though there was very little in terms of body to my hair, I had thick hair and the drying process was long and tedious. By the time, I was done my hair was curled and pulled into a soft twist at the nap of my neck with loose curls framing my face. The makeup took only thirty minutes, which was longer than I ever took to do it. By the time they were done with me I looked like an entirely different hellborn. The makeup was subtle except for the eyes. My eyes were done in a more dramatic fashion with silver and black. The colors made my eyes stand out even more. We left the salon with both of us smiling instead of just Meri. She had been right about everything that was happening. If I wanted to have a little happiness with my mate I had to create it myself. I couldn't let Matthew or Dante stop us. If I did the bad would swallow us up.

The venue was not far from our home. An area within a small forest of trees had been made into a beautiful venue for parties. There was an off white building set up with changing rooms and private bathrooms for individuals to get ready. Along with public restrooms for party guests. The rooms were small, no larger than eleven by ten with a dressing table and a few chairs. It was perfect for Meri and I to get dressed for the ceremony.

The outside was decorated with dozens of white twinkle lights strung over long tables, from pole to pole set up on the edge of the venue. The dance floor was set about six feet in front of the tables. There was enough space for the witch, Santiago, and myself to stand between the guests and the dance floor. We would perform the ceremony and then slide right into the reception. The reception was not part of witches or vampires mating ceremony but we were having one because the guest list was made up of not just friends but political figures from the city.

Meri and I got dressed. My dress was a perfect fit as Miss Radmaker had said it would be. Meri had to help me into the corset and then zipped me into the dress. When I first put the corset on, I wasn't sure breathing was an option as Meri cenched the thing tight around my body. The longer I wore it the more I grew used to it. I helped Meri do the same with her dress.

I stood in front of the full length mirror taking it all in. We had been mated for the last three months by vampire standards. I had given my oath to Hugo, promising to be with Santiago forever and accepted into the clan. With all of that, I was nervous and had no clue as to why. This ceremony would be more of the witch's traditions than the vampires. Just as the ring Santiago had given me was. I stepped away from the mirror and took a seat in the chair at the dressing table. I slid into my shoes and turned, adding diamond

studded earrings to each of my ears. As I got the backs of my earrings on, a knock sounded at the door. Meri answered it.

"Cristian, what are you doing here?" she asked.

"Santiago, asked me to deliver this to Savannah."

Meri stepped away from the door letting him in. Cristian was
dressed in a soft grey suit with a black shirt and grey tie. He carried
in his hands a wide black velvet box in his hands. I had forgotten
about the necklace until I saw the box.

"Santiago wanted you to have this for today," he pulled the lid
open to reveal a breathtaking necklace of diamonds. The diamonds
were arranged in a holly wreath pattern. I lifted the necklace from
the box, lost for words. I had never thought in a million years I
would be having a mating ceremony nor wearing anything close to
what I was wearing. I turned to the mirror and placed the necklace
around my neck.

"Meri, can you fasten it?" I asked in a shaky voice.

"Yeah," she stepped up and latched the necklace closed. It sat at
the base of my neck. I had never been a jewelry kind of girl or one
to wear dresses but I was for Santiago. I actually liked getting dolled
up from time to time. He made me feel beautiful even when I was
in a pair of yoga pants and a ratty T-shirt. I had to clear my throat
twice of my emotions before I spoke.

"Tell Santiago thank you and I love it."

Cristian bowed his head and turned leaving Meri and I alone.
She stood behind me smiling.

"Santiago has great taste," she said.

"Yeah, he does."

THIRTY MINUTES LATER guests had arrived and were in their
seats. I stood back from the glass doors. The lights were lit as the
sun was beginning, it's decent in the west. The long tables were set

with pristine white tablecloths. White and gold plates decorated the tables. Cherry blossoms and gardenias were in small vases down the center of each table. I watched as Santiago headed down the line of tables in a tux that was tailored to his body. Kabel was standing with Santiago, which confused me. We had hired a witch for the ceremony? Where was she?

"Meri where is Celeste?" I asked.

"Well ... You see ...Santiago called me while you were getting your hair done. Turns out she wasn't comfortable doing the ceremony. So we had to find a back up."

"You guys chose Kabel?" I asked, flabbergasted at their choice.

"He's good with crowds and was more than willing to do it."

He was good with crowds. I wasn't sure he knew what he was doing. I just shook my head and hoped he did.

"Are you ready?" she asked me.

"Yes," I said. Meri held out her hand and I took it. She was the only family, I had which meant she was the one who was to present me to my mate. Liam and Cristian opened both doors as we stepped up. We descended the two steps and made our way down the white cloth that had been spread down the walk way. I glanced at the guests seeing friendly faces at the tables on either side of me. Cain was there, with no date. Ryan was next to him with his wife, who was just as graceful as I had pictured her to be. She had soft blond hair pulled back from her thin face. Watts was there next to Ainsley. They were smiling at one another. Damian was at the table on my right with Tess as his date. Her normally colored hair was a soft grey today. She wore a red dress that hugged her lean body. I smiled at the two of them as I made my way down to my mate. Meri and I stopped our progress two feet from Santiago.

"Please present this female to her mate," Kabel said with a smile.

"I, Meri Ember, sister of Savannah, give with my blessing this female to Santiago De los Rios of The Black Grove Clan."

I hugged Meri and stepped over, taking Santiago's hand. Meri stepped back taking a seat at the table closest to the ceremony next to Duncan.

"Thank you all for being here for this joyous occasion," Kabel's voice boomed. "I need to warn all of you, I am new to this officiating thing, so bear with me," Kabel looked down at a piece of paper before he started again.

"Are you both here of your own choosing?" he asked.

"Yes," we both said in unison.

"Good. I am going to ad-lib a little right now so just stick with me."

"Oh no," I groaned softly.

"Trust me female, it'll be good. These two hellborns are the best I have ever known. They are both kickass fighters, just ask my arm, what this male did only days ago to it. They both know how to throw a party or I at least hope they do," that got the crowd laughing. "And they love each other deeply. Prior to Savannah, Santiago was a bit of a stick in the mud as many of us know all too well. Something about this female changed everything for him. For that I say thank you, Savannah," he placed a hand on his chest giving me a small bow.

I tried to not laugh at the last part but failed. Santiago just shook his head with a grin.

"We are all happy you are part of our clan if nothing else for the fights you will provide us. Now let's move on," There were a few cheers at his last statement. What had I gotten myself into? "Turn to one another. Wrists up."

Santiago and I turned with our wrist turned up exposing the veins. Kabel drew out a small dagger from his pocket. With quick work he cut both of our wrists, blood welled up to the surface. He placed Santiago's wrist onto mine and began to wrap two ribbons that were intertwined around our wrists binding them loosely together. He looked down at his paper once more.

"As your blood mingles into one, please speak your oath to one another. Santiago, please go first."

"Mi Amor, I have loved you for as long as I have known you. I swear to be with you no matter what comes our way. I swear to you I will love you until my final breath. You are my beginning, my middle, my end. I swear my loyalty to you from this day forth. This is my oath to you."

I could feel my eyes tearing up and had no way to stop the flow that was threatening to start."

"Savannah," Kabel prompted me.

"Santiago, you are the love of my life. I swear to be with you no matter what comes our way. I swear to you I will love you until my final breath. You are my beginning, my middle, my end. I swear my loyalty to you from this day forth. This is my oath to you."

"Good job, guys," Kabel said, giving us both a big grin. That got a small laugh from our audience. "Now for the blessing. This is the part where I go off script again."

I shook my head at him.

"The last one was good, have a little faith," he said to me. He smiled before he started. Instead of looking at the crowd he looked at us. There was humor in those eyes but there was also a touch of seriousness too. "Santiago and Savannah, you two are amazing. Prior to this mating the two of you were well known throughout our clan and the city. Some good and some bad but since the two of you have joined forces our futures are looking up. You are amazing and the love you share for one another is what we all hope to find. Today, I give my own vow to the two of you to be forever your friend and to always have your back," he finished.

Kabel was right, it was a good blessing. I smiled at him.

"Now with oaths given all around, I now am happy to say you are happily mated ...again," Kabel concluded smiling mischievously.

The ribbons that bond us were pulled from our wrists. Santiago pulled me to him, kissing me as we were greeted with cheers. I was officially mated under vampire law and witch law. In that moment, I knew that even though we were about to be faced with a war and a sociopath or two we would make it to the other side as one.

Chapter Forty

Dinner was served after the ceremony. Santiago and I sat at a table with our people around us. There was chatter and smiles around throughout the night. We made the rounds to every table. I met the mayor and the deputy mayor. I had never met them and wasn't sure what they thought of the entire ceremony. I was happy to move on as soon as the niceties were over. The chief of police were also in attendance. It was the first time I had met him in all the years I had worked with SCPD. He gave me a big thanks for the work my team and I had done on the Daring case. I brought Ryan and Cain over making sure I pointed out it was with their help, we had been so successful in our efforts. Ryan was embarrassed at the bragging I did about his leadership. His face turned red as I talked about his work as a lieutenant. Cain on the other hand, was in his element as his chest puffed out at my praise of how good of a detective he was. I was happy when the music started up because it meant I was done with the meet and greet of all of the city politicians.

"Dance with me, Mi Amor?" Santiago said as we walked back to our seats.

"Of course," I said.

He took my hand leading me to the dance floor. Our last dance had not ended the way either of us had wanted or planned. This one would. He moved me around the dance floor as we held one another close.

"You have said nothing about the song?"

In truth I hadn't really been listening to the music. I had been enjoying the moment of just the two of us in a crowd of many. I listened to the song playing as memories from when we were getting to know one another came back.

"All I Ever Need," I said the song title.

"I thought it was the perfect song for you and I today."

I smiled at him as we moved.

"You know human couples have songs they dance to at their matings, we don't."

"Some human traditions I feel all of us should have, this is one of them. You look wonderful this evening."

"I guess I made the right choice in dresses."

"You took my breath away when you stepped out," he replied.

I kissed him as we moved, a cheer broke out. I turned to see Cain, Watts, and Kabel making the noise. I smiled at them as we kept dancing. When the song ended Santiago walked us off the floor. I saw Damian staring at us as he sat in his seat. Tess was nowhere to be seen.

"Give me a minute and I'll meet you back at our table?" I asked.

"Take your time," he gave me a kiss before he departed.

I walked over to Damian and took the seat next to him.

"Where's your date?" I asked.

"She's mingling."

"Why aren't you?"

"I talk enough with these humans on a regular basis, I don't want to on social occasions," he smiled.

"Yeah. I can understand that," I replied. "How are you doing?"

"Better than the last time we saw one another."

Damian had the grace to look embarrassed.

"I'm glad to hear that, Damian."

"The council is pushing me to start dating again," he said.

"How do you feel about it?"

"I'm not sure I'm ready. You know the last female being a traitor makes you leery to date again."

"You have to at some point," I replied.

He nodded his head.

"You two looked good out there. You know, I don't ever remember us dancing?"

"Thanks. No, you and I never danced. You weren't open to it," I answered.

"Yeah, sorry about that."

"I don't hold it against you. It was just one of those things that we didn't have in common," I said.

"I'm happy for you and Santiago."

"Thank you."

"I heard about the rescue you guys did a couple days ago."

"Not shocked it's been all over the news. Mind you, Hugo couldn't be more delighted with the coverage."

"How are the young?" Damian asked.

"They're healing and hopefully will be okay. We're still trying to sort through their files. There is still a lot we are piecing together," I explained.

"You could have called, we would have helped."

"I appreciate that but this was something we had to do."

"I'm happy to help when I can in the future."

I thought of the young who had been injected with wolf blood. I knew little of where the female was going once she was well enough but I was confident finding a home for her would be difficult. Vampires wouldn't want her and neither would a witch. Maybe Damian was the solution.

Many of the young were going to be taken in by clan members in their hometown. The ones who had been kidnapped would be returned to their families. The ones no one wanted we were still working out details for. I needed to talk to Hugo about them.

"There may be something you can help me with. Can I call you tomorrow?" I asked.

"Sure. Anything I can do to help."

"Thanks."

I saw as Tess was making her way back to Damian. She was wearing a tight, red cocktail dress that showed off the few curves she had. The color made her eyes shine. She looked stunning in the dress. I was so used to seeing the wolf in her black pants and tank tops, it was a nice change to see her in something different.

"I should go find my mate," I said as I stood up. "You should get up and go dance with Tess," I suggested.

"I'm still not much of a dancer."

"Maybe not but I think she would like it and maybe you would too," I smiled.

"You know the last time we saw each other you hinted to something about Tess and me."

"And I stand by what I said then. For once listen to me," I patted him on the shoulder.

Tess approached us with a smile on her face.

"Savannah, congratulations," she said.

"Thanks Tess. I'm glad you two could come. You look great."

"Uhm...Thank you," she looked uncomfortable.

I walked away and heard as Damian asked her to dance. I turned and watched as the two headed for the dance floor. Damian took her hand as they moved with one another. I watched as they smiled and talked. They moved back and forth, not really moving their feet, just swaying together. Damian was right, dancing was not his specialty. It didn't matter or at least not to Tess. I watched as her entire face lit up. They looked good together. A hand slid around my waist pulling me against his wide body. I leaned into the embrace.

"They look good together," Santiago said.

"They do."

"Would you care to dance one more time or would you rather sneak away and finish what we did not get to last night?" Santiago asked, his voice was husky.

"Are you sure we can sneak away without anyone noticing?" I turned to face him, draping an arm around his neck.

"This party will carry on for hours. No one will notice our departure. Besides, I am dying to see you in nothing but that necklace."

That was all my male had to say to me.

"Lead the way," I said.

He took my hand and led me to the door I had exited out of for the ceremony. We were just inside the threshold when Meri caught us.

"Where do you two think you are going?"

"I should have known," I hissed, dropping my head.

"As should I," Santiago said.

I turned to look at my best friend who was smiling a little too cheerful.

"You really thought you could walk out of here?" Meri smiled.

"We hoped we could," I shot back.

"Hugo wants you to make a speech, Santiago. You know the thanks for coming speech," Meri informed us.

We both looked at one another.

"It will be another hour before we have another chance, Mi Amor," Santiago brushed a hand across my cheek.

"An hour it is."

We walked back out hand in hand. Meri was grinning from ear to ear at our ruined getaway. As much as I loved her, she could be annoying. It took another thirty minutes before Santiago could give his thank you speech. There was another round of hand shaking and smiles. Ryan and his wife left shortly after. We tried one more time to leave again, on the way to our exit Cain and Kabel stopped us. I was beginning to think someone was plotting against us. It took us another two hours to finally bid our goodbyes.

The Panamera handled perfectly on the back roads as we headed home. As great as the night had been, I was ready to have time with Santiago. Soon enough we would be faced with my transition and I wanted as much time with him as I could get. I had a few calls to make the next day but I would take care of those early. The rest of the day would be spent with him and with any luck in bed.

The drive took twenty minutes. As soon as we walked in and the door was closed, his lips found mine with urgency. My back hit the door as we kissed. I went for his tie pulling it loose. He broke the kiss.

"Get up stairs," he whispered.

He turned to the alarm as I moved up the stairs. I was heading down the hall when he reached me. He spun me around claiming my lips once more. The urgency was there as his tongue licked its way into my mouth. My core tightened with anticipation. I wanted him now. I broke the kiss taking his hand and pulling him to our room.

As soon as we were in our room he slammed the door shut and went for the back of my dress. He slowed himself down enough to get the dress off of me without ripping it. It slid to the floor as I pulled my arms free. Santiago looked at the black corset for only a second before he was on top of me. I pulled at his shirt until the buttons gave way. I heard as buttons bounced off surfaces as he backed us across the room to the bed. He had one arm around my waist as the other was in my hair. I pulled the shirt free of his body and went for his pants. Before I had them undone he picked me up placing me on the bed. Santiago pulled my lace panties off of me a second later, his mouth locked on my core. I gasped as his tongue worked in and out of me. Each lick going deeper inside of me. He kept at me until I was coming against his mouth. I felt as his tongue moved out of me, working my clit. His fingers sliding inside of me as his tongue teased. I moaned his name as I came again, around his fingers.

Santiago stood up as I tried to relearn to breathe. He licked his lips tasting what I had left on them. I watched as he sucked the taste of me off his fingers. Santiago stripped his body free of his pants. His erection sprung free. I sat up and grabbed him and began to stroke his hard sex. Santiago's head fell back on his spine as I moved my hand up and down his shaft. I kissed his mark on his chest and moved down his body slowly while my hand continued its steady movement. I found his nipple with my mouth and sucked on it hard for a moment

"Mi Amor," he moaned as my mouth began to move farther down his body again.

I wanted him in my mouth before he entered me. I made to slide off the bed, which brought his focus back to me. Santiago pushed me back on the bed forcing me to release my hold on him. He bit through the bodice of the corset I was wearing. The poor material stood no chance of survival. As soon as my breasts were free his mouth was on one, then the other. Sucking and nipping at my nipples. I ran one hand in his hair as he sucked on my body. I was on the verge of coming again and wanted him inside of me before I did.

"I need you in me," I breathed.

He looked at me as he continued to play with my nipple. His eyes were hungry as he watched me. I watched as he pulled on the nipple until it was too much for me and my back was arching up. Santiago climbed up on the bed sliding his cock inside of me. It wasn't gentle in the least but the sensation as our bodies came together was enough to make me come as soon as he was inside of me. My hands found his back as he moved inside of me. Nails digging into his flesh. He pushed in and out of my body, hard and fast

. Santiago dropped his head and I knew he wanted my vein. I tilted my head to the side, allowing him to drink from me. His fangs sank into my skin with the same need he had kissed me with. My nails dug into Santiago's skin harder as he rode my body and drank from me, I came once more as he did. I released my hold on him as our bodies stilled. Santiago drank from me for only a moment longer before he released my vein. The feel of his body against mine made me want more of him. His lids were low when he met my stare.

"I love you," I whispered.

"And I love you."

It took no time for him to start moving in me again, taking me over the edge repeatedly.

Chapter Forty-One

Santiago and I spent the rest of the night and early hours of the morning making love. I fell asleep lying on his chest. I woke several hours later, my body sore but in the best way possible. I lifted my head finding Santiago awake staring down at me. He brushed my hair behind my ear as he smiled.

"I never got to tell you how beautiful the necklace looks on you," Santiago said.

I scooted up his body and kissed him as my legs fell around his body. The kiss was less urgent than it had been the night before but the need was still there. His arms came around me holding me against him. As sore as I was, I craved him like no other male. From the moment we started a relationship, I craved him. The craving seemed to intensify the longer we were together. I could feel his hard erection as it pressed against the outside of my sex. I angled myself and pushed my upper body up above him. The movement was enough as I slid down his hard shaft. He gasped at the sensation of me surrounding his hard length. I moved slowly as he placed one hand on my neck and one hand slid slowly down my back until he found my ass. I stared down at him as our bodies moved together. He was a gorgeous sight under me as I rolled my hips back and forth, meeting his. Santiago's hand that had been on my neck moved down my chest finding my nipple. He brushed it softly with his thumb making me catch my breath. He smiled at me as he pulled me down to him. We kissed as I continued to ride him slowly. It took no time for either of us to find our release. I collapsed on top of Santiago's chest, listening to his heart beat. The feel of his hard body was amazing. Our bodies, still connected. We stayed that way for a while before he spoke.

"What shall we do today?" he asked.

"I have to make a few calls but after that I'm all yours for the rest of the day," I replied.

"All mine?"

"Yes," I smiled.

"What shall I do with you."

"I guess we will have to figure out what to do with our time."

I wiggled my body a little, reminding him I was still locked around him. He moaned. The sound made me smile.

"As much as I would love to have more of you, I believe I should feed you first," he rolled me onto my back as he pulled himself free from my body.

"We could stay in bed a little longer."

"I drank from you quite a bit the last two nights. I believe you need to eat before we do anything else. Besides this gives you time to make your calls. I will bring you your phone."

"Fine, if you insist," I shrugged.

"I do insist," Santiago smiled, giving me a kiss.

He climbed out of bed as I stretched out. I watched as he moved around the room collecting the clothes we had left on the floor. He headed to the closet with them as I watched him. A few minutes later he came out in his pajama pants. He moved with such grace. His large muscular body was like a work of art. His perfectly sculpted arms with his broad chest that was well defined to his flat stomach. I wrapped myself up in the blanket wishing he was back in bed with me. We had today and part of tomorrow to be together before I went through the transformation of being a hybrid. I wanted as much time as I could get with Santiago. I told him I wouldn't die only two days ago but the truth was I could die. Nothing like the possibility of dying in the near future to make you appreciate what you had. I thought of what was to come. I hoped I would survive the transition. I didn't know if there was anything I could do to ensure it. I had been doing research on becoming a hybrid in hopes I could learn something, anything to increase our chances of success. So far I had found nothing. Maybe my sheer willpower to survive would be enough.

"Mi Amor, are you okay?" Santiago asked standing in the doorway. He had my bag from the car in his hand.

"Yeah."

"I can smell the change in your scent. What is bothering you?"

"I'm just thinking about tomorrow night."

I watched as his body sagged slightly at my words. He moved to the bed not meeting my eyes. He dropped the bag at the foot of the bed before sitting down. He brushed my hair back from my face.

"We do not have to do this. Not yet," he spoke softly.

"Yes, we do. Dante is going to be Hugo's mate. He will be more of a threat to everyone who hates him. Waiting will only delay the inevitable. Not to mention what if we wait too long? This is not something that can't be done quickly. It can take anywhere from two or three hours to a full day."

"I do not wish to lose you."

"Nor do I want to lose you but you know as well as I do that this is the best window we will have."

He nodded his head.

"Okay. Make your calls, I will cook breakfast for you," Santiago pulled me to him, placing a quick kiss on my forehead before he left. I watched him go, memorizing every inch of him until he turned the corner. I pulled the bag towards me and began to dig through it. I had no clue when the bag had been packed in the car but I was grateful that it had. I hadn't thought about it last night. My only thought had been for my mate and getting under him. It wasn't a bad thought on a whole but the idea seemed to distract me more than was probably healthy. I mentally shrugged at the thought and moved on. I found my phone in the bottom of the bag. I pulled it out seeing it was almost dead, and plugged it into the charger I kept next to the bed. I checked my messages first and then my email before I dialed Damian. I hadn't used his number in almost a year, it was weird hitting his contact number after so long. I had grown used to him being almost nonexistent in my life. In the past, when I had called I had always had anticipation, now there was none of that.

"Hello," he answered groggily.

"Did I wake you?" I asked, looking at my own clock. It was almost nine in the morning.

"Savannah?"

"Yeah."

Damian had always been an early riser; the fact that he was asleep was a little shocking.

"Sorry. We didn't leave your party until around two. I have to say your vampires know how to keep a party going," Damian said, his voice was rough.

"You have no clue."

"So...uhm... you said you needed my help."

"Yeah, I did. I don't know how much the media is reporting about what happened at H & W, but one of the young was injected with wolf DNA."

"Wait...What did you say?" now he was awake.

"The young we rescued, they were being experimented on, in the hope they could turn the young into witches, killing the vampire DNA."

"Okay," Damian said hesitantly.

"One of the female young was given wolf DNA. She now has fur and no one knows how to make the hair recede or how to help her. I was wondering if you can help."

"Wolves and witches can't breed. Our DNA is completely different from yours."

"I know but for some reason this female survived what they did to her."

"I don't know what I can do to help?" he asked.

"I was wondering if you can come to the hospital and meet her. I don't know if you can help but no one will want her. No witch will want her because she is a hybrid to the extreme. Vampires won't because of the fact she has wolf DNA. I don't even know if any wolf will want her."

"I don't know, Savannah."

"Will you meet her and see what we are dealing with? If you can't help her, then fine. I will figure out another option," trying to convince him.

"Does she have any other wolf characteristics?"

"I don't know."

He was quiet for a long moment.

"Okay, when can we do this."

"I'll call the hospital to see if we can see her this afternoon," I answered.

"Text me the time and I'll be there."

"Thank you, Damian."

"Don't thank me yet, Savannah," he warned. It almost felt like a normal conversation.

I hung up as Santiago came in with a tray of food.

"You called Damian?" Santiago asked as he set the tray down in front of me. The tray was full of eggs, bacon, and toast. There was a bowl of fruit as well. A glass of orange juice completed the meal. The smell of the food made my stomach growl. I took a piece of bacon and bit into the crispiness, enjoying the flavor.

"The young we saved in the raid, the one with wolf DNA," I said around the bite. "She has nowhere to go. I was thinking maybe Damian or his pack can help with that."

"Is he willing to?"

"He's willing to try. Whether he can or not I don't know. The only way to find out is to go meet her."

He nodded his head.

"Does this mean you and Damian are friends once more?" he asked as I ate.

"I don't know. Maybe? Does it worry you?"

"No. I know you are mine. Your friendship with Damian is good for both of you. It is also is good for the wolves and the clan. I do not wish for you two to be at odds."

I pulled his face to mine and laid a soft kiss on his lips. Santiago responded and moved closer to me. I started to lay back on the bed when he stopped me.

"You need to eat. You will need your strength today." I smiled at him and did what I was told for once in my life. "I am going to draw us a bath while you eat," he said as he climbed off the bed.

I ate my breakfast and then called the hospital. The young were doing better. Many of them were having night terrors but they would be ready for visitors soon. The young we needed to see was named Natalie, which was the first time I was learning her name. The doctors were still trying to figure out if they could reverse the effects of the wolf DNA. If it hadn't been for the fact they had no clue what to do with her or the fact I was Santiago's mate I wouldn't have been granted access to her or any information. I was scheduled to come see the female at four in the afternoon. I sent Damian a text message saying I would meet him at the hospital at four.

I walked into the bathroom seeing the tub was almost filled. Santiago was pulling fresh towels from the cabinet. I looked in the mirror seeing my neck for the first time. The bite marks from two days ago had been almost healed up until they were reopened at some point during the night. I had a new set of marks on my shoulder as well. If we kept this up, I wasn't going to have anywhere else for him to bite. My mate came up behind me pulling me close to his body.

"Our bath is ready," he whispered against my skin.

He was naked as he led me to the tub. Santiago helped me in before stepping in himself. The water was hot but I paid little attention to it. I wanted my male and in that moment nothing else mattered.

Chapter Forty-Two

We took our time in the bath until the water turned cold. The rest of the day was spent in bed until it was time to get ready to go to the hospital. As I dressed, I began to wish I had waited to schedule this meeting, it was time Santiago and I could spend dealing with business instead of with one another. The thought of what awaited for me the next afternoon meant I was right to set it up now. Santiago's words "what if you die", rushed at me. What if I did die, this little female would be lost in a terrible foster care system with no home or love. No, I needed to do this today just in case.

"Are you sure you wish me to come with you?" Santiago asked as he finished getting dressed.

"Yes, I am. If we can see the other young. It's important you're there in case we need to make any additional arrangements for any of them. Besides after the hospital, you and I can have dinner and spend the rest of the evening together."

"I cannot wait," he said before he kissed me.

WE ARRIVED AT THE HOSPITAL a few minutes before four. Damian and Tess were already waiting for us at the entrance. Tess was back in her regular clothes as she stood next to her Alpha.

"Thanks for coming," I said as we approached.

"Yeah. I'm not sure what I can do to help but I'm willing to try."

"We are not sure ourselves but you may be her last hope," Santiago said.

"Let's go in," I said.

Santiago and I walked hand in hand, as Tess and Damian fell into step behind us. The children's ward was on the third floor. The walls were painted in bright colors in hopes of keeping the patients in a positive mood. A mural, painted on the walls of the waiting room, was a jungle scene with animals. There was a monkey swinging from a tree with a tiger below it. An elephant could be seen in the distance as it moved. Birds were flying in the painted blue sky. I approached the nurses' station with my identification.

"Hi, my name is Savannah De los Rios. I spoke with Dr. Bradson about seeing one of the young from H&W Clinical."

"Your the one who got them out," the nurse stated with a smile.

"I am. I have brought my mate, Santiago De los Rios, who was also there that day and Damian Vanguard from the Falls Wolf Pack to meet Natalie."

"I'm Hailey," she introduced herself. Hailey was shorter than myself and a little on the round side. She had a kind smile and I could see her lavender eyes were full of knowledge. She wore pink scrubs like the rest of the nurses on the pediatric floor. "That poor child. Come with me."

"How's she doing?" I asked.

"She's scared mostly. She growls and backs away from us. It took us an hour to get her to eat on the first day. All of the young have been leery of the food. A few of the younger ones are speaking to us. The older ones not so much," she explained.

I tightened my hold on Santiago as I listened to the nurse.

"Is she finally eating?" Damian asked.

"Yes but we believe she is requiring blood. The records the facility kept were detailed. The problem is none of their names are listed in the charts. We're still sorting out the information we were given."

We stopped in front of the room three fifty-one.

"Good luck," the nurse said with sadness.

I opened the door hearing a small growl. We enter the room to find a little brown haired female in a corner, crouched down on her legs. She had hair poking out of her hands and cheeks. I could see under the hospital gown thick patches of hair on her legs. Her hazel eyes looked at us bouncing from one to the other. Her teeth were sharp like a wolf's teeth.

I squatted down to put myself on the same level as her.

"I'm Savannah and I was one of the individuals who found you," I spoke softly. More growls came from the girl. "I wanted to talk with you. Can we do that?" The female growled at me again, shifting into an attack position. She was scared. I stayed where I was not taking my eyes off of her. A small bark escaped her lips, more hair began to pop up as I stayed still.

"Let me try," Damian said as he stepped up beside me. I stood up and took a step back, which made the young female jump.

"I'm Damian. I'm a wolf. It looks as if you're having trouble with transitioning."

The girl's eyes narrowed at the sight of Damian. He stuck out his arm and shifted the arm. We all watched as bones popped and moved creating a paw with sharp claws. Hair sprotted out of the limb. The girl stood as her mouth fell open. The growling stopped. I could see some of the hair on her face was receding into her skin.

"How did you do that?" she asked in a small voice.

"Well, I focus on what I want my body to do and it does what I tell it to."

He transformed his arm back to a male's arm.

"It hurts to change," she whimpered.

"Can I come over to you? I think I can help you," Damian spoke to her in a kind voice.

She looked at all of us before her eyes landed on Damian. There was an uncertainty there. I didn't blame her for not wanting to trust anyone. She, like all the others, had been to Hell and back.

"I won't hurt you. I swear," Damian reassured her.

"Just you," she spoke quietly.

Damian moved slowly to the girl. He sat down in front of her and offered his hand to her. It took her a minute to place a hand in his.

"Now I want you to close your eyes and picture what you would look like without the fur. Can you do that?" he asked.

She nodded her head. It took ten minutes for it to work but we all watched as the fur retreated back into her skin. Her teeth shrinking to normal size except her canines that stayed long. Somehow this girl was the super hybrid of hybrids. I wondered what it would mean for her later in life.

She looked at her hands seeing little girls hands. Tears started to roll down her face.

"How did I do that?"

"Like every wolf does."

"Is that what I am now?" she asked.

"Part of you is," Damian answered.

"No one will want me because I'm a freak. That's what they called me."

She sobbed as she sat back down on the floor.

"You are different but you are not a freak," Damian said.

"I was supposed to be destroyed the day they took us out of there," she nodded her head indicating me. "I was a freak before this, now I'm even more. My mother didn't want me and now no one will."

Her words were tearing me to pieces.

"My pack wants you," Damian said.

"What?"

I looked at Damian in shock at his words. I wanted his help. I had no clue he would take it this far.

"How would you feel about living with us?"

"But I'm not just a wolf. What if I can't transform all the way?"

"It doesn't matter," he answered with a shake of his head.

"You are also more than welcome to spend time with us," Santiago smiled at her.

"What if I hurt someone?" she asked.

Santiago stepped up and bent down next to Damian.

"My name is Santiago. I am a friend of Damian's. We will make sure you do not harm yourself or anyone," Santiago promised.

"But you're a vampire. How can you be friends?" she asked.

"We are both hellborns, just as you are. That is how," Sanitago explained.

"You both want to help me?

"Yes," Santiago answered.

"Natalie, would you like to come live with the Falls Wolf Pack?" Damian asked. She was looking at Damian with a look that questioned if he was being serious. There was a long pause as she sized up Damian. I could see the distrust in her eyes as she stared at Damian. "I want you to be part of my pack."

Those words shifted something in the young.

"Yes, please."

"Good," Damian said before he looked at the rest of us. "Why don't we ask the others to leave us and we can get to know each other better. Are you okay with that?" Damian asked her.

"Yes, please," she said.

"Good," he replied. Damian looked at us. "Why don't you find something else to do?" Damian said.

"Alpha, I'm supposed to stay with you," Tess pointed out.

"This is Tess, she is one of my wolves. Would it be okay if she stays?"

Natalie looked at Tess as if she was sizing her up. There was knowledge in the young's eyes that should not have been there at such a young age. She finally nodded her head.

"Santiago and I will go check on some of the other young," I said.

"See you later," Damian answered. I could hear their voices as they began a conversation. Damian was telling her all about the pack. It was good seeing him smile as he talked to Natalie. It felt as if it had been forever since anyone had seen that look on his face. Calling Damian had been the right move for Natalie, maybe even the right move for him. What would become of her as she grew was anyone's guess. Between the vampires and the wolves she would have plenty of support.

Santiago and I found Hailey down the hall. She was at a computer station adding notes to a chart.

"Hailey, I'm sorry to bother you but could we visit with a few of the other young?" I asked.

"I have to speak with the doctor. It shouldn't be a problem," she said as she finished typing. "How did it go with Natalie?" she asked.

"She's making friends with the Alpha of the wolf pack now."

Hailey stopped typing looking at me as if I had two heads.

"Is she really?"

"Yes."

"Let me try to get ahold of Dr. Bradson."

Santiago and I stepped away from her, giving her time to make the call.

"It was a very good idea having Damian approach that young."

"I wasn't sure it was going to work," I admitted.

"She will be the only one of her kind."

"I know," I said sadly.

The wolves would treat her as one of their own or at least most of them would. I was happy that she would have a home. The worry I had was, she would never feel like she belonged. I spent most of my life feeling that way. It was hard on the soul. Santiago made me feel as if I had a home. I was hopeful Natalie's wolf side would take control of her transition, eventually drowning out the vampire side.

Hailey approached us.

"We have three who are well enough to be seen. The first is a five year old, her name is Siobhan. She had been in the facility from what we gathered for about a month. She is doing well. Nights are rough for her. From what we can tell she wasn't tested on more than a few blood draws and scans," Hailey informed us.

"I guess there is some good news. Do we have any idea who her family is?"

"No, she hasn't said anything about a family."

We followed Hailey into the room where a little brunette female with electric blue eyes was playing. She was the girl Meri and I had pulled from the fire. She had been hiding under a bed. Her eyes were bright as she looked up at us.

"Siobhan. This is Savannah and Santiago. They wanted to meet you," Hailey said in a cheerful voice.

The female looked at me and ran at me. Her little body hit my legs as she hugged me.

"She's the one who got me out. She was with a vampire, like him," she pointed at Santiago as she spoke to Hailey.

I had no clue what to do as the girl hugged me. I had never had a lot of experience with young and now one was hugging me.

"Can you show me how to do that thing you did?" she asked as she finally stepped back.

"Uhm...Well... can I ask what kind of witch you are?" I asked.

"I'm like you. See," she said as she produced a magenta flame in her hand. "I also have to feed like a vampire," she sounded sad about it.

Santiago bent down in front of her.

"It is not so bad being a vampire," he said.

"I got in trouble at the group home for feeding on a boy. I was so hungry and they wouldn't listen. Then I ended up in that place and they wouldn't let me feed either. If I wasn't a hybrid someone would want me."

"What if I can get someone to feed you today?" he asked.

Her face lit up at the idea of being fed.

"I'm so hungry."

"Let me make a call," Santiago stood up and headed outside.

"So can you teach me to control my magic?" she asked.

"Let's have a seat." I suggested. She hopped over to the bed.

"If I could control my magic maybe a family would like me. At the last home, right before I bit that boy, I set a trashcan on fire."

"Siobhan, I would be more than happy to work with you," I said.

"You will!" she squealed.

"Can I ask you where you're from?"

"Phoenix. Do I have to go back there?"

"I don't know. We have to talk with the vampire clan there. They may want you to live with them, unless we find your family."

"I don't have one of those."

She sounded too comfortable with that statement. Siobhan reminded me of myself at that age. If the clan in Phoenix didn't want her, I would find her a home with one of our vampires. Someone who would understand her vampire needs and would allow me to help her to control her magic. For a leyline witch it was hard when you were young to control your magic. Strong emotions could cause your magic to materialize without knowing how to stop it. It took time and patience. Earth witches had it easier in many ways. They worked with charms and their own blood. Spirit talkers or ley line magic had a harder time.

"I am making a vow to you, I will find you a family," I placed my hand on my heart.

"You are born to a family," she said matter of factly.

"There are two kinds of family. The one you are born into and the one you choose."

"What kind do you have?"

"The one I chose. My mate is a vampire and so is my sister. But I also have a few humans who I am close with and a wolf who is a very good friend as well."

"And they're your family?" she was shocked.

"Yup."

Santiago came back into the room.

"I have a human who will be arriving shortly to feed you, Siobhan. She is happy to help."

We sat with Siobhan and talked while we waited. Ansiley arrived with a human within the hour. Santiago and I stepped to the side while Siobhan's needs were met. I told Santiago the little I had learned from the girl. He would call the Phoenix Clans and see if anyone claimed her. He was confident no one would. The fact no one wanted her, just made everything worse. She was a sweet little female who had already learned the harshness life could deal.

"If no one claims her, we need to find her a home with one of our vampires."

"Mi Amor, do you think it wise we be the ones to do it?" he asked.

"Yes, I do."

"The humans will want to do the placing of these young."

"Normally yes but they have no clue what we, as hellborns, need. Siobhan was starved in the group home she was in because they had no clue what she required. Then was starved again at H&W because no one cared. I made her a vow I would find her a family. We need to do this," I explained.

Santiago gave me a measured look.

"Then we will do what we can. I am going to warn you, many of them will more than likely find homes with clans elsewhere."

"I understand but we need to make sure they're good homes. And Siobhan gets a home here in our city. She needs to be a part of our clan," I demanded.

He smiled at me as his hand wrapped around the back of my neck. He pulled my head to him laying a soft kiss on my forehead.

"You have an amazing heart," he said.

"Just don't tell anyone, it will ruin my reputation."

"It will be our secret," Santiago smiled.

Chapter Forty-Three

S antiago and I visited two other young. One of the young was a male who was seventeen, he had been in the facility since he was six years old. He was one of our missing young we knew about. Andrew Corker had survived what many had not. He had been experimented on with drugs, they had injected him with stem cells from humans as well. He had almost died from the various treatments they had tested on him. The medications they had given him at one point had caused him to become ill to the point he could not stand, nor eat. Andrew had tried to escape three years ago and had been severely beaten for his attempt. From what Andrew had told us, they were fed small meals twice a day. If you received any negative reports from staff, your meals were cut in half. His small frame showed the abuse he had endured. Andrew looked like he was ten not seventeen. His body was thin to the point where you could see the bones in his arms and legs. There were scars covering his body from the abuse and the look in his eyes was one of trauma. His story as he spoke, made me want to go back to H&W and kill all of them again. Andrew was unsure about seeing his mother when I mentioned her. The staff at H&W had told him his mother had sold him in order to fix him. I had spoken to the female. It was as far from the truth as you could get. I would continue my visits with Andrew and hopefully he would find a way to be okay with all he had endured.

The other young we met was a fourteen year old female. Her name was Darlene. She had been held at H&W for the last eight years. She had received the same treatment as Andrew, except as soon as she turned thirteen two of the male staff members had began to rape her as a form of punishment. The mental wounds she was dealing with were going to last for years. She was doing as well as could be expected. Santiago kept his distance as I spoke with her. Her eyes never left him, Darlene wanted to ensure he would not come near her. There were so many others that I hadn't spoken to as of yet and I would imagine their stories were just as hard to hear as Andrew and Darlene's had been. I was happy to be heading home for the night after the time we had spent listening to a few of the stories. I asked Hailey to call me if anything changed with any of the young.

SANTIAGO AND I TOOK the rest of our last twenty-fours to be with one another. Santiago had started to look for a home for Siobhan as soon as we left the hospital. Anyone interested in taking the young in would contact Cristian until after my transition. We spent most of our evening lounging around, watching movies, curled up next to one another. The time we had was relaxing but only to a point. I could feel the tension in his body as I curled into him. As the hours ticked by, the worse it would become. I could feel my own anxiety building as Santiago's grew. At one point I almost called the entire thing off but I couldn't do that. This was something I had to do either by my own choosing or by Hugo forcing it upon us. In my mind it was better for me to do it on my terms than someone else's. The Matthew factor also hung over our heads. He had made no other contact with me since the night of Hugo's party. It was only a matter of time before he did. What if his next contact was in person? Becoming a hybrid may be my only way of survival against Matthew.

We left our home an hour before we had agreed to meet Meri at the club. Fear rode through me as we arrived at the club. Santiago parked in the back of the building as I tried to calm myself. Normally, we would have been in his Porsche but we took my vehicle instead. As soon as the transition was done, I wanted to be home in our bed. My car allowed for me to lie down in the back while he drove. He reached over taking a hold of my hand. I looked at him as we sat there.

"Are you sure you are ready for this?" Santiago asked.

"No, I'm not but when else do we have the time? I have the next five days off, which means I have time to recuperate and adjust to a new normal."

"We can find another..." he began.

I leaned across the seat, placing my free hand on his cheek.

"No, we do this now. You, Meri and Duncan will keep me safe while I go through it. We will get through this."

"Months ago I was ready for you to do this. Now that the moment is here I am terrified," Santiago admitted.

That made the two of us was what I said in my head. What came out of my mouth was totally different.

"I will make it through this. Do you hear me? Death may try to take me but he is going to have one hell of a fight if he thinks I will go quietly."

He rested his forehead against mine as we sat there. He released my hand taking my face in both of his hands, drawing my lips to his. The kiss was gentle as he licked his way into my mouth. I pulled back looking into those dark eyes.

"I will survive this," I said reassuring him. I gave him a quick kiss as a pair of headlights swung into the spot next to us. I glanced over to see Meri and Duncan pulling in.

"It is time," he said.

"Come on."

We climbed out of the car. Santiago stood at the front end of the SUV as I waited for them to climb out of their car. Meri looked at me with a serious look on her face as she opened the door. Duncan climbed out of the drivers side and gave me a quick hug. Neither of us were huggers, so the fact he had hugged me meant he was just as nervous as the rest of us.

"Thank you for being here," I said.

"I told you before you're family. This is what we do for family."

He walked away joining Santiago as I waited for Meri to come around. She hugged me, which was just as weird as Duncan hugging me, maybe more.

"I need a moment with you," I whispered into her ear.

"Shall we proceed inside?" Santiago's voice was tight.

"Give us a minute, please," I said.

He gave me a look before he nodded his head.

"I will stand by the door. When you are ready, knock," he instructed me.

I watched as the two males proceeded inside through the back door. I waited until the door was shut before I turned to Meri. I took both her hands in mine.

"Listen, if this all goes sideways I need you to take over the company. I already added your name to the ownership paperwork and filed them with the state. But I need to know Ryan and the guys are covered."

"Don't even go there right..."

"No, I have to because there is a chance that the transition could go bad. Look, I'm going to tell you the same thing I told Santiago. If death thinks he can just ride in here and take me, he has another think coming but we both know I could die. So I need your word."

"Dammit! Why do you have to do this now?" She pulled her hands away from me, placing them on her hips.

"Because it's now or never."

She looked at me, seeing the resolve on my face.

"Fine. I will. Okay?" Meri all but grumbled.

"One more thing. If I do die, you have to promise me you won't let Santiago do anything stupid."

"I can't guarantee that."

"Duncan will take care of you. He will prevent you from doing something stupid. But I need someone doing that for Santiago just as you would do for me. Promise me!" I pleaded.

"I really hate you right now."

"You love me or you wouldn't be here right now," I tried to smile at her.

"If you die, I swear I will find a way to bring you back and kill you again for this moment right here."

"Is that a promise?"

"I promise I will take care of your mate, if you die," she growled.

I took a deep breath before I hugged her one more time and headed for the door. I pounded on the door with resolve. It swung open with Santiago there to hold it open. We walked down the stairs saying nothing as we went. I kept telling myself to breathe as we moved. It took no time to reach Santiago's office. I headed across the room to the door of his former living quarters as I heard the office door shut behind me.

"Where do you want us?" Meri asked.

"Uhm... I want you to start out here. The first part should be just the two of us. Once it starts you can decide where you want to be." Meri didn't look happy about my decision. Before she could say anything Duncan intervened.

"You got it," Duncan replied. He took his mate's hand holding her in place.

Santiago crossed the room joining me near the living quarters door. He opened the door for me allowing me to enter first. I was confident he gave the other two a final look before he followed.

The room was exactly as we had left it three months ago. All the furniture was gone except for the king size platform bed that sat in the middle of the room. The sheets looked fresh as I approached the bed. Dark red sheets with a heavy goose down, black comforter covered the bed. Santiago was standing behind me. He placed a hand on my shoulder as we stood looking at the bed.

"Are you sure this is the right time?" Santiago asked once more.

I stepped up to the side of the bed and folded the bedding back before I climbed up onto the bed. The mattress was just as I had remembered it. Soft to the point it felt as if I was sinking into it. I took off my gun belt and hung it off the headboard before I kicked my shoes off. I laid down and looked at my mate.

He seemed to release a breath in defeat as I stared at him. He moved slowly to the other side of the bed and slipped out of his shoes. He got on the bed next to me, sliding as close as he could get. Santiago stroked my check as he looked into my eyes.

"I love you, Savannah."

"And I love you," I replied as I laid a kiss on his wrist.

He took the wrist I had just kissed and scored it with his teeth. I watched as blood welled to the surface. His hand was shaking as he moved it towards my mouth. He hesitated just inches from my lips. I could see the fear he was feeling. If we were going to do this I would have to draw him to me. I grabbed a hold of his wrist and leaned my head towards the wound. As soon as my lips touched his skin he shuddered. I began to suck slowly allowing the taste of him to flood my system. I knew the taste of blood all too well. I had expected it to taste like copper, as my own did. Santiago's blood was different; it was a bolder taste and more enjoyable than I thought it would be. The taste was close to his scent. The taste was clean and of oak. I sucked on his wrist as he watched me. I looked into his eyes as I took from him, I had to survive this. I wanted more time with him and those eyes. He was beautiful in so many ways.

I continued to take from him, for what seemed like forever before I could feel the first change in my body. A cold sensation had begun to spread from my lips, down my body. It felt as if I was in a tub of ice as I lay there. The coldness was taking over my system and I could feel as a shiver ran down my body, followed closely by another. Weakness was also there. I had to rest my head on the pillow beneath me, taking Santiago's wrist with me and still I fed from him. The shiver that had started was now a continuous wave. I tried to look at my mate only to find I didn't have the energy to open my eyes. As weak as I was, I continued to drink. No additional symptoms came for several minutes. I had the thought that this isn't so bad, when a new sensation hit my body. Spasms started to tighten the muscles in my arms and legs. At first, the pain was small and easy to ignore. Soon the pain grew in intensity. I moaned as the pain became worse by the minute until I had to finally release his wrist. I threw my head back as pain became the only sensation I could feel. The spasms grew even worse, as if my limbs were about to break off from my body. I heard a ragged scream tear from my throat. The spasms spread to my chest next and moved down through my body. Breathing was becoming a challenge as the spasms felt like bands wrapping around me, squeezing across my chest. I could feel as wetness swept down my face. I tried to stop myself from screaming again. I was confident Santiago was on the verge of panic, as he watched it all unfold. God only knew how Meri was doing. It felt as if my body was about to burst open as the spasms continued and a new feeling of fire filled my chest. I felt as my back arched off the bed, a new even worse scream filled the space. A distant sound came from my left. It sounded as if it was miles away. I had no clue what it was because the pain overrode all of my senses. I screamed and screamed until I could hear nothing else. It felt as if my body was going to be consumed by flames. It took a moment to realize that I no longer could hear myself. I could feel my mouth was open wide but I could hear nothing. The world had gone silent or maybe I had. The pain was there and I begged for the end to come. I opened my eyes finding it hard to see, Santiago's face was above mine and I could see as tears streaked his face. His lips were moving but I had no idea what he was saying. My vision was becoming blurry and dark around the edges. I watched as slowly my vision became clouded and then the pain intensified one more time. I didn't know how it could get any worse from what it had been but it did. Blackness took my vision, which set off a new panic inside of me. My heart was hammering against my ribs. It was pounding so hard I wasn't sure if the fire was going to kill me or my heart, when it finally beat a path out of my chest. I had one final thought of Santiago before I was swallowed by the pain.

I DIDN'T KNOW HOW LONG I had been unconscious but slowly sensations were coming back. I could hear voices as I lay there. I couldn't figure out who they were but they sounded far away. The next thing that returned was the feel of the soft sheets around me. I tried to move but found my body was sore and stiff. As time continued to pass, more of my senses were coming back on line. My hearing was getting better and better, so was my sense of smell. I could smell citrus in the room that was mingling with the scent of aged wood. It was a nice and relaxing scent in all honesty. There was another scent as well, a hint of lavender that was deep in the smell of mahogany. It was the smell of Santiago but the scent was ten times stronger than it had ever been before. There was also another smell; it was less charming than the others. It was the smell of acid, as if the room had an open container of vinegar. It burned my nose. I tried to raise my hand to cover my nose. A moan escaped me as I tried to find the energy. All conversation stopped as the smell of acid grew stronger. All at once my hearing came back in a flood. I could hear the shuffle of feet and the sounds of their clothes as they all moved.

"Savannah! Can you hear me?" came the panicked voice of my mate.

"I ...ahem...yeah... I can," I said. My throat felt as if I had swallowed a ton of sand. I opened my eyes seeing those beautiful dark brown eyes above me. It was the best sight in the world. The smell of acid disappeared and the other scents replaced them. I tried to sit up finding my body was weak.

"We were worried you would not wake up. I am very happy to see your eyes open," my mate said with relief clear on his face. He kissed me on the forehead.

"Help me sit up, please?" I said.

Santiago slid an arm under my back and pulled me up slowly. As I got up right the world tilted on its axis. I closed my eyes allowing the head spins to stop. There was the scent of acid again. I opened my eyes seeing Meri and Duncan standing at the foot of the bed. The muscles in their faces were drawn tight as they watched me. The scent I had been smelling since I had awoken, had been their fear. Interesting, I could sense emotions now. Well that was going to come in handy, wasn't it.

"I'm okay guys, just a little dizzy."

"Are you sure?" Meri asked.

"Yes," I replied.

The smell disappeared again. I took in their appearances as I got re-oriented with life. Meri and Duncan were both in jeans but they had on different shirts than they had when we arrived. Duncan had shown up in a black graphic T-shirt with something to do with coffee on it. I couldn't remember exactly what it had on it past a coffee cup. Now he had on a navy blue one with a red crab in the center of the chest. Meri had started out in a black razor back tank and had changed into a long sleeve purple top. Why had they changed? I looked at my mate seeing he was still in his workmen jeans, he wore when he was working with wood and a black collared shirt that had seen better days. I looked at his wrist seeing the skin had mended, only a slight pink still lingered.

"How long was I out?"

They all looked at each other before Santiago answered me.

"A day and a half."

"Wait ...What?" I said in disbelief.

A day and a half! Holy Hell! No wonder they had all been scared.

"You were conscious for the first four hours of your transition and when it became too much, you passed out. For a while you moaned and your arms would twitch and then you just fell silent. You did not move or make any noise," Santiago explained.

Four hours. I had lasted four hours in that Hell. I forced my brain to move on. Santiago looked weak. I could see his coloring was off. The bite mark on his wrist should have healed if I had been out almost two days.

"How much did I take from you?"

"You took a substantial amount," he answered.

"Oh God, you need to feed," The smell of fear was there again except it was coming from me.

"I will once I know how you are doing."

"You need to feed," I ordered.

He sat down next to me placing one hand on my cheek.

"I swear I am fine. Are you hungry?"

I stopped and thought about it. My throat still felt like I had eaten sand, so water was a must. I ran my tongue over my canines. They were longer than I remembered them being but they were not as long as the three vampires standing in front of me. I took inventory of my body. I was sore but it was minor. My stomach rumbled. I was hungry... for food.

"I'm hungry for food, not blood."

"Well then that answers that question," Duncan said.

"What question?"

"If you would need to feed. When you go through a transition the first thing you want is blood. You don't, which tells us you don't require blood for survival," Duncan explained.

"Which leads us to the other question. What piece of vampire have you taken on?" Meri asked, eyeing me.

A new smell filled the room; it smelled like lemons. Interesting.

"My sense of smell is better. Before I was fully awake I could smell acid," I answered.

"You were smelling our fear," Santiago replied.

"Yeah."

"What else has changed?" he asked.

I took stock again and my hearing was excellent. There was someone in the office, I was confident of that. There was a sound of feet moving. I didn't think my sight had altered but I could be wrong. I flexed my hand. I needed food before I could see if I had more strength there.

"Whose in your office?" I asked.

"Hugo. He has been waiting for you to wake as well."

"I take it he wishes to see me?" My voice sounded tired.

"Yes," my mate smiled at me. I smiled back at him.

"Then let him come in and see me."

"I can ask him to wait until you have been fed properly."

"No. I would rather get this done with and then go home and eat." He looked at me unsure of my plans. I gave him a nod, which caused the room to spin again. "Please."

"As you wish, Mi Amor," he replied. He kissed my forehead once more before he got up and crossed the room. I leaned back against the pillows, pulling the bedding up slightly. A moment later Hugo entered the room with Santiago behind him. Meri and Duncan bowed their heads, as did I. The spinning started once more. I was hoping Hugo would make this quick. I really needed to eat.

"Dearest Savannah, you have arrived on the other side," he smiled down at me.

"Hello, Hugo."

"You have small fangs, I take it you will not need to feed then?" Hugo looked at Santiago.

"It appears she will not require blood," Santiago answered.

"You look breathtaking, Savannah," Hugo complimented me.

"Do I?" I asked.

"Yes. Your mate's blood seems to have given you youth. I cannot wait to see what else will become of you," he smiled.

"Thank you," I said unsure of how to respond. Hugo was the only one who had that effect on me when it came to what to say. I usually had an answer for everything, not when it came to Hugo.

"Now I know you wish to go home but there is some business we must complete, you and I," Hugo said.

"Hugo, surely this can wait until tomorrow," Santiago tried to intervene.

"My dear Santiago, there are things that must be done."

The next exchange was all in Spanish as the two went back and forth. Santiago's arm shot out pointing at me. I let them carry on for a few minutes before I stepped in.

"Santiago... Santiago!" the arguments stopped at my raised voice.

"Let's just do it and then you can take me home. Please. I have only a few more days before I return to work and I want that time with you. So I will do it now."

Hugo smiled at Santiago as if he had won a prize. Hugo walked around to my side of the bed. I pushed myself back up. I was just happy I could sit up myself this time. Hugo offered me his wrist.

"Savannah De los Rios do you vow to honor the Black Grove Clan? To uphold our laws? Do you swear your loyalty to us?"

"Yes."

"Take my vein, dearest Savannah."

I had no clue what I was actually doing in that moment. My fangs hit his flesh and I pushed them deep into his vein. I drank from him as I had from my mate. I could feel all eyes were on me as I drank. He tasted sweet but not nearly as good as Santiago. He touched my shoulder, which I took to mean I was done. I pulled free from his vein, finding some of his blood was on my lip. I licked it off, which made Hugo smile.

"Thank you, Savannah. Now I require your vein as well."

This was news to me. Hugo saw the confusion on my face.

"You are part of my family and I require a small taste of you as I have with each of my members."

I offered up my wrist to the vampire. His thin delicate hand wrapped around my wrist, gently as his fangs pierced the skin. I gasped at the sharpness of his bite. Santiago had begun to growl as he watched his friend and leader drink from me. It lasted only a minute. Hugo pulled his fangs from my flesh and kissed my wrist.

"You taste very similar to your mate, with a sweetness I have never tasted before," Hugo said. I could see he wanted more from me. His head hung still over my wrist. Santiago growled loudly, as the room grew cold. "I am sorry, my dear friend. You may go home with your mate," he replied, turning his eyes on Santiago. "Santiago, I will see you in three days time. Enjoy your time with your mate."

Santiago bowed to Hugo as he headed for the door. Santiago didn't wait for the door to shut before he stepped over to me. The smell of fire filled my senses. I looked at my mate seeing the same look in his eyes I had seen only days ago, when Matthew had left me roses. He had not liked any of this one bit.

"Will you please take me home?" I asked.

"Yes," Santiago answered with a smile.

I tried to get out of bed finding my legs were shaky as I stood up. My head did its number once again. I really needed to eat. I sat back down on the bed collecting myself before I tried again.

"I will be carrying you to the car," Santiago said, standing in front of me.

"No, I can walk. I just need a moment."

He didn't respond, he picked me up as if I weighed nothing.

"You are going to allow me to carry you. You will not fight me on this," Santiago said with finality.

I wanted to fight him but it felt good being in his arms. I rested my head on his shoulder as he moved.

"Meri can you please collect her weapon from the headboard."

"I'm on it," Meri answered.

He moved gracefully down the hall and up the backstairs. The sun was already making its descent in the sky. I heard the car alarm beep. Santiago shifted me slightly opening the back seat door and placed me gently on the seat. I watched as Meri kissed Duncan and they smiled at each other. Santiago climbed into the back seat with me as Meri took the driver's seat. They had obviously worked this out while I was out. I slid myself into the middle seat and leaned against him. Santiago placed an arm around me as Meri adjusted everything. The feel of him was the greatest feeling in the world. During the transition I had almost begged for my death, the pain had been so great. I had been unsure if I would ever get to feel his arms around me again. Now I was grateful I had survived just to be in his arms again. His scent filled me as I breathed him in. I loved the smell of my male. It was the smell of home.

Chapter Forty-Four

We arrived home without any issues. I had a difficult time staying awake as Meri drove, Santiago never released his hold on me. As soon as we arrived home, Santiago carried me from the car to the house, I insisted on walking but he would hear none of it. This was one of those moments where it was better to give your mate what he wanted instead of fighting it. He carried me up the stairs to our room, placing me gently on the bed. Meri sat down next to me as he bustled back down the stairs for food. The lack of substance in my body was becoming more apparent the longer I went without food. The dizziness I felt at the club had now turned to shaking. I tried to ignore it as Meri stared at me. I could see the worry in her eyes, as the smell of vinegar filled the room.

"Are you going to sit here by my side fretting all night?" I asked.

"Until I know you're okay, yes I am."

"I'm awake and sitting up mostly. All I need is food. You should go home with your mate."

"No, not yet," she said.

"For God sakes, I'm fine."

"Savannah, I have seen a lot of transitions, most of them last a matter of hours. Your's lasted almost two days. We weren't sure if you were going to wake up or not. No, I'm staying here for a little longer."

"Have you ever seen a hybrid transition?" I questioned.

"No," she answered.

"Maybe that's all it was. When a witch goes through the change, the vampire and witch DNA's are fighting the transition that has been started. I swear I'm okay."

"Maybe but I'm staying for a little while longer," Meri said stubbornly.

"For the love of God! Is there anything I can say that will get you to leave?" I demanded.

"Nope."

I thought for a moment before I switched tactics.

"I'm going to be feeding my mate after I eat, that usually involves sex. So are you sure you want to stay?"

"Well I have always wondered..." Meri smiled, not completing her sentence.

"And that's where your wondering ends."

She smiled at me as Santiago brought a tray of food to me.

"You need to eat immediately, so I chose simple foods. A sandwich and fruit."

"Thank you."

The turkey sandwich was delicious with thick slices of meat, lettuce, and tomato. I tried to take my time as I ate but found it difficult. My body was deprived of food so all I wanted to do was scarf all of it down. I had eaten about half the sandwich when I realized the two of them were looking at me.

"Will you two stop watching me?" I snapped around a bite of my sandwich.

"Perhaps I will see if we have any more of those little cakes you like so much?" Santiago offered.

"You need to sit down until I can feed you. The Ding Dong will wait until after I eat." I replied.

"No. I will call someone to feed me," he said.

I set my sandwich down with Santiago's comment. Like hell someone was going to feed him, other than me.

"No you won't. Look, we have determined I don't need to feed from a vein, correct."

"Yes but..."

"Then I can feed you just as I have done so for the last three months," I cut him off.

"Mi Amor, be reasonable."

"I am. Once I eat I will be well enough to feed you. You will not be taking any other vein other than mine. Now sit down before you collapse," I demanded. "And you," I said pointing at Meri. "Go home. If something changes, I swear Santiago will call you and you can rush right over," I snapped at Meri.

Meri looked at me unsure if she should do what I was demanding. She looked at Santiago who looked tired.

"Okay but you better call me in the morning."

"How about I send you a text?" I offered.

"No, I want a call."

"Fine, I will call you. If you will just go home," I said.

She gave me a crushing hug before she left. Santiago walked her downstairs while I enjoyed the rest of my food in peace. I loved both of them but the hovering needed to stop before we found out how my magic had changed, right now.

Santiago was back a few minutes later.

"I know you requested to wait until you were done eating but I brought you one anyway," he held up the Ding Dong.

I wanted to stay irritated with his nervous nilly routine but couldn't. It was probably why he brought me the Ding Dong. He knew chocolate always softened me up.

"Thank you."

"I am sorry for our behavior. You frightened us during your transition. When you didn't wake after eight hours I began to panic. Eight hours turned into twenty-four hours, which turned into thirty-six. I was on the verge of calling an ambulance when you woke," he sat down next to me.

"I understand why you're hovering. If I wasn't okay then I wouldn't be awake and eating now."

"You do not understand. I felt I had lost you twice in one week, Savannah. I cannot handle anymore near death experiences when it comes to you, at least not right away," he replied. He stood up and moved to the foot of the bed. "It has been too much. When we began to date I accepted all of it as part of you. I still do but you have had one too many close calls as of late."

I reached my hand out to him. I could smell the stench of fear as it rolled off of him. He took my hand and sat back down next to me.

"I can't promise I won't have anymore near death experiences again. I can promise you I won't be so reckless as I was during the fire. I can also promise I won't have anymore this week."

"When I told you if you die I will as well. I was not being dramatic, I was being honest," he looked at me with sadness in his eyes. The smell of cold winter rain replaced the smell of fear.

"I know you were. And I would feel the same if it was you."

He pulled me against him. The smell of sadness was still there but it was slowly easing away. He released me.

"Now finish eating," Santiago ordered me as he set the Ding Dong down on the tray.

I ATE ALL THE FOOD on the tray and then some. Santiago ended up making me another sandwich before I was full. I sat back in bed as Santiago took the tray back downstairs. I was feeling stronger than I had when I had first woken up. The dizziness and shaky feeling was gone thanks to my mate feeding me. I looked down at the clothes I was wearing realizing I was still in what I had worn when we had started the transition. I wanted a shower and fresh set of clothes. I headed for the bathroom not waiting for Santiago to return. He could always come and join me. I turned the shower on not looking in the mirror at first. I grabbed a clean set of clothes from the closet and set them on the counter. I began to strip out of my clothes when I looked into the large mirror and saw my reflection for the first time. The marks Santiago had left on my neck were gone, as was the soreness I had had when I awoke. My eyes were a brighter shade of blue and my hair was an absolute mess. I ran my brush through it as I looked at my fair skin. Any bruising I had received from the raid on H&W was now gone, as if it had never been there. My new sense of smell had been the first thing I noticed when I woke. It appeared I also had the healing capability of vampires as well. I had to admit I was looking forward to that part of it. A smell of mahogany, mint, and lavender floated into the room. I turned to see Santiago as he entered the room. His smell intensified at the sight of me. It was the scent of arousal, it had to be. I drew my eyes down his body seeing he was hard under his jeans. Any fear he had been feeling evaporated into thin air.

"You are supposed to be resting," he said as he took in my body.

" I am doing just fine. I needed to get out of those clothes and I am in desperate need of a shower. In fact, since eating I feel better," I took a few steps towards him. "Now are you going to stand there and watch me in the shower or are you going to join me?"

"Mi Amor, I do not wish to push your body too far on the first night after your transition."

I walked over to him and began to undo the buttons on his shirt slowly.

"And I am saying I want my mate to come join me in the shower."

I pulled his shirt open and touched his broad chest with a gentle hand. My hands slowly moved to his pants. He stood still as I undid the button.

"I know you want to," I whispered against his skin as I laid a kiss on his chest

"Do you?"

"Yes," I whispered as I slid his pants down from his body.

My hand stroked his hard sex as he tried to resist me. I met his eyes as he watched me. I could see the fire in his eyes as his scent filled the space. A new smell was mingling with his. It smelled like strawberries. It had to be my own smell. The mix of the two was intoxicating. My mouth found his nipple and I sucked on it hard. He was almost panting as I played with his nipple and cock at the same time. I looked at him again as I moved my mouth down his body. I dropped to my knees and licked the tip of his cock. I felt as he shuddered. I looked up to see his eyes on me. I extended my tongue again and circled it around the head of his cock. Santiago was trembling as he fought to resist me. I sucked on the tip of him as I stroked him with my hand. A growl rolled through him, as I found a rhythm with my mouth and hand moving as one. I kept going until he could do nothing but growl. I let go of his cock and slid all the way down his hard shaft with my mouth.

"Savannah," bit out. I pulled back from his sex.

His hands drew me up from the floor pulling me against him. The kiss was as it had been the night of our mating ceremony, urgant and full of need. Santiago grabbed the back of my neck holding me to him. My lips parted for him as his tongue moved into my mouth. The feel of him was different in some way, as if I was feeling more of him than I ever did before. He ended the kiss just as fast as it started. He kept a hold of the back of my neck.

"Get in the shower, female," he growled. I smiled at the sound of his voice. It was all predator. If I thought the day Matthew had delivered his roses had been predatory it was nothing to what was about to happen. Santiago released his hold on me. I walked to the shower as he pulled his jeans from his legs. I stepped into the shower with Santiago following. The spray was hot or maybe that was just our bodies, as he spun me to face him. Santiago forced my body against the tile as he lifted me up. His large hands on my ass.

I wrapped my legs around him as we kissed. One of my arms went around his neck while the other was in his hair. The water from all three shower heads rained down on us as I kissed him. There was no prelude to it, just his hard cock pushing into my body in one hard thrust. I cried out at the feel of him inside of me. He pushed in and out like a piston as I held onto him. He pulled his mouth from mine. His dark eyes watched me as I moaned his name. The feel of him as he moved was mind blowing. It was like nothing I had ever experienced with Santiago before. He was holding none of himself back as we had sex. The only thing Santiago was resisting was my vein. I could see as his lips pulled back exposing his fangs. I angled my head to the side and still he resisted. I could feel the tension in his shoulders and hands as his fingers dug into my flesh.

"Drink Santiago," I urged.

He growled in response.

"Please. I want you to take from me," I panted. His eyes met mine and traveled down my neck. "Please Santiago, take from me," I begged.

It was all too much for him to resist his thirst any longer. Santiago moved quickly, bending my head at a sharper angle. His fangs punctured my flesh as hard as his erection had entered my core. He took from me as his body worked in and out of me. I came as he fucked me against the wall of the shower. The feel of his lips and his cock taking from me at the same time left me withering against him. As a witch it had felt amazing but this was mind blowing on a new level. Santiago had been holding back, fearing he would hurt me. I had always wondered if he had but this was confirmation. Now that I was a hybrid he wasn't holding back. I felt as his hips changed rhythm and angles slightly. He was entering me with a deeper faster stroke, as his cock hit the end of me. Santiago's lips continued to suck at my neck, drinking in all he needed. I came again calling his name, this time loudly. He continued to pound into me hitting the barrier each time he slid back in. I cried out as he came inside of me. He pulled his lips from my throat. Santiago's stare was heavy as if he was drunk.

"Are you okay?" he panted.

"I'm perfect."

"Good because I am not done with you yet," he was still hard. At the prospect of having more of him, my body tightened again.

We ended up on the floor of the shower. Santiago kept the pace he had when we were upright. I felt nothing but him. He kissed me, as he screwed me into a mind numbing bliss. His tongue moving with mine.

He released my lips abruptly. The next thing I knew his mouth on the nipple sucking hard. I felt as one of his fangs nicked it and he sucked even harder on me. His hips kept up the pace as his mouth sucked on my nipple. I intertwined my hands in his hair holding his head in place. I came over and over again as he kept at me. His mouth released my nipple and moved to the other one. It received the same treatment as the first. I could do nothing but wither under him with his name on my lips as the waves of pleasure continued to roll through my body. Santiago finally met his own release. My arms fell away from him as he released my nipple. He ran a tongue around the nipple before he collapsed on top of me.

Santiago tried to raise his body from mine but I could see he was having a difficult time. His eye lids were low, almost closed.

"Are you okay?" I asked, worried.

"You... were always the best taste... I have ever had but now... now you are intoxicating," he breathed heavily.

It took Santiago another minute before he lifted his body up, pulling himself free of my body. He helped me to my feet slowly.

"Are you okay?" he asked. His worry was there once more.

"I am more than okay," I leaned into his chest using his body to stabilize me as I kissed him. Santiago's hands brushed the side of my face as we kissed. This time our kiss was filled with everything he and I felt for one another. I pulled away from him.

"I need to ask, do you need to feed more?" I asked.

"No, I am sated."

I tasted the air around us. There was no other scent aside from our own.

"So you can still take from me," I pointed out.

"Yes. In fact your blood is even more potent than it was before. I am a bit drunk from it. I have heard of vampires becoming intoxicated but I have not experienced it until now," he smiled slowly.

"Is that a good thing?" I questioned.

"Yes," he whispered. I felt as he unleashed his power over me. It was like a giant wave of ecstasy washing over me. I started to come as I leaned against him. Santiago's ability had always been powerful but this was a new level of power. The smell of his desire swirled around us as I stood, leaning against him. "It appears your blood strengthens me," he spoke, throwing his ability at me again. I gasped as the feeling washed over me, yet again.

"Holy Hell," I gasped at him. Normally, I would have been angry with him for using his power on me but in that moment I didn't care. The feel of it brought back every sensation of him inside of me.

He kissed me as I tried to learn to breathe once more. The kiss didn't help the whole breathing issue I was having but at that moment I didn't care. I could have suffocated to death in that moment and it would not have made a difference. I wanted more of my mate and believe me I got what I wanted.

Chapter Forty-Five

Santiago and I eventually left the shower and ended up back in bed until the next morning. My new bite marks were almost completely healed by morning, which was a testament to what being a hybrid was going to be for me. I woke the next morning feeling no soreness or fatigue as I stretched. I took stock, checking my body mentally finding nothing wrong with it. Today, I would pull on a line and see what would happen. My blood was making Santiago stronger so it made me wonder what the vampire side of me would do to my magic. Part of me wanted to stay where I was. The other part of me was curious to know if anything had changed.

"What are you thinking about?" Santiago asked from behind me. His voice was heavy with sleep.

"Thinking about today."

"You're still off from work, correct?"

"Yes, I am."

"Then we have nothing pressing we must handle," he drew me in closer to him.

"Technically, that is correct but I want to see what being a hybrid has done to my magic."

"Are you sure you do not wish to wait another day."

"So far you drinking from me has given you more strength. I can smell emotions now and have some form of fangs but I don't need to drink. So what else is different? The only way to know is to try it out," I reasoned.

"If you are sure," Santiago ran a hand down my arm, leaving goosebumps behind.

"I am," I drew his arms around me tighter as we lay in bed.

The feel of his hard body against mine brought back images of the night before. It had been an amazing night. If everything went well today, he and I could have more nights like that until we both had to return to work. When I had the week before the ceremony off, I had not been concerned about being bored. There had been plenty to do that would have kept me busy. I wasn't a female to take time off and neither was Santiago. In fact both of us were work horses. When I was given the time after the ceremony off I had worried both of us would go crazy. Now I was more concerned about what would get us out of bed. If we kept up the way we were going neither of us would want to go back to work.

Santiago must have sensed where my thoughts had gone. His hips rolled against me and I felt his hard cock as he began to kiss my shoulder. I rolled my hips back to meet his sex. There was a growl of approval, which made me smile. I was just about to roll over to face him when my phone started to ring. I ignored it, continuing my turn and pushing Santiago on his back as my lips claimed his. The ringing stopped for a few seconds before it started again. He ended the kiss.

"You may want to answer your phone or it may not stop ringing."

I grumbled as I rolled off of my mate and looked at the caller I.D. I should have known.

"I told you I would call you this morning. I just didn't say when I would," I said as I answered.

Santiago curled up behind me and returned to kissing my shoulders and neck.

"When I didn't hear from you I got worried," Meri responded.

"I'm good. Trust me when I say that I'm all good," I growled at her.

Santiago was now moving slowly down my back leaving a trail of kisses behind.

"Did I interrupt something?" I could hear the smile in voice.

"Actually you did. Now I will call you later," Santiago's kisses had reached my hip. He rolled me over to my back. His mouth continued its movement south. I opened my legs as he moved between them.

"Well maybe I should talk to you a little while longer?"

"Or I could just hang up on you," I threatened.

She laughed at me.

"Seriously is there anything you need. I mean outside of sex?" she asked.

Santiago's hand was sliding down my thigh. If he kept this going, I would not be able to stay focused much longer. As it was I was having a hard time remembering the question.

"Can you be here in two hours?"

I was trying to speak normally but I was having a hard time. My voice had gone breathy. Santiago's lips were now on my inner thigh.

"Yeah. Why?" Meri giggled.

I felt as the feeling of ecstasy washed over me as it had last night. I was practically panting now. He placed a kiss at the top of my sex. I looked down at him as his tongue extended giving my already wet core a quick lick.

"I'll explain later. Bye." I replied as I cut off the call. I wasn't even sure I said bye before I hit the end button. My phone hit the floor as he began to lick my sex slowly, his eyes watching me as I gasped. He took his time as he licked me.

"You cannot do that while I'm on the phone," I panted. Another wave of pure ecstasy washed over me as his tongue entered me. His tongue darting in and out of me . He went slow, driving me insane as he drove me slowly to the edge. He released his ability on me as his tongue continued to move deep inside my core. I came against his mouth. He pulled his mouth from me, his lips wet. Santiago licked them as if he was enjoying the taste of me on his lips.

He bent down and kissed me slowly keeping his body above me. I placed a hand on his chest. He knew what I wanted as he wrapped an arm around my waist and rolled us.

"You are having way too much fun with this new strength of yours," I said as I climbed on top of him.

"Would you like me to stop, Mi Amor?" he said his voice heavy with sex.

My answer was in the kiss I gave him. It was all the answer he needed.

TWO HOURS LATER I WAS dressed and waiting for Meri to arrive. Santiago was in his office making a few calls. We had submitted the paperwork to his lawyer for the name change, not only myself but also my business. Santiago was doing follow-up on both. He also was checking on the club. Cristian was running the show in Santiago's absence. It wasn't that Santiago had a lack of confidence in the vampire, it was more about the fact my mate liked being the one who did everything. In other words he was a control freak just as much as I was.

As I waited for Meri, I slowly pulled on a line near our home. The feel of the line was different than it had been before. As a ley line witch I always felt the lines as I moved. I always carried a small amount of energy in my body. The energy was like a subtle hum inside of me. It was always there but nothing I took notice of as I went through my day. The hum was still there but as I pulled on the line the feel of the line was stronger, more electrifying. I lifted my hand and watched as blue flames grew in my hand. The fire I usually created sat in the palm of my hand. This flame was not like that, this engulfed my hand. It was as if my hand was the flame. I turned my hand examining the magic I was performing.

"That's cool," Meri said as she walked in.

I pulled the flame back into my skin, feeling as the magic flowed back into my body.

"It kind of is," I answered.

"I see your neck is clear. Does that mean Santiago has to feed from a human?"

Meri sat down next to me on the sofa.

"No, my neck is already healed."

"Wait, are you saying he can still feed from you."

"Yup and it seems my blood makes him stronger," I explained.

"In what way?"

"His ability. We discovered that last night."

"Do tell," Meri smiled at me.

"That's all you get."

"You're no fun." She pouted as I rolled my eyes at her. "Why did you need me to come over?"

"I need to see what becoming a hybrid has done to my magic."

"I'm not letting you throw energy balls at me," she said before I could explain more.

"I wouldn't expect you to. I want to see what happens when I throw up a shield. I want to see if it's different."

"Does your magic feel different?" Meri asked.

"It does. It feels more powerful. I mean you saw the fire I created. It was like my hand became the flame."

"Where do you want to try this out?"

"In our office."

Meri looked at me as if I was crazy.

"Are you sure outside wouldn't be a better idea?"

"Probably would but I can only guess that Matthew is watching us. He was a few days ago. I don't want to put everything on display."

"Okay."

We headed down to our office. The basement was large enough that we would still have room to move. Meri leaned her butt against her desk as I faced her. I still had a firm grip on the line I was holding onto as I sat waiting for her to arrive. As soon as the thought of a shield came to mind I watched as a blue wall began to form. Usually it took a small amount of focus to bring one up but not this time. Meri looked at the wall then at her desk. She knew how my magic worked. I watched as she picked up a pen from her desk and tossed it at the shield. The pen bounced off of the wall hitting the floor. She took a mug that had been sitting on Watts' desk and tossed at it as well. The cup hit the wall and shattered. Generally, I would feel the hits my shield took, this time it was like a blip on my screen. Meri began to look around the room for something larger.

"Not the computers or a desk," I said.

"How about a chair?"

I steadied myself as she picked up one of the chairs and threw it across the room. The chair hit the shield and bounced off as if it was an actual wall. The chair hit the floor with a loud clatter as it met the floor. Two of the wheels popping off.

"Are you sure we can't try a desk?" she asked with a smile.

"What in the bloody hell are you two doing?" Santiago demanded from the stairs.

"Testing out her shield," Meri explained.

"By throwing chairs?"

"I wanted to see how strong it is now," I said as I let go of the shield. It came down and flowed right through me.

Santiago shook his head at us.

"I heard crashing noises from upstairs. You must warn me when you plan to be destructive."

"Maybe Santiago should try to throw something at you. You said he's more powerful with feeding from you. He would be the real test," Meri offered.

"That's a thought," I replied.

"No," he looked at both of us as if we had lost our minds.

"Come on, she needs to see what she's dealing with."

"What if I harm her? I could not live with the thought I had harmed my mate," he explained.

"Fine, have it your way. I guess we'll try one of the desks next," Meri shot back.

"You will not be throwing any desks at her," he ordered eyeing both of us.

"She was joking," I laughed.

"No I wasn't," she said under her breath.

I gave her a look that told her to shut the hell up. Santiago walked back up the stairs, cursing in Spanish as he went. I nodded at her as my shield slid back up into place.

Chapter Forty-Six

M eri and I spent a few more hours testing out my magic and laughing. It had felt like we hadn't had any time to just be friends in a while. She didn't throw a desk at me but she did throw a few other things, which brought my mate running down the stairs again. He finally put a stop to our behavior, both of us laughing about it. Becoming a hybrid had been scary but it was showing its upside the more I learned about the new me.

THE HYBRID YOUNG WERE making great strides in terms of health or at least most of them were. We lost three of the young due to infections that developed from surgeries they had endured in the past month. Two other of the young died as well, one from sucide. He had been a seventeen year old male who had been held at H&W for most of his life. He had been abused in more than one way. Unfortunately, the memories of the years had proven too much for him to live with. We lost another to heart failure. The young, a ten year old had been in bad shape when she was brought in, she never recovered from the medical experiments they had done.

The other young were slowly on the mend. Natalie, our vampire, witch, wolf hybrid was being fostered by the wolf pack. Damian called me a week after he met her. He would be the foster parent in the eyes of the humans but the pack would all be stepping up to help her. Damian and Santiago were working on a feeding schedule for her to ensure her vampire side was taken care of.

Siobhan was going to be living with Ainsley. She and the girl had bonded. Ainsley was different from many vampires. She had an ability that made others nervous and made her an outsider. She understood Siobhan and not being wanted. The two were a good match. The humans who work for the Department of Children's Services were lost as to what to do with the hybrids who had no family to return them to. It took our clan and clans from where the young had originated from to find them homes. Santiago, Cristian, and I spent weeks ensuring they were going to good homes. Eventually, we were able to do right by them all.

Out of the eight children Illingworth had brought to us, three died inside of H&W. Faith Holden had died during a procedure. According to her file she had been undergoing a plasmapheresis treatment. Generally, it is a procedure, which is used to remove harmful antibodies from the bloodstream. They had tried to remove the vampire side of her through the process. During the procedure the female died. She was only there for two months before she died. I wasn't sure if it was a blessing she died after two months or not.

Denise Clark died after a year of being taken. She died of liver failure. H&W had been trying to create a drug that would reverse the hybrid process. The only way for them to know if it worked was to test the drugs. The combinations she was given were more than her little body could handle.

Callie Rider died of malnourishment. Her vampire side was starved to see if that was a way to kill the vampire DNA. She ended up trying to feed from her own vein. Between the malnourishment and biting herself her body couldn't recover.

In total they killed four hundred and ninety-six hybrid young over the course of twenty years. The fact that they had been able to get away with it, had been a shock to the country as a whole. Hellborns were less surprised and were demanding the federal government do more for hellborns. I wasn't sure if the federal government was willing to do more for our safety.

Troy Salazar was put to death four days after his surgery to fix his wrist. I had wanted to be the hunter to do it but it was given to another. Even though the WPG leader was dead, it didn't mean the organization fell. No, hate groups were like Hydras. You cut one head off and another grew, keeping the beast going. There was always someone to take the place of a fallen leader.

Lucy Whitbar died in a federal penitentiary. She was found with her wrists slit. She never even made it to her sentencing hearing. She had been alive when it was lights out and by morning she was dead. It was listed as a sucide. I knew better. Matthew was responsible or at least his ability. If I was right about what he was, he used his ability to force her to kill herself. Hell, I wouldn't have been shocked if he handed her the shiv to do it. Illingworth said she had no visitors while she was locked up. I didn't know how Matthew had done it but I knew he had. There was no way that human wanted to die.

RYAN WAS ABLE TO OBTAIN a warrant for the Brazens. They had helped in the kidnaping of their granddaughter. I waited to serve the warrant until I was back at work. As much as I had wanted to be the one to kill Troy Salazar, I had made a promise I would come for them.

Meri and I arrived at their home just after midnight, waiting and watching. We sat on the house for two hours. There was no knocking when we approached the door. We went in quietly, picking the lock. We found their room in the back of the house, both of them asleep, side by side. I walked around the bed to stand over Gemma Brazen while Meri stood by Emerson. We looked at each other, giving a nod.

"Emerson," Meri spoke next to the witch's face. "Wakey, wakey." He came awake slowly. His hand folded into the curl of Meri's hand as she touched his face softly. It took him a moment to realize it was not his consort touching him. He shouted aloud, which woke Gemma. She popped straight up and into my hand. My hand wrapped around her throat cutting off her airway. I'll give her credit; instead of looking panicked she gave me a look of pure evil. Emerson on the other hand was panicking as Meri dragged him from his bed.

"I told you I would come for you," I said into Gemma's face.

"You have..."

I squeezed her throat tighter, cutting her off.

"I have a warrant for your death. You are guilty of kidnapping, poisoning, and holding a young against her will."

I brought up my hand as blue flames engulfed it and pressed the fire into Gemma Brazen's chest. Her screams filled the night as she burned on her bedroom floor. I threw a shield around her body as she burned. Meri went for Emerson's carotid artery, ripping it open. He bled out within minutes. I called Ryan when they were both dead. When I served a warrant there was always a small part of me that felt something for those I had executed. The Brazens I didn't have that feeling with. Maybe it was because I was losing a piece of me. Maybe it was my own mommy issues. Or maybe it was because they were that evil. Either way, I was glad to see them dead. I didn't focus on the lack of feelings for them. I moved on.

We had better things to worry about than my lack of feelings for two terrible hellborns. Hugo was making his plans for his mating ceremony. As the head of the vampires, Hugo would have a ceremony just as Santiago and I had. It would be public with all the big wigs of the city there to watch. Santiago and I were watching the beginning stages of the planning. Santiago would be writing a press release for them soon enough announcing to the city the news. Most of our clan was not happy about the mating. We all put on smiling faces but that was all it was, smiling faces. The vampires were becoming nervous with what this mating would mean for our clan. The only ones excited about it were those Dante used as pawns. You could tell who they were. They were vampires who had been alive for less than five years. They were also the weakest. They had no interest in being more than Dante's followers. Part of me hoped one or two of them would throw a challenge at me. I would enjoy teaching them all a lesson.

Santiago and I kept the strength the two of us were gaining with my change a secret. The only ones who knew were Meri and Duncan. Santiago and I had made the decision to keep it quiet because of Dante. If he knew of the power either of us had developed, then Matthew would know as well. Dante was a threat but Matthew was the bigger threat. The more Matthew knew, the closer it felt he was getting to me. Most days I could ignore any thoughts of the vampire but from time to time it felt as if he was at my back following my every step. The feel of those eyes as they watched me from a distance. A big part of me wanted to find Matthew so I could kill him. The other part of me feared I would fail. Santiago wanted the vampire dead at his hand. I feared Santiago going against him just as much as he feared me doing the same.

For now my mate and I were going to live in as much bliss as we possibly could. When we were home together we talked less about the problems we were facing and more about enjoyable things. With the growth of my business, meant I was able to take a night off once a week. Santiago had started to do the same. Cristian had handled the club perfectly or as close to perfect as he could. There had been a few ordering issues but nothing that couldn't be fixed. It gave Santiago confidence he could take a night off without everything turning to a nightmare for him. Those nights were the best of my life. Santiago and I had a full day of peace with one another. What could be better than that? I'll you, nothing in the entire freaking world.

Don't miss out!

Visit the website below and you can sign up to receive emails whenever Sammantha Anderson publishes a new book. There's no charge and no obligation.

https://books2read.com/r/B-A-VJNI-TWQFB

BOOKS 2 READ

Connecting independent readers to independent writers.

About the Author

Sammantha Anderson is the writer of The Hellborn Series. Most of her days, she spends working with Savannah to create the hellborn world. When she is not busy talking to her characters, you can find Sammantha with her two active children, reading, workout or binge watching Grey's Anatomy.

Read more at https://www.facebook.com/authorsammanthaanderson.

CPSIA information can be obtained
at www.ICGtesting.com
Printed in the USA
BVHW031926240520
580239BV00001B/1